Also by Gary K. Wolf

Killerbowl
A Generation Removed
The Resurrectionist
Who Censored Roger Rabbit?

WHO
P-P-P-PLUGGED
ROGER
RABBIT?

WHO P-P-P-PLUGGED ROGER RABBIT?

BY

Gary K. Wolf

VILLARD BOOKS

NEW YORK

1991

Copyright © 1991 by Cry Wolf, Inc.
Published in the United States by Villard Books, a division
of Random House, Inc., New York, and simultaneously in Canada by
Random House of Canada Limited, Toronto.
Villard Books is a registered trademark of Random House, Inc.
Library of Congress Cataloging-in-Publication Data
Wolf, Gary K.
    Who p-p-p-plugged Roger Rabbit?/by Gary K. Wolf.
        p. cm.
    ISBN 0-679-40094-X
    I. Title.
    PS3573.0483W55 1991
    813'.54—dc20 90-50673
Designed by Robert Bull Design
Manufactured in the United States of America
9 8 7 6 5 4 3 2
First Edition

To Michael, Jeffrey, Steven, Bob Z, Dick, Bob H, Charlie, and Kathleen.

You're a 24-carrot bunch.

A MEMO TO MY CLIENTS

Roger Rabbit and his screwball buddies play fast and loose with historical accuracy.

That's the way things happen in Toontown.

Take a tip from a guy who's been there. Relax, hang on, and enjoy the ride.

Eddie Valiant
Private Eye
Los Angeles, California
1947, more or less

WHO
P-P-P-PLUGGED
ROGER
RABBIT?

I knocked on the rabbit's door.

A curtain shivered in a second-floor window, and I caught a flash of ears. The window flew open.

A word balloon sailed out.

It turned edge-on, slicing the air like the business end of a guillotine, and shattered on the stoop. Six inches farther left, and I'd own one less private eye.

I jigsawed the pieces together with my toe. "Eddie Valiant," it said, followed by a single exclamation point the size of a major leaguer's bat and ball.

I looked up. There he stood in the open doorway. Six feet tall and change, counting his eighteen-inch ears. His carroty cowlick flopped forward to the tops of his blue-lagoon eyes. Cotton candy ear canals, marshmallow fur, and lemon-drop mittens put him next in line to replace Shirley Temple as First Mate on the Good Ship Lollipop. His red corduroy overalls fit him the way spiderwebs drape the Headless Horseman's hat rack.

"P-p-p-please come in," he said out loud, spraying me with enough saliva to irrigate the San Fernando Valley.

I entered the low-ceilinged warren he called a living room.

He'd decorated it on the cheap, with props from his movies. I spotted a sofa from *Tummy Trouble*, a beach chair from *Roller Coaster Rabbit*, and dishes from *Waiter, There's a Hare in My Stew*.

I recognized his Oriental rug from the flying scene in *Baby Baba and the Forty Thieves*. It still bore the stain where Baby Herman had wet his pantaloons during one of Roger's hare-pin turns.

One whole wall displayed autographed photos of famous celebs. Studio prexy Walt Disney and his adopted nephew Mickey. Roger and Baby Herman flanking publicity agent Large Mouth Bassinger. Benny the Cab out for an evening of engine revving with Fangio, the Spanish race car driver. Baby Herman making goo-goo eyes at Carole Lombard and her making them back.

• • • • • • • • • • • 3

Roger even had one of me and Doris. Together and happy. A collector's item if ever there was one.

A faded chunk of wall space contained a hook but no likeness. In a nearby wastebasket, I spied a silver picture frame. I eyeballed its eight by ten. Jessica Rabbit, Roger's hot-cha wife. She looked terrific, even scraped and torn by broken glass.

Roger opened the breastplate in the suit of armor he'd worn in *Sleepless Knights*. With its straight-up-and-pointy iron ears, it would have made a perfect cocktail fork for the giant who lived at the top of Jack's bean stalk. Roger had a better use for it. He'd converted its hollow innards into a bar. "Drink?"

"Every chance I get."

He set out glasses—decaled with his likeness—and poured from a bottle of bourbon with more years on it than a perpetual calendar. I'll say one thing in the rabbit's favor. He didn't know when to stop.

We both drank up.

I lit a smoke and tried to ignore Roger whooping, turning colors, smoking at the ears, pinwheeling his eyes, and careening around the room with the wobbly abandon of a lopsided sky-rocket.

I counted seven points in his imperfect landing. He skidded to a stop with his head stuck in a large vase. He twisted it side to side and levered it with his feet, but it refused to come off.

Wearing his Ming turban, he groped his way blindly around the coffee table until he came to several recent copies of *Variety* and *The Hollywood Reporter*. He held them up. "Do you read the trades?" His words popped out of the vase individually, strung together like links in a chain.

"Sure."

"Then you know about the plans to film *Gone With the Wind*."

"Yeah." Frankly, I didn't give a damn. The only movies that copped my six bits showed John Wayne whaling the living tar out of galoots wearing black ten-gallon hats.

Roger puffed his scrawny chest. "I'm a leading candidate to play Rhett."

Hop hop hooray for Hollywood. With the whole Civil War for chaos, why did *Gone With the Wind* need Roger Rabbit?

"The producer, David O. Selznick, loved me in *Song of the*

South." His word balloon formed a circle the size of a buttermilk biscuit. The writing inside had the broad, swooping mushiness of a pen dipped in grits. When the word bubble popped, it was with a fragrant whiff of honeysuckle.

"It's a long way, chum, from Br'er Rabbit to Br'er Butler."

"And getting longer every day. That's why I wanted to see you." By touch and feel, he located a wad of newspaper clippings. He handed them in my general direction.

They'd been ripped out of the *Toontown Telltale*. I gave them a once-over. According to "unnamed but in-the-know sources" Jessica Rabbit was baking her carrot cakes for Clark Gable. The clippings gave the whats, whens, and wherefores in embarrassing detail.

I tossed the articles on an end table. They hit with a juicy smack. "Rabbits will be rabbits."

Roger muttered a string of the gobbledygook you get dragging your finger along the top row of a typewriter. "You can't believe that garbage."

"They can't print what isn't true. First Amendment. Look it up."

The steam coming out of his ears blew the vase off his noodle. It shattered against the wall. Too bad his head wasn't still inside. The impact might have jolted some sense into him. "I want you to make them stop."

"I'm the wrong man for the job. You need a shyster."

The rabbit helped himself to a Big Red One, a brand of cigar artificially colored to resemble a stick of dynamite. Sometimes the goofballs who roll and paint them slip a few of the real thing into the box. That's why so many Toons have only four fingers. Roger lit the fuse. I held my ears. Nothing came out but smell and pollution. "I already contacted one. He told me a lawsuit could drag on for years. By then the damage will have been done."

"What damage?"

"I can't afford a scandal at this point in my career. Mr. Selznick is risking millions on *Gone With the Wind*. He can't have his major star tainted by even a hint of impropriety. Even though the story's a total fabrication, if the *Telltale* keeps running this . . . this bilge about Jessica, I'll lose my chance to be Rhett."

"Sorry, Roger. I promised Doris. No more muscle work."

"I'll pay any price you want."

"My principles can't be bought."

He quoted me a figure that would rent them for a while.

"OK. I'll lean on the the *Telltale*. But I warn you, they're liable to lean back."

"I have faith in you, Eddie. You'll make everything right. You always do."

WHO P-P-P-PLUGGED ROGER RABBIT?

I opened my office door and held my hat in front of it. My fedora came back with no holes. Which meant Doris had either forgiven me or run out of bullets.

I turned out to be only half wrong.

Doris wasn't around, at least not any place I could see. Maybe she was hiding in my bottom desk drawer. I checked. Nope. Nothing in there but that nasty old bottle of firewater. I put it to my lips and tilted it back.

Not a drop dripped out.

I spotted her note. She'd stuffed it down the bottle's neck. The one place she knew I'd find it.

I read her writing through a liquid haze.

"I'm leaving you, Eddie," she wrote in her tiny, precise hand. The booze, or maybe a tear, had smeared the ink that formed my name. "I'm a simple girl. I'd be real happy living in a tiny cottage, raising a couple of kids, married to a common working stiff with a better-than-average chance of living to a ripe old age. Maybe, in time, I could learn to abide your crazy schedule, your financial peaks and valleys, and your low-life friends. But I'm afraid I'll never shake the dreadful feeling that one day I'll find a policeman on my doorstep come to tell me the worst news a woman can hear." I twisted the bottle around, and the next line swam into view. "Don't bother calling, and don't try to see me. You can't change my mind." She signed it simply, "Doris."

I emptied the bottle by pouring it down my throat. I hooked her note out with a pencil. It didn't read any better blotted dry.

I heaved the empty out my office window. We both hit bottom in a dead heat.

* * *

A stiff Santa Ana would send the Toontown Telltale Building sailing out into the Pacific. Considering its fishy journalism, maybe that's where it belonged.

The building's four massive corner columns duplicated in painted stucco the muckraking mutton heads who changed the *Toontown Telltale* from a paper that wrapped garbage to one that printed it. The one called Sleazy had the pained, elongated snout of a constipated alligator. Slimey, with his triangular face, grayish pink pallor, sharply right-angled ears, and prominent, bony nose, resembled a fresh pork chop. An X-shaped scar crisscrossed Dreck's cheek like the carved-on signature of an illiterate buccaneer. Profane had the profile of a wrecked four-hole Buick.

I tried a nearby parking lot, but the attendant had a medical problem. He refused to touch eyesores, so I docked my heap on the street.

I entered the publisher's office.

His plain-Jane receptionist with her shiny nose, dull lipstick, bun-coiled hair, pince-nez, and ruffled, high-collared frock had "Agnes Smoot" engraved on her nameplate, and permanent spinster stamped across her forehead.

I flashed dear, sweet Agnes my badge. After reading the front, she checked the back for a dime store price tag. She take me for a fool? I washed it off last month, same time I laundered my underwear and socks. Agnes relayed my essentials to her boss. He told her to show me in.

I entered an office twice the size of my biggest aspiration.

The *Telltale*'s publisher, Delancey Duck, waddled out from behind his desk atop a webbed pair of orange size-fourteens. In a Mr. Universe contest, he'd lose to the fat soprano who sang the national anthem. His skinny white arms were just the right size for fishing quarters out of sidewalk grates. A basketball could roll between his legs and not touch either knee. An orange bill the wobbly shape of a sledgehammered pumpkin underlined a bulging pair of hard-boiled-egg-and-black-olive eyes. He measured three feet even but that included the good four inches of ruffled head fuzz you'd call a ducklick.

He sported a tan cutaway with expanding shoulders for freer wing movement, a matching vest also tailored loose in the flappers, a buttoned-down duck cloth shirt in goosey gander white, canvas-

WHO P-P-P-PLUGGED ROGER RABBIT?

back pants with extra give in the drumsticks, and a set of spats borrowed from his tropical cousin, the blue-footed booby. His feathery handshake removed the lint from my shirt cuff.

He motioned me to a seat in an antique side chair. The duck shinnied up the leg of a ditto and plunked himself atop a plush eiderdown cushion.

He coaxed a great impersonation of the Chattanooga Choo Choo out of an expensive Havana corona-corona. My mouth watered, but the implication rolled right off his back. He tipped the end of his butt into a gold-crested ashtray, a souvenir from the Stork Club.

"You're wasting your time, Mr. Valiant. Our reputation for spurious journalistic ethics far belies situational reality." His balloon was as crisp as an English muffin. Printer's devils could sort his letters and use them to set type for his morning edition.

"Translate that for me."

A string of musical notes floated from a concealed speaker and tinkled into broken circles and stems against the wall. *Swan Lake*. "We print the truth, the whole truth, and nothing but the truth."

I hauled out today's edition and read him the cover headline. " 'Husband reborn as parrot. Says he never loved her.' " I flipped it in his face.

His smile proved ducks do have teeth, and sharp ones. "We inform. We also entertain." Delancey shinnied down his chair leg, duck-walked to the wall behind me, and fastidiously wiped a bit of grime off a diploma, magna cum laude from Drake.

"What category does your story on Jessica Rabbit fall into?"

"To which one do you refer? There have been so many over the years." He opened a cupboard beneath his sheepskin and hauled out a chilled bottle of Cold Duck. He exhaled a transparent balloon, poked it into goblet shape with his thumb, and filled it full of bubbly. "She's one of our reliables, so to speak." I watched in thirsty silence as he took a sip, sip here, and a sip, sip there. "We can always count on Jessica Rabbit whenever circulation, or male blood pressures, need a boost."

"I'm talking about the pieces of smudge romantically linking her with Clark Gable."

"Ah, yes. Some of our more recent efforts. If memory serves me correctly, and it usually does, those fall into the category of absolutely true. They were researched and written by Louise Wrightliter. One of our best and most tenacious reporters." Delancey Duck spread his tail feathers open. It turned him into a dead ringer for the centerpiece at the signing of the Declaration of Independence. "I personally taught her everything she knows."

"She's following in the foot webs of the master."

"So to speak."

"Where'd she get her information?"

He opened his center desk drawer and hauled out a word balloon. He sailed it across the room. I caught it on the fly.

I examined it, front and back. Typical size, eighteen inches across, the grayish color of cheap newsprint. I fanned it under my nose. It smelled faintly of perfume. It said "Jessica Rabbit and Clark Gable" in pasted-on letters sliced from other balloons.

"That came to me in the mail. Just as you see it there. No return address. I passed it along to Louise. She checked it out and returned with the goods."

I handed it back. "Or the no-goods."

"I have every confidence in Louise's integrity."

"That why you took her under your wing?"

Two angry golf balls of smoke blew out of his ears. Either he was inhaling his cigar into crossed cranial plumbing, or he didn't take kindly to ethnic jokes. Remind me never to ask him how many Toons it takes to screw in a light bulb. "Miss Smoot will escort you to Louise's office. I'll instruct Louise to cooperate fully in your investigation. She will answer all of your questions, within the confines of journalistic privilege." He couldn't shoehorn that many polysyllabic words into one balloon. He needed two. They emerged a translucent, milky white, brittle, with narrow gold rims, like the plates stuffy dowagers use to serve crumpets.

I walked over them on my way out, crushing them to slivers under my heel. For a lark.

WHO P-P-P-PLUGGED ROGER RABBIT?

Miss Smoot pointed me down a hallway. "Third door on the left."

I grabbed her by the elbow. "A friendly word of advice, Toots. Paint something bright and red on that mouth, invest in a tight sweater, let your hair down, and buy some rhinestone eyeglasses. You'd give Dixie Dugan a run for the money."

She slapped my hand loose. "Go flounce a floozy. I want a man with an IQ higher than his hat size." She walked away twisting her bushel just enough to let me catch a brief glimpse of the light that glowed underneath.

Louise Wrightliter had an age-yellowed slip of notepaper thumbtacked to her door. "Out on assignment," it said. A cardboard clock with "Will return at" printed across the bottom hung from her doorknob. Both of the hands were missing.

I checked the door. Locked, with a pot metal dead bolt too cheesy for Mortimer Mouse. I popped it open without even scuffing my nails.

I needed a machete to hack through her jungle of books. Judging from the titles of those that fell on my toe, they covered every weirdity from eyewitness accounts of outer space invasions to psychic predictions to horoscopes to how-to-do-it manuals for hexing your neighbor. A complete collection of the hokum every good *Telltale* reporter needs to know.

Caribbean travel brochures layered her desk top three deep. Glancing through them brought back memories of Doris, me, and my brother Freddy in Cuba.

Freddy came into the business with me after a Toon killed my brother Teddy. Freddy and I were a pretty good team, real hotshot operatives, free-lancing for Pinkertons. Doris answered our phones, opened our mail, balanced our two sets of accounting ledgers, and, in her spare time, accepted my proposal of marriage.

Pinkertons sent us to Cuba to check security at one of the big casinos. The job took a week—we caught a pit bull pit boss with his paw in the till—and we stayed a week extra. Call it a trial honeymoon for me and Doris, with Freddy along to referee. With a fat Pinkertons paycheck burning a hole in our balance sheet, and the promise of plenty more where that came from, our prospects looked rosy indeed.

We drank gallons of rum and Coke, pumped Wurlitzers full of nickels, learned to dance the Carioca from a parrot named Jose, lazed in the sun, and gambled. Doris and I broke about even at craps. Freddy lost his shirt to roulette and his heart to Lupe Chihuahua, the Latin Spitfire.

Between bit roles in the horror movies studios shot on the cheap down there, Lupe performed at Baba de Rum, the wild Havana nightery. She sang and danced in a costume made entirely of fruit. Unlike Freddy, I'm not that attracted to lady Toons, but I must admit Lupe looked better in a bunch of grapes than most women did in a Paris frock. And that was before she peeled!

The plot thickened to the consistency of lumpy gruel after Lupe turned out to be the more or less steady girlfriend of Tom Tom LeTuit, chief of the Cuban secret police.

The trip left me and Doris with horrible sunburns, worse hangovers, and another broken engagement.

Freddy? I don't know. I never saw him again. I went to his room the morning we were scheduled to sail back to Miami, and he was gone. No note, nothing.

I combed the room inch by inch. I found eight cigar butts, a pineapple stem, and a busted castanet—the three blind mice who worked as maids in this joint missed any piece of trash smaller than the Rock of Gibraltar—but nothing to help me find Freddy.

I reported his disappearance to the police. Tom Tom LeTuit surprised me by bounding into action. He assigned a hundred men to the case, and kept them on it for at least half a minute.

No trace of Freddy ever surfaced.

Louise Wrightliter's brochures described Cuba as the Paradise of the Caribbean. I called it worse.

I put the travel brochures back and rifled her drawers.

She chewed spearmint gum and number-two pencils. She never washed her coffee cup or paid her speeding tickets. She smoked my brand and drank it, too, masking her vices with Sen Sen. If the automatic I found in the bottom of her Kleenex box had been two calibers larger, we could have passed for twins.

I rolled her next day's column out of her Remington. She wasn't quite halfway completed and she'd already managed to tally four of the *Telltale*'s five Ns: nefarious, nasty, naughty, and nudity. If she could find a way to work necrophilia into a story about a young, blonde girl storming her way into a country cottage occupied by three bears, she'd score a full house.

I hate that kind of lewd, crude drivel. In my era you learned about the birds and the bees the good old-fashioned way, from your savvy buddies out on the streets. Today kids read about it in the scandal sheets. Or worse. They get it as part of a well-balanced, formal education. Smut 101. What's the world coming to when kids go to school to watch dirty movies? Put that stuff back in the stag parties and smokers where it belongs.

I went through Wrightliter's filing cabinet and located the folders on Jessica Rabbit and Clark Gable. They were color coded, Jessica's in valentine red (naturally), Gable's in yellow. The two folders were the largest she had, each easily twice the size of any other. I'd need two solid days to read them cover to cover. I settled for grabbing a handful of papers at random off the top of each, and returned the leftovers.

I fished one of my cards out of my wallet, wrote a note on it asking Louise to call me, "Urgent," and tacked it to her door.

I walked back to my car in the dark.

Nighttime falls quick in L.A. Like everybody else who works steady in this burg, Old Mister Sun's a union man. The minute his shift's over, he pulls the plug, reels in his beams, and goes home.

I fumbled out my car key under a streetlight that gave off less shine than a two-year-old's birthday cake. All of a sudden the streetlight went dark, and so did I.

Whoever sapped me walloped me pro style, above and slightly behind my ear, with just enough oomph to cave in my knees. He planted his foot in the small of my back and booted me forward into the running board.

My assailant delivered another kick which sent me halfway to la-la land. As I drifted in and out of consciousness, he unplugged my heater from under my armpit.

He slapped my eyes open and rolled me sideways enough to shove a balloon into my puss. "Box, and you could get hurt," it said.

He sapped me again.

I woke up stretched out in the gutter. I'd been there before, plenty of times, but this was the first visit I didn't have only myself to blame.

I lurched to hands and knees, and stumbled to my feet, plenty the worse for wear. My head spun. My breath came in short, painful gasps. Drops of blood wept off my cheek. I'd cracked bones I hadn't thought about since I counted them for my high school biology final. My hands trembled like a pair of palsied moths.

I dragged a butt out of my pack and nailed it to my lips, twisted my head sideways to shield my match from the wind, and scraped my nose on the guy's balloon. It hung over my shoulder, dried to the brittle shape of a taco shell. His words were on the inner surface; from my side I saw them backwards. I carefully lifted it off and held it to the side-view mirror, rotating it slowly to bring the whole sentence into view. I blinked a few million times to clear my vision. Yep. "Box, and you could get hurt." That's what it said. It seemed like an obvious point to me. Why nearly kill me to make it?

I popped open my trunk, wrapped the frizzled balloon in the coveralls I keep for dirty work, and bundled the package into my spare tire.

I climbed into the front seat and reached into the glove compartment. Thank God! He'd spared Granddad. I poured the old geezer down until the dent in his bottle matched the size of the one in my head.

WHO P-P-P-PLUGGED ROGER RABBIT?

I slept in my jalopy and showered in the morning mist that blows off the ocean. My chenille seat cover toweled me dry. I finished my toilette by lathering on enough Ben Gay to parboil a yam, then dressed standing on the curb.

My mood brightened right along with the landscape as Big Sol punched in for work right on schedule and threw the master switch that drapes this town with tinsel.

A Toon mockingbird flew by, littering the landscape with a bad impression of a canary. I brushed its ersatz warbles off my car before they cracked open and blistered the paint.

I cranked up my engine and headed on down the yellow brick freeway.

Breakfast consisted of auto exhaust and two Almond Joys nutty side up chased with the dynamic duo, a shot of gargle and a gasper.

I paid a quick visit and twenty bucks to Arnie Johnson, Doctor of Veterinary Medicine. I didn't have an appointment, but Arnie squeezed me in, between a mangy dog and a bloated goldfish. He taped my cracked ribs, stuck three stitches in my head, advised me to find a safer line of work, and agreed, as usual, not to report my assorted bumps, cuts, and bruises to the proper authorities.

He updated my chart, informing me that my head now bore only three less stitches than a regulation Spalding baseball, and was only ten shy of a world's record. He told me to hurry up and take a few more lumps so he could secure his place in medical history. I promised to do my best.

I found Professor Ring Wordhollow in his office, surrounded by piles and piles of Toon balloons.

With his slender, rounded appendages and limber joints, Wordhollow resembled a stick doll manufactured out of LifeSavers and rubber bands. He wore a shapeless pair of nubbly blue wool trousers, a white shirt, an ink-spotted green tie tucked into his waistband, and a belted shooting jacket with half a dozen pens and pencils filling the loops designed to hold shotgun shells.

As head of UCLA's Visual Linguistics Department, Wordhollow devoted his life to the study of Toon conversation. He pored over balloons the way touts read the racing form. He could point out subtle—and to him, thrilling—differences in texture, thickness, circumference, lettering style. As a human, he had a major handicap in the exercise of his chosen academic specialty. A scholar of American history could easily learn to speak English. Wordhollow could hold his nose and blow until his face turned blue. He'd never produce a balloon.

I gave him the one my attacker left behind.

He promised to take a look.

A revolving circle of Toons picketed the entrance to Schwab's. Seems Hollywood's most famous drugstore discriminated. It refused to serve Toons their daily dose of tutti-frutti.

I say throw open the door and invite them inside. They want to spend five bits for a two-bit soda, let them. They want to sit next to humans and gobble overpriced french fries, who cares? Eddie Valiant's definition of civil rights. Their money's as good as anybody else's. I ought to know. I'm the one working for a rabbit.

I ducked my head, stiffened my arm, and plowed into the tightly packed bubble clusters of protest which blocked the front door. It was like swimming through the sting and pop in a bottle of beer.

Once you got past the turmoil, it was a typical day at Schwab's. Out-of-work actors and actresses hogged the counter stools nursing cheeseburgers, lime rickeys, and the hope of being discovered. The only stars I saw sparkled in the eyes of the rubbernecked tourists lined up for booths.

On my way to the fountain, I checked out the counter dollies. I tallied four pairs of pretty good legs, one set of blue eyes so fiery they could melt the Tin Man, and enough angora sweaters to wrap King Kong's high-school ring. My purely unofficial opinion was good quality, but not great. Nobody likely to replace Jean Harlow this year. Or any year, for that matter.

WHO P-P-P-PLUGGED ROGER RABBIT?

Skipper, the counter boy, had his nose buried in a Hollywood fan magazine. His lips moved as he read. I watched his mouth and caught the gist. *Baby Herman confesses to being Heddy Lamar's love child.* For this they turn perfectly good trees into paper?

"Any messages?" I asked.

Without raising his eyes, Skipper reached under the counter. He handed me a single note. A phone message. "Slow week," he said. I never heard Skipper utter more than two words running. He aspired to laconic, saw himself as the drugstore Gary Cooper. I slapped half a buck into his open palm.

"Thanks, Eddie," he said with his usual one, two. He tried doing George Raft flipping the silver but muffed the catch. Miss Liberty plopped in the sink. "Oh, drat." I left him up to his elbows in Lux detergent and warned him to beware of sharks. He laughed. But he would. He yuks at anything. Skipper's the kind Toons were made for.

A mean eye and hostile attitude swept the Iowa hayseeds out of my usual booth. I slid in and unfolded Louise Wrightliter's notes.

I set the two stars side by side and ran an eenie meenie miney moe. I caught Jessica Rabbit by the toe. I picked her up and started to read.

Less than two pages later, with a five-alarm fire pouring smoke out from under my collar, I signaled Skipper to draw me a seltzer, light on spritz, heavy on ice. I needed cooling, and I needed it bad. The last time I read anything this spicy, it spelled *Burp* and exploded out of a Toon who'd overindulged in a chili parlor.

A hot number, Jessica Rabbit. Louise Wrightliter meticulously itemized times, dates, and places of Jessica's multiple rendezvous with Gable. Plus, Louise had a battalion of witnesses—hotel clerks and bellboys, mostly—who had seen the two together. Louise even snapped photos of the happy couple. One showed them clinking champagne glasses and wearing the monogrammed cashmere bathrobes that come with a fruit basket and complete discretion if you rent a bungalow at one of the swankier Hollywood hideaways.

In the pictures of them on the street, both wore sunglasses, slouch hats, trench coats, and baggy britches. Adequate disguises for most people, but not this pair. Anybody on the short side of total myopia would recognize Jessica Rabbit even stuffed in a gunnysack. As for Gable, there was no mistaking him, either. I only saw one other with ears as big as his, and he answered to the name of Dumbo. Forget ordinary earmuffs. Give Gable a set of fur-lined peach baskets.

"Your seltzer," said Skipper without taking his nose out of his magazine or his mind out of the sewer.

I slipped the wasp-waisted glass discreetly under the table, added a dollop of joy juice from my hip flask, and swizzled the mix with my tonsils.

This was the poop Louise had used to write her exposés, and it backed her up six ways to Sunday. I folded the report and stuck it back in my pocket. Looked like I'd have to tell Roger he didn't have a case. Judging from the swill in Louise Wrightliter's journalistic garbage pail, maybe he didn't have a wife anymore, either.

Even though Jessica's material told the tale, I took a gander at Gable's anyway. The mark of the consummate professional.

Wrightliter had turned over one of Gable's stones and found an ugly serpent lurking underneath. According to a "reliable" source, Gable wasn't the man's man he appeared to be. He swung more toward a hint of mint, if you get my drift.

Rumors that Hollywood's premier heartthrob was a nancy. That was a revelation that would rock a neighborhood Bijou or two. I wondered why Louise Wrightliter hadn't branded her byline on that juicy tidbit. And what did that do to Gable's supposed romance with Jessica Rabbit?

On the bottom of Gable's heap was a medical bill from a Doctor Wallace Ford. Five hundred eighty-six bucks for unspecified services rendered. Arnie Johnson came a lot cheaper, but I bet Gable's problems didn't result from fleas, ticks, or a porcupine quill in the snout.

Fortunately for my bank account, this case wasn't over yet. I could milk this cow another day or two easy. Thank God for closet queens, jealous rabbits, and philandering wives.

Time to smell the rest of the roses cooking on my burner. I hauled out my phone message.

Charley Ferris, the day manager, backed out of the walk-in freezer cradling a half-gallon carton as tenderly as a mother would her child. He wore Blondie Bumstead's white apron, Mary Worth's sensible shoes, and Steve Canyon's slit cap except Charley's came in white paper instead of khaki twill. Charley eats, breathes, sleeps and sneezes ice cream. To him, Heaven's a frozen cloud of moo juice and Hell's a busted churn. He turned around and saw me sitting in my accustomed spot.

"Hey, you, Valiant," he shouted, so enraged he threatened me with his armload of hand-packed. I shivered at the thought before I calculated the odds. Let him conk me to his heart's content. His bludgeon would melt to slush a good half an hour before I went senseless. "Quit using my establishment for an auxiliary office. I ought to bill you rent for the booth. And your phone calls! One more bookie, one more loan shark, one more bazoomie rings my number looking for Eddie Valiant, and I start charging you secretarial rates."

I toasted him with a sip of seltzer. "Sure, sure. Add it on my tab."

Charley slammed his flavor of the month on the table and drew his stainless steel ice cream packing spoon out of his apron string. "Your tab. You mean the one you didn't pay last month, or the one you're not going to pay next month?"

The first rule of a private eye. Never let them see you sweat, a procedure which got a lot easier once I started wearing my shoulder pads under my arms instead of over. "Live and let live, Charley. Hermie Schwab pays you fifty simoleons a week, and you act like you own the place."

He stuck his spoon under my beezer. I caught a deliciously nutty whiff of pistachio, my favorite. If I had to die at the end of a scoop, at least I'd expire happy. "Yeah, yeah, wise guy," taunted Charley. "How much did you make last week? Come on. Tell me. I'm waiting." He waved his spoon around the room. "Tell everybody. We'd all like to hear."

Charley knew how to hurt a guy, but I was born wearing cast-iron underwear. "I got potential." I fluttered my phone message at him like it mattered a hill of beans.

With surprising speed for a guy with frostbitten fingers, Charley snatched it out of my mitt. "Oh, yeah? Big, important shamus. Hotshot private dick. Peeper to the stars. Let's measure the vast amount of potential you got." I tried to grab it back, but he smacked my hand with his spoon.

I relieved the sting with a slug of tonic as Charley read my note out loud. " 'I must see you immediately,' " he said. " 'I have a mystery which only you can solve. Cost is no object. I'll pay anything. Please. Help me. You're the only one I trust.' Signed . . .'' At this point Charley lost his voice. He tried to talk, but only a harsh, froggy croak came out.

Every eye in the place was on us. You could have heard an egg cream plop. I slid out of the booth, heisted the note away from him, and read the name he couldn't. " 'David O. Selznick.' " I folded it up real tiny. "Selznick, Selznick, where have I heard that name before?" I slid the wadded note across his extended spoon to soak up some flavor. "Oh, yeah. I remember. He's only the most powerful producer in Hollywood." I stuffed it into his open mouth. "So, Charley. You were asking me to take my business elsewhere?" I headed for the door.

Charley gulped hard and swallowed my message. He ran after me and caught me by the arm. He elbowed a paying customer off her stool, wiped it clean with his sleeve, and forced me to sit.

He motioned for Skipper to whip me up a Schwab's Special, the double banana split. "Right, boss," said Skipper, hauling out his steam shovel and building a four-mounded creation to rival the Pyramids of Giza. He dropped it in front of me. It registered six point one on the Richter scale. If he ever served two of these at once, his customers would have to eat them in the basement because the combined weight would drive the counter straight through the floor. Skipper used his fan magazine for a place mat, fulfilling my lifetime fantasy: to lick butterscotch syrup off Betty Grable's face.

"Thanks," I said.

"No problem," Skipper responded with his usual, stupid grin.

I'm not much for health food, and the special came loaded with it—bananas, pineapple, strawberries, cherries, nuts—but I'm also not one to turn down a free lunch. I ate it left to right, saving the chocolate end for dessert.

As I spooned down the last bite, Charley leaned in real close. His breath reeked of peppermint, the schnapps, not the chewing gum. "You like it, Eddie? If it's not made right, I'll do you another myself."

"It's fine, Charley. Perfect."

WHO P-P-P-PLUGGED ROGER RABBIT?

He handed me a paper napkin, an extraneous gesture since I'd already wiped my mouth on my sleeve. "You want anything else?" asked Charley. "Maybe a malt to wash it down? Or something stronger?" His voice dropped. "Promise me you won't tell Hermie, but I keep hootch in the freezer."

No kidding. "You're angling me for a favor."

"Your bill." Skipper laid down my check.

Charley grabbed for the tab, not that he had any competition, rolled it into a ball, and dropped it into an ashtray.

"Eddie. Eddie, my friend," he said, lighting my leafer and giving me his matches to keep. "I got a niece on my wife's side. Trudy Hammerschlemmer's her stage name. The old lady keeps pushing me to introduce her to a big-time producer. As if one would ever come in here. No self-respecting mogul's gonna hang out in a drugstore. That Lana Turner thing? That was pure publicity eyewash. Just between us girls, Hermie slipped Metro a wad to say they discovered her here." Charley peeled off his paper cap. A piece of the front end tore loose and stuck to his sweaty forehead. He worried it loose with his fingernail. "If you could maybe give Mr. Selznick Trudy's portfolio, I'd personally make sure that you never paid for another soda as long as you live."

This was taking on all the aspects of big potential. "No more complaints about Skipper fielding my calls?"

He crossed where his heart would be if he had one. "As God is my witness."

Being the only rider on the merry-go-round, I had my best chance ever at grabbing the brass ring. "I want one of those cardboard reserved signs left permanently on my booth."

His face flashed dark. Who pushed him harder, me or his missus? No contest. He nodded. His wife's a woman I'd hate to meet in a dark alley.

I wiggled my fingers. "Gimmee the goods."

He reached over the counter and grabbed a leather book he kept at the ready beside the frozen frappé glasses.

I took a gander at her eight-by-ten glossy. Surprise, surprise! Long, silky hair. Big brown eyes. Soft nose. Wide mouth. Plenty of teeth. Charley's niece had a future in the movies, all right.

Whenever Lassie needed a double. Woof, woof. "I'll do what I can."

Always one to push my luck, I stopped at the cash register and helped myself to a stogey.

Charley smiled and presented me with the whole box.

In my town, in my business, it's all in who you know.

WHO P-P-P-PLUGGED ROGER RABBIT?

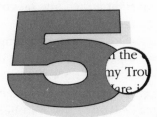

I tugged open the heavy, green-painted door at Joe Bazooka's Gym. A terrific wind belted me in the face, nearly hard enough to bowl me over. For a minute I thought the janitor had replaced the ceiling fans with airplane propellers, but the breeze came from Joe's lightning jabs as he shadowboxed the opponent provided him by the hundred-watt bulb shining over his shoulder.

Wham, bam! He flattened the shadow with a combination too quick for the human eye to see.

Joe Bazooka, the one and only retired, undefeated, heavyweight champ of the world. I took a seat on an overturned spit bucket and watched a genius at work.

Joe spotted me and gave his shadowy opponent a final bang-on-target one-two flurry. The shadow doubled over. Joe spared him the indignity of total collapse by reaching overhead and turning out the light. The shadow froze in place. Its edges crinkled and lifted, and it peeled slowly off the wall. Joe scooped it up and tossed it into a large wheeled cart half full of wet towels. "Hey, uh . . ." Joe scratched his tousled blonde head. After three hundred fights, the ink in Joe's well didn't flow easy anymore.

"Eddie," I reminded him.

"Yeah, Eddie." His large, solid, punching-bag-shaped balloon hung motionless in the air. I rapped it, none too gently, with my knuckles. It arced away, though in true championship tradition, it came right back for more.

Joe extended a hand the size and color of a baked ham. "I'm Joe Bazooka." As if I didn't know.

He turned to the wall and eyeballed the levelness of a photo already aligned with a transit. He rapped the bottom right side with his fingertip, moving it a gnat's eyebrow closer to perfection. "This is me and Jersey Joe Walcott. Madison Square Garden, June 16, 1934. That's the night I won the title." Joe sunk into a crouch.

Left arm slightly out, right tucked into his chin. "I came out hard at the opening bell . . ."

If I don't have much of a future, I don't mind reliving the past, but right now I had a paying customer. "Great fight. I saw the newsreels on the Cavalcade of Sports."

Joe's arms dropped to his side, his face not far behind them. "Right," he said in a balloon so low it scuffed my shoes. "I guess you know, then. About the night I won the crown." He dusted the picture with his sleeve. "This your first visit?"

If you didn't count twice a week for the past five years. "Yeah."

"Glad to have you." He pointed proudly around. "We got a full range of weights. Light and heavy body bags. Incline boards. Speed bags. Weighted jump ropes. You here for a workout or you planning to take up boxing as a career?"

Boxing could get me hurt, I'd recently been told. "Strictly exercise."

He sized me up. "Just as well." He peppered his stomach with his fists, duplicating the sound of twin woodpeckers beating against a steel flagpole. "Try to remember. You are what you eat."

Given my diet, that makes me a beer nut.

Joe looped his arm around my shoulders with enough reach left over to do it again. "You need help, holler. I'm always around."

Joe cocked a cauliflowered ear toward the silent wall phone. "I better answer that."

He handed me a shadow from out of the cart and picked up the telephone's earpiece, surprised to find nobody on the other end. He jiggled the hang-up hook. I left him telling the operator about 1934, the glorious night he decked Jersey Joe in two.

I went into the locker room and stripped to my underwear. I tightened my thigh garters a notch, slipped back into my steel-toed black brogans, strapped on a pair of Everlasts, and went looking for a fight.

I found it in the person of Joe's ancient, white-haired manager, Knuckles Woburn.

We climbed into one of the gym's two practice rings. Normally, I sparred without headgear, but, out of respect for Arnie Johnson's cranial quilting, I strapped on a leather helmet. Knuckles gave my basted noggin and my battered face the once-over. "Don't tell me. I oughta see the other guy. Who was it this time? A client, a cop, a husband, a bouncer?"

"How about one of those evil, no-good lawbreakers I've sworn to eradicate?"

"Cut the hooey. This is the old Knuckler you're talking to." He exhaled an empty balloon, crushed it into grit, sprinkled the residue on the floor, and shuffled it into the soles of his shoes. "Let's have the straight poop."

We touched gloves and squared off. I quick-punched him hard in the kisser. "You want the truth? OK. A Toon came at me out of the dark and hit me when I wasn't looking."

"That's what they all say," said Knuckles. He faked a left.

I took my eyes off him to read his chatter. I'd done it a million times before with never a problem. Two maybe three hundred rounds he'd never laid a glove on me. This time, his right cross walloped my chin with the force of a sledgehammer.

"Looking then?" taunted Knuckles.

Nobody, for sure no Toon, does that to Eddie Valiant and gets away with it. I waded in swinging. "Ever hear the phrase 'Box, and you could get hurt'?"

"Regularly. From my dear, departed mother." Knuckles foiled my efforts to end it quick by hiding behind his balloon. "I should have listened."

When I reached forward to brush his balloon away, he ducked out, came in under my arm, and socked me with another power-house right. It staggered me. I backed off and jabbed at him, waiting for my head to clear.

"Gable still coming around?"

"Pretty much." Knuckles popped me with another potent right. "He does the circuit. Goes a few with Joe. Ought to make a prizefighting movie, he should. Terrific build on him. Fast hands, too. He's a game cock, he is. I remember once Joe bopped his nose. Broke it clean. I offered to straighten it out. Gable told me not to bother. Said the studio kept a high-powered doctor on special retainer for him. Said he'd let the sawbones earn his fee. Walked out of here calm as you please with a swollen honker that would have had a lesser man screaming for an ambulance. You gotta respect his moxie."

His right stung me again. One more like that, he'd win by a KO, and there goes my undefeated record. "Gable mention this medic's name?"

"As I recollect, he had the same moniker as Gable's car. Dusenberg, Stutz, Bugatti . . ."

"Not Ford?"

"Right." He smacked me another good one. "I remember thinking, here's a star can drive whatever foreign jobbie he wants, and he buys American. A regular guy."

I was fading fast. Time to put the old-timer to sleep, by hook or by crook. "Hey, Knuckles." I pointed at the canvas. "Your shoe's untied."

He backed away and glanced down. "So's yours."

"What kind of boob you take me for?"

He shrugged. "Don't come crying when you trip and fall."

We traded shots, nothing major. "Hear any gossip about Gable?" I asked.

"He's stepping out with Jessica Rabbit."

"Deeper than that, and darker." I blocked his right with my forearm and lost feeling to my elbow.

"Don't tell me Gable's a crossover Toon!"

"Not that bad."

"What, then?"

"How about a poof?"

Knuckles laughed. "We talking about the same Gable? Clark? Tall guy, big side flaps? Eddie, I've seen this guy in the showers. He's got half the women in town tattooed on his chest. He's as straight as the train track through the Valley." Knuckles dropped his guard.

I stepped in close, cocked my arm, and tripped on my untied shoelace. As I fell backwards, Knuckles rapped me with his last balloon.

I woke up with rosin on my back and ammonia in my nostrils. Knuckles pulled me to my feet.

"You sandbagged me. That's illegal." I used my teeth, thankful that I still had them, to unloosen my gloves.

"You got a beef, take it to the boxing commission." Knuckles unlaced his left glove and pulled it off. "Gable a poufah. Don't that

WHO P-P-P-PLUGGED ROGER RABBIT?

beat all." He removed his right. His clenched fist gripped a roll of quarters. He held them up between his thumb and forefinger and winked.

"That *is* illegal."

"So's beating up on an old man every week."

"What are you talking about? You're a Toon. You like it."

"Sure. Same way Joan of Arc enjoyed a good barbecue."

I slipped my suit back on and went into the steam room. Since I had it all to myself, I cranked the temperature up to the level that percolates out bad food and worse whiskey.

I sat on the lowest bench and watched myself drip down the drain.

The door opened and closed. Young Harry the Hedgehog waddled in and tugged at my pants leg. "Swab job, Eddie?" He rolled his chocolate-pudding eyes. I'm a sucker for chocolate-pudding eyes.

"Sure, sure, why not?" I told him. I penciled his two-bit charge into my expense book. But how to itemize it to score it legit? "What do you hear, Young Harry?"

Young Harry hopped up on my lap. "Uuuuuh, not much."

Reliable informant. I closed the book and returned it to my inside breast pocket.

Young Harry chinned his way to my shoulder, inched around to the back of my head, grabbed my collar in his tiny paws, and draped himself upside down over my noggin. As he tick-tocked side to side, his furry stomach swabbed my forehead.

A cold breeze rattled my kneecaps as the steam-room door opened and stayed that way.

"You born in a barn?" I complained to the newcomer without thinking that around here the answer could be yes. "Come in or get out before the hot stuff leaks away."

The door closed. I couldn't see a thing. Squishy, menacing, rubbery footsteps moved in my direction. "Who's there?" I said.

I didn't get a response.

Young Harry ceased his swabbing.

The footsteps came closer.

Young Harry scampered over my shoulder and ducked behind my back. He knew my business and wanted no part of it. Right about now I couldn't say I blamed him.

I moved against the side wall and checked out the ceiling. In the six inches of clear air between the steam and the roof, a pointy pair of great white shark fins headed straight for me. My heart pounded louder than the overture to *Moby Dick.*

I grabbed Young Harry by the hind legs. Soaking wet, he hefted about the same as a calf-length argyle full of BBs. "Who's there?" I repeated.

A balloon poked through the steam and bopped me on the nose. Condensation had filled it half full of water. The letters inside floated like skim on a bowl of alphabet soup. Using Young Harry's tail as a rearranging tool, I deciphered the message. "Eddie! Thank goodness. Am I glad I found you. I've been looking *everywhere.*" The approaching shark fins dipped out of the vapor and became the ends of Roger Rabbit's pointy ears.

I leveled a thumb at the door. "Members only, chum."

"But I am, Eddie. I joined today. Joe gave me his special, limited time only, introductory offer." He calculated the cost on his fingertips. "One month at half price, half a month at a third the price, a third of a month at a quarter the price . . ."

I threaded Young Harry through the collar of my jacket and out the bottom. I grabbed him by both ends, stretched him long, and whipsawed him across my back.

". . . and twenty minutes *FREE!*" Roger's fingers interlocked in a tight weave. He untangled his digits and plunked himself down beside me. His wishboney hips weren't wide enough to anchor his Turkish towel, so he held it up with clip-on suspenders. His shower cap with its two ear holes resembled Clarabelle Cow's milk warmer. For watertightness, the ear holes drew shut with red drawstrings which Roger had looped into large, intricate bows that would have been the envy of Pollyanna's pigtails. To keep his toes cozy, he sported bright yellow galoshes. His arms held a sponge, a squeegee, a mop, and an armload of dishrags.

Roger launched another soppy, indecipherable balloon.

"Knock off the gasbags and talk normal, will you? I can't read a word you're saying."

WHO P-P-P-PLUGGED ROGER RABBIT?

"Sure, Eddie," he said in his breathy squeak. "You name it. My p-p-p-pleasure." He yanked off his boots and poured the sweat out of them with a noise that made Niagara Falls sound like a drizzly squirt from a kid's water gun. As he squiggled back into his footwear, he eyeballed my attire and launched enough question marks to supply the collected works of Sherlock Holmes.

"I wear my suit in the steam room because it saves on dry cleaning, all right?" I tugged my lapels to iron out the wrinkles. "You know, curiosity killed the cat."

"Lucky for me I'm a rabbit!" He unrolled his tongue and ran his squeegee down the length of it. His eyes crossed as they followed the squeegee's progress.

"This so important it can't wait for regular office hours?"

He shook his noodle to restart the rolling marbles that activated his brain. He pushed his nose. His extended tongue reeled in like the steel tape measure a criminologist would use to administer a lie detector test to Pinocchio. "There's been a truly frightening development in my case." He ran his mop across his puss, nearly taking my head off as he swung the handle. "I'm terrified, Eddie. Scared nearly out of my wits."

That didn't stop him from draping the mop top over his noggin and pouting his eyes in a pretty fair impression of Tallulah Bankhead. Encouraged by that success, he stood up on the bench, hung the mop head around his waist, and demonstrated his hula-hula.

While he figured out a hundred and one ways to have fun with a mop, the heat and the wetness got to him. He blurred around the borders. "Oh, my golly," Roger said with grave concern. He grabbed for the red emergency can of laundry starch clipped to the wall. He doused it liberally on his parameters as he dove headlong through the door. It shut behind him with a tired hiss.

I upended the hedgehog and slid him teeth first down each of my pants legs.

The door opened and Roger dashed back inside. His contours had nearly resumed their normal sharpness. "Aren't you coming?" he asked in great big letters.

I leaned backwards against the bench behind me, lifted my arms, and locked my fingers behind my head. "Eventually."

"Now! P-p-p-please! It's really important, Eddie. Honest it is."
He zipped out the door. His parallel black speed lines fell to the
floor with a glockenspiel tinkle.

"I'll be out when I'm good and ready," I said to nobody in
particular.

The hedgehog finished my pressing and held out his paw. I
paid him off and added a big tip, the name of a sure thing in the
fifth at Santa Anita.

I followed my client out the door.

Roger emerged from the locker room wearing a brown worsted suit, padded to bring his shoulders out even with his cheeks;
a wrinkled, belted, double-breasted overcoat born in the trenches
of Spade, Marlow, and Hammer; and a slouchy hat with a brim
wide enough for peewee roller derby. Worse, I was wearing the
exact same thing! I hated Mom dressing me and Teddy, or me and
Teddy and Freddy, or me and Teddy and Freddy and my sister
Heddy alike. You can imagine how I felt about twinning Roger
Rabbit.

Joe walked by and gave us a take. "Geez, are you two related
or something?"

"Oh, brother," I said.

"Oh, brothers!" Joe responded. "I should have picked it up
from the family resemblance."

I sprung for lunch at my favorite cart, Dad's Dogs and Other
Fine Cuisine.

Dad ran it out of a motorized hot-dog cart, his theory being
that a rolling restaurant gathers no visits from the sanitation inspector. He set up shop wherever fate and the traffic flow took him,
so you never knew exactly where he'd homestead day to day.

The health department must have been hot on his wheels. He
wasn't set up for business at any of his usual haunts. After half an
hour of foodless searching, I drove through a neighborhood
where every third person evidenced crossed eyes, a puckered
green face, and a doubling-over case of stomach cramps. Back-
tracking a trail of discarded, half-eaten franks, I found Dad's in an
out-of-the-way alley. Parked, as usual, heading out for a fast getaway.

I docked my boat and went ashore. Roger stayed inside. "You coming, or what?" I asked him.

"That's where you want to eat?" His balloon formed a pair of hands which grabbed him by the neck and strangled him until his eyes bugged out to the cone shape of paper water cups. Why did this fuzzy clown insist on turning every side show into a three-ring circus?

"Hasn't killed me yet. What are you, squeamish?"

"To be honest, yes." He thought up a road map and marked our position with a big, red, *You Are Here* arrow. "I know a restaurant not far away." The arrow moved, got lost, reversed direction, took a shortcut through the La Brea tar pits, and arrived at its destination with half the street names in L.A. adhered to its sticky black tail. "I bet you'd love it. Best carrot soup ever. Great steamed broccoli, fresh lettuce, juicy . . ."

I was starving, my head ached, and I was in no mood to argue with a reluctant rabbit. I snabbed him by the ears and yanked him out through the window. "Trust me on this one. It's better than it looks."

His balloon had to squeeze itself pencil thin to worm its way through my fist. "That won't be hard. It looks disgusting."

Trust a Toon to overexaggerate. Granted, Dad wasn't one to go in for excessive cleanliness. Grease dripped off the underside of his striped umbrella. His steak meat got that way by losing too many races at Hollywood Park. He reused his paper plates. And you had to cover your face with a handkerchief when you ordered to filter out the thick, acid smoke overhanging the grill. But who cares about a lack of minor amenities? Could that man cook! He's the only *rotisserier* I ever found who roasted and toasted hot dogs exactly the way I like them, one ember shy of a charcoal briquette.

"How's business, Dad?"

"A mite slow today, Eddie." Dad was married to the hot-dog art. Like anybody who stays hitched long enough, he'd come to resemble his mate. Dad wasn't much bigger around than a Polish sausage. His oversized Army surplus great coat encased him like a brown wool bun. Standing beside a flaming grill day in and day out had reddened his complexion to the color of a bratwurst. Dad advertised his selection of condiments—ketchup, mustard, relish, and horseradish—with large blobs on the front of his apron.

Way back when, he wore a traditional chef's hat, but his low-hanging umbrella kept knocking it off. So he trimmed his headgear to fit under his bumbershoot, which left him sporting a white band and three inches of plume, like a paper booty snitched from a giant lamb chop. "You dining on dog?" he asked me. "Got one's been over the flame since yesterday noon."

"Sounds tempting, but a single frank's not gonna cut the mustard today. I'm hungry enough to wolf a horse." Keeping my hand low, out of Dad's sight, I motioned for Roger to step forward. "I brought you another hungry customer. Famous fellow. Recognize him?" I pointed beside me to a hunk of empty air.

"Casper the Friendly Ghost?" tried Dad. He flipped a burger off the griddle, sniffed it, crinkled his nose, and threw it back on the slats to cook for another few hours. "The Invisible Man?" He tossed a batter-covered hot-dog-on-a-stick into a vat of frying oil suspiciously similar to the Quaker State that lubed my coupe's engine.

I checked around for Roger.

Dad scratched his head. "Harvey?"

"You're warm, very warm."

Despite my assurances, Roger hung back. I motioned him forward. Reluctantly, he joined me at the stand-up counter.

"Well I'll be dipped, Roger Rabbit," said Dad. "You're one famous galoot! You're gonna eat here? I don't believe it." He handed me his barbecue fork. "Jab me hard in the arm, Eddie, to prove I ain't dreaming."

I begged off. "Take my word, Dad. He's as real as life and twice as ugly."

"Do me a favor, would ya?" said Dad to Roger. "Sign an autograph? It's not for me, mind you, it's for my missus. She's one of your biggest fans." He checked under the counter. "Got some blank paper somewhere." He came up empty. "How about this?" He handed Roger a hard slice of day-old white bread.

Roger inscribed it in mustard, "To Mom," added his paw print, and handed it back.

Dad gave the bread a curious look. "How'd you know her name?"

"Lucky guess."

WHO P-P-P-PLUGGED ROGER RABBIT?

"She'll treasure this forever." Dad stored it in his toaster for safekeeping.

Dad slapped menus in front of us. "Trout's especially fine today." He reached into his larder and wrestled a half-eaten skeleton away from his cat. "Also some terrific specials." He rattled them off. Rabbit stew, hasenpfeffer, rabbit dip, Welsh rabbit, rabbit McMuffin, and country fried rabbit, all you can eat.

Decisions, decisions. I ordered the sampler platter and a cup of black.

Roger, pleading a finicky stomach, went with Caesar salad to start, chef's salad with a side order of spinach salad as a main course, and Waldorf salad for dessert.

Dad served our selections on two of the magazines he used for trays. Mine, a recent *Photoplay*, showed Loretta Young looking great even under yesterday's relish stains. Roger's *Life* pictured a smiling bookseller peeking out from behind a small mountain of *Gone With the Wind*s.

We carried lunch to the car, spread it on the hood, and sat on the fender.

I took a bite. Dad must have picked up this recipe during his world tour of garlic festivals. "What's eating you?" I asked around a mouth full of rabbit's foot.

Roger reached inside his trench coat and withdrew a stuffed Roger Rabbit doll. "This." He held it up.

Looked identical to hundreds of others I'd seen since Roger became a star. On sale in any toy store. The hottest item going, so I hear. Even available in a handy five-pack for kids who couldn't afford a china bisque set of Dionne quints. "If you're trying to peddle it, I pass. My teddy bear would get jealous."

"You don't understand!" Roger's eyelids fluttered like a babbling semaphore. "I heard a knock on my door this morning. I answered it, but I found nobody there. Only this doll, propped on the welcome mat."

"Dolls talk, they cry, a few even wet their britches. Maybe this one sells Fuller brushes door to door."

"Not a chance." Roger flipped the doll over and displayed its rear end. "Look at it closer."

A word balloon hung from a hatpin poked into the quarter-inch hole where the doll's missing cottontail used to be. The balloon said "Dead rabbits carry no tails." I recognized the voice. It matched the one I gave Wordhollow.

Roger locked his hands behind his back and paced the hood side to side, rising and falling with the slope like a hiker touring the foothills of Hell. "I've been under such pressure lately. This business with Jessica, my screen test for *Gone With the Wind*. Now a threat to my life. I ask you, Eddie, what's a rabbit supposed to do?"

There's a question could keep a philosopher occupied for the rest of the century. I climbed into the car. "Come on. I'll drive you home."

As Roger slid down the fender he slapped a balloon flat against my windshield. "Could you maybe," it said, "if it's not too much trouble, tell me how it's going with the *Toontown Telltale*? Were you able to persuade that vile rag to print a retraction?"

I thumbed the starter button. "Not quite." Three swipes of my wiper sent his question to oblivion. Roger eased open the door and slipped into the seat beside me. At first I thought he'd grown a second Adam's apple, but it was his heart raising the extra lump in his throat. "There's a major detail that still needs to be worked out." Roger's *Life* magazine wrapped itself around my radio antenna and hung there flapping in the wind.

"Let me hear it," he said.

I told it the only way I know how, fast and ugly. "The story's probably true. The *Telltale* has photos, eyewitness reports, hotel receipts, the works. I've seen murderers convicted on less evidence. If I had to judge based on my observations, I'd say Jessica's cooching Gable."

"She's not!" Roger collapsed forward and bopped his noggin on the dashboard. "She's not!" The impact sailed him backward. He smacked his cranberry on the rear of the seat. "She's not." He would have bing-bonged back and forth denying the obvious for the rest of the trip if I hadn't grabbed his ears and shaken some sense into him.

"Don't take it so hard, chum. It's the story of life. Happens every day. A beautiful woman plays a rabbit for a sap. If it wasn't for that, half the town's columnists and three quarters of the divorce lawyers would go out of business."

WHO P-P-P-PLUGGED ROGER RABBIT?

Roger pulled loose and stuck his whole upper body out the window. His ears flew parallel with my coon tail, and his fists shook to Heaven. What he yelled tore loose in the windstream. I read it in my rearview mirror. "It's a lie," it proclaimed before the car behind me ran it into the asphalt.

I yanked Roger back inside, reached across him, and cranked up the window. "I don't want to raise your hopes, but there's a chance, a slim one, you might be right."

Roger's face brightened so visibly he blinded an old lady in an oncoming Stanley Steamer. "Why do you think that?" he asked.

"It has to do with Gable. I want to check him over. See if he's everything he's cracked up to be."

"Whatever it takes, Eddie. However much it costs. I'm behind you one hundred percent. Is there anything I can do to help?"

"Yeah, maybe. You know Gable? Ever meet him personally? Have any dealings with him?"

Roger settled back in his seat. "No, never. And if I did, I'd . . . I'd . . . I'd *ignore* him."

"You're a feisty rabbit."

"Darn right." Roger's balloon fluttered its edges but couldn't muster the strength to soar. It caught on his forelock and flopped like a patch across his right eye. Too bad the Hathaway folks couldn't see him. He'd be perfect for an ad if they ever designed a shirt boasting a three-inch neck and no shoulders.

I pulled into Roger's driveway. Roger got out and shambled toward his front door.

I peeled his *Life* off my antenna. It was open to a picture of him schmoozing with David Selznick in the MGM canteen. "Hey, Roger. For your scrapbook." I tossed it to him.

He caught it on the fly and read it as he walked away.

I backed the car out of the driveway, fiddled it into first gear, and punched the gas pedal.

Next thing I knew, Roger bounded into the middle of the road as only a hopping mad rabbit can. He stood directly in front of me, holding his yellow paw outstretched. I put on the brakes, thankful for quick reflexes and a wheezy engine.

"That's a good way to kill yourself," I yelled at him out the window.

He jumped onto my running board and shoved the *Life* photo in my puss. "Eddie, this isn't me."

I took a second gander. Looked exactly like the Roger clinging to my door breathing swamp gas in my face. "You sure?"

"Of course I'm sure. Don't you think I can recognize myself when I see me? I'm telling you, this rabbit's a wolf in sheep's clothing."

I ripped out the page and stuck it in my pocket. "I'll drop by Selznick's office and ask him."

He cocked his head. "Are you kidding? David Selznick's a very important man. He only sees Hollywood's top dogs."

"Call me Pluto."

I stopped in a gin mill for a pack of smokes. One thing led to another and pretty soon there were five empty bottles of Schlitz on the bar, I'd lost an arm-wrestling match to a white-haired woman who called me Whippersnapper, I told my one good joke where I turn my pants pockets inside out and impersonate an elephant, and MGM was closed for the day.

A Boy Scout abandoned a hobbling grannie mid-street to help me to my car.

After I figured out how to start it and kicked it into gear, I did the same as I always do the times my hard head needed a soft shoulder. I drove over to see Doris.

I parked outside her bungalow. Since she didn't answer her doorbell or come to the bedroom window after I broke it with a rock, I deduced she wasn't home. Nothing to it. Any correspondence school hawkshaw could have figured it out. I poured myself a time waster out of the glove compartment, and settled back to wait.

About three hours later, just as my glove box ran dry and I was debating whether to tap the radiator for a refill, Doris showed up.

She was with a guy, a three-piece blue suit, pressed shirt, clean necktie, neat haircut, shiny shoes, solid citizen type. Maybe I was reading too much into appearances, but he looked like the dull, stodgy variety who would give her a steady paycheck, a house in the suburbs and three lovable kids, and would never stagger home late at night reeking of booze or riddled with buckshot.

WHO P-P-P-PLUGGED ROGER RABBIT?

They shared a laugh as he tripped over a rosebush walking her to the door. They laughed again as she rummaged through her purse for her keys. They quit laughing a few seconds or two before he smooched her good-night.

They weren't laughing, either, as she invited him in.

I stuck around for a few more hours until I began to see it as a lost cause.

I wished Doris pleasant dreams and a happy life. God knows, after the one she'd been through with me, she deserved it.

I let the air out of Mr. Right's tires and drove up to Mulholland to catch some Z's.

I parked next to a Roman chariot and said, "Morning." No answer. "Any chance of cadging a lift over to Davey Selznick's office?" Silence. I stroked its fender. Sometimes that loosens their tongues.

A gorgeous young actress walked by reading a thick script. She glanced at me and snickered, I couldn't guess why. A hasty quality check showed my socks matched, my hat faced more or less forward, my jacket was on right side out, the old barn door was closed and shuttered. She left me standing with my arm around a mute Toon as she walked off alone into a painted sunset.

A prop handler drove up in a studio quarter ton. I asked him directions to Selznick's office, and he all but drew me a map. He then picked up the chariot and threw it into the back of his truck. The chariot wasn't a Toon, it was a plywood dummy. I hated to think what that made me.

As I hoofed it across the Metro complex, I detoured down memory lane, Soundstage 16, the big outdoor back lot where Teddy and I worked as stuntmen in the Westerns the studio once cranked out at the rate of two a week. Teddy fell off moving horses; I tumbled over cliffs. Nobody did either better. Or more often. I once calculated that between us we'd fallen on our beans five hundred and eighty-six times. To be fair, I credited Teddy with two for one because at a full gallop he always bounced twice. I hit harder but stayed put.

We left the movie stunt business because we couldn't compete, not with Toons willing to fall farther, faster, and land with a bigger squish.

Now I'm a private eye instead of a stuntman, but not much else has changed. I still take regular headers, the other guy always gets the girl, and I can rarely follow the plot. Though there are two differences. The bullets are real, and I write my own lines.

On Soundstage 16, the West had flown south for the winter

to make room for *Gone With the Wind*. Crumbling brick Atlanta mansions replaced the plain pine boxes of Dodge City. The pies were pecan instead of cow. Evenly spaced whitewashed pickets had converted the OK Corral into a garden fence. The Long-branch Saloon had been renamed the Atlanta Hotel. It advertised hot water baths and afternoon tea. There wasn't a gun being slung. The men walking the streets were as fancy as the ladies.

I watched a row of cactus plants and tumbleweeds audition for bit parts as magnolia trees. Those that couldn't prune their talents trundled back to nursery school.

Horatio Horsecollar rode past costumed as a Yankee captain. He sat four hands tall in the saddle. Underneath him, Ward Bond gave a pretty good supporting performance in the role of Horatio's horse.

I spotted the beautiful young extra who had caught me chinning with the scenery. She was costumed as a Southern belle and surrounded by a cotillion of likewises. She saw me and spread her hoop skirt so it obscured the camera truck behind her. "Hide your flivvers, ladies," she said with a lightly Limey accent. "We've a man in our midst with a yen for inanimate objects."

I smooched the nearest camera dolly—who says I can't take a joke?—and beat a hasty retreat.

The full-relief doohickey on Selznick's polished mahogany door reproduced the wooden crest projected on-screen at the opening of his movies, except this one was cast out of solid gold. Shielding my eyes from the glare of wanton greed, I yanked at a few protruding heraldic escutcheons, but the unchivalrous rascals refused to break loose. I cursed the vainglory that drives a man to forge a coat of arms solid enough to survive the next ice age.

The sofas and chairs in Selznick's outer office came from one of those German architectural colonies where form follows function—if you happen to be shaped like the steel tack hammer that built your davenport. His artwork resembled something Krazy the Kat dragged in. The wall-mounted lighting was as subtly indirect as a teenager angling for a good-night kiss.

His carpet undulated slightly as I closed the door. I watched my step. An entire tribe of pygmies could be hiding in the nap. I rolled out my Lawn Boy and mowed a path to his secretary's desk.

She was straight out of Central Casting, a perfect cross between Rita Hayworth and a busted watch—gorgeous as Gilda, but she wouldn't give me the time of day.

She flipped on her intercom with a fingernail slightly shorter than a strawberry Popsicle but just as red, whispered into the speaker, and seemed surprised at the words it whispered back.

She returned my slightly tarnished badge, pinching it between thumb and forefinger the same way the safety manuals instruct you to hold a bubonic rat, and told me to enter Sleznick's inner sanctum. I promised to stop back on my way out and collect the quarter she owed me for cutting her rug. She flipped me two bits and told me not to bother.

Enclosed spaces the size of Selznick's office usually belonged to breweries who used them to age barrels of beer. His housed a Civil Warrior's garage sale, a wall-to-wall assortment of swords, boots, scabbards, sashes, epaulets, tunics, and striped trousers.

A small arsenal of incredible shootware caught my eye. I'm a gun fancier, and I'd never seen guns fancier. Rifles, muskets, carbines interlocked into bivouac tripods. Pistols nestled side by side in wooden crates bearing faint traces of Army serial number gobbledygook that hadn't changed much since Hannibal's quartermaster stenciled it on the side of his pachyderms.

I picked up a matched pair of gorgeous, like-new Colt .44 Dragoons with polished bone grips and hardened brass cylinders. Each weighed as much as a steam locomotive and was almost as long, but they balanced in my grip like a teeter-totter with identical twins straddling either end. I'd never seen one of these babies in action, but I knew them by reputation. They packed the smack to blow a hole clear through Saint Louis. These smelled faintly of Cosmoline and carried a full load of ammunition. I put them back before they became too attached to my hand.

Selznick might know everything and its uncle about movie making, but in dealing with the general public, he could learn a lesson from Montgomery Wards. For starters, his office needed overhead signs—or better yet, aisles. From where I stood, I couldn't see anything beyond Men's Period Outer Garments.

I navigated my way to Selznick's desk in less time than it took

Stewart Granger to find King Solomon's Mines, though granted I didn't have Deborah Kerr along to slow me down.

I had heard Selznick was a perfectionist, that he insisted on strict historical accuracy. I heard he personally inspected and approved every prop and every costume used in his movies. That's what I hope I found him doing.

Selznick stood facing a full-length mirror. He was holding a floor-length calico print dress to his chest. He flicked its narrow, stand-up collar. He fluffed its puffy shoulders. He extended his arm and checked the inseam for puckers. He kicked out an ankle to see how the skirt draped his leg. He slid his hand down the long row of buttons securing the bodice. He stopped halfway, lifted one of the buttons between his fingers, and ripped it loose. He penciled a note on a clipboard attached to the mirror's frame. When he caught me peeking, he returned his frock to a rack containing twenty-six others identical to it except that each was slightly more, or less, tattered, soiled, faded, or scorched than the one beside it.

"Mr. Valiant," he said. "How do you do? I'm David Selznick Junior." If the Producers' Union ever got a load of this guy, he'd be banned from the fraternity for life. Movie producers were required by law to wear shapeless, heavily pleated, houndstooth-checked, wool gabardine slacks; a glove-leather belt with first, last, and middle initials curlicued in that order onto the gold buckle; a blousey rayon shirt with cuff links the size of Rolls-Royce headlights; a silk ascot tacked into place with a stickpin too flashy for Diamond Jim Brady; two-toned saddle shoes; and an oversized sport coat with a pattern as far removed from the trousers as you could get and still be on this planet. A beret was required headgear outdoors, optional, though highly recommended, in.

Selznick didn't only break the mold, he pulverized it to sand. A tall, stocky man, he wore a conservative blue suit perfectly tailored to accentuate his positive; a simple white shirt; plain black tasseled loafers; a slightly tattered, grandfatherly, blue cardigan sweater I wouldn't wear to a dogfight; and a zigzag-patterned tie that I would. His wristwatch came from the five-and-dime and ticked louder than a tower clock. He wore no other jewelry except for a broad gold wedding band. He combed his thick dark hair straight back and parted it in the middle. He had a baby's beard, or maybe he shaved every hour. The brass fan twirling behind him blew me a faint whiff of lilac cologne. His eyeglasses were the same plain hard steel as his handshake. "My God, man," he said, wide-eyed, "are you feeling all right? You look like you slept in your car and dressed on the street."

"A minor case of all-night surveillance. I'll recover."

"Can I offer you a drink?" He pointed to six Oriental metal tea chests each as large as a clothes hamper. "A cup of hot herbal tea, perhaps? I have an extensive selection."

He must pal around with a lot of biddies. One man alone could brew nonstop for the rest of his life and never finish that much orange Pekoe. I noticed he had a large earthen jug encased in a cocoon of woven wicker. "A nip of that'll do me fine."

Selznick followed my gaze. "I doubt it. The bottle's suitably aged, but the liquor's colored water."

"I thought you always went in for absolute accuracy."

"One hundred percent, but never ninety proof." He saluted me with a plain white crockery mug full of steaming hot tea. "I'm not a Puritan. If whiskey's your preference, I maintain a fully stocked bar." He pointed to a spot somewhere over the rainbow. "Against the far wall. Feel free to help yourself."

I figured under the best of conditions an hour to get there, the same to get back. "Thanks anyways," I told him. I had my choice of places to light, a lady's sidesaddle slung across a sawhorse, or a fancy parlor chair with the spindly legs of a malnourished spider. I pulled up the chair, spun it around, and mounted it from behind. It groaned, but not half as loudly as I would have. "I understand you've got a problem."

"Indeed I do, Mr. Valiant. A very serious one." He turned his back to me and gazed out his picture window. It gave him a clear line of sight to the Washington Monument. Painted plywood and ten feet high, it still beat the air shaft and brick wall my office landlord peddled as a room with a view. "I'm in the midst of the biggest production of my career. I have a million details begging for my attention. Major decisions to make. Yet I can't proceed, I can't accomplish another thing, until you solve a mystery for me."

I'm a man of few words. So far he hadn't said any of them. "Skip the soliloquy. Here's my terms. You tell me what, where, and when. I tell you who, why, and how much."

WHO P-P-P-PLUGGED ROGER RABBIT?

Selznick took a seat in his desk chair, a high-backed, gold-leafed monstrosity with faded upholstery, rosebuds twined across the headrest, rickety racked legs, and unpadded arms. It was undoubtedly genuine Louis the Roman Numeral. A dowager would probably mortgage her tiara for it but I'd cart it straight to the dump. He slid an eight-by-ten glossy into his desk drawer, casually, so I'd think it wasn't important—which meant that it was. "I admire directness," he said. The edges of his mouth inched closer to his cheeks. It wasn't quite a smile but seemed the best he could manage under the circumstances. "I see so little of it in my industry." His basso profundo rumble duplicated the throaty shush of the Pacific Ocean vacuuming Malibu Beach. "Let's begin at the end. How much. I'll pay you four times your current going rate. One hundred dollars a day plus expenses. I trust that sum will be sufficient."

I shrugged. "Depends. I'd strangle your grandmother for it. Ask me to strangle mine, it's going to cost you more. Tell me the job, and I'll decide which granny gets the throttle."

This time I got a real smile, a big one the size of a hangnail moon. "Nothing half so grisly as grandmatricide. I'm paying you a premium because I require and expect the absolute essence of tact and discretion."

My turn to grin. "In that case, hire Jeeves, the gentleman's gentleman. You want a zipped lip, you're barking up the wrong guy."

"I don't think so." He took the top off a clear crystal humidor and offered me a sniff of a pretty good argument for declaring Virginia broadleaf a national treasure. "I admired your handling of the Roger Rabbit frame-up a while back. A lesser man would have trumpeted his success with a blatant round of self-promotion."

Little did he know. Men don't come any lesser than me. Citing the city ordinance against bad taste, every newspaper in L.A. declined to print my ad. "I'm a saint."

"I wouldn't go that far." Selznick stuffed an iota of his prime burly into a corncob pipe you could buy from any street corner news vendor at three for a buck. A hasty mental calculation told me a pinch of his tobacco cost a hundred times as much as the furnace that sent it to blazes. "I checked you out with the police. A Captain Cleaver."

Oh oh. We got trouble in River City. "He gave me a glowing endorsement?"

Selznick lit his cooker and took a long, slow drag. He exhaled the sludge straight in my face. "He described you as a human weevil, a parasite who lives by chewing holes in the fabric of society."

Clever Cleaver, consistently voted L.A.P.D.'s Poet Lariat for the way he tied me into knots. "Guilty as charged, Your Honor. Yet you dialed my number, anyway."

He tapped a yellow Ticonderoga against his desk blotter hard enough to break the lead. "For my task, I require a man of, shall we say, dubious credentials." He set his pipe into a polished marble ashtray while he repointed his pencil with a red plastic sharpener.

"Shall we say what exactly you want me to do?"

He put a polish on his pencil point by rubbing it across the stilettoed edge of a letter opener that could gut an envelope or the postman who delivered it. "As you may know, I'm producing *Gone With the Wind*."

A Confederate campaign hat hung on my chair back's center spindle. I lifted it off and twirled it on my finger. Whoop-de-do. "I couldn't have guessed."

"I plan to make it a classic, a musical comedy which will live in the memory forever. Songs by Rodgers and Hammerstein. Choreography by Busby Berkeley. Comedic routines by Buster Keaton."

He sucked the life back into his tobacco kiln, sending up a cloud of smoke larger than the one that announced the election of a pope. "To be done right, the project requires great quantities of money." Bitsy whiffets of smoky aroma leaked out of his stem, about an inch from the end, where he'd chewed it through with his teeth. "Unfortunately, I've reached a temporary impasse with my backers. They refuse to provide any more financing until I cast the main role.

"They don't understand that this is not a decision to be made arbitrarily, or in haste. The lead will make or break this movie." His smoke drifted to the ceiling, where his revolving fan tortured it for a while before cutting it to ribbons.

"Initially, I wanted an unknown to play the part. I felt it would infuse the project with appeal to the common man. I conducted talent searches in hamlets across the country." He showed me a stack of audition ads he'd run in near 'bout every hick weekly between here and Podunk Junction. "I wasted months. My efforts proved fruitless. My mythical newcomer doesn't exist.

"My lead will be an established star." He reached into his desk drawer and removed a trio of manila folders. I craned over and caught a glimpse of the photo he seemed so anxious to hide. A cheesecake shot, of the Brit I'd met on the soundstage. Her legs matched her vowels, long and well rounded. "I've narrowed the field to these." He fanned the folders in front of me. "Any one of them would satisfy my backers and get me the money I need to continue. Of greater importance, any one of them would imbue the film with the energy, the wit, and the extraordinary talent it needs to succeed on a monumental scale. This is the role of a lifetime, and it's mine to bestow. The star I select achieves filmic immortality. Tell me, Mr. Valiant, how do I choose?"

I binked one at random with my pinkie. "One potato, two potato always works for me."

He raised up the folder I'd settled on. "Under normal circumstances, for me, too. But not this time." He laid the folders flat on his desk and shuffled them around each other like a street corner slick angling for a game of three-card monte. "One of these stars is undeserving." He spaced the folders across his desk. "One of these stars is a thief."

A floor-to-ceiling bookcase on Selznick's near side wall hinged outward with a loud, lingering creak. It revealed a doorway filled, side to side, top to bottom, front to back, by a man with moose antler shoulders, a wastrel's belly, and a butte of a butt. He filled his clothes the way helium fills a blimp. An American Legion troop with a broken howitzer could parade him around instead. He had the clotted, pugnacious face of an immigrant thug. His malicious black eyes strained daylight through a narrow slit between a beetled brow and cheeks wrinklier than a tin washboard. "Bad news, Davey," he growled, and I mean *growled* like a junkyard Rottweiler. It might have been my imagination, but I swear he slobbered, too.

Empty costumes reached off their hangers to touch him as he walked past. Either he was a fabric Messiah, or his sky-blue sharkskin suit carried a charge of static electricity that could short out the Underwriters' Lab.

He walked with a bumpity limp, like Long John Silver, and for the same reason. He wore a shoe on one foot, a broomstick on the other.

Selznick made introductions. "Eddie Valiant, meet Pepper Potts."

My handshake was a vise. Potts's was the hydraulic press that forged it, strong enough to squeeze blood out of a turnip.

"I stunted in a Western a few years back," I said, "starred a peg-legged man name Pepper Potts."

Potts shrugged, a motion equivalent to twin derricks pumping oil. "I been in a few flicks in my day."

"The Pepper Potts I'm remembering always played the villain. Loved nothing better than tying a perky young lass to a railroad track and watching her wiggle while the Iron Horse bore down. Always seemed real disappointed seeing the hero gallop in at the last minute to slice her loose. Ornery cuss, this Pepper Potts. Rustled cattle, murdered lawmen, terrorized womenfolk, pillaged ranch houses, and never died easy. 'Course that was only pretend. In real life, he could be a whole 'nother story."

Potts's voice dropped half an octave, from the screechy mutter of a maltuned bass fiddle to the dissonant wheeze of a leaky bassoon. "You making a point, or just flapping your gums to breeze the room?"

"The peg-legged Pepper Potts I knew was a Toon."

"Lets me out." He and Frankenstein shared the same lipless smile with one minor difference. Frankenstein stole his from a moldy cadaver. Potts came by it naturally. "I'm human as they come."

Selznick, apparently no fan of sparkling repartee, snapped his fingers. "What have you got for me, Pepper?" He reached out to Potts the same way the empty costumes had.

Potts handed Selznick a sheaf of printed surveys. "The upshoots of my meet with our West Coast distribs."

Selznick leafed through the forms. It didn't take long. Very few of the respondees had answered the questions. Most had summarized their response by scrawling one word, four letters long, horizontally across the page. Selznick whipped through the sheets like they were a deck of animated flash cards and the faster he flipped, the smoother their moving image would appear.

"It's exactly the way I told you, Davey," said Potts. "Costume epics is dead as door mice. You got the poop right in front of you. Read it and weep. Theater owners don't want any more movies where everybody writes with feathers."

With a single backhanded stroke, Selznick swept the surveys into his trash basket. He pointed his index finger at his desk top. "See that? There?" His flat-ended fingernail underscored faint traces of dark blue ink. "Henry Fonda used this desk to sign the Emancipation Proclamation in *Young Mister Lincoln*. Last year. With a quill pen. In front of sizable audiences."

Potts's rumbly laugh rattled the room with the smack of a ten-ton blockbuster coming home to roost. "You're living in a cloud, Davey. Times change. Nobody wants the movie you're selling."

If Selznick had been a dynamite stick, I'd have pitched him out the window, he was that close to exploding. "For goodness sake, man, it's your job to convince them! Why else am I paying you?" Selznick arose so quickly his ancient chair toppled backwards. It hit his throw rug and splintered into a messy pile of pick-up sticks. "Get me their support," said Selznick softly. I'd heard such hushiness before. Once, in the tropics, in the middle of a typhoon.

"Bring them into line." Selznick pressed his back against his wall. "Put a halt to their incessant carping." He couldn't stand where he was for long or the steam leaking out from under his collar would peel his wallpaper. "I don't care how." He shifted around to relieve the stabbing pressure between his shoulder blades caused by a gilt-framed photo of him accepting some sob sister society's Humanitarian Award.

Potts smirked with uncivilized glee, like Attila the first time a fellow barbarian called him "Hun." "Whatever's your pleasure, Davey." One of his caterpillar eyebrows wiggled in its cocoon. "It would be a big helper if I could leak who was going to headline."

Selznick rapped the baseboard with his heel. "How can I tell you if I don't know myself?" He turned his gaze on me. His tightened lips creased slightly upward at the corners. "You want a star?" He jerked his hip in my direction. "Persuade Mr. Valiant to work faster. He's the man who's holding up my decision."

Potts said "Do tell" and looked at me like I was the roadblock standing between him and the stairway to Paradise.

He chugged over and stuck his puss in mine. His bucked teeth, Neanderthal forehead, and tuberous honker raced to see who could get to me first. His nose won by a hair. "I need a name." He bonked my chest with an ox-bludgeon finger. "Don't keep me waiting, chum. Not if you know what's good for you."

He kicked out his good leg and spun around on his pin. He plowed his way toward the bookcase, which had the good sense to Open Sesame before he reached it.

Selznick leaned his head backwards and closed his eyes. Air wheezed out of his mouth, deflating his chest like one of Woody Woodpecker's rat-a-tattered balloons. He shambled listlessly back to his desk, where he evaluated his fallen chair by tickling it with his toe. He could use it for chopsticks the next time he ordered moo goo gai pan. For sure he'd never sit on it again. He kicked it out of his way and pulled up another, a modern one shaped like an angle-sliced egg. He plopped himself into the deep leather cushions. He sat with his arms stretched limply across his desk top and his chin touching his chest. His pale, clammy skin; unblinking, wide-pupiled eyes; and shallow, raspy breathing would get him VIP treatment at any emergency room in town.

No question, he was down. One more kick wouldn't hurt. "I got news for you, Junior. Your history book's short a reel. I saw that movie about Honest Abe. It ended with him getting elected Prez and leaving for Washington." I reached across and tapped his desk top's dark-blue doodling. "All he signed in that film was a few autographs before he climbed on the train."

Selznick raised his head a whisker and stared at the writing, bracketed on either end by his boneless arms. "I wrote it myself." His face went from sour to sweet with the elastic ease of Gumby transforming himself into a rubber tree plant. "I alter the story to suit my point." He straightened up, stuck his pipe between his smiling lips, and kissed it to life. "Works rather well, don't you agree?"

"Probably would if I was in a better frame of mind, but, to tell you the truth, I'm up to my gills with make-believe today. You got a job for me to do, swell. Give me the details, a hefty down payment, and a hundred-yard head start on your gimpy friend."

WHO P-P-P-PLUGGED ROGER RABBIT?

"Done, done, and done." For as quick as he answered, I knew I'd sold myself short. I should have gone for two hundred yards.

"The problem is quite straightforward." He handed me his three manila folders. "These are the contenders for the role of Rhett Butler. Two days ago, I invited them to my office for a side-by-side comparison. We chatted together in various groupings for perhaps an hour. After they left, I discovered one of them had stolen a small metal box I keep on my desk."

"No chance you misplaced it? Maybe somebody copped it before them, or later?"

"Absolutely not. It was here when they arrived. It was gone when they departed." He rummaged through his center drawer and pulled out an eight-by-ten publicity still of him in shirtsleeves working in this office, at this selfsame desk. In grease pencil he circled a box. It nestled inconspicuously between a sooty ashtray and a round procelain match holder. As boxes went, it was no great shakes, made of pitted gray pot metal and small, about the size of a mousey eater's bread basket. Its only notable feature was a small, heart-shaped iron padlock stuck through its rusty hasp.

"This box valuable?"

"Hardly. I've never had it appraised, but I can't imagine it's worth more than ten dollars. It serves me as a paperweight."

"Where'd you get it?"

"Here, there. I can't recall." He removed his goggles and polished them on his tie. "I seem to recollect receiving it as a present. I don't remember from whom. I'm sorry, but even the occasion slips my mind. I kept it because I found it appealing in a primitive way." He held his eyeglasses in front of his face and squinted at me. He must not have liked what he saw since he wrapped his peepers back in his tie and repeated the buffing process. "Why do you care where it came from? Its origins make no difference to the matter at hand."

"Most likely you're right. I ask the question mainly to show I'm a thorough guy, so you know you're getting your money's worth." I folded the photo with the box facing out and slipped it into my pocket. "By the way, what's in it?"

I realized why he soused his hair so liberally with Brylcreem. The oily white grease strangled the brushfires he ignited scratching his scalp with his pipe stem. "I have no idea. It was locked when

I got it, and came without a key. I suspect from the age and the style that it contains some insignificant, sentimental, romantic, Victorian geegaw. A lock of hair most likely. Possibly a cut-paper silhouette."

Outside his window, a stagehand accidentally smacked the Washington Monument with a stepladder and tilted it six inches off plumb.

"Let me emphasize that the box per se isn't your primary focus," said Selznick. "I'm not that concerned about getting it back. I'm more interested in finding out who took it, because that will indicate a deep character flaw which will eliminate that particular star from my consideration."

"Leaving you with a simple flip of the coin." I opened the folders. "Let's see who we got for suspects." I took a gander at the tidbit every gossip columnist in Hollywood would kill to find out: the three finalists for the role of Rhett Butler.

Roger Rabbit had made the cut. To make matters even more ridiculous, so had his perennial nemesis Baby Herman. The third candidate was a dark horse, a player named Kirk Enigman. Two buffoons and a cypher. I wouldn't pay a wooden nickel to watch any of these three burn Scarlet O'Hara, and I doubt many others would, either.

"You seem pensive, Mr. Valiant. Is there a problem?"

Not if you didn't count the conflict of interest if I started investigating my only other client. "None whatsoever."

"Good. Remember, pursue this matter with utmost discretion. If word leaks out that I suspect one of my principal candidates of felonious conduct, the scandal would ruin any chance of my movie's success." He handed me a check. "I believe you requested a retainer."

It was written in the same dark blue ink as Selznick's forgery of Fonda's impersonation of Lincoln's John Henry. It contained more zeros than a winning game of tic-tac-toe. I slipped it into my wallet, very slowly so as not to wake the moths.

"One question." In my line of work there're things you're better off not knowing. There're questions you don't want to ask. That's why I often get the feeling I'm in the wrong line of work. "Why me? Why not one of the studio's security boys?"

He picked up a wax millinery head, a rosy-cheeked lady with

full, pouting lips and marble swirl eyes. He covered her chestnut ringlets with a lady's bonnet and held her at arm's length to check the fit. "You're better than they are."

"Only at spotting a lie if I hear one."

He removed the sunbonnet and replaced it with a widow's veil. It did its job one hundred percent. You'd need a fluoroscope to see the happenings underneath. "Very well, then. I chose you because you're totally expendable. If the press gets wind of the fact that you're snooping around, or if one of the three stars complains, I'll deny we ever met and feed you to the sharks." He whipped off the manikin's black silk shroud. He and she flashed me the same inhuman smile. "Anything else you want to know?"

"As a matter of fact." I pulled out the *Life* magazine picture of him and Roger in the MGM canteen. "What's going on here between you and the rabbit?"

"Another of your irrelevancies?" He took the picture and shot it a glance. "Offhand, I'd say lunch." He wadded it and played bombs away with his circular file. "Do me the favor, Mr. Valiant, of sparing me further demonstrations of due diligence. Find a more positive way to convince me of your worth."

"Gladly. How's about you gimmee the slack." I rescued the picture from its stainless-steel grave, smoothed it flat, and dangled it between us. "I repeat. What'd you two talk about?"

"Why could that possibly make a difference?"

"This isn't Roger Rabbit."

"That's absurd." He snatched the photo out of my grasp and looked at it closer this time. "Of course it is. Who says it's not?"

I tapped Roger's nose with my knuckle. "Him truly, and he's the one oughta know."

I punched a rivet out of my funeral urn and offered Selznick one of the same. He took it automatically and held it to his mouth. I stoked us both off the same match.

"Ridiculous," said Selznick, dragging deep and holding it there. "The rabbit must be insane." He dangled the ciggie off his lower lip, like any common stew bum.

"Normally, I'd say yes-siree-Bob, in spades, but here I think otherwise. Roger says no, and I believe him."

Selznick stashed his specs on his crown while he examined the photo through a magnifying lens the thickness of the stargazer on

Palomar Mountain. He held it close to the paper as he moved it across the rabbit's face. "If that's not Roger, it's a rabbit bearing a remarkable resemblance."

"Exactly my comment, and Roger's, too. Now, care to tell me the gist of this meet?"

He rubbed the red, half-moon indentations his eyepieces had left on the bridge of his nose. "I can't exactly recall. I take hundreds of meetings a week. But it will be noted in here."

He opened a side drawer and hauled out a leather-bound diary. He checked the date on the photo caption and flipped to the diary's corresponding page. "According to my notation, we *weren't* having lunch together that day. Roger accidentally ran into me in the canteen. And I mean that literally. Roger came galumping around a corner, and we collided. He hit me so hard, he knocked me over. He apologized profusely, and helped me to my feet. We chatted amiably for a moment. The studio publicist and his photographer happened by and snapped our picture. That's all there was to it."

He read farther down the page. "No, wait. There's more. Later that day, I discovered a pickpocket had stolen my wallet!" He raised his head. "My wallet, my box, my God! That deceitful fur ball was there both times. By George, man! You've solved the case." He closed the book on Roger Rabbit. "The hare's the thief."

I returned the photo to my pocket. "Don't jump to conclusions. Leave that to me."

He proved the feasibility of one-handed applauding by drumming his desk with his palm. "With pleasure. I've no complaints thus far." His Lucky shortened to the length of his nose, and the smoke drifted straight up into his nostril. He yanked the ciggie out of his mouth and looked at it like he'd never seen one before. "Can you believe this? I quit these eight years ago. Amazing how one regresses under stress." He mashed the offending butt to death in his ashtray. "Anything else I can tell you? No holds barred. Nothing off-limits. Whatever you want to know."

Might as well go for broke. "Cut me in on the big secret. Who's playing Scarlet O'Hara?"

He held his hands up shoulder high and shoulder wide. "Who

else?" He traced a figure in the air. It would order him a bottle of Coke at any bar in the country.

I got the picture. Jessica Rabbit. The best-built redhead in town. She got my vote too, hands down. That shot the rabbit's theory about sleazy publicity ruining any chance for stardom. "One more thing." I showed him Trudy Hammerschlemmer's likeness. "Got a part in your picture for her?"

He held a frilly ball gown below the picture. He exchanged the frock for a bridle and bit. "That's better. Have her talk to my head wrangler." He handed me the picture back. "If there's nothing further . . ."

I took that as my cue to leave.

I found my trail of bread crumbs and was almost out of the woods when Selznick snapped his fingers like Admiral Byrd did after realizing he'd gone off without packing his compass. "I almost forgot. After you find the box . . ." Selznick's face harbored more perils than Pauline. ". . . whatever you do, don't open it."

I picked up one of the Colt Dragoons and twirled it around on my trigger finger. "No peeking?" I did a hand-to-hand Durango shift, surprisingly slick considering my lack of practice, and slipped the gun into my empty shoulder holster. "No problem."

He didn't say a word.

The state's vehicular motor code requires a full and complete stop at a flashing red light. I passed one flashing "Jake's Saloon." Law-abiding citizen that I am, I immediately pulled over and stopped my motor.

I never interrogate a suspect on a dry whistle. Call it tradition, superstition, anything you want. Point is, it got me where I am today, and why rock the bottle?

Jake was my style of barkeep, a big, beefy galoot with jackhammer arms, a nose the size of a pickled egg and the color of jerky, a crosshatched facial scar that could pass for a railroad siding, butch-cut hair, a vocabulary limited to "Name your poison," and a repertoire of libations that began and ended with whiskey, neat.

Jake pumped a gallon of high test into my tank while I breezed Enigman's file.

First and foremost, Enigman needed to pop for a new shutterbug. The clicker who snapped his publicity still was doing him more harm than good. It's not that the photo wasn't unflattering. It wasn't anything! The image showed Enigman's head in full silhouette against a light background, strictly black on white. You could squint until your eyelids fused together and not make out a single detail of Enigman's face. That's no way to get work in a profession where you live or die by the depth of your chin dimple.

According to Enigman's bio, he'd done his early professional work on the legitimate stage with bit parts in *Shadows in the Night* and *Dark Shadows*.

From there he graduated to the movies. First as a chorus boy. He was one of the hoofers behind Fred Astaire in the "Me and My Shadow" routine. Next he grabbed the title role in *Shadow of the Thin Man*, where he got third billing behind William Powell and Myrna Loy. His big breakthrough came playing the killer in Hitchcock's *Shadow of a Doubt*. He coasted from that success into the highly acclaimed *Shadow on the Window* and the equally well received sequel, *Shadow on the Wall*. He co-starred in the cult classic Caribbean-lensed goose bumper *Shadow of Evil*. In his most recent outing, he acted the part of Lamont Cranston's alter ego. Ty Power played Cranston the man. Enigman did him as *The Shadow*.

Under awards, he noted a Tony nomination for a Broadway play about Javanese shadow puppets.

I could sense a pattern emerging out of this tangled yarn, but darned if I could pick the woof apart from the weave.

Enigman's black cat gardener crossed the black asphalt driveway in front of me, riding on a black sheep who mowed the blackberry ground cover by nibbling off the leaves.

I parked under a stand of black walnut trees, got out, and kicked away an overly friendly black Labrador retriever intent on coercing my leg to mother his child.

Since you never know how a guy's going to react after you call him a thief, I packed my powers of persuasion under my arm. Lucky for me I had an open-bottomed shoulder holster, since the barrel of Selznick's Dragoon hung to my pelvic bone. I had to tuck the muzzle into my pants, otherwise it would have stuck out under the bottom of my coat.

I climbed the black agate steps to the front door.

Enigman must have had a swell time getting fire insurance. He had built his house out of coal, six-by-twelve blocks of prime, Appalachian anthracite, the hard, shiny kind that burns smoky and slow.

Enigman's doorbell played the opening notes from "Old Black Magic." I touched my hand to the outer wall. It came away looking like I'd slapped a minstrel. I wiped the powdery black residue off on my shirt, under my armpit where it wouldn't show.

A raven in black livery opened the ebony door. I told him why I'd come. He guided me through a lightless hallway and parked me in a pitch-dark living room. From what I could see, and that wasn't much, Enigman's furniture came from that Bavarian forest where trolls chisel stately black maples into overpriced hassocks. I stumbled my way to a sofa the color of the ring around my bathtub.

Somebody, I couldn't see who, entered the room. I caught a

strong whiff of Black Jack chewing gum. I stuck out my hand. "How do. I'm Eddie Valiant, private eye."

"Kirk Enigman," proclaimed a vice-versa balloon, neon white lettering on a black background. The wide, scrolly script showed me an affinity for the dramatic. The precisely scribed letters indicated he took himself seriously. The clipped-out space between words told me he didn't waste time. Give me another sentence, and I'd have the color of his underwear. "Pleased to make your acquaintance."

"Silk boxers, solid black, custom tailored, changed fresh every morning, with your initials embroidered on the seat."

His words popped out at a cockamamie angle as my BVD bull's-eye tilted his attitude toward the side of caution. "I beg your pardon? Have we met before? In a locker room perhaps?" His blinking questions floated past a bank of display shelves and illuminated his collection. Chess pieces. You know the color.

"Could we throw some lamps on in here, Kirk?"

"I'm afraid not." A bat would ruin his eyes trying to read by the candle power of Enigman's balloon. "Exposure to light blisters my skin."

"Dracula pleaded the same case."

"Except in my situation the problem is medical, not metaphysical." To illuminate his joke, a string of balloons flashed in short, brilliant bursts, like news hounds photogging the stars at a Grauman's premiere. "May I offer you a libation? I'm having Johnny Walker Black."

"I can't see a man drink alone."

Old owl eyes pressed a hefty glass of black lightning into my hand. He offered me a snack but I passed, having no taste for dark raisin-rye bread spread with black pepper jam.

He touched his glass to mine. "May the cold dark o' dyin' give ye a rest from the cruel light o' day."

"Your toast doesn't come with much butter."

"It's an old family proverb. A heritage of my nationality."

"Which is?"

"Black Irish." He formed his capital letters out of bent and twisted shillelaghs. It's amazing the silliness you can create out of thin air and a warped mentality. "Might I inquire what brings a private detective to my humble abode? Since it can't be anything

I've done, I assume you're here to interview me regarding someone else." His balloon came out pure as the driven snow. Two more like it and I could build my own Frosty.

"No guilty secrets tucked away in a dark closet?"

"None so heinous as to attract a minion of the law."

You can crack open a man's facade slowly by gently tapping away at it with a velvet hammer, or explode it to pieces in one whack by piercing it with an ice pick. I chose the sharp pointy method and stuck it to Enigman right in the eye. "Cut the Gorgonzola, Enigman. You know why I'm here. Selznick wants his box back."

"His box?" Enigman's balloon corkscrewed aimlessly in circles the way they do if they lose their bearings and can't tell which way is up. "I'm sorry. I don't have the slightest idea what you're talking about." In the few seconds before his floater faded, I caught enough light from its incandescent white words to get a make on him. He stood about my height, although with the wispiness of a vapor. He had the squiggly profile of an ink blot. He wore a black tie, black frocked coat, and black trousers with a crease that would slice his legs if he ever crossed them. He held his black silk cravat in place with a black sapphire stickpin. I just knew his favorite candy was licorice, and he took his coffee without cream.

"You had a meeting day before yesterday with David Selznick. You, Roger Rabbit, and Baby Herman. Remember?"

"Naturally." He lit a smoke, cupping his hands outward so the sparkle of the match wouldn't crinkle his photosensitive husk. "David's none-too-subtle method of evaluating the contenders. I took the meeting because it played to my advantage. In a straightforward, side-by-side comparison with such ridiculous competition, I can't help but shine." His ciggie flared against a set of choppers as perfectly squared as a box of dotless dominoes. "It's intuitively obvious. By any standard, I'm the superior choice. Let David name his criteria. Reputation, acting ability, physical stature, personal attractiveness, demeanor. Not to mention intelligence. Why, I'd win on my brightness alone!" The wattage of that statement's rosy glow left spots parading in front of my eyes. "Choose a facetious rabbit or a morally stunted middle-aged toddler? Over me? Fat chance."

"Hold on to your black socks, Enigman. You're not the patent leather shoe-in you think you are." I goosed my eyelids up to hummingbird speed to clear away the coronas. "Selznick's got a prejudice problem. He hates thieves."

"How could that possibly disqualify me?"

"Easy. When you strolled out of Selznick's office, this box went with you." I held up the picture. I don't know if he saw it. I'm not sure I had it right side up or pointed in his direction.

"There were three of us in that room. What gives me the black eye?"

"Availability of hiding places. You're the only one of the trio who wears clothes with pockets."

I'd have swapped a bonded bottle for a two-cell flashlight just to see the look on his face. "If I admit you're right, which I'm not, and I return the box, I'd be knocking myself out of contention for the role of a lifetime. Wimpy would have a better chance of playing Rhett Butler. Why would I do such a thing? Incriminate myself to the man who can make or break my career?"

"Remorse. An overpowering desire to clear your conscience. Happens a lot with me on the case. Goes under the name of deathbed confession."

His words came so close to my nose they spluttered bluster on my chin. "Is that a threat, Mr. Valiant?"

I turned his balloon around and jammed it back in his kisser. "Read into it whatever you want."

His next balloon was more down to earth, so much so I had to bend over to read it. "Browbeat me to your heart's content, Mr. Valiant. We're debating a moot point. I don't have Selznick's box."

"Sez you."

"You don't believe me? Feel free to search my house. I assume you know Braille." His cackling laugh swirled the air between us the way a witch's broom handle stirs a cauldron. "I'm an ambitious man, Mr. Valiant. There's nothing I wouldn't do to achieve my goal, and nobody I wouldn't do it to." He demonstrated his evil inclinations by scraping his fingernails across his blackboard wall. "I want that role. I deserve it. One glance at me and any fool can see I'm the perfect Rhett Butler."

WHO P-P-P-PLUGGED ROGER RABBIT?

"You're also the perfect thief. And that's how I'm reporting it to Selznick."

"Don't be stupid. Do that, and it's you who'll be blue."

"I'll believe that when I see it in Technicolor."

His teeth clicked together with the distant, faintly disturbing, rat-a-tat rhythm of a rascally rodent tap-dancing inside a pantry wall. "If you insist."

His unadorned statement twisted and bent into a bulb-encrusted arrow which tried to herd me along with alternating flashes of razzle and dazzle. I stood my ground. I'd wander aimlessly through the dark until I died of starvation before I'd take orders from a half-watt balloon. But the arrow refused to cease and desist. It none too gently prodded my behind, forcing me to concede its point. I followed it along a snaky, black mambo hallway, through a swinging blackout door, into a vat of pure India ink.

I collided with a long, solid, waist-high obstruction. My hand caressed hardwood, metal, fuzzy mohair, and petrified chewing gum. No mistaking that combination, not with my background in the movies. I've never in my life gotten to a flicker on time. I've spent longer groping my way through darkened popcorn palaces than it took to film *Birth of a Nation*. Even in the pitchiest dark, I recognized theater seats when I fell over them.

I sent Mr. Arrow flying. From here on, I could manage fine on my own. I high-stepped over the back of the row, lowered the spring-loaded cushion, and settled in for the show.

With the ominous slap of an ill wind churning the Black Lagoon, Enigman settled in beside me. "Welcome to my private screening room, Mr. Valiant. I insist upon viewing films in the same environment as my public. To that end, I've gone to great lengths to duplicate the layout, style, and ambience of an actual cinema."

I must admit, he came close. Add a box of Good & Plenty, a pocket full of JuJu Bees, a red licorice whip, sticky floors, two kids smooching in the upper deck, and a crusty geezer to tromp on my arch supports on his way out to the can, and I wouldn't know this from my local Bijou. "Whatever you're planning to show me, save your electricity. It won't change my mind."

"Oh, quite to the contrary, Mr. Valiant. It most definitely

will." His hand caressed a button on a control panel between us. A projector clattered, and the screen flickered to life. "Relax, and enjoy the show."

That wasn't going to be easy. Enigman's sprocket reeler opened the same way as one of those artsy, boring documentaries that substitutes a point of view for a plot line. First up came a grainy, overexposed, and unfocused wide-angle of a head-high stone wall.

The camera swung around to show a panorama of empty lawn. The shot had as much interest and drama as an ant's-eye vista of a green-felt pool table.

"No newsreel? No short subject? No titles? No music? No sound?"

"Wait, Mr. Valiant, wait. If you're not impressed by the vision before you, I'll cheerfully refund the price of your admission."

While I panned the film, the film panned a tennis court, a softball diamond, and a croquet setup. On the edge of the frame, standing between a bucket of fungo balls and a cart of wooden mallets, I could have sworn I glimpsed a khaki-coated bullyboy toting a tommy gun, but it could have been my imagination, which plays nasty tricks on me while I watch movies about toe dancers, Kansas in August, or brewing farina.

Finally, I got some action, if action's your idea of a couple of Toons lounging beside a swimming pool, dangling their tootsies in the crystal-clear.

They both had their backs to the camera.

The one of the male persuasion sported a flowered silk shirt, white starched baggy shorts identical to the ones worn by tropical cops, and a wide-brimmed white straw plantation hat. His biceps were big enough to move out, get a job, and rent their own apartment. He swigged a dark liquid.

His companion gave the lie to the term "better half." She had him beat by at least three quarters, maybe seven eighths. Her outfit must have been designed by Oscar de la Mayer, since only a sausage machine could stuff her body into her suit. I couldn't see her hair. She wore it tucked under a paisley scarf knotted in the complicated manner perfected by women, swamis, and sheiks of Araby. She overdid the gold bracelets a tad. Heaven help her if she fell in the water, because she'd sink straight to the bottom and tarnish to death. Her drink came in a hollow pineapple topped by a rice-paper-and-bamboo umbrella.

She tilted her head slightly to the rear, listening to somebody. I prayed it was the cameraman instructing her to turn around. She nodded and did just that.

My whole world turned around with her.

Lucky for me I hadn't shaved that morning. Without a fishnet of stubble to rope it in place, my jaw would have fallen off my face. The woman I found myself gaping at was none other than Lupe Chihuahua!

She waved at the lens in the same lovey-dovey, come-hither way she'd waved at my brother Freddy from the stage of the Baba de Rum.

Just as I decided this was as bad as life got, it got worse. Lupe prodded her male companion to turn around and give the camera a full frontal view. He none too gently waved her off. She pleaded the way only a gorgeous dolly can until he finally succumbed to the pressure of her lips on his ear. But he didn't like it and didn't pretend to. He glanced over his shoulder and sneered disdainfully at the shutter.

My spine turned to Jell-O and took my brain along with it. The man on the screen was Tom Tom LeTuit! "You want to explain this?"

"Be patient, Mr. Valiant, and everything will come clear."

LeTuit drained his glass and snapped his fingers for another hit. The waiter who delivered his shot moved like the drum major from *Zombies on Parade*. His legs didn't bend at the knees nor his arms at the elbows, a grotesque hump topped his backbone, and his head tilted so far left his earlobe touched his shoulder. The camera zoomed in for a close-up on his tortured, contorted, tongue-dangling face.

I leaped to my feet. "Freddy!" I screamed. "My God, Freddy!" But even *that* wasn't the worst.

I'm an adaptable sort. Given time, I could learn to live with my beloved baby brother being a zombie. The real shocker, which I could never accept, was that someway, somehow, that vicious, no-good, bastard LeTuit had turned Freddy into a *Toon*!

The spool of film pulled off the reel and slapped itself silly against the projector. The on-screen image flickered and died right along with my slender hope that I'd one day find my brother alive and little the worse for wear. "It's impossible. Something that horrible can't happen to a human being."

I was already as dizzy as a man trapped on a runaway Tilt-a-Whirl. Enigman's words made it worse by coming out tiny and shrill, buzzing my head like a bee burgling a begonia. "Indeed it can, and it has. You've seen it yourself."

"It's trick photography," I said. I jerked my thumb at the screen. "That's not really Freddy."

"I can assure you, your brother is everything he appears to be." Enigman stroked my arm the way a vet calms an anxious puppy. "You needn't worry about him. Freddy's perfectly happy with his new lot in life."

I shook loose of his hand and grabbed him by the lapels. "Where is he? Where's Freddy? Who's got him?"

Enigman wiggled loose of my grip. "You want to be reunited with your brother? I can arrange it. But not without a quid pro quo." His balloon took the shape of a highway sign indicating the only exit off a bumpy, dead-end road. "Tell David Selznick that one of the other two stole his box."

I would have strangled him, and gladly, except a choked man always dies with an imitation smile on his puss, and I didn't want Enigman to expire even *looking* happy. "I got a better idea."

At six pounds apiece, his words carried the same weight as a solid brick wall. "My suggestion is not negotiable. I won't listen to counterproposals."

"You'll hear mine and so will your neighbors for two blocks on either side." I reached under my coat and pulled out the Dragoon. "Tell me where my brother is, or I paint the ceiling with the walnuts rattling inside your head."

"Holster your peacemaker, Wyatt," said Enigman nonchalantly, "or I'll be forced to counter violence with violence." His balloon curled up at either end and grinned at me. "The law requires me to inform you that I'm a master of jujitsu."

"Black belt?"

He hesitated half a beat. "Only brown, but that doesn't alter the fact that my hands are registered as lethal weapons."

"So's my gun."

His response unrolled slowly, his words interlocked like the fence forest rangers erect to separate careless hikers from two hundred feet of straight down. "Before you make a mistake you'll regret for the rest of your life, there's an important fact you should consider."

"Tell it to Saint Peter, bub."

He exhaled two small chuckles. "Do I understand correctly? Are you threatening to kill me?"

"Darn right."

"That, Mr. Valiant, would be a grave, no pun intended, mistake. You see, we're not in this room alone."

I slid my free hand around his statement and caught my thumb on a raggedy precipice of panic. "You're lying through your black-hearted teeth."

His balloon came out side-on. From my perspective, I saw it as a glowing white line the height of a hobgoblin and the width of a scud. I tapped it with my gun barrel and revolved it around to where I could read it. "Prove it to him," it said.

I started to utter "You can't bluff me," but I never got the chance.

Somebody, I couldn't see who, grabbed my hand, the one with the gun in it.

"Convinced?" asked Enigman.

My mystery assailant extended my gun hand forward.

"What are you doing? Stop! Valiant!" said Enigman. The Dragoon's front sight pointed bang-on at the tag end of the curved tail connecting his balloon to his mouth. I couldn't see squat in the dark, but if I could, I had a hunch I wouldn't like the looks of this. "Valiant, no!" he said out loud.

Whoever had a hold of my hand squeezed my trigger finger. The Dragoon went off with a thunderous roar.

Enigman yelled in my direction, but the white flash from the gun barrel fouled up his contrast control. His balloon whistled past my noggin way too shady to read. He hit the floor with a loud thump.

My gun hand dangled free.

I heard a snicker. I felt the vibration of running feet. Enigman's thick carpet muffled the sound.

I lit a match.

The sight I saw knotted my stomach, lumped my throat, and

dried my mouth. Enigman was spread out on the floor like the oil slick in a garage.

Drained of bravado, Enigman was only three quarters of an inch away from being two-dimensional. He looked like a squashed black olive.

I could see a square yard of matte black rug through the hole my bullet had punched in his gut. My match did me the courtesy of expiring so I wouldn't have to watch myself get sick.

I found a newspaper, rolled it into a cone, and torched it.

I burned away the city section locating Enigman's last balloon. I found it wedged under his sealskin sofa. It was as long, narrow, and flat as an alligator's tongue depressor and the color of a dirty puddle. I wasted half the sports page trying to decipher its message before I realized that would take more light than I could wring out of the morning edition. I'd have to set fire to something bigger, say the house.

Rigor mortis was setting in; Enigman's balloon was hardening fast. I didn't relish the thought of leaving Toontown with a death-bed balloon the size of an ironing board sticking out the window of my jalop. Any cop with more than a pea for a brain would haul me over in a second. I folded it over and over again into an easily-carried-and-concealed package the size of a gadabout's valise.

I dug my bullet out of the wall. I know, I know. Destroying evidence. Small potatoes compared to the murder rap I faced if I left it. It still shined with a faintly greenish cast, and smelled strongly of acetone and benzene. Just my luck to be carrying a load of dip-tipped. The only bullets that'll kill a Toon.

I spent the rest of my light on a general look around. The film of Freddy was gone. I didn't find Selznick's box, either.

The newspaper expired between my fingers.

I weighed my options. They tallied zilch. If I wanted to stand any chance of hanging on to my license, there was only one thing I could do. And I did it.

I beat it the heck out of there before somebody called the cops.

WHO P-P-P-PLUGGED ROGER RABBIT?

8

I taped the incriminating murder weapon to the folded hunk of Enigman's final balloon—which said "Valiant! Don't shoot me"—and skimmed them across the Malibu surf. They skipped into the sunset and sank without a trace.

Heddy and Ferd owned a three-bedroom ranch house in Hobson's Choice, a sprawling, ramshackle development built on poured slab foundations thinner than the credit it took to buy one. Hobson's no-money-downers were split about equally between blue-collar humans and dog-collared Toons. The two traditionally antagonistic contingents lived more or less peacefully side by side, the attitude being you don't boot your neighbor if you're living on a shoestring yourself.

Heddy's bad dream house was prefabricated by the same cardboard cutup who built cracker boxes for Saltine. Given light winds, no rain, and a mutant generation of toothless termites, it might last half the thirty years it would take to pay off the mortgage.

I pulled up. Heddy was outside molding hardscrabble clay into lawn. She'd do better if she swapped her grass seed and fertilizer for a paint sprayer and ten gallons of forest green. Better yet, a hundred gallons. She could coat every yard on the street and earn what she needed to move someplace nice.

She wore a long-sleeved red jersey, Oshkosh bib overalls, clodhopper boots, and a red bandanna that knotted in back and covered her hair. Give her a John Deere tractor, a plow, five hundred acres of prime farmland, and she'd still look like a city slicker playing Old MacDonald.

I honked.

She ceased her dirt scratching and gazed up at me with the same vacant, lifeless stare I'd already seen in one sibling too many.

I got out of my car, doffed my fedora, and swept it under my gut with a deep bow that set the death of chivalry back at least twenty years. "Good morning, fair damsel."

"I beg your pardon," she responded in a tone only slightly less grating than the metal knuckle scraper chefs use to pulverize cheese. "Do I know you?"

I grabbed her around the waist and nailed her with a big, wet smooch. "Come off it, Sis. It hasn't been that long."

"Oh, hasn't it?" She rubbed my juicy welcome off her lips, replacing it with a wide streak of garden-variety dirt. "How many kids do I have?"

"Huh?"

She jabbed my stomach with the business end of a trowel. "Your nephews, jerkwater. How many are there?"

"Jeez, Heddy, you know I'm not so hot with names."

The muddy point of her trowel stained the babe on my hand-painted tie. "I'm not asking for names, just numbers. Count them off."

I made a few quick calculations and guessed two.

She cupped her hands to her mouth as soon as she saw my smug smile. "Boys," she yelled, and three wild Indians came galumping around the corner.

"Uncle Eddie, Uncle Eddie, Uncle Eddie!" They greeted me the way a steeplejack attacks a slate-tiled roof. Rug rat climbed to my knees. Fiddle in the middle made it to my belt buckle. Chip off the old block planted his toe on my earlobe and claimed my head for Spain.

"Remember these little guys, Eddie? Your *three* nephews? "Ferd Junior, Ferd the Second, and Ferd the Third."

I shook them off and lined them up at attention. They had Heddy's face and their father's stocky, cowbell body. They sported matching baseball caps, matching short-sleeved pullover shirts, matching gym shorts, and matching black-dot Keds. Poor kids. Heddy had obviously inherited Mother's tendency toward sartorial duplication.

I debated giving them each a dime to buy clothes of their own, but not wanting to spoil them rotten, I flipped them a single nickel and told them to split it three ways. When last seen, they were hunting for their daddy's hacksaw.

WHO P-P-P-PLUGGED ROGER RABBIT?

"So, Eddie." Heddy and I walked up onto the front porch. "Tell me the flavor of stew you've gotten yourself into this time."

I held open a punctured screen door that wouldn't bar any creature smaller than a muskrat. "Why do you think I'm in hot water?"

"I know you, Eddie. You're all give and no take." She jerked her thumb at a sofa with more dips to it than a roller coaster. "You only come around if you need help." Heddy possessed our mother's classic features, and the same aversion to putting them on display. She cropped her hair unfashionably short, never powdered her face, didn't even own a tube of lipstick or a bottle of perfume.

"This time, sweet cakes, you got it one hundred percent wrong." I wiggled myself into a gully of cushion. "I just wrapped up a big case. I'm taking time off. Catching up on family obligations."

"Hi-de-ho-ho-ho. That'll be the day." She ducked into the bedroom and came back a minute later wearing a lumberjack shirt, Army fatigue pants, and worn leather moccasins. Heddy prided her ability to assemble outfits out of odds and ends, a fact which enhanced her reputation as family eccentric. Pop referred to Heddy as Harpo. Every Christmas he threatened to buy her a bicycle horn.

She uncorked a fresh fifth and poured me a snootful, fixing it exactly the way I like it, big. Then she settled into her one good piece of furniture, Grandmother's pressed-oak rocking chair, picked up her knitting, and draped it over her lap.

"Good-looking bedspread," I told her.

"It's a sweater." The whole family could fit inside it with room left over for their coal furnace. "Can you stay for dinner?" she asked.

"You making anything good?"

"Pot roast."

"Mother's recipe?"

"Naturally."

Mother cooked pot roast you couldn't slice with a fireman's ax. I loved it. "Set me a plate."

"How's Doris?"

"Happy, contented, not a care in the world."

"She tossed you over, then."

"More or less."

Heddy leaked some juice into the radio, and we caught the last half inch of Glen Miller's *String of Pearls* platter. Heddy hummed the tune. Her needles clicked harmony.

I struck a match on a sprung spring and set fire to a cough. "Where's your lesser half?"

She played roulette with the radio's tuning dial and won a serenade from Vic Damone. "Do you really care?"

"I want to pay my respects. Nothing strange about that."

"Except you've never gone an inch out of your way to say boo to him before."

"I'm mellowing in my old age."

"Sure. Like Daddy did. Hi-de-ho-ho-ho." We both laughed. He'd mellowed. From raw sulfuric acid to crumbly quick lime. Either way, he'd eat you full of holes, the only difference being the older he got, the longer it took, and the more you suffered.

The radio announcer sliced Damone's throat for an important news bulletin concerning the murder of a famous screen star. I leaped to the RCA and strangled the story before it strangled me.

"Hey! I wanted to hear that," Heddy complained.

"I've had it to the ham hocks with this city's crime wave. I'd rather listen to you play the piano."

"Really?"

I lifted the keyboard cover and pulled out the bench.

She stood and laid her knitting across the rocker's rear slats. The weight tipped the chair over backwards. She left it for the maid.

Heddy took a seat at the family upright. "Real or otherwise?"

"You pick it."

"I'm kind of rusty for real."

"I've got nothing against otherwise."

"Hi-de-ho-ho-ho." She smiled sweetly at me. "You always were my favorite brother." She opened the double doors above the keyboard and read aloud the legend on the roll. "I'm Only a Bird in a Gilded Cage."

"Number one on my hit parade."

She shut the doors, threw the play lever to "automatic," and pumped the foot pedals to beat the band. The roll started to move, and the piano tinkled out its honky-tonk melody.

For practice, Heddy moved her fingers above the eighty-eights. Try as she might, she remained a good four bars behind the bobbing black and whites. Twenty years of piano lessons, and she couldn't keep up with a piece of paper full of holes. But you had to admire her gristle. She never stopped trying.

I leaned against the side of the piano. That put me eye level with a long lace doily showcasing a framed display of happier times. The Kodachrome hitting hardest pictured me with more hair, less weight, and two live brothers.

I picked it up.

Like every photo in the Valiant family album, a black, nickel-sized half-moon obscured the lower left-hand corner. Mother's finger over the lens.

This shot had been snapped the day Teddy graduated from high school. He held his diploma proudly at chest level and flashed the Devil-may-care grin he'd swiped off an Army Air Corps recruiting poster.

I wore my only suit, equal amounts of shoe polish and hair oil, and a suitably serious expression.

Freddy, rakishly attired in newsboy cap, cotton twill shirt, sleeveless argyle sweater, arm garters, and pleated gabardine trousers, stood between us. He'd been trying for weeks to grow a beard, but freckles still outnumbered his chin whiskers five to one. He had his arms draped over our shoulders. His extended first and second fingers formed V-for-Victorys above our heads. The family cutup, Freddy. He took after Pop.

Pop didn't make it. He had better things to do than sit in a hot gym and applaud the first Valiant to graduate from a school that didn't have the word "reform" in front of it. One of his old circus pals came by the morning of the ceremony and begged Pop to unretire. They needed a sub for a guy with a hot appendix. Pop promptly hauled his zebra-striped clown suit out of the rag barrel, dug through Heddy's toy box until he found his fuzzy green wig, stole his red rubber nose ball back from the dog, grabbed his Big Bang backside paddle off the mountings over the fireplace, and made a beeline for the klieg lights.

Pop spent Teddy's graduation day cruising the Big Top, crammed inside a teeny car with twenty other bozos.

Next morning, Pop gave Teddy a Kewpie doll he'd won knocking rag cats off a shelf. That naked Kewpie decorated Teddy's mantel right up to the day he died. It's on my bureau, now.

Heddy caught me wiping my eye. "Salt water," I told her. "Left over from my last trip to the beach."

"I go to that same sand dune myself quite a lot." She stopped pumping, and the piano wheezed to silence. "Hi-de-ho-ho-ho."

Heddy held out her hand. I gave her the picture. She looked at it squinty eyed and close up, the same way she used to study the drawings in her fairy-tale book about Oz. "We had great times together. You, me, Teddy, bless his heart, and . . ." Her moist, warm breath formed a misty halo on the glass. She wiped it away with her thumb, leaving Freddy's face an island of sparkling purity in a rectangle of dust. She looked up at me with that sweet innocence that had been wrapping me around her finger ever since she realized I bent. "Are you having any luck finding Freddy? Will I ever see him again?"

"You know the old saying." I took the picture, cleaned the rest of it with my elbow, and returned it to the piano top. "No news is good news."

"Wrong. No news is no news." She took hold of my hand and pulled me onto the bench beside her. "Do me a favor, Eddie."

"Name it."

"Be careful." She held my hand so tightly I couldn't have pulled it loose without leaving a finger behind. "I lost Teddy, I lost Freddy, I don't want to lose you."

"The danger in my line of work comes highly overrated. I've got more of a risk falling in the bathtub."

"Hi-de-ho-ho-ho. Save the fog for killing mosquitoes. I'm a cop's wife. I know how you make your living."

"Catch the sudden concern for my health and welfare. I never heard you utter a word of protest when Pop shot me out of a cannon."

She flicked open my suit coat, exposing my empty gat holder. "Now you pack a cannon of your own, and a stubborn inclination to shoot back."

WHO P-P-P-PLUGGED ROGER RABBIT?

A word balloon snaked under the front door, manacled itself to my ankle, and yanked. "Move your flocking rattletrap, scum frugger," it said. "You're blocking my frigging driveway."

"How can you not love a guy with that kind of command over the English language?" I whacked Ferd's balloon with a brass ashtray. It shattered to pieces except for the blue words, which congealed into lumps. Heddy scooped them up with a piece of sheet music before they stained the carpet. Judging from the indigo patterns blotting the broadloom, she didn't always succeed.

I sauntered casually outside and stood on the sidewalk.

Ferd sat in his heap, craning his neck to see over the heavy, dark cloud of fuming, angry impatience that rose almost to his chin.

I loved to watch Ferd steam.

He reversed his defroster. Twin jets of heated vapor whooshed out of his side air vents. The smoke inside his car descended to the level of his shaking fist.

I gave him a jaunty wave, eased into my six-banger, punched it to life, and slowpoked out of his way.

I goosed the engine once for luck and shut it down.

Ferd welcomed me to the neighborhood by yanking my car door off its hinges. "Careful," I said. "I wouldn't want my favorite brother-in-law busting a gut."

He scaled my door into the street, where it skipped once and decapitated a trash can. "Cut the farking sludge, shamus." Ferd sported a snorter the size of a watering can. He aimed it at me and flared the dual wheat fields he used for nostrils. "What the frick are you doing here?"

I got out of my car. We faced off across an open bag of grass seed. "I came to pay you my respects."

"Bull froggers you did." Ferd and I matched up in one dimension. He was as wide as I was tall. He put a hand on my shoulder and pressed down, sinking my feet into Heddy's newly tilled clay. "You're here because you forking need something."

"That's where you're wrong."

"You mark my flarking words, before you flicking leave, you'll ask me for a flooking favor."

Heddy shouted "Heads up!" and lobbed out a pair of brews. Ferd popped the caps with his bottom teeth and handed one to me.

"Ink in your eye," he toasted, "and lead in your pencil." We both drank to that.

"What they got you working on?" I asked.

"A famucking ring of hooch haulers running shine into Toontown. Until this afternoon. The big boys pulled everybody off the feeping streets for a big forking murder case."

"Anybody I know?"

"Not fupping likely." He knotted his dangly ears under his chin to keep them from falling into his mouth when he tilted his head back to swig. "This one's way out of your fooping league, Shearluck. And strictly hush-hush. I don't fipping know if I ought to even tell you about it."

"Why not? I'll read it in the papers."

"You learned to freeping read?" Ferd plunked himself on the porch swing and set it in motion, tugging his waistband out so the moving air would blow through. "Promise you'll keep it under your fornicking hat?"

"Absolutely."

He stopped the swing and leaned in close. His tiny words elbowed each other for space inside a balloon the size of a gnat's whisper. "Famous famucking movie star. Kirk Enigman. Took one in the fleeping pumper. Big bore. The doc thinks a fumping forty-four, though I can't fligging remember the last time I saw one of those."

"Any leads?"

"Yeah. We got us a real fudding break for a change. A neighbor eyeballed the farfing killer. Gave us a perfect description. Squat, heavyset monkey. Porky pig jowls, caterpillar eyebrows. Wearing a rumpled brown suit. Drove away in a prewar Plymouth coupe, two-tone, tan over rust."

Me to a T, right to the rusty bucket. "Any suspects?"

"Nobody yet, but it won't be long. With that fligging description to go on, I could draw you his picture."

"Who's in charge?"

He took a long, slow, delicious swig. "Sergeant Bulldog Bascomb."

That meant problems. Bulldog Bascomb was a sleuth hound so dogged he made Mike Hammer look like a mutt. Bascomb treated P.I.s in general, and me in particular, with the respect he bestowed on the nearest fire hydrant. "Do me a favor, would you?"

Ferd smacked his hands together, exploding his beer can, and spraying himself with busted suds. "I famouching knew it!"

"Naw, nothing major. Let Heddy know I remembered something I gotta do. Tell her I'll take a rain check on dinner."

He cleansed his hands by combing his fingers through his chest fur. "Always glad to deliver the frinching news that you're fleaving leaving."

"One other thing."

He tossed his split can over the porch railing. It landed in a bush already festooned with more crumpled metal than a Christmas tree. "Here it comes."

"Yeah, Ferd. I'm gonna ask you to run a check for me. But it's for Heddy, too."

His vacant expression told me he needed a stronger wind to get my drift.

"I got a line on Freddy."

"He's alive?"

"That's hard to answer. He sort of is, and he sort of isn't."

"I don't get it." His finger scratched at the top of his head but didn't make a dent.

"Trust me on this one, Ferd. Do it, and don't tell Heddy."

Puffs of exhaust fume blew out of his ears as the gears whirled inside his noggin. From the clanking, he needed a rebuilt transmission. "Give me the scoop."

"I need everything you can dig up about a Cuban butcher boy named Tom Tom LeTuit. His activities for the past couple of years, and where he's currently calling home."

"You better not be yanking my tail, gumfoot." He underscored his metaphor by reaching behind himself and jerking his shaggy rump. It sent him somersaulting paws over jaws across the back of the swing and off the porch. Toons.

"Would I lie to you?"

He stood and dusted Heddy's rosebushes off his fur. "Absofooping-lutely."

I headed for my wheels. Ferd grabbed my arm.

"Driving that fleeking heap is like prancing around in a fupping sandwich board reading 'I shot Kirk Enigman.' Leave it here," he said. "I'll hide it in my garage. Take mine, instead."

I asked the obvious question. "Why?"

"I don't want Heddy losing her last brother to the gas chamber."

At last something we agreed on.

He exhaled a string of steel-colored BBs, looped them through his car key, and snapped them shut. "I find you're slobbering me, I'll skin you bare and boil the bones." He draped his improvised key chain around my thumb and twisted it hard enough to tingle. "A word to the wise, Eddie. Let it be sufficient."

The dashboard of Ferd's Toon Buggy boasted more screwy levers, meters, switches, gears, knobs, and push buttons than Doc Frankenstein's erector set. I tickled the starter, eased the slush box into giddyup, dropped my feet through the floorboard, and gave the engine a running start.

Philco Phil, Ferd's dashboard dipole, asked me my pleasure. I opted for news. He fiddled his innards. A crosshatched balloon peeled off his loose-mesh grill cloth. Philco Phil grabbed the broadcast in his knobs, gargled his tonsils, and began to read.

"Welcome to *Person to Person* with your host, Edward R. Murrow."

MURROW: My guest this evening. A gull, a donkey, a booby, a goose, a cootie, a cat's paw? Or a deeply thoughtful lagomorph with profound, hare-brainy insights into his cony nature. You decide.

ROGER RABBIT: Jumping jibbers, that's a toughie!

"Change the station," I told the airhead. He ignored me. They always do.

MURROW: How did you begin your theatrical career?

ROGER: As a powder puff in a burlesque house. Talk about getting show business under your skin! I'm really brown with orange polka dots or yellow with green stripes. I forget.

WHO P-P-P-PLUGGED ROGER RABBIT?

Ferd's rearview mirror distorted the cars behind me, making them look skinny on top, fat on the bottom. That's why it took me a minute to peg the buggy behind me for an unmarked patrol car.

MURROW: What's hardest about being a Toon?
ROGER: Avoiding erasers. No, fading in sunlight. No, being stuffed into trombones. No, keeping a straight face at operas.

The patrol car sniffed my tail pipe.

MURROW: How do you feel about sex in the cinema?
ROGER: Personally, I prefer popcorn.

The cruiser spouted a gum ball dispenser and flashed it red. Philco Phil coughed out another piece of repartee.

MURROW: Disprove the widely held belief that Toons can't resist getting a laugh. Tell a joke and leave off the punch line.
ROGER: That's easy. Name Ignatz Insect's favorite radio show.
MURROW: I give up.
ROGER: *Davy Cricket.*
MURROW: You told the punch line.
ROGER: No, I didn't. It's *Name That Toon.*

I weighed making a run for it, but when I goosed the gas pedal, the grinder under the hood couldn't shake out another ounce of pepper. I dropped anchor. It caught on a lamp pole and jerked me off the road.

MURROW: How has stardom changed your life?
ROGER: I don't get mistaken for the Easter Bunny as much.

A car door slammed. Flat feet crunched pea gravel. The law's paws rapped my rear fender.

MURROW: What do you do for fun?
ROGER: Everything!

A twelve-gauge load of kennel breath blasted me through the window. "I ought to slap you behind bars, Valiant."

A zillion cops to choose from, and I get hauled over by Bulldog Bascomb. "You got a specific charge, Sarge?"

"I'll ask the questions," woofed Bascomb.

MURROW: Who turned the lights out?

"Shut up," I whispered to Philco Phil.

"You got big worries," Boscomb snarled.

"Name one."

"Kirk Enigman, the famous movie star. He bit the onion a couple of hours ago." Bascomb's porcupine eyebrows locked elbows, rolled over, and pointed their poisoned quills at me. "I'm hot on the trail of his cold-blooded killer."

"Let me know the minute you catch him. I always wanted to see one up close."

Bascomb put a match to the rigor mortised grunion he called a stogie. "I got a witness saw a dumpy hard apple in chocolate worsted fleeing the scene." He fingered my nubbly brown lapel.

"Like it? Eight bucks off the rack. I buy 'em by the dozen."

"The killer made his getaway in a battered Plymouth rust bucket."

"Case solved. Find the louse who raided my closet and stole my car."

"Don't play cute with me," Bascomb snorted. "You're in this murder up to your bloodshot eye sockets, and I'm the pooch who's gonna prove it."

"Sorry, Sarge. I plead total and complete ignorance."

"That's the one excuse a jury's likely to believe of you." His gruff, throaty chuckle jingled his Army K-9 corps dog tags and the metallic blue disk proclaiming him rabies-free. "The name David O. Selznick ring a bell?"

"Let me guess. He wants you to play a loose cannon in *Gone With the Wind.*"

"That's good, Valiant. Funny." He tested his jaws to see if they opened wide enough to rip off my head. They did. Easy. "Selznick told me that Kirk Enigman, Baby Herman, and Roger Rabbit were up for the same great big juicy role. Rhett Butler, if you can believe it. I couldn't."

WHO P-P-P-PLUGGED ROGER RABBIT?

"You landing any time soon," I said, "or you gonna keep circling around in the ozone all night?"

"I'm coming down, you bet. Right on your case." He planked his foot on my running board. "Enigman's unfortunate passing leaves Roger Rabbit and Baby Herman minus a major competitor. It also puts them neck and neck in the race for prime suspect."

"Why aren't you out chasing them?"

"I am, more or less. Check my logic on this and see if it don't make sense. You've been known to work for Roger Rabbit. The rabbit wants Enigman bumped. A scamp greatly resembling you does the deed. Ain't that a funny coincidence? Sounds like murder for hire to me."

He scratched his head just behind his ear. His leg gave an involuntary shake. "What did I forget? Of course, the gun. Did I mention the gun? No? How could I skip that juicy tidbit. Selznick tells me you left his office today in possession of a big-bore forty-four. Exactly the size howitzer used to slick Enigman." He inverted his paw, turning it pad up, and made a spidery motion with his fingers. "You want to give me that gun, Eddie?"

He stuck one of his fingers under my lapel and raised it up, displaying my empty holster. "Save your breath. You're gonna tell me somebody swiped it. You're gonna tell me you ain't got it no more. Right?"

"Along those lines, or words to that effect."

He chucked me under the chin with his dew claw. It raised a welt the size of a barnacle. "I'm proud owner of a perfect record, Eddie. I've solved every case I've ever tackled. My method's real simple. I figure out up front who did it, and then I stick to them like ticks to my uncle until I prove it."

His next balloon assumed the shape of a hangman's necktie. Bascomb's not one for subtlety. "You're gonna take the fall for this, Valiant. Count on it. You might as well confess now, save us both a lot of time. Think about it awhile. When you're ready, whistle. I'll be right around your corner."

He signaled the squad car. It pulled up beside us. Bascomb yanked open the door and jumped in on the fly.

First, I stoked my gut furnace with a shot of liquid coal. Then, I pulled one of Philco Phil's buttons, a little harder than I had to.

"Oh, my goodness," the radio yelped. "You won't believe the excitement you missed." Philco Phil gathered up the jumbled program. "Stay tuned for a minute while I put these in order."

"Skip the verbatims," I told him. "Spout the gist."

Philco Phil's nickel-plated nameplate drooped at either end, disappointed.

"The studio went dark, and a gunshot rang out. Then a body hit the floor."

"That's ridiculous. Who'd want to kill Edward R. Murrow?"

"Senator McCarthy for one, but it wasn't Murrow who took delivery."

"You're telling me a triggerman plugged . . ."

"Roger Rabbit. One and the same."

Back when the world was a ball of ferns, when a good front lawn was a half acre of bubbling slime, a giant amoeba split in two. The front half, the end with the brains, called itself Los Angeles. The butt end became Toontown.

I live in a bungalow apartment near the border.

My landlady swears my place comes with a great view. If so, I never saw it. L.A. air's too fouled with dense, hazy, aimlessly drifting babble. I wouldn't mind if it said anything important. I'm not after philosophy. I'd settle for a weather report or yesterday's ball scores. Instead I get "Yikes," "Zowwee," "Bam," "Pow." And worse. Vinegary swear words that water my eyes.

I hear the sky's still clear in the mountains. I'm tempted to make the climb, homestead a cave, invent a religion. Ponder the nature of truth while I gaze at the stars. Except yaks and incense make me sneeze. And I look awful wearing a bed sheet.

An inebriated Toonmobile dozed in my parking slot. I didn't wake him. On nights I exceeded my recommended octane level, and my hands and knees gave out short of my doorstep, I'd slept between those old white lines myself. I know how cozy warm wavy asphalt can be.

I stored Ferd's heap on the street and left Louise Wrightliter's folders in the glove compartment. They'd be as safe there as anyplace. I walked into my courtyard.

The super had drained the swimming pool again. He used it as a grease pit to swap oil in his Model A. The water, after he refilled it, sported a perpetual slick the thickness of a zoot suiter's pompadour. Let one breaststroking lightning bug flash his phosphorous, and the whole complex would go up in flames.

I checked my Simple Simon burglar alarm, a strand of gossamer I loop low across my door. I found it busted clean. As Baby Bear would say, somebody'd been nosing my porridge. Far as I knew, he was still in there, licking the bowl.

I eased open the front window and wiggled in through the venetian blinds. I came out the other side knowing how a loaf of pumpernickel feels after do-si-doing a bread slicer.

I hit rolling and landed on my belly, senses crackling.

I scoped out the living room. Empty.

I fished my backup heater out of the cookie jar. I skipped searching the kitchenette. If my intruder was hiding in my wheezy Frigidaire, the poor sucker was wilted to a puddle by now. Anybody concealed in my toaster was too little to worry about.

I peered around the door frame into my bedroom. I saw somebody sleeping in my bunk. I prayed for Goldilocks. My luck favored the Big Bad Wolf.

I two-fingered back the covers and exposed a bumpus swathed in a baggy white cotton diaper. A baby? I wasn't taking chances. I been led down the garden path by babes in scanties before. I pistol-poked the nappie and shouted "Freeze!"

"Sure, Eddie. My p-p-p-pleasure," said Roger Rabbit, jerking awake from under the blankets. He wrapped himself in his macaroni arms, turned frosty blue, and chattered his single bucked tooth. "How's this? Cold enough for you?"

I nearly pulled the trigger. I'd plead justifiable homicide. Testify that a sweet, lovable, wisecracking bunny drove me, a hardboiled, two-fisted, brass-knuckled private op to cold-blooded murder. Would any jury in the country convict me? You bet. In a minute.

I holstered my peashooter. I opened my nightstand drawer. Roger had beaten me to my punch. I shook the hollow brown jug in his fuzzy face. "Ninety-six proofs and you couldn't leave me one?"

"I'm sorry, Eddie. I got a terrible case of the jumpin' jitters." My hooch hadn't calmed him much. His words bebopped around the black borders of his balloon like sock hoppers at a kangaroo cotillion.

He pointed to his nether region. He wasn't wearing a diaper but a bandage. "Somebody p-p-p-plugged me, Eddie! Just like the note said would happen. You gotta help me, or I'm a goner. A cooked goose. A p-p-p-plucked p-p-p-parrot. A skinned cat. A dead dog." He stuck his head under my pillow. Probably searching for more similes. He'd find only gun oil and lint.

WHO P-P-P-PLUGGED ROGER RABBIT?

"Calm down. Tell it straight and simple."

He stood up and strolled the knolls of my Posturepedic. "I was on the radio tonight. With Edward R. Murrow. He asked me terribly hard questions, one after another, but I handled them bippety boppety boop."

"I know. I heard."

He stopped short. His hangnail eyebrows boomeranged to the top of his forehead. "You gave up Edgar Bergen and Charlie McCarthy for me?"

"Sure. It wasn't even a contest." I never bought the notion of a ventriloquist on the radio. Who's to say he's not moving his lips?

Roger's pencil-lead mouth squiggled itself into a goofy grin. His yellow hands moved up and out. I sniffed a bunny hug aborning. I reached for my gat. I would have used it too, I swear. Except the rabbit, in a rare display of good judgment, cocked his noggin, rotated his mitts around to palms out, and backed off. Though his inky-dinky grin still split open his face like the snaky residue of a shaky-handed shave.

He resumed his pacing. "Halfway through the program, the studio lights went dark." My bedsprings groaned. I would too if I got tromped by tootsies the shape and circumference of snowshoes. "I heard a shot. *Ka-pow!*" His onomatopoetic exclamation drifted out the open window. Another senseless expression of violence polluting the landscape.

"I felt a stinging pain in my"—he blushed—"overalls. The lights came on, and I found myself holding this."

He showed me yet another Roger Rabbit doll. They sell in stores for a buck. This one would go for twenty percent less. It had no head.

Roger handed me a balloon. "This was stuffed . . ." He pointed to the gaping hole where the neck bone connected to the breastbone.

"You've got the box, and I want it," read the balloon. It matched the ones left by the rascal who clobbered me and deposited the tailless rabbit at Roger's front door. "Put it into a plain paper sack. Bring it tomorrow night to the Toontown graveyard. Leave it outside the Crypt of the Dipped on the stroke of midnight. Come alone. Don't try anything cute. I will be watching."

He'd signed it with a hand-drawn skull and crossbones under

which he'd added a P.S.: "Cross me, and forget about hats, fright wigs, baseball caps, propeller beanies, eyeglasses, nose cozies, wax lips, chin straps, or anything else worn above the shoulders."

I crammed the note back in the chest hole it came from. "You know the box he's talking about?"

Roger's ears bent outward at right angles. They shrugged. You got no shoulders, you improvise. A light bulb oozed out of his head and plopped onto my pillowcase. It switched on, filling the room with the fire-sale odor of scorched percale. "My lunch box, my bread box, my shoe box, my tool box, my itty bitty ditty box?"

"How about the one that belongs to Davey Selznick?"

"A box seat!"

"Not hardly. Remember the day you, Kirk Enigman, and Baby Herman went to Selznick's office to palaver about *Gone With the Wind*?"

"Of course. I dressed in my finest apparel. Red overalls with *brass* buttons. I cut quite the impressive figure, if I do say so myself."

"When you three skedaddled, a box belonging to Selznick snuck out with you." I gave him the rundown.

The accumulated weight of the mogul's accusation pressed him low. By the end of it, he was under the carpet with yesterday's dust. "Mr. Selznick thinks I swiped his dumb box? That's ridiculous. I'm as honest as . . . as . . ."

I braced myself for another round of parallels on parade. He didn't disappoint.

". . . as the day is long. As the mountain is high. As the river is deep. As the cheese is binding. As the . . ."

"Spare me the indignation." I went into the living room. I propped Trudy Hammerschlemmer's photo against my fish tank, figuring it might keep the scum at bay. I threw the mutilated rabbit doll under my coffee table, out of Roger's sight. "I can square you on the rap. Enigman took the box. He as much as admitted it to me. Before person unknown booted his bucket."

Roger's jaw took the elevator to the basement. "Kirk Enigman's dead?"

"Done in, unless I miss my guess, by the sharpshooter who

slung lead at you. The box holds the key. I find it, unlock it, and I throw this case wide open."

"Do it, Eddie, and quick. Or I'll be playing the lead in *The Headless Horseman of Sleepy Hollow*." He bent his fruitcake backwards and tucked it under his arm, worming his neck into the shape of a bar pretzel.

A fist hit my front door with the impact of a rutting goat. "Open up, scuzz hamper." Pepper Potts. There went my hundred-yard head start.

I shoved Roger into my hall closet.

"Hold it," he protested, his head snapping out from under his armpit with the whooshing velocity of Jack Kramer's second serve. "I'm your buddy, your sidekick. I go where you go, do what you do, see who you—"

I slammed the door on his balloon, tore off the half circle caught on the outside, and flipped it under an easy chair.

I threw the dead bolt and opened the front door.

"Took you long enough," snarled Potts.

"Sorry, I was in the greenhouse pollinating my posies."

He shoved me aside and hobbled in. His phony leg clattered like a castanet on the linoleum.

"You need a pedicure, chum. Hang on. I'll fetch my rasp."

"Don't crack wise, peeper." He kicked my early American rocker so hard its maple slats wept pancake syrup.

"Pick on something your own size. The sofa, maybe, or the daybed."

"You're a piece of work, Valiant. A regular Wisenheimer." He wore baggy-knee britches and a matching back-belted jacket the color and texture of a mangy ferret. "We got a problem, you and me."

"Let's solve it quick. I had a long, tiring day. I'm bushed. I need my beauty rest."

"Har har. That's a pip. You could sleep through to the next stone age and still be plug-ugly." He leaned on my bookshelf, his shoulder next to my fish tank. "I got a job to do, and you're standing in my way."

"I'll move aside and let you past if it gets you out of my life."

He picked up the picture of Charley's niece. "Quite a looker."

His ligneous leg rubbed against the bookcase with sufficient friction to start his calf smoking.

"I'll introduce you."

"Skip it. I'd owe you, and I wouldn't want that." He took two steps toward me. His spindle sank to the ankle through my cast-iron heating grate.

"Need a saw?"

"What I need is a star for *Gone With the Wind*." He lifted his pin and two square feet of metal grate came with it. He took another step. The extra weight didn't slow him, but the noise, the sound of a tap-dancing telephone pole, stopped him dead. "What I got is a dead actor and two prime suspects. That ain't gonna hack it with my financiers." He stamped his gimp hard enough to dent the underside of China. The iron grate snapped in half. "Mr. Selznick is not a happy man. The cops been sniffing around. Davey don't like it when cops ask him questions. It's bad for his image. Not to mention it upsets him. He can't work. And when Davey's testy, I'm an absolute screaming banshee."

I uncorked my volcano and flowed molten lava into a matched set of jelly glasses. I handed one to him.

"Never touch the stuff." The smell of rum on his clothes said otherwise, but I wasn't about to argue. More booze for me. "Mr. Selznick wants this matter wrapped up pronto. Before any further damage gets done." Potts laced his digits together, turned them inside out, and crunched them, producing the pop a firebug makes when he snaps his kindling. "To that end, Davey authorized me to persuade you to hurry it up."

I got a flash of what literates call déjà view. Meaning I don't have to get hit in the head to know I'm about to get hit in the head. I made what fly-boys call a preemptive strike, meaning I cheap-kicked Porter low with sufficient force to pulverize any stone short of a diamond. Men hit that way will double over, fall down, choke, turn blue, puke, pass out, die, or worse. Porter reacted like I'd tickled him with a feather.

He stepped forward and planted his wooden size one on my instep. While the force of his broom handle pinned me upright, he played xylophone on my ribs, and glockenspiel on my kisser.

When he'd finished his recital, he lifted his pinion and let me sink to the floor. By the light of the constellation of stars whirling around me, I made a quick calculation. According to my unofficial tally, I'd taken more beatings than an old maid's living-room carpet.

Potts sunk his spindle into my gut. "Davey says you've gotten too notorious for him to deal with direct. He don't want you calling him or coming around his office. From now on, you deal with yours truly and nobody else. This box Davey's got you hunting for. You tell me who stole it. You give it to me and only me when you get it back." He peeled open my eyelid. "Clear?" He let loose of my head. It hit the floor. Potts mashed my puss for luck. "You get a break in this case, you call me on the horn."

"French or fluegel?"

"Keep talking like that and it'll be a bugle blowing taps over your casket."

As he walked out, he tromped on Roger's beheaded doll. His leg went through its stomach. "Remember, Valiant. Davey don't want to see you, hear you, smell you, or taste you. From here on, you deal with me." The doll impaled on his pinewood muffled the sound of his leaving.

I sterilized my wounds with Potts's untouched drink, then opened my hall closet. Roger had fallen asleep draped over the hanger supporting my green checked slacks. I lifted his head, laid it on the shoulder of my raincoat, and let him snooze.

I drove to Arnie Johnson's. He complained when I woke him until he realized he'd just secured Guinness Book of Records immortality for most stitches laced into a single head.

I returned home, went to bed, and tried logging Z's but didn't have much success. I've slept through earthquakes, but none rattled me as much as Pepper Potts.

10

A suicide squadron of chirps and trills kamikazed my upwind ear canal. I tilted my head and palm-smacked the opposite temple. The tiny eighth and quarter notes popped loose, but the bigger halfs and fulls burrowed in deeper, warbling to beat the band.

I named that tune in nine notes.

"Wake up, wake up, wake up, you sleepy head, get up, get up, get up, get up, get out of bed. . . ."

I burrowed out from under my top sheet.

Roger stood facing my open bedroom window. The morning sunlight reflecting off his polar-white fur ice-picked my pupils, inflicting the worst case of snow blindness south of Nanook of the North.

A boisterous choir of bluebirds perched on the edge of the sill. Clothespins shielded their beaks from the aroma of the stinkweed overgrowing my window box. Roger led them in rosy song. For a baton, he had rolled up the rent-overdue-pay-up-or-get-out notice which the super shoved daily under my door.

". . . cheer up, cheer up, cheer up, the sun is red. Live, love, laugh and be . . ."

I threw my pillow at the merry songsters. In a scene out of Mr. Disney's sticky sweetest fairy tale, they encircled it in the air and caught it on the fly. Holding it in their tiny beaks, they flew it back to me and tucked it under my head.

There's never a scattergun handy when you need one. "Shoo those squawk boxes out of here," I yelled at my morning maestro, "before they give me diabetes."

Roger sent his tweeters flying. "I thought you'd like a wake-up song."

For six months in boot camp I rousted to bugle music. I'd toss Peggy Lee out of my sack if she tickled her tonsils before noon. "You thought wrong."

I did my morning exercises. Twenty push-ups, ten squats, five leg lifters, two shots. Roger shadowed me one for one including the deuce of snifters, then he followed me into the bathroom. "What's our modus operandi, chief?"

I gave him the boot and slammed the door.

I scrubbed my snags with Ipana, tamed my cowlick with Wildroot, frosted my chops with Burma Shave, mowed them with a double-edged Gillette, and anointed my armpits with Old Spice. I stepped back and rated the results. My mirror told me the wicked queen could quit worrying. Her position as fairest in the land was safe for another day.

When I went back into my bedroom, I discovered how Dorothy felt when she went from Kansas to color.

Roger had tidied up, and how! My wallow hadn't been this neat and mud-free since Doris handed in her latchkey. A geometry teacher could use my bed-sheet corners to illustrate isosceles triangles. My plumped pillows resembled the rear view of a Dandie Dinmont. Gymnasts trampoline on fabric looser than my bedspread.

The rabbit had washed and ironed my argyles and underwear. A spotless shirt hung on the closet door. He'd pressed my brown plaid suit. He'd even mended the old bullet hole. With a green square cross-stitched on with yellow thread to match my tie!

In my circles, neat relates to whiskey not clothes. If I wore this regalia, my friends would think I'd gone Ritzy, or crackers. Or both. I ripped off the patch, rumpled my suit and shirt, and dowsed a pair of skiffs with bay rum to loosen the starch.

I accessorized my outfit with my snap-draw shoulder holster and my spare .38.

Roger was in the kitchenette, hunched over my Formica table. He'd dumped out the contents of an entire cereal box and was picking through the flakes. He wasn't being a finicky eater. He was hunting for buried treasure.

He whooped, held up a clear cellophane packet, and ripped it open. It contained a Captain Midnight Secret Decoder, round and solid brass, the size of a lady's compact, embossed with the year and Midnight's emblem. A revolving metal dial set the code of the day.

"Yippee! I can't believe it!" I've wrapped Christmas presents in paper less colorful than his balloon. "I've searched through a hundred boxes for this!"

"And you found it in *my* Wheaties."

His gasbag crumpled. Glumly, he handed me the decoder.

"Keep it," I told him. "I use the Jack Armstrong model."

"He's got one too?"

I scowled.

Roger split a grin the size and shape of a melon slice. "Gee, thanks, Eddie. You're swell." He dropped the premium in his pocket.

He eyed my outfit. "I must have missed those. Take them off, and I'll iron them."

"Skip it." I scraped a bowl of cereal off the table and ate it standing up. "I got to get to work."

"I'll get ready." Roger ducked into my closet. He came out wearing my belted trencher, collar up, and a wide-brimmed hat. "How do I look?"

"Like Humphrey Bogart on Halloween." If he wanted stroking, let him move to a petting zoo. I dialed the phone.

"Oh, boy, here we go," said Roger. "Official detective business." He pulled out a leather notebook. He wetted his pencil point on his tongue. "Who you calling?"

"The casting director at MGM."

Using his ear for a straightedge, Roger divided his page neatly into four equal columns. He wrote "CD/MGM" in the first, noted the time in the second, the date in the third, and poised his pencil above the fourth. "What's he got to do with the price of peanuts in Paraguay?"

"None of your beeswax."

Roger winked. "That's a test, right? To see if I've got the moxie to overcome resistance when interrogating a suspect. Fine. I accept the challenge." He bent over and aerialed his ears around my head. "I'll switch to aural surveillance."

I smacked his bean with the telephone, raising a lump the size of my kitchen table. He didn't need Captain Midnight to decode that message.

The casting director came on the wire. In exchange for the

promise of a double sawbuck, he gave me a daytime phone number, a car wash on the Strip. No surprise. If not that, it would have been a hash house, a juke joint, a bookshop, a department store, or a soda fountain, the traditional meal tickets of daydreamers.

The maître d' at the auto laundry ordered me and Roger to vacate while our buggy took a bath. I flashed him a peek at my heater. He wished us bon voyage and hooked us to the treadmill. We rolled headlong into a humid hellhole of soap bubbles and water.

"I'm baffled," said Roger from the backseat. "What nefarious skullduggery goes on in here?"

The automatic scrub brushes shoo-shoo-boogied the length of the car and backed off. The passenger door opened. A female attendant piled inside. She wore loose-fitting white coveralls and a long-billed blue twill cap of the sort sported by elderly fishermen and Donald Duck. A cinnamon-backed, black-bellied, plug-ugly male anteater with toenails as long and prickly as scimitars hopped in after her.

The dame came armed with a spritzer of Windex and a handful of rags. The rodent packed a snout the length, breadth, and color of Paul Bunyon's Coney Island red-hot. Both were sopped to the skin, which displayed the contours hidden beneath white denim and fur, respectively. Underneath his bristly exterior, the anteater resembled a shriveled desert carcass. Road crews shovel up and bury better. The woman was another story. Unless she wore a Mae West and a tool belt stuffed with extra sponges, she curved front to back, side to side in exactly the right places.

The rodent and I bookended the frail.

She moved me over with an elbow shot to the ribs. "Another cheap thrill seeker," she said to her partner in grime. "Hoping to pinch my wuzzle while I scrub his glass."

The anteater ignored her, me, everything but the ashtray into which he stuck his snifter and snorted.

"One touch, mate," she warned as she squirted my windshield, "and I yell for the bobbies."

"Save your lungs." I showed her my photostat. "I'm legit."

She held my license an inch from her nose and squinted at the likeness. "I know you," she said in her lilting, lightly Limey accent. "Last time we met, you were talking to a prop."

"Second to last. We met once after."

"So we did. I forgot."

"Beautiful women usually do."

Her nose dimpled on the end when she smiled. "I admire a man with the linguistic ability to pay a lady a compliment and disparage himself in a single four-word sentence."

"Smart girl, dumb luck." I grinned. She clapped her wet hands. I took as much of a bow as you can while wedged behind the steering wheel of a Hupmobile.

The anteater finished vacuuming the front floor mats and started on the back. He should have looked before he lipped. He inhaled Roger's left ear.

"Don't tell me what happens next," she said to me. "I know." She sprayed the seats with the same solution she'd used on the windows. "You beat me with a rubber hose until I squeal. Isn't that the way detectives operate?"

Roger braced his feet on the anteater's forehead and yanked to no avail.

"What gave you that idea?"

The anteater sneezed louder than the chief inspector in a pepper mill, but couldn't clear the ear out of his throat.

She extended her index fingers, raised her thumbs, and lined them into an imaginary machine gun. She sprayed a burst into my craw. "My daddy was a great fan of your American gangster films. He carted me to every one that played in London."

"Sorry, toots. Life don't imitate art in this burg. I haven't seen a Thompson since Normandy Beach. I looked you up to buy you lunch."

"Really?" She removed her cap, wrung it out, and mopped her brow with it. "Let me warn you. I haven't eaten a decent meal for weeks. I might gorge myself and not be able to walk away from the table."

"I'll bring my wheelbarrow."

Her warm laugh dried the car from the inside out. She knighted my shoulder with her headgear. "I have tomorrow off. Pick me up at my place." She gave me the address.

WHO P-P-P-PLUGGED ROGER RABBIT?

The anteater hawked. Roger's top third blew out of his honker along with six pounds of dust.

The lady and the anteater climbed out. They ran down the line to catch the next boat through the canal, a bright yellow Rolls.

"Hey," I called after her. "What's your name?"

She yelled it over a snake hiss of steam. "Vivien Leigh."

Roger tumbled into the front seat, his left ear bent to the shape of the anteater's innards. "We wasted half the morning, and I nearly lost a lobe just to get you a date?" He formed his thumb and first digit into a circle and ran it stem to stern along his kinked appendage. It straightened with the sound of pigs popping their knuckles. "How can you possibly justify that?"

"Love makes the world go 'round, chum."

He blinked like I'd speared him through the heart. "You're right." He unleashed a torrent of tears having the high arc of a one-handed jump shot. They splattered me with brine. "What's life without romance? Without wooing and cooing? How I miss the bliss of her kiss." I folded his bright red, lacy-edged balloon lengthwise and tucked it away. It would save me a dime, assuming I clicked with a skirt by Valentine's Day.

"Forget about the assassin," he said. "Forget about Mr. Selznick's dumb box. Forget about Rhett Butler, Baby Herman, Kirk Enigman, *Gone With the Wind*. None of it matters a hill of beans, not compared to what's really important. Eddie, I have to know."

He stood on the seat and faced me, pleating himself across the middle so he wouldn't have to stoop. "Is Jessica cheating on me or not?"

I kicked the gas. The acceleration sproinged open the accordion folds across his stomach, leaving him wedged firmly between seat cushion and roof. "Let's find out."

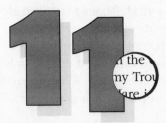

11

We pulled into an office park built entirely out of the Jolly Green Giant's old toy blocks. The developer had simply hollowed them out, added doors and windows, and stacked them in piles. Architectural critics took one gander at his hodgepodged square wooden buildings, embossed on the sides with brightly colored silhouettes of circus clowns, choo-choo trains, and barnyard livestock, and proclaimed the brilliant dawn of *style naïveté*. Space here leased for an arm and a leg per foot. "Wow," said Roger. "These streets are paved with gold!"

The rabbit needed spectacles. The road we traveled was common macadam, a bit less bumpy than most. It led to the medical offices of Dr. Wallace Ford.

A small brass door plaque displayed his name followed by enough letters to stir envy in an eye chart.

I unwrapped a large bar of Ivory and handed it to Roger. "Chew this up good before we go in."

"What? Eat soap? Are you nuts? It could kill me."

"Not a chance. It's ninety-nine and forty-four one hundreths percent pure." I shoved it into his craw. He munched it up and swallowed.

Ford's starchy, lemon-pussed receptionist informed me nobody sees the doctor without an appointment. His first open slot? Two weeks into the next decade.

I pleaded emergency. Told her I had a rabid rabbit on my hands. Roger stood beside me, obligingly foaming at the mouth.

She ushered us into an examination room, *posthaste*.

Dr. Ford entered a few minutes later. He was as thin and sterile as a scalpel. I hoped he wasn't as sharp. He added a final notation to his last patient's file and dropped it into a wall-hung metal basket. He slipped a fresh form into his clipboard. His brisk, efficient manner epitomized the medical profession's motto: *Impellite Eos, Expellite Eos* ("Move 'em in, move 'em out"). Another reason I saw a vet. "What seems to be the problem?"

Roger belched a quantity of soapsuds sufficient to swab the decks of a battleship.

Ford grabbed a handful, rubbed them between his fingers, and sniffed the residue. "Definitely not rabies. Any family history of saponaceousness?"

"Only the sap part."

"Let's have a look." Ford shined a flashlight into Roger's ear. A shadow picture of squirrels storing nuts for the winter appeared on the wall beyond.

"You come highly recommended by a friend of mine," I said. "Clark Gable."

"Ah, yes. Clark, the dear boy. I haven't seen him for ages." Ford tapped the back of Roger's head with a silver hammer. It rang like a lumberjack axing a hollow oak.

"When he heard I was coming here, he asked me to do him a favor. You sent him a bill." I showed him the copy I'd cadged from Louise Wrightliter's Gable file. "He can't remember what it's for. Maybe you could refresh his memory."

Ford glanced at it and nodded. "That was incurred by a friend of his. A lady friend." He flat-handed Roger between the shoulder blades. Roger coughed out a balloon filled with froth.

"Clark requested I send the bill to him personally rather than to her or the studio." Ford snapped Roger's balloon onto a back-lighted viewing box. He studied it through a magnifying glass. "I obliged."

"Clark figured it for that."

"I'm surprised the matter slipped his memory." Ford wrapped a blood-pressure cuff around Roger's neck, stuck a bicycle pump in his mouth, and inflated him to three times normal size. "Considering the circumstances."

He put his stethoscope on Roger's nose and pulled out the air tube. "It's not every day a man requests me to examine Jessica Rabbit. Especially for what he gave her."

Roger deflated to the thickness of an ironing board.

Ford slipped Roger under a fluoroscope and turned on the juice. The screen showed a cranium full of bubbles. Ford noted it on Roger's chart. "Remarkably clean-minded chap."

Hardly. I saw murder in Roger's pancaked eyes, and that's as dirty as thinking gets.

"I prescribe a vacuum purge," said Ford. He stuffed Roger into his stainless-steel sterilizer, slammed the door, spun the spoked metal lock, and set the timer for thirty minutes.

With Roger out of earshot, I asked Ford the sixty-four-dollar doozy. "What exactly did Jessica Rabbit catch from Gable?"

He chuckled. "A case of morning sickness. The lady is pregnant."

I paid a street-corner urchin six bits for a map of the stars. It told me Gable resided in what real-estate hawkers call an ethnically undifferentiated, upscale neighborhood. That means everybody's invited, Toons and humans alike, but show a fat wallet at the door.

The names on Gable's street read like *Who's Who*. Movie stars, athletes, politicians, industrialists, more movers and shakers than you'd find at a bulldozer's reunion.

His driveway snaked so far back from the road I earned a few extra bucks in mileage money, and so far up it practically gave me a nosebleed. Gable lived in a suction cup that clung to the leveled-off top of the hillside the way flies stick to a wall. One good swat from Mother Earthquake and he'd ride the world's only twenty-six-bedroom toboggan.

The actor wasn't as egalitarian as Knuckles presumed. He had a Ford all right, but I have a hunch he only drove it when sweaty. His personal parking lot also boasted a Stutz Bearcat, a LaSalle, and a Duesenberg.

I parked next to an Indian Chief motorcycle. A leather helmet and goggles hung from the handlebar. Comforting to know even he-men worry about bug-spotted foreheads.

The soap suds had melted away, but raw fury and gall had kept Roger lathered. When I dowsed the engine, he exploded with the roar of a match down a gas pipe. "Gable! That p-p-p-parsimonious p-p-p-popinjay. That p-p-p-prodigious p-p-p-pederast. I'll p-p-p-parboil his p-p-p-porridge. I'll p-p-p-pulverize his p-p-p-petunias. I'll p-p-p-punch his p-p-p-parasol to p-p-p-pieces."

"Hold on, champ, before you lay on the blame. Last I heard, it takes two to tango."

The lump in his throat blocked off his balloon. When it swelled to the size of a terminal goiter, I thumped him hard and shook it loose. I should have let him rupture. "I'm coming in with you," he said.

"Over my dead body." I got out of the car and headed for the door.

He hopped around and kneeled in front of me. "P-p-p-pretty p-p-p-please?" I left my heel marks on his chest. He grabbed me around the knees. "I'll be good, honest I will."

I'll say this. He was tenacious. I like that in a rabbit. "You'll keep your yap shut?"

He zipped his lip.

"You so much as raise your pinkie, and you spend the rest of this case locked in the trunk."

He gave me a look of innocence that would have sailed him past the screening committee to the hereafter.

As we walked to the front door, I noticed him slip a nickel out of his pocket. He ran it the full length of Gable's Stutz. It left a gouge almost as wide but not quite as deep as the one in his ticker.

A bronze plaque on the door frame designated Gable's cliff-hanger as a National Historical Wowser. Seems Daddy Warbucks built it in the twenties as a one-upper to his arch rival, William Randolph Hearst. He scoured the globe for French and Dutch doors, Grecian formula columns, Venetian blinds, and Roman candle holders. He crowned it with a Chinese-checkered paint job. The end result resembled the outhouse at the United Nations. Though admittedly my taste in castles runs to white ones that sell cheap hamburgers.

Gable's butler was an English bulldog from the wrong side of the Thames. He was tall and lanky with not an ounce of puppy fat. He had his breed's typical pushed-in face, but his went back farther than most, like he'd run full-tilt down one too many dead-end streets. He'd never take Best of Show at Westchester, but he'd go good rounds with any dogcatcher in town.

His words came out pure Cockney, dry as a day-old basket of fish and chips. The master was in the backyard enjoying a swim in the pool. Roger and I could cut through the house so long as we promised not to let our feet touch the floor.

We entered Gable's inner sanctum. Roger pulled up short

when he saw what hung over the mantel. An oil portrait of Jessica. Her eyes twinkled brighter than the star I wished on every night. She had hair the color of a strawberry sundae, always my favorite dessert. A plastic surgeon could have made a career out of giving other women her nose. Her smile out-candlepowered Rudolph the Reindeer. The portrait ended just below her bare shoulders and left me wishing for twelve inches more canvas.

Roger's ears drooped like the side flaps on a moose hunter's hat. I grabbed him by his limp auricles and dragged him onto the veranda.

If not for the Great Salt Lake, Gable's freestanding, cantilevered pool would have been the biggest body of water west of the Mississippi. A strong wind could raise waves high enough to swamp his garage.

I picked binoculars off a small patio table and scanned the horizon. I spotted him paddling around on the far side of the island. He swam to shore with the effortless grace of a water sprite.

He pulled himself out of the pool and toweled off, starting with his long black hair and working his way down. I've met my share of movie actors. Most make as much of an impression as a gnat's foot on wet sand. Not Gable. An advertising huckster seeking a ruggedly handsome face to drift the high plains in praise of a cigarette need look no further. His nose, perfect. His mouth, perfect. His chin, his teeth, his eyebrows, his mustache, even his nose hairs were perfect. When he smiled, his face became a sheet of slightly crinkled bronze foil recently unwrapped from a very expensive piece of Anglo-American toffee. In those movie posters showing him with his shirt off, his muscles came from pressing iron, not from the end of an airbrush. Ladies nowadays called him a dreamboat. I'd classify him heavier and more dangerous, a light cruiser or a PT. Crowds would part to let this man through, and so, probably, would the Red Sea.

There was only one slight flaw in his otherwise perfect demeanor. With his ears, he'd be well advised to stay out of high winds and elephant herds.

I handed him my card. "A private eye, huh?" He sized me up, not caring for what he saw. "What can I do for you gents?" He turned to Roger.

Technically, Roger kept his promise. His dander was way up,

flaking off him in a white blizzard that could serve as the before picture in an ad for hare conditioner. But he didn't mouth off. He didn't have a chance. Gable took one gander at him, said "Not you again," and decked him with a right cross. I've heard directors complain that Roger can't produce stars when he's bonked on the bean. You couldn't prove it by Gable's punch. Roger created enough five-pointers to overpopulate the Milky Way. He collapsed into a heap.

"What'd you do that for?" I asked.

Gable slipped on a robe, heavy terry cloth with the nap of a good throw rug. He stepped over the unconscious rabbit, walked to the table, and poured a glass of orange juice. "The hairy little weasel's trying to bribe me."

"You got him confused with another hairy weasel."

Gable rolled him over with the tip of his toe. "Roger Rabbit. I'd know those flying-saucer eyes, those Popsicle ears, that bell-bottom body . . ."

"What'd he do to rattle your snake?"

Gable extricated his foot from the rabbit's belly and let him fall back to the concrete. "The crumb bum came here yesterday. He offered me a sizable amount of money. All I had to do in return was interrogate my best pal."

"And who might that be?"

"Baby Herman. He's a good stiff. Me and the Babe have done more than our fair share of bar crawling. Not to mention racing our cycles together up in the hills. He's a game little mudlark, a suicide rider, flat out and won't stop for anything. Though that might have something to do with the fact his legs don't reach the brakes."

"What was the rabbit after?"

"He wanted me to pump the Babes about a stupid box."

Gable's butler spread Roger flat and rolled him up from feet to head.

"I told the rabbit to take a hop." Gable lit a smoke, a fancy brand that sells for a dime a pack. "I kicked him. Hard. Check under that bandage he's wearing. I'll bet you'll find an imprint of my shoelaces."

The butler tied Roger into a bundle knotted with his own ears.

"The rabbit grind any personal axes during his visit?"

Gable vitamin-enriched his juice with four ounces of fermented potato. "Give me a clue."

"The subject of you and his wife."

Gable's thumb traced a pattern on his frosty glass, either a bull's-eye or a zero. "Rumors. I pay a press agent big money to spread them. They bolster my reputation."

"According to Old Doc Ford, one of those rumors took seed. He says Jessica's in a family way, and you're the culprit."

Gable sipped his drink. "That's a private matter a gentleman doesn't discuss. You want to know, I suggest you ask the lady in question."

"So far I'm aught for two here in the rumors-confirmed department. Let's try for strike three. There's a story going around that you're not the man you're cracked up to be, if you get my drift."

That one drew a response. He smacked his fist so hard on the patio table he dented the metal.

"They're saying you're not a red-blooded male. They're saying your bloodlines might be closer to shocking pink."

He pointed a finger between my eyes. "That's plenty, buster. Give it a rest. You've drawn the lines, you don't have to color in the picture."

"In other words, I don't need to ask you the truth of that morsel."

"Not if you value your head."

"Any idea where it came from?"

"Who knows. I'm not a well-liked man in Hollywood. This is a company town, and I keep the wrong company. That's why my career's stagnating."

I followed him into the house. "You're getting your share of parts."

"For the wrong reasons." Fifty sets of glass animal eyes stared down at me from the walls. Frank Buck brought 'em back alive. Gable brought 'em back stuffed and mounted on boards. "I'm always cast as a pretty boy. Nobody acknowledges my acting. I don't want to leave this world with a tombstone that reads 'He was only a pretty face.' I want to accomplish something significant."

"Choose another profession. Switch your major to physics. Sit under a tree and get beaned with an apple, or drop a pizza off a leaning tower. You'll get credit for changing the world."

WHO P-P-P-PLUGGED ROGER RABBIT?

He wasn't about to take my advice, but rewarded the sentiment by going to the bar and pouring us both a short message from my favorite sponsor. "Excuse the vodka," he said. "I much prefer rum at this time of day, but I'm having trouble getting it lately."

I ought to put Gable in touch with Pepper Potts. They could break the law of supply and demand. One has no rum, the other bathes in it.

I tracked him up the stairs to his bedroom. While he dressed, I stood outside the door and fiddled with the loose threads dangling off my buttonholes.

"When I told the rabbit I wouldn't play ball," Gable said to me through six inches of polished Philippine mahogany, "he let fly with a word balloon so profane it blistered the paint." Gable wasn't exaggerating. I noticed a bare spot three by three on the ceiling slightly right of the porcelain chandelier.

Gable came out. When I suit up every morning, I pick my apparel by pulling stuff out of my closet and drawers until I've got the proper number of items—which, by trial and error, I learned to be eleven. If I don't have on eleven items, I've left something out. Which explains why I've gone to work wearing no belt and two pairs of shorts. Color? Who cares. It all goes pink in the wash. Style? I wear my undershirts inside out to give my Fruit of the Loom label equal time in a world of alligators and polo ponies.

Gable, on the other hand, with his monogrammed gold buttons, double-breasted blue blazer, gray slacks, white shirt, and V-necked white sweater, stepped right off the cover of *Esquire.* A straw boater added just the right touch of *savoir faire,* which, for you who don't speak the sartorial, means proper breeding. "What happened after you booted the rabbit?"

"He threatened me. Said he had contacts in high places. He promised me I'd never work in this town again. He took a poke at me. He missed. I didn't."

"Leave any marks?"

"I blacked his eye."

The butler had left Roger rolled up by the front door. I hoisted him up by his ear knot and checked his face. His nose was pushed clear to his tonsils, but there wasn't any sucker's halo around his lamps. "I think you got your rabbits confused."

Gable checked for himself. "If it wasn't him, it was his identical twin bunny, right down to the stutter. 'D-d-d-do what I tell you or you're d-d-d-dog d-d-d-donuts.' That's what he said. Wish he'd been there to spray me with saliva when I was in the Mojave shooting *Red Dust*."

Together, we carried Roger out to my car. We walked side by side, the prince and the pauper. No question which part I played.

Gable opened the door and we threw the comatose rabbit into the backseat. "Tell the little imp I'm sorry if I made a mistake. I'm normally better at keeping my temper under control. I've been under a great deal of stress lately."

"The rumors, the career."

"That I can handle. I'm being bothered by the age-old story."

Gable's butler pulled around to the front of the house. His chauffeur's cap was way too small for him. The Duesenberg he drove wasn't. "I read the same book," I said. "*Cherchez* the dame."

"I'll give you this much, buster. You know the ropes. Seems the love of my life's been cheating on me with another man. I'd kill the guy if I knew his name."

If Roger wasn't already out cold, the shock of hearing this would put him there. "Jessica's trysting with somebody else?"

Gable's laugh rattled out of him like an empty corn husk, brittle and dry. "Probably, but it's not her who's slicing my heartstring."

"Care to share a name?"

He shrugged. "Why not. You'll read about it in the *Telltale* sooner or later anyway. It's Carole Lombard."

I recollected the photo I saw hanging on Roger's wall, a lovey-dovey glossy of Lombard and that diminutive rake around town, Gable's cycling buddy, Baby Herman. Imagine that. I had to hand it to the Baby. Stealing his best friend's girl. The little man had a big, big cheek.

I tailgated a GrayLine Tour Bus along the twisting Malibu beach road. The double-decker slowing my parade had a PA system so loud hoedowners could use it to call square dances during an air raid. Even with my windows up, I got a blaring earful of the guide welcoming his Als and Allisons to Wonderland.

The bus slowed as it went past an isolated beach house. A red-tiled roof and smooth, buff-colored walls tossed the place into the Spanish stucco bin, though in size it came closer to King Ferdinand's villa than to Father Sierra's mission. The loudspeaker ahead of me identified the place as the getaway of that terrific twosome Jessica Rabbit. Remind me to laugh.

I turned into the pea-graveled driveway.

Roger was still dead to the world. Mute testimony to the force of Gable's wallop. Or maybe my luck was turning.

I stretched him out in the trunk. His head rested on my spare tire, his legs straddled my jack handle. He blipped out a stream of hazy, black-and-white balloons, visions of him wailing the tar out of Gable. Only in his dreams. I took off my belt and tied the trunk shut, leaving it open a smidgen so his apparitions wouldn't fill the space to overflowing and suffocate him.

Jessica opened the door in person, and that's quite a person, indeed. "Why, Mr. Valiant. How nice to see you again." Her delicately petaled balloons could easily pass for a bouquet of gardenias, especially since they exuded the same hint of secret passions and gave off a similar aroma of forbidden delight.

Too bad I only knew two words that rhymed, "moon" and "June," because this was the woman wordsmiths invented poetry for. "Always a pleasure being in your neighborhood."

Young girls across the country faddishly aped Jessica's arched eyebrows, butterfly lashes, virgin-blush cheeks, passion-purple eye shadow, rosy-red smackers, and peekaboo hair. The girls of my youth leaned toward Tugboat Annie. How times change.

In the flesh, no pun intended, Jessica wore a bright blue swimming suit that left little to my scanty imagination. I needed a window-shade roller to stuff my tongue back into my mouth. I shouldn't have left my gat in the car. I could have gotten a free reload from the way she made me sweat bullets. Except for my one and only scruple, never mess with married women, I'd camp outside her window every night strumming romantic ditties on my lute.

"Won't you come in," she said warmly enough to melt butter-scotch.

She held a brace of wooden dumbbells. Working on her pecs, she said. I volunteered to lend a hand. She winked, exhaled a pair of appropriately sized balloons, and blew them in my direction. I reached out with the surefingered poise of a Harlem Globetrotter demonstrating how to palm basketballs. The instant I touched them, they turned to jaggedy-jawed mousetraps and sprang shut with the vicious snap of an overwound set of chattering teeth. Lucky I got quick reflexes. I barely escaped having no further use for gloves with fingers. I love a woman with a sense of humor.

"I'm going to finish off my workout with a swim," she said. "Perhaps you'd care to join me."

"I didn't bring my suit."

"That's not a problem." She chucked me under the chin with a red fingernail the shape of an ironing board. "It's a very private beach."

She took my hand and led me down a long wooden staircase to the water. She plunged into the surf and motioned for me to join her.

I stripped to my unmentionables and followed her into the drink. Our idyllic cavort lasted only until I watched her do the breaststroke. My jaw hung so far open I swallowed a gallon of salt water. She dragged me out, laid me facedown on the sand, straddled my back, and pumped me dry.

"I had a dream last night, Mr. Valiant." She switched from artificial respiration to back massage. "Do you ever have dreams?"

"I'm having one right now."

"You were in my dream."

"Makes us even. You're in all of mine."

WHO P-P-P-PLUGGED ROGER RABBIT?

My explosive starts as a human cannonball had left me with a perpetual kink in my shoulders. She found it and rubbed it with her palm until it heated to near boiling. She had strong hands for a woman. "I dreamt Roger killed a man. Then somebody killed Roger."

I tried to roll over and face her, but she knew how to keep a man pinned to the ground. "If this story goes on much longer, I'll need a week to come back to Earth."

"Stay put, it's almost over. You straightened everything out. You discovered who censored Roger Rabbit, you even cleared him of a murder you knew he committed. Because you'd grown fond of my little honey bunny."

"My soul drips with compassion."

"It was so real, Mr. Valiant." She jammed her fist into my deltoid and twisted. My knot dissolved. "I awoke in a cold shiver, convinced my beloved was gone forever. Imagine my surprise when I went into the bathroom, opened the shower door, and there he was, cute as ever, lathered tip to toe." She rolled off me, stretched out, leaned on one elbow and stared me in the eye. Drops of seawater, or maybe perspiration, trickled off the end of her dainty, upturned nose. "What do you make of my dream?"

"About a quarter of a million dollars from any movie studio in town. Call it the story of a man, a woman, and a rabbit in a triangle of trouble. Ending needs work. Only a nincompoop would believe that shower scene."

We air-dried lying side by side on the sand, me on my stomach, her on her back. Her silhouette reminded me of a picture postcard I once got from a friend in the Alps. "Is this social, Mr. Valiant?" Her thick red hair pillowed her head. "Or business?"

"I guess you'd say a bit of both. You been too social. That makes it my business."

"I'm sorry. I don't follow."

"Let me spell it out for you as genteel as I can. I'm looking to find out what's going on between you and Clark Gable."

She gripped a handful of sand and squeezed it tightly enough to fuse it into glass. "By whom? Who hired you? Roger?"

"That's confidential info. I can't divulge the name of my client."

She moistened a fingertip with her tongue and ran it into my hair, at the sensitive spot where temple meets ear. "Not even to Jessie Wessie?"

It would take stronger than me, Sampson or Goliath maybe, to resist. "Davey Selznick. He's checking up on the stars for his Southern extravaganza. He doesn't want any scandal blotting his bottom line."

She rolled over, front down. I never thought I would envy sand. "You can tell Mr. Selznick I resent his intrusion into my personal life."

"That doesn't answer my question."

"Then how about this. Clark and I are good friends. Period. You know Hollywood. You keep bumping into the same people."

"The way I hear it, you've been bumping into Gable in some of our better hotels."

If looks could kill, I'd have spent the rest of eternity six feet under that patch of beach. "We have fun together, Clark and I. Gay parties, wading in fountains, racing the streets of Hollywood in his Stutz, mountains of caviar, oceans of imported champagne. You know the feeling."

"Sorry, sweetheart. In my version, folks sit around coldwater flats with a bucket of beer. Where's your hubby while you're out hobnobbing with the fast life?"

She opened her fist. Sand ran out in a fast stream, like the last residue of time tumbling from an hourglass. "Roger is a stay-at-home rabbit. I'm not. I enjoy a good frolic out on the town. And so does Clark. But that's as far as it goes."

A car door slammed on the road above, a Packard or Cadillac from the solid clunk. "I invited a few girl friends over for a swim," Jessica said. "I hope you don't mind."

Mind? Her three friends came laughing and sashaying down the wooden stairs. A voice from out of my wildest fantasy said, "Eddie Valiant, meet Rita Hayworth, Betty Gable, and Mae West." The three women who kept my heart throbbing while I slogged through Europe making the world safe and free for democracy. In swimming suits that didn't contain enough material among them to upholster a footstool.

Betty requested that I lather her with suntan oil. Rita told me I reminded her of a bullfighter she'd once seduced. Mae asked me to hold her beach balls while she slipped out of her sandals. Purely my pleasure, believe me.

The trio of lovelies invited me to join them for a splash. Jessica held me back. They went without me. Paradise lost. The sacrifices I make to earn a buck.

"Don't be fooled by appearances, Mr. Valiant." Jessica pulled her knees to her chin and wrapped her arms around her stems. "I love my husband very much." Her sentiment came forth in the puppy-love lettering a high-school girl uses to see how her name looks sandwiched between "Mrs." and her biology teacher.

"Is that what you tell the desk clerk at the Beverly Hills Hotel when you and Gable register as Mr. and Mrs. Jones?"

"I've said everything I'm going to say concerning my relationship with Clark."

"Maybe I'll have to browbeat the juicies out of your friends." I indicated the three lovelies frolicking in the foam.

"Save your breath. Even if they knew, which they don't, they wouldn't tattle. It's the age-old law of womanhood. Girls stick together."

I pitched her the change-up. "I know why you went to see Dr. Wallace Ford."

What a great actress! When she told me, "I never heard of the man," and stuck to the story, I almost believed her.

It was an hour later when I pulled into Ferd's slot in the Police Department parking lot.

Roger, sprawled on the seat behind me, woke up swinging. He kayoed a cubic yard of air. "He sucker p-p-p-punched me. The big p-p-p-palooka hit me when I wasn't looking."

"You always stutter when you talk?"

Roger crawled into the front seat. "P-p-p-practically never. Only when I'm nervous or excited or especially adorable, and then just on words beginning with p-p-p-p-p-p-p . . ."

"Never stutter on words starting with D?"

He struck an oratorical pose, one hand gripping the front of his overalls, the other with index finger extended pointed into the air. "Dorothy dug doohickeys down by the dump."

"Wait here." I got out. "While I see a man about a dog." I

walked into the station. The rabbit's balloon caught me as I opened the door.

"My no-good half cousin Dodger. He stutters on D's."

"Where is he now?" I yelled back.

"Last I heard, he was in p-p-p-p-p-p-p . . . jail!"

So much grousing overhung Ferd's desk it resembled a balloon concession at the park. Seems the powers that be had yanked him off the Enigman case and put him back chasing the Toontown hooch haulers. What's one dead actor, more or less? Rumrunners, on the other hand, cheat the state out of tax revenue. Besides, word had it that Bulldog Bascomb had the Enigman case one nail away from shut. I had a good hunch who was about to get hammered.

I asked Ferd what he'd dug up on Tom Tom LeTuit.

"Swell company you're keeping, shoo fly," he said. He slipped an official file folder out of his desk. "Guy's a famuzzing scuzz ball. As soon kill you as call you a cab." He opened the folder and went for a cup of coffee.

He didn't make it totally easy for me. I did have to lean over to read it. I learned LeTuit was suspected of being drug smuggling's Kingpin of the Caribbean. He was living high on the hog at the penthouse suite of the Toontown Ritzy. Carbuncle Chameleon, undercover cop *extraordinaire*, had him under twenty-four-hour surveillance. No word on the whereabouts of Lupe Chihuahua.

When Ferd returned, I asked him to run a check on Dodger Rabbit. Find out if he was still vacationing at a government resort.

I used Ferd's city line to call my answering service. Skipper told me I had a number of messages from Louise Wrightliter. Charley Ferris commandeered the horn and asked if I'd gotten his niece a starring role. I told him it was only a matter of time. So was the end of the world.

We drove past Grauman's Chinese. The marquee announced a special memorial tribute to the late, great Kirk Enigman. A round-the-clock nonstop showing of all his movies. Ain't Hollywood grand? Your wake consists of insomniacs sitting in the dark eating popcorn.

WHO P-P-P-PLUGGED ROGER RABBIT?

A poster for *Shadow of Evil* caught my eye. I braked to a halt. Could it be . . . ?

I headed for the curb. "Let's take in a movie," I told Roger.

"Right now?" said Roger. "In the middle of our case? I strongly protest. We should be hopping and bopping, shaking and quaking, moving and grooving."

I handed him his ticket.

We sat in the balcony. The lights went down. *Shadow of Evil* came on the screen. The opening credits rolled.

I got up and left.

"Eddie," said Roger, hopping after me. "Where you going? You haven't seen anything yet. The movie's just starting."

The rabbit had it dead wrong. I'd seen plenty.

Baby Herman shot his daily newspaper strip in a swanky photography studio in Pasadena.

We found him sitting in his personalized canvas director's chair surrounded by the dialogue he'd been rehearsing, a milky, slightly rancid heap of gee gee and ga ga balloons.

He was taking a break while his prop man restocked the day's supply of seltzer bottles.

A line of tourists snaked through the studio. One at a time they stepped up and stood next to the Baby. In return for five bucks, a photographer snapped a quickie of them with the star. For an extra fin, the Baby tweaked their noses. For a double saw, he goosed them in the knickers. Plush-bottomed women got the ten-dollar extra free.

A makeup lady powdered Herman's face and realigned the red ribbon tying his spit curl. As she worked over him, his head lolled sideways. An infantile inability to hold it upright? Nope. A better angle for peeking down the front of her dress.

"Valiant," bellowed Herman when he saw me, "you old sack of shingles. How they hugging?"

The photographer asked Herman to open his mouth into a wide circle. He took a light level on Herman's tonsil for the Baby's big bawling scene. Herman obliged, producing a cavern to rival Carlsbad.

"And Roger," said Herman. "Still got the rabbit habit?" Roger and Baby Herman exchanged the elbow-slapping, nose-tweaking, eyeball-gouging foolishness that constitutes a handshake in Toon circles.

Herman pulled us both to him and put his tiny arms around our shoulders. "The poon platoon, the beaver brigade, together again. All for one, and one for all." With a lecherous wink, he pointed at an attractive woman waiting in line. "That's the one I'll give my all for."

With the aid of a small stepladder, he climbed off his director's chair. He hung a sign on the back reading "Gone to Lunch" and motioned for us to follow him into his dressing room.

A disgruntled tourist bolted out of line and blocked our way. "Where you think you're going, pip-squeak?" he said. "I been waiting an hour to get snapped with you. You ain't walking out when I'm next."

Simba and Somba, the two gorillas Herman employed as bodyguards, shambled forward, their brassed knuckles scraping the concrete floor. Herman waved them off.

"One more," he told his shutterbug. Herman held out his arms. The tourist picked him up. Baby Herman reached into his diaper and hauled out a box Brownie. He pointed it at the tourist. Herman and the shutterbug popped their cameras at the same time. The Hasselblad flashed. Herman's Brownie squirted a stream of faintly brackish water, hitting the tourist full in the face. He loved it. He vowed he'd never wash his kisser again.

"Butt brain," whispered Herman under his breath as we walked away. "I make wee wee in this." He tucked his Brownie back into his diaper. "You try being thirty-six years old and still not potty trained. It ain't funny, McGee. And the baby talk. Always the baby talk. If another old lady chucks me under the chin and says 'Kitchee kitchee coo,' I'll spit up on her."

We entered his dressing room. "Take a gander at this." Herman held up an ordinary picture frame holding a photo of Theda Bara. "Mandrake the Magician designed it special for me." He touched the glass. Bara's picture disappeared, replaced by one of Clara Bow. "This guarantees that the thrill of the hour always sees her smiling puss on display in my crib." In quick succession he flashed photos of a dozen well-known screen lovelies. Including Carole Lombard.

Herman opened a wooden cabinet with a picture of Little Bo Peep stenciled on the front. It held all the comforts of home, assuming you lived in a good bar. He poured heavy shots of high-test mother's milk into baby bottles. He handed me and Roger the ones without nipples. "Here's to dry didees," he toasted, and started to suck.

Roger took one drink and went into his patented pinwheel routine. I opened the door, nudged him out, and watched him spin away. At his velocity, he'd stay high for a good ten minutes.

"Hang on for a second, buckaroo," said Herman. "I'm writing my memoirs. Seeing Rog reminded me of a poignant tidbit. Let me get it down before I forget."

Herman picked up a recorder molded in the shape of Mickey Mouse. "People think I'm an overnight success," said the Baby. "To that I say cockie doo doo." Mickey's automated arm grabbed Herman's balloon and slipped it into a canvas bag slung over his mousey shoulder. "I spent years learning the trade. I started out blowing up word balloons for a newspaper comic strip. I enrolled nights at Stooge U, where I studied the classics. The eye poke, the foot squash, the fur singe, the ear twist, the body crumple.

"I met Roger Rabbit about then. At a gas station. When one of my girl friends brought me in for a lube job and diaper change."

He turned off the recorder. "I got to get it down before I forget." He tapped his tiny skull. "The memory's the second thing to go, you know." He gave his crotch a tussle. "Lucky for me I still got the memory of an elephant, if you know what I mean."

He sat in a blonde oak chair specially manufactured to his diminutive scale. "What no-good poop-a-doop brings you sniffing around?"

I couldn't fit into his furniture so I perched on his toy box. "For starters, I'm checking to see if your best friend knows you been stepping out with his girl."

Herman gave me the obscene smirk you see at strip shows and bachelor parties. "Be more specific. I got a lot of best friends. I've introduced my dinky to most of their darlings."

"Try Gable and Lombard."

"Oh, them." He scratched the single tuft of hair desecrating his scalp. "Nothing to it. Me and Carole are just kissing cousins." I swear he leered when he said "kissing," but it could have been trapped gas. You know babies. "We'd never put the horns on our good buddy Clark."

"We?"

He pointed at the front fold of his diaper. "Me and Dinky Do Right."

"You and Dinky know anything about Davey Selznick's missing box?"

WHO P-P-P-PLUGGED ROGER RABBIT?

"Probably. What's her name?" He hiccupped with such force his chair scooted back.

"It's not a she, it's a what."

"What's a what?"

"The box. Selznick's box."

"Selznick? That reminds me." He picked up a telephone made in his own image. "I got to call my agent."

He indicated his phone. "You want one of these? I can get you a good deal. They're going out of production. Low sales. I can't imagine why."

I could. Who wants to put their ear to a baby's rear end?

"What do you hear from Selznick?" he said when his agent came on the line. Herman nodded a few times and smiled. He stuck a big cork into the mouthpiece to keep his balloon out of the handset. "With Enigman out of the way, I'm a shoo-in for Rhett Butler! Warm up the casting couch, Mother. We're testing O'Haras tonight."

He pulled out the cork. "How about the Andy Hardy series?" He didn't like what he heard. "What do you mean, I'm too old? I know I'm thirty-six, but I can play younger." Apparently his agent didn't agree, since Herman yanked his self-likeness out of the wall and smashed it on the floor. He pulled on his bottle with a fuming vengeance.

"A man of his word, that Enigman. We had a meeting, him, Roger, and me, with Selznick. I heard Enigman tell Selznick he'd die for that role. He did, and I got it!" He picked up Mickey. "Memo. Send a thank-you bouquet to Kirk Enigman's funeral."

"Where were you about four o'clock yesterday afternoon?"

"That's when Enigman fell off his stroller?"

I nodded.

"I was home taking a nap."

"So you've got no alibi."

"Up your wazoo-zoo, Valiant." He winked. "I never go beddy-bye alone."

"This naptime companion got a name?"

"Yeah. And so does her husband. You ain't getting either one."

Roger Rabbit walked in with his arm around Bulldog Bascomb. "I love to garden," said Roger to Bascomb. "Mostly carrots. A hybrid variety exactly the width of my front tooth. Give me a dozen to get my rhythm, and I can mince those babies faster than a Veg-O-Matic. I also grow tomatoes because they're homebodies and stay put. Not like peas and corn, which are always sneaking off to vegetable beds to make succotash."

Bascomb's dewlaps went atwitter. "I love this goofy rabbit," he said to me. "I'm his biggest fan." Somewhere, down on the lower rung of Bascomb's pedigree, a hunting hound rolled over in his grave.

"Who are you?" asked Herman.

Bascomb flashed the tin.

"Well, it's about time. I report a burglary, I want action. I am a star."

"Different division," said Bascomb. "I'm Homicide." His stainless-steel balloon softened to the consistency of mush. "I got a few littermates would love your autograph," he said to Roger. "If you would oblige."

"My p-p-p-pleasure," said Roger.

Bascomb pulled out his police notebook. He handed it to the rabbit. "One to Buster, one to Bowser, one to Biter, one to Barney . . ."

"You had a break-in?" I asked Herman.

"Last night." He freshened his makeup with a dash of baby powder, one puff on each end. "While I was . . . napping, they robbed my house."

"You didn't hear them?"

"My . . . naps tend to be loud and raucous."

"What'd they take?"

"That's the odd part. Nothing that I could tell. I checked. I still got my little black book, my eight pagers, my marital aids, my spurs, my electric—"

"Maybe they were looking for the secret of eternal youth."

"I keep that with me." He wiggled his diaper pin.

". . . and finally Big Bad Bob," said Bascomb.

Roger signed his name with a flourish.

I waited for Bascomb to make his move. It turned out to be a hitchhiking motion, aimed at the door. "Beat it, Valiant," he growled. "I got questions for the Baby."

WHO P-P-P-PLUGGED ROGER RABBIT?

I was glad to oblige. Roger followed me out.

"Roger," said Bascomb.

The rabbit turned.

Bascomb waved his two-inch stack of autographs. "Thanks a heap."

"Gee, Bulldog Bascomb's a swell dog," said Roger as we walked. "A regular pussycat."

I stopped in front of a scenery panel, a front view of the Phantom's Skull Cave, to light a cigarette.

"No smoking allowed in here, Valiant," said Pepper Potts, clippety-thumping out through the cave's painted lips. Two hundred yards. I should have asked for two hundred yards. "It's the law." He extended a hand holding a burning match. "Not that I ever let Johnny Law stand between me and the object of my desires."

I took my time taking his light. He held the match steady even when it burned so low it singed his fingertips. "You look real natural holding a flaming torch," I said. "If the movie business slows, I hear they got an opening in New York Harbor as a stand-in for the Statue of Liberty."

"The problem with that is the clientele. I can tolerate the tired, even the huddled masses. But I could never stomach the poor."

"Associating with them, or being one yourself?"

"Take your choice." In a movement worthy of a flamingo, he balanced on his broomstick while his good leg scratched his backside. "How goes the hunt?"

"A lot better if you'd quit cramping my action. Detecting requires a certain amount of incognito. I can't get that with you shagging me."

"Don't give yourself that much credit, peeper. You're not the reason I'm here. Mr. Selznick's got a major interest in Baby Herman's comic strip. He adapts them for theatrical shorts."

"Theatrical shorts. Sounds like rhinestone underwear."

"You're quite the funny man."

"*Au contrary,*" said Roger in a long, thin balloon shaped like a loaf of fractured French bread. "He's not funny at all."

"Take a hike, Roger," I whispered.

"I wonder how hard you're gonna laugh when Bulldog Bascomb gets a surprise package in the mail. A certain . . ." Potts's hand slipped into his jacket pocket.

"Aren't you going to introduce me to your friend?" asked Roger.

"No."

"Then I'll do it myself. Roger Rabbit," he said cheerily. "Pleased to make your acquaintance."

Potts ignored the rabbit's extended paw. "I know who you are. I ain't impressed. Me and the peep, we got business between us. How's about you take a flying hop."

Roger belligerently puffed out his chest. It added maybe a quarter inch to his girth. "You can't talk to me that way. I'm almost about to become a very big star!"

Potts picked him up by the ears, spun him around, and flung him the length of the studio.

"Where was I?" said Potts. "Oh, yeah. My surprise package for Bascomb." His voice was as hard and cold as the anvils blacksmiths use to forge shoes for jackasses.

He took a gun out of his coat pocket. He had it taped up inside a clear cellophane bag. He held it up where I could look but not touch. It was the mate to the Dragoon I threw in the drink. I didn't need bifocals to see my prints on the handle. "Mr. Selznick will swear on a stack of Bibles that this is the gun you took from his office. And I'll swear the same."

Potts exchanged the bagged Colt for a jackknife as long and thin as a honed garter snake. He ran it beneath his fingernails to the depth a torturer would insert a bamboo strip. "Bascomb's going to come after you with a warrant in one hand and a warden in the other." He tapped the tip of his blade on the bridge of my nose.

"You're in bad trouble, shoo fly." He folded his jackknife shut and returned it to his pocket. "Don't cross me." He caught a passing balloon by the tail and whammed it on a filler light suspended over my head. The impact produced a spiderweb of fractured glass with me framed in the middle.

He slipped back into the studio darkness the way a submarine submerges into the ocean deep after slamming a torpedo into a battlewagon.

"What was that about?" asked Roger.

"Don't ask."

"Does it have anything to do with our case?"

"Don't ask."

"What's in his surprise package for Sergeant Bascomb?"

"Don't ask."

"Why are you so testy all of a sudden?" He took the hint without me giving it. "I know, I know. Don't ask."

I checked my rear view. I saw what I'd seen for the last couple of miles, a big, mustard-colored Toon sedan. Blackout paint covered its chrome grillwork, all but a narrow slit on its headlamps and all but a foot-square section of its front window. Wide, slick tires built for speed more than comfort stuck out from under its hooped fender skirts. It rode stiffly raked, like it had pogo sticks for shock absorbers, higher in back than in front. Cars like that run fast and loose. They race each other for gas money on straight stretches of 101, or for hundred-dollar purses on dirt tracks at county fairs. The ones that win graduate to faster action. Providing getaway services for liquor-store bandits. Or outrunning border patrols on smuggling junkets into Mexico.

Driving Ferd's bucket of bolts, I could lose a tail only if somebody sliced it off with a rocking chair. Besides, I like to know who's on my bumpus, and why. I quit feeding peanuts to the engine. The car rolled to a slow halt.

The sedan angled in ahead of me, blocking my exit. The sole occupant, a woman, got out and walked toward me. Her swing and sway rivaled Sammy Kaye. Her short, tightly-permed brown hair had the shape of a doughboy's helmet. The belt on her trench coat didn't hold enough holes to cinch her waist. She'd tied it into a knot. Her legs were heavier than most men liked, but I wasn't most men.

She stuck her head in my window. The front of her trench coat pulled open, as did the expensive burgundy silk blouse she wore underneath. Roger averted his eyes. I didn't.

"You're Eddie Valiant," she said, her voice more gravel than sand.

"So my mother told me."

"I'm Louise Wrightliter. You have something I want."

She knew I had stolen her info. "Fine by me. I'll trade for a few tidbits of information."

"That's all?"

"I come cheap."

"You sure do." She went around to the passenger side and opened the door.

I told Roger to go up and chew the rag with the sedan. He climbed out, Louise climbed in. It's true what travel agents say. The change of scenery did wonders for my outlook.

"Ask your questions," she said.

From out of her purse she pulled a glass pocket flask covered with filigreed Victorian silver. Pinch me, Mama, I think I'm falling in love!

"Who's spreading the rumor that Gable has a limp wrist?"

She filled the two shot glasses nesting under the cap of her portable bar, and handed one to me. I took a lick. It was top-quality rum. "I got it right from the baby's mouth," she said.

"A baby named Herman?"

She poured me a refill. "One and the same."

Gable's bosomest buddy strikes again. "An item that juicy, how come the *Talltale* never ran it?"

"Let me give you a lesson in the economics of yellow journalism." She leaned back against the seat. I never had a teacher look so good. "Label Gable a Mabel, it buys you one big issue and ends his career. Link him with a married rabbit's wife, and you cook up a scandal that feeds your circulation for months. Next question."

"You heard any stories linking Carole Lombard to Baby Herman?"

"No, I haven't." She capped her flask and put it away a lot sooner than I would have. "Though it wouldn't surprise me. Herman's undiapered more babes than most maternity wards. Anything else?"

"Nope. That's about it. Here's my end of the bargain." I pulled her file papers out of the glove box and handed them over.

WHO P-P-P-PLUGGED ROGER RABBIT?

She flipped once quickly through the pages. "What's with these?"

"Your files. The ones I stole."

She flung them over her shoulder. They landed in a jumbled heap on the backseat. "Who cares about these? Everything in them is either a bald-faced lie or stored on microfilm. I can re-create the contents anytime I want."

"Then what is it you're after?"

"A certain objet d'art."

"Give me a better clue. Business has been slow lately. My powers of deduction have atrophied."

She pulled off her kidskin gloves a finger at a time, revealing tattered nails that spent more time on a typewriter than on a manicurist's table. "David Selznick's box."

"Sorry, toots. No deal. I can get a lot more than worthless gossip for that goody. Why, I know people talking high two figures, at least."

She laughed. "That puts the bidding way out of my range. Maybe I can persuade you with something besides money."

"Tempting, but no thanks."

"I meant a story. A particularly good one." She drew her gloves between her thumb and first finger with the same motion a farmer uses to decapitate a chicken. "Seems I was tracking a tip that Kirk Enigman was involved in a highly illegal enterprise. To get proof, I broke into his house."

"They teach you that at the Columbia School of Journalism?"

"Try the school of hard knocks. It's chiseled in stone over the door: 'Whatever works.' " She lit a cigarette, the strong, stubby variety much in fashion with burly stevedores who muscle crates around the docks. "I was poking through his belongings, seeing what I could see, and that wasn't much. Dark as an aardvark's ark hole in there. I don't know exactly where I ended up, but wherever it was, Enigman himself came in. And guess what. You were with him. I realized I was in his screening room. I ducked under the front row of seats and waited for the show to start."

"You saw the movie?"

She nodded. "I saw Enigman tell you about Selznick's box.

Needless to say, the *Telltale* would pay a major bonus for a peek at anything that important to so many high-powered big wigs."

"Then you also saw whoever else was in the room."

"Sorry. All I saw, or didn't see, was you."

She pulled her coat more tightly around her, though I was the one catching the chill. "I heard you threaten Enigman. I heard the gun go off, your gun. What's more, I got Enigman's last three balloons on film. I'd show them to you except the film's hidden away. I will tell you one thing. His dying words make you look guilty as sin."

Of that I had no doubt. "How do I know *you* didn't kill him?"

"Maybe I did. Why don't you try and prove it?" She flipped the remnant of her glowing cigarette out the window into the scrub grass lining the road. Obviously a woman unconcerned about starting fires. "Either I get the box, or the film goes to Bulldog Bascomb. After the *Telltale* runs a series of stills on page one." She opened her purse. "That's a better deal than you'll get from David Selznick."

She replaced the lipstick her ciggie had kissed away. "Here's an exclusive scoop for you. Selznick's backers are one step away from pulling their money out of his Civil War musical, lock, stock, and cannon barrel. Selznick's near bankruptcy. He doesn't have the money to pay your fee let alone produce *Gone With the Wind*."

Life was so much simpler when my only worry was matching the day of the week with the word embroidered on my underwear. "The box is yours."

"You better not forget." She got out of the car. She pointed a finger at me gun fashion through the window and pulled the trigger. "Or you can tell it to Saint Peter, bub."

Exactly my next-to-next-to-last words to Enigman before somebody iced him.

Roger came back. "That car's got a bad drinking problem," he said. "He positively reeks of rum. What'd you find out?"

"You can't trust a woman." Of course I already suspected that.

I had a hunch about the devious Miss Wrightliter, and it smelled of lots worse than rum. I gave Roger the wheel plus everything that went with it and told him to follow her car.

WHO P-P-P-PLUGGED ROGER RABBIT?

I grabbed a hack to the Toontown Ritzy. I found Carbuncle Chameleon rolled out three feet wide, eight feet long, a quarter-inch thick, masquerading as the hotel's front doormat.

I squatted beside his flattened body. "How you doing, Carbuncle."

"Eddie," he said in a balloon as thin as a pauper's pocketbook. "What brings you around?"

"Tom Tom LeTuit."

Carbuncle reached up with his snaky arm and held the door open for an elderly swell and her pet poodle. "My but we're looking lovely today," he told her. His balloon assumed the shape of a tin cup. The lady tossed him a nickel. He flipped out his tongue and caught the coin on the fly. He dropped it into his pocket. He was spread so thin I could count his change. A dollar twenty-three. "Never heard of him."

"Let me refresh your memory. LeTuit amscrayed my brother. Five years ago. About the same time that murdering burglar Farnsworth Fenestration found out his egress of choice was really a cop, and I saved your casement. Remember?"

Carbuncle's throat coiled tight enough to hogtie a dogie. "It's coming back, yup." Three of his letters blinked. The I, the O, and the U. "Follow me." Chameleon got off the sidewalk, curled himself into a sphere, and bounced along ahead of me, making me feel like a guy blind-dating a basketball.

We entered the employees' lounge. There, Carbuncle assumed his normal shape, tall and thin, with the deadly tension of a cocked bowstring. His jet-black hair, greased shiny and plastered flat, gave his head the sheen of a highly polished bowling ball.

If you work plainclothes detail in the tonier sections of Toontown, you dress to the nines. In Carbuncle's case, that meant a wide-shouldered brown worsted suit, a monogrammed silk shirt, and buffed leather wing tips that would go sixty bucks easy in a

Beverly Hills footery. Tough to handle on a cop's pay. So Carbuncle patronized the trunk of Filo Fence's car and called it a victimless crime.

"What I'm telling you stays between us." Lucky I took a speed-reading class. Carbuncle's balloon stuck around for barely an instant before turning to smoke.

"You know me."

He nodded. "LeTuit's staying in the penthouse, but he hasn't been around for a couple of days." He poured himself a cup of coffee and another for me.

I sweetened my java with the nectar of the gods. "Any idea where he's gone?"

"None." He sat down the easy way. He turned himself into a chair, a plush, heavy, claw-footed winger upholstered in crewel. The undisputed King of Camouflage. A mummer with a magnifying glass couldn't tell him from any other chair in the room. "LeTuit shook his tail and disappeared. I'm waiting for him to show so we can place him under surveillance again."

"What's his play?"

Carbuncle crossed his leg apron over his seat cushion. "He's smack in the middle of a major drug deal."

"Powder, pellets, tablets, crystal, weed?"

"None of the above. Liquid. Formulated by a Cuban *compadre* of LeTuit's. Dr. Jackal. The title's bogus. He swiped it along with a white coat and stethoscope when he escaped from the nuthouse."

"What's his potion do?"

"Don't know, but I understand it's worth a wad of bucks."

"Heard any names?"

He wigwagged his wings.

"How about LeTuit's girlfriend? A bowser named Lupe Chihuahua."

He returned to normal in time to avoid being plopped on by a three-hundred-pound maintenance man. He formed himself into a circle and rolled back to his post, letting inertia do his work. "A couple of months back Lupe breezed LeTuit for another mug. She dropped out of sight shortly thereafter. I would too. Can't imagine LeTuit taking kindly to a Dear Tom Tom letter."

I couldn't either.

Carbuncle no sooner stretched back out on the sidewalk than

a happy camper in waffle-soled hiking boots strolled the length of his back, leaving him resembling what goes under a helping of pancake syrup. "Be careful, Eddie," Carbuncle warned me in a balloon as squarely peaked and valleyed as he was. "LeTuit's a mean, lean, ugly machine."

The news wasn't all bad. At least I matched my quarry in the first and last categories.

I strolled the Boulevard.

Millions of Toon bulb heads illuminated the advertising signs and theater marquees on either side. I've seen buses rolling in from Podunk that glowed in the dark, full of incandescent pilgrims eager to put their luminescent craniums up in the limelight. A few, the very brightest, would rise to the klieg level. Most would spend a few years spelling out "Coca-Cola" for scale before they gave up and went back home to their annual star turn as the bright spot on top of the hometown Christmas tree.

I walked into Playhouse of the August Moon Mullins, a theater so far off Broadway it might as well be on Mars.

A rusty tin sign screwed to the cornerstone informed me that forty years ago this playhouse premiered the original version of *Gasoline Alley*. The theater must have run out of ethyl soon thereafter. Reluctant to destroy a candidate in the contest for lousiest lyceum in L.A., the owners hadn't so much as freshened the paint since Michaelangelo's untalented cousin slapped it on.

Ring Wordhollow moonlighted nights here as dialogue coach for a Toon Revue.

The performers consisted of barnyards, house pets, humanoids, small appliances, and, for comic relief, a few connect-the-dots, the Toons with numbers for elbows and knees.

I joined Wordhollow in the last row. "All the world's a stage," I said, "and all the talking toasters and flatulent furniture merely players."

He lowered his head, not in shame, only to peer at me over the top of his spectacles. "Facetiousness does not become you, Eddie. Even in the literary genre of detective fiction, where traditions tend to linger, witty repartee has largely passed out of vogue."

"I'm an old-fashioned guy. I've been hard-boiled too long to go back to sunny-side up."

Wordhollow reached into the embroidered carpetbag that served him as home away from home and pulled out the balloon I'd given him. There wasn't much left. What he hadn't snipped to ribbons or dunked into chemicals had shredded to dust on its own. "I'll be honest with you, Eddie. I've seen a great quantity of these in my day, but never one even remotely resembling this. It's unique, although I can't quite lay my finger on the reason why. It's a Toon balloon, but yet it's not. Of course that's flatly impossible. It must be one or the other."

The Toons resumed their play. One of them muffed a line. Wordhollow searched through his bag until he found a balloon showing how the line should have been spoken. He marched up on stage and displayed it to the actor, comparing the flubbed line letter by letter with the good.

I considered the remnants of my balloon. As airy as unenriched white bread, yet it had the potential of knocking my whole world topsy-turvy.

My office was within sight of the perennial rainbow that stretched from one end of T-town to the other. Travel writers describe it as a fitting metaphor, symbolic of the carefree life-style in Happy Valley. I call it a tourist gimmick, a way to attract the rubes from Kansas. Beneath those furry, fuzzy, feathery Toon exteriors runs a vicious streak that's totally unhuman. Pop a close gander at the daily strips or Maroon's cartoons. Squish, pop, bang, pow. You call that entertainment? So did the Marquis de Sade.

Either somebody left a pair of pink surfboards on my desk top, or Roger was sitting in my swiveler with his tootsies propped. I uncorked the office tool kit and poured myself a gut wrench. "Where'd Wrightliter go?" I asked the rabbit. "What'd she do?"

"I know exactly. I wrote it down." He pulled out a pocket notebook with Dick Tracy's smiling likeness on the cover. "She drove to a seedy warehouse in Burbank. She met up with a dozen more cars like the one she was driving. You know. With that queer black paint on their windows and headlights, and those big wide tires, and that funny slant. The bunch of them stood in line at the warehouse loading dock and took on gas."

"They got fueled at a warehouse?"

"Abso-rootey-toot-tootley. An attendant pumped them from a long rubber hose." He closed his notebook. "Made me hungry to watch."

"How so?"

"The whole place smelled like a big fruitcake."

Proof positive that it takes one to know one. I shooed Roger out from behind my desk and called Ferd. I asked him what he'd turned up on Roger's prodigal cousin Dodger.

Seems Dodger escaped from the hoosegow six months ago. The hare hadn't been heard from nor seen hide of since.

I asked Ferd to find out if Dodger had ever left the country. He groused and groaned but eventually promised to run a request past a buddy of his at the State Department.

Lastly, I hit Ferd up for details on Baby Herman's burglary. He agreed to check, mostly to get me off his back.

I rewarded him with a Lucky Strike extra. I told him to meet me at the entrance to Toontown at half past midnight. I suggested he bring along a squad of his biggest, meanest friends.

Even in my worst scrambled egg and pepperoni nightmare, I never saw anything as horrifying as the stiff stone whatnots guarding the drawbridge leading into the Toontown Graveyard. Ugh. Squat, reptilian bodies supported snaky necks with sulphurous eyes and heads the shape of upended spittoons. Their sculptor modeled their ears after the parts of a chicken that people throw away. Pitchforked tongues flicked through lips ripe as rotten tomatoes. Cold sores substituted for noses. Clustered stingers tipped their serpentine tails. Talons extended from each of their four stumpy fingers and three bootless toes.

They reminded me of the plastic horror toys which a few sharp twists transformed into innocuous household devices. Their finely honed, double-edged eyeteeth or perhaps their bread bowl bellies suggested that these two might metamorphose into Mixmasters.

Roger and I parked next to a large wooden rack full of broomsticks, the docking lot for the boneyard's resident witches. We walked through an archway shaped like the mouth of a mummified Sultan.

I toted a paper bag concealing a brick the size of Selznick's box.

"Gee, Eddie, I'm glad you're here," said Roger, his teeth clattering with a sharp staccato rhythm a flamenco dancer would envy. "I'm not scared with you along to p-p-p-protect me."

We found the Crypt of the Dipped. The graveyard's boogey women straddled the roof. They wore the union uniform, peaked hats and billowy black robes. They were ugly as sin, and in this town, that's as ugly as ugly gets. Their skin reflected every shade of green from seasick to serpent. Line up their noses end to end and you'd walk an extremely crooked mile. Huck Finn could have worked his way through Mississippi State selling them wart remover.

I recognized one as the crone in *Snow White*. With her death-rattling cackle and her poisoned apple, she'd scared the popcorn out of half the kids in America. Rumor said she came by her talent naturally, and I don't mean acting. Word was if you crossed her she'd vex you, hex you, pox you, and box you. I didn't believe it. I'm your basic Doubting Eddie. Still, when she flashed me her evil eye, it made me wish I'd worn my garlic necktie.

"Maybe he won't show," said Roger. From the lightness of his lettering, he expected that theory to disintegrate in the slightest passing breeze, and it did. He puckered his lips to whistle a happy tune. Discordant static came out. Every body part south of his nose chattered. He was scared half out of his wits, dangerous since he didn't have a full compliment to start with.

In the distance, a steeple clock struck midnight. The Hell's Hobgoblins mounted their broomsticks and rode away into the moonset.

I bent over and left the sack, as instructed, outside the crypt. When I turned around, Roger was gone! "Hey, fur ball." I figured he'd discovered a secret passage. I tapped the crypt's polished marble wall. Solid as Gibraltar. "Knock off the foolishness. I got no time for hide-and-seek. Ollie ollie oxen free."

A motion caught my eye. I saw Roger, two rows over, standing in front of the Crypt of the Slipped, a repository for Toons who broke their necks on banana peels. He had his arms upraised. His torso shook with the uncontrolled abandon of a bee-bitten belly dancer. Then I saw why. Somebody standing in the shadows had him covered with a gun. My gun! I'd found the spit bucket who clipped me and stole my rod. I couldn't rush him without getting my client exterminated, and that's generally rotten for business.

The stark terror radiating out of Roger's balloon lit up an area three rows by three, turning the graveyard into a tic-tac-toe game with headstones for X's and O's. "Refrain from pulling the trigger," pleaded Roger. "Please, please, please!"

Roger's supplication bought him a single blast at point-blank range.

I would have been hard-pressed to miss at that distance, and I'm the world's worst pistol shot. It runs in the family. Me, Teddy, Freddy; we inherited it from Dad, who couldn't hit the broad side of a barn with his cannon. Yet that's exactly what happened. Red flag. Betty's bloomers. Goose egg. Zilch. Out of the onion. The bullet went wild, cracking the Almond Joys off a marble cherub. The little angel wouldn't miss them.

Roger examined his hands, surprised they weren't holding a harp. He checked himself for extraneous holes. When he found none, he hitched his britches like the Lone Ranger confronting a bloodthirsty renegade. "Miss me, miss me, now you have to kiss me." Ah, the new West.

Roger's assailant wasn't about to smooch a rabbit *or* make the same mistake twice. He pressed his pistol barrel directly against the rabbit's chest and emptied his load. Five dip-tipped slugs ripped through the rabbit like hot pokers through lard. The impact carried him ten yards backwards. He landed like a swatted bug, on his back with his legs and arms poking straight up in the air.

By the time I drew my hog leg and reached the action, the shooter had taken a powder along with my gun.

I checked the rabbit. His pulse, normally a sprightly marimba beat, thudded at the rate of a funeral dirge. Empty balloons gurgled out of him the way muddy water burbles from a dried-up well pump. I dismissed artificial respiration. I'd need a pneumatic tire pump to respirate him in his leaky condition. I'd need corks the circumference of poker chips to plug the holes in his chest. "Who did it?" I asked him. "Who shot you? Tell me a name."

Roger motioned me closer. I leaned forward and put my head next to his mouth. He stuck his wet sticky tongue in my ear and went "BLAAAAAT!"

He died laughing.

Apparently, Roger hadn't been the goody-goody he pretended. A transparent likeness emerged out of his chest. It sported horns, carried a pitchfork, and took the escalator, express, to the basement.

Hard to predict how fast a dead Toon will decompose. Enigman hung around. The one at my feet melted faster than an ice-cube omelette. In seconds, Roger went from star of stage, screen, and comic strip to puddle on the ground. I gave him the best funeral possible under the circumstances. I kicked a clod of dirt over him. I skipped the eulogy. What can you say about a dead rabbit?

I went back to the Crypt of the Dipped. My sack was gone.

WHO P-P-P-PLUGGED ROGER RABBIT?

Roger's killer had plugged him for nothing more than a common brick.

I put the Toontown Graveyard a couple of miles behind me. I wished I could do the same for this case.

I uncorked my liquid hammer and beat a few brain cells to death, but they must have been in the wrong quadrant. The memories lingered on. What's worse, they intensified. I swear I could smell that dumb bunny's cologne. *Eau de phew*.

As I returned the bottle to the glove compartment, a hand reached out from behind my seat and pincered my shoulder.

I rammed the car into a light pole. The jarring impact slipped me out of his grip. I whipped out my cannon, thumbed the hammer, whirled in my seat, and stuck the barrel halfway up the dastard's snout.

"P-p-p-please don't be mad at me, Eddie, for getting scared and running away."

"Roger?"

He sneezed my gat out of his honker. "I'm so sorry. I'll do anything you say to make it up. I'll be your p-p-p-personal slave. Say the word. I'll wash your board, I'll scrub your bucket, I'll whisk your broom, I'll clean your clock." He climbed into the front seat. "Don't hate me just because I'm not as brave as you are."

"You miserable, good-for-nothing twerp," I yelled at him. "Why aren't you dead? I watched you die."

"Which movie?"

"Real life!"

His balloon took the shape of a ghost. "You must have been hallucinating. Graveyards have that effect."

Not on a hard-bitten dick like me. There was only one explanation that made sense. "This cousin of yours. Dodger Rabbit. He look like you?"

Roger shook his head so forcefully the ends of his ears cracked like bullwhips. "Don't be silly. I'm unique in all of rabbitdom. Nobody ever mixes up me and Dodger. We're totally different. He parts his hair in the middle."

"You always stutter on P's? No exceptions?"

"P-p-p-pretty much."

The dead rabbit hadn't. "That picture of you and Selznick. Could that have been *Dodger* and Selznick instead?"

Roger shut his eyes. A mental vision of the photo floated in the air between us. He pulled out a magnifying glass the circumference of a moose's monocle and went over the picture inch by inch. "By golly, you're right. It *is* Dodger. That scurrilous scamp's been impersonating me! That rabbidy rat. He nearly got me killed!" Roger wrapped his stubby hands around the floating image of his cousin's neck. He strangled a half quart of air.

"He's always been the black sheep of the Rabbit family." Roger closed his eyes so he wouldn't see what he said next. "I never thought I'd wish this on any relation of mine, but that foul foolish fellow deserves to be incarcerated. Eddie, when you catch him, make sure he gets five years in Sing Sing, at least."

"I got good news for you, buddy. He's serving a longer sentence, in a lot worse place."

16

I met Ferd at the entrance to Toontown. His backup contingent wore baggy twill pants and knee-length blue uniform coats. They packed oversized soft rubber nightsticks and pistols that shot seltzer water. Two-quart helmets covered their one-quart heads clear to their googly eyes. To amuse themselves, they played Ping-Pong across the hood of their paddy wagon. For paddles, they used their flat-footed, splay-ended uniform shoes. Toontown's finest.

"Call roll," I told Ferd. "I don't see Larry, Moe, and Curly."

"Be famucking happy with what you frugitty got." Ferd slid into the front seat beside me.

"Watch your feet," I told him. Roger sat in the backseat, bawling his oblong eyes out. He'd covered the floorboards with a quarter inch of tears.

"What's with blubber bunny?" asked Ferd.

"Death in the family," I said.

"I adored that rotten, miserable, sneaky, scum-sucking louse," wailed Roger.

I offered Ferd a shot of courage. He cleansed the bottle of cooties by rubbing the open mouth with his palm. "The captain would rip out my fuzzucking guts and eat them for breakfast if he knew I was dragging out the troops to help the likes of you." He gave me my turn at the spigot. "Hand me a fadduking hint. What's going on here?"

"I got a hunch there's nasty business coming down the road."

"Nothing more concrete than that?" He took back the sauce. He didn't wipe the bottle this time. He wanted plenty of germs present to infect the wound when he clubbed open my skull. "You dragged me and a frigadigging contingent out in the frugadugging middle of the frogadogging night based on a lousy hunch?"

"Don't knock it, Ferd. Those hunches of mine got me where I am."

"Which is living next door to nowhere." From out of his coat pocket he produced a bag of potato chips and a government envelope. He ripped open both with a single pass between his teeth. He kept the chips and handed me a sheet of government stationery. "My buddy at State ran a check on Dodger Rabbit."

"Waaaaa," wailed Roger. "I loved that rabbit like a half cousin once removed."

Dodger had been out of the country once in his life. On a packaged gambling junket to Cuba.

Ferd tucked his bag of chips between his legs, the one place he knew I wouldn't reach for a handful. He flipped through his official police-issue notebook. Dick Tracy was pictured on the outside of his too, but here Dick held a gun and he definitely wasn't smiling. "Here's the skinny on the Baby Herman caper. Burglar came in through an open window. Spent maybe an hour, hour and a half there. Tossed the place pretty good. Must have made a terrible racket what with the rattles, drums, and clacker toys lying around. Herman insists he didn't hear squat. He was entertaining a very vocal lady friend in that den of iniquity he calls a playpen. I checked with her and she confirms the basics. We got one suspect. A suspicious clod wallander a next-door neighbor saw prowling around."

"Toon or human?"

"That's the odd part. The neighbor couldn't tell. The jaboney acted like a Toon, walked like a man. You figure it out."

We settled back to wait, parked at the base of the miniature mountain range Angelenos erected to keep Toons in their place. For size, it put San Francisco's Great Wall of Chinatown to shame. Visionaries who dream up what you can see from places you've never been claim it's one of the few man-made objects visible from the moon.

The bungle brigade had polished off its hundreth game of clip-clop, Ferd and I had done the same to my quart of amber inspiration, when a convoy of Toon sedans came hightailing past, speeding into Toontown lickety-split. They rode low in back, filled to the gills with heavy cargo. A familiar black four-door sedan led the way. "Chalk up another win for Valiant's famous hunches," I announced. "Your rumrunners, Ferd."

"You're kidding," said Ferd.

"If I'm lying, I'm dying."

WHO P-P-P-PLUGGED ROGER RABBIT?

"And I'm the one who'll kill you." Ferd drew his pistol, filled it from his canteen, and joined his men at the barricade they'd erected across the road.

"Is there going to be shooting?" asked Roger.

"Count on it, chum."

"If you don't mind," said Roger, "I'll stay on the floor until it's over. I've already lost one dearly beloved family member today. I don't want to lose another." A bright yellow stripe ran the length of his balloon.

The convoy crashed headlong into the barricade. After a short, vicious gun battle in which I, in all modesty, acquitted myself handsomely, the sedans threw in the grease rag.

The motor mouths immediately started honking for their lawyers. The cops slapped Denver boots on them to keep them from skedaddling.

I walked to the lead sedan and yanked open the rear door. "Well, well, well. Look what the cat dragged in."

Louise Wrightliter stretched out the length of the rear seat. "It's not what you think, Valiant." She'd thrown a car blanket over herself. Not much of a hiding place for a woman with more ups and downs than the Dow Jones average. "I was only along for the ride."

"You should have turned left before you hit the skids." I scooted her aside and pried loose the phony seat cushion concealing the fifty-gallon tank suspended between the wheels. I unscrewed the cap, wetted my fingers with the liquid inside, and took a sniff. Straight rum, the brand she'd poured me before. Also what grannies use to lace fruitcakes. Score a point for Roger's sniffer. He'd smelled right at the Burbank warehouse. "You're in hot potatoes, lady."

She lit a smoke, despite the fact she was sitting on sufficient high-octane alcohol to turn us both into crepes suzette. "I'm no rum dummy. You know that. It's the story I'm after."

Ferd loped up behind me riding piggyback on the blithe spirit of his biggest arrest ever. "What've we got here?"

I winked at him. "None other than the notorious Bonnie Parker. Murderess, bank robber, car thief. Last time I checked, she was number eight on the FBI's hit parade and rising fast."

"What are you trying to pull, Valiant?" She snuffed her butt on the rum tank. "Officer, my name's Louise Wrightliter. I'm a nationally renowned journalist. I work for the *Toontown Telltale*."

"You got ID to that effect?" asked Ferd.

"Don't be ridiculous. I'd be a fool to carry my press credentials during an illegal activity."

"She left them home," I said. "Clyde's baby-sitting them and her spare burp gun."

Ferd studied her face close up, a not-unpleasant assignment. "Quit juking me, lady. I know who you are. I recognized you right off. I seen your picture in the papers." For a refreshing change, Ferd played my game. "And your mug on the post-office wall. You're Bonnie Parker, no question about it. I'll win a medal for hauling you in." He snapped steel bracelets over Louise's delicate wrists.

"Hold it," she shouted.

He dragged her unceremoniously out of the car and shoved her towards his prowler.

"Stop!" She dug in her heels but only succeeded in snapping both her three-inch spikes. "Call my boss. Delancey Duck. He'll vouch for me."

"Sorry, tootsie," said Ferd. "I'm fresh out of nickels, and payday ain't until a week from Friday. I'll check you out when I got spare change and an extra minute. Until then, I'm gonna dump you in the hoosegow with the geeks and stumps and drools and drizzles and sad apples. Don't worry. If you're really who you say you are, sooner or later I'll find out, and set you free."

"How long is that likely to take?" she asked sarcastically.

"By the time I do the paperwork, put it through channels, get an answer from the powers upstairs, I don't know. The rate the gears turn in Toontown, you might be out come next Armistice Day. Plus or minus a month either way."

"I hope you brought a change of underwear," I said.

"I want a lawyer."

"You bet. 'Course there's only one in Toontown," said Ferd. "Owen Cantrell. Just left on a month's vacation. I'll tack a note on his screen door. Tell him you want to see him first thing when he comes back."

"You can't do that to me. You can't hold me incommunicado without charge. I've got my rights."

WHO P-P-P-PLUGGED ROGER RABBIT?

"Not in Toontown, you don't," said Ferd.

She fooled me. I figured she'd last at least a few days in the squalid Toontown slammer before she offered a deal. "Let's negotiate, shall we, Officer? Perhaps we can strike a bargain."

"What do you think, Eddie? Is this a transaction I care to negotiate?"

"I don't know. She's a vicious, amoral, homicidal gun moll. Yet I sense that deep down she's a good person. I vote you hear her out."

Ferd bobbed his coconut. "What you got?"

She directed her words to Ferd. Her smoldering eyes locked on me. "Release me, and I'll hand you Kirk Enigman's killer."

Not at all the deal I wanted! "Whoa," I said. "You're swimming in the wrong kettle of fish. The officer's after the name and current location of the Toontown jackboot who's running rum."

"Is that what you're after, Officer?" she cooed. "Really? Too bad, since I can give you so much more."

Ferd weighed me against her. I fell two tons short. "Can it, Valiant. I'll decide what I'm looking for and what I'm not."

Thus encouraged, Wrightliter reached into her brassiere and pulled out a small spool of film. Some secret hiding spot. Though I must admit, it was the first place I thought to look. "Take a peek at this." She handed the spool to Ferd. "Decide for yourself whether or not it buys me my freedom." She indicated me with her thumb. "And loses him his."

"What the famafooming frigadoozies is she talking about, Eddie?"

I pulled Ferd aside and spilled my guts into his droopy earlobe. "Buddy boy, brother-in-law of mine, there's a few words on that film which I wouldn't want Bulldog Bascomb to see."

He held the spool out at arm's length, upside down between his first and second fingers, the same way you'd carry a dead skunk. "You're telling me I'm going to play the score of Enigman's murder and watch you singing lead."

"I didn't croak Enigman."

"Like I'm a monkey's uncle."

He wasn't and never would be. Ferd was an only chimp. "Give me a chance to prove it. Lose the skirt in the system. Grill her about the rumrunners. You drag out of her where I can find their head cheese, and I'll deliver Enigman's killer split on a spit."

He buried the spool in his pocket along with his oath to place law above family. "Twenty-four hours, Eddie. After that, me, the broad, the film, the whole sorry forfumpalumping story goes to Bascomb."

I discovered how rabbits mourn their dearly departed. By pumping nickels into a roadhouse jukebox and dancing sprightly jigs atop the linoleum lunch counter. I spent the wake in a back booth wailing over a cup of java and a long stack of buckwheats.

A newsboy came in and peddled me a paper, the *Telltale*'s early-bird edition. The banner headline sent a shiver down my spine that rattled Mr. Richter's scales. Roger wouldn't be the only one grieving today. Half the town's women would be wearing black. Baby Herman had been killed!

Details were sketchy. Herman had finished shooting a magazine ad for Sweet Herman's Pabulum, the brand he endorsed. He had been relaxing his usual way, making the rounds of late-night jazz joints.

He was last seen in a dive called Dingles. His diaper was drooping and so were his standards. He was hustling anything with a skirt, including the tableclothed barrels surrounding the dance floor. He left about midnight, cocked to the gills, his baby buggy pushed by a Toonette the other patrons described as a cross between a battle-ax and a burro.

Early this morning, a downtown construction crew spotted Herman's carriage ditched in their excavation hole. The Homicide cops, under the command of Bulldog Bascomb, searched the vehicle. Inside, they found an ice bucket and a magnum of nose tickler; a box of Cuban stogies; a trick lighter in the shape of a brass monkey; four quarts of beer: a cast-iron bottle opener with a randy lady for a popper; a twelve-inch bundle of monogrammed didees; a wind-up Victrola and a dozen pressings of *Bolero*; an emergency road repair kit consisting of talcum powder, safety pins, burping cloths, and spare bibs; a family-sized jar of Vasoline; a gallon of milk; a gross of slicks in assorted colors; an assortment of fireworks to celebrate occasions when the Earth moved; a solid gold, diamond-studded rattle; a pacifier autographed by Hedy Lamarr; a steamy love letter signed C.L.; and a whalebone shoehorn, which, I suppose, the Baby needed for squeezing himself in with all that junk.

Bascomb's prime suspect was currently doing a soft-shoe routine on a clear glass donut cover. Right. According to the *Telltale*, Bascomb believed Roger Rabbit had cacked Herman, and Kirk Enigman too. The motive was ambition, a common cause of felonies in Hollywood. Bascomb reasoned Roger did it to eliminate competition for the Rhett Butler role in *Gone With the Wind*. Roger's self-proclaimed biggest fan had issued a warrant for the rabbit's arrest. Ah, the fleeting nature of fame.

I grabbed Roger's ears in the middle of a passable buck-and-wing. "Eddie, p-p-p-please! Have some respect for the dead."

I stuck the tabloid under his fuzzy pink nose. His eyes crossed as he read.

"That nice Bulldog Bascomb's after me? For murdering Baby Herman? That's absurd. It's worse than absurd. It's *doubly* absurd." A midwestern plowboy could plant an acre of corn in the furrows creased into Roger's forehead. "He wouldn't railroad an innocent rabbit. Would he?"

"Bascomb would swap his kidney for a conviction."

"I can't go to jail," said Roger in a balloon the texture of sackcloth and ashes. "Horrible things happen to rabbits in jail. I've heard of rabbits being used for . . . earmuffs!" He sucked in his mouth until his nose was halfway down his throat. "I'll go underground."

"You ever done it before?"

"No, but I'm sure it's in my genes."

"Trust me on this one. I've tucked away a fugitive or two in my day. I know the perfect place. Safe and sound as Fort Knox."

"Lead me to it."

"A locker at the bus station? I'm not hiding out in a locker at the bus station." Roger stiffened his arms and legs against the opening.

I huffed and I puffed, but I couldn't jam him in. "You got a better suggestion, let's hear it."

His answer bubbled out in one of the clear, beaker-shaped balloons that usually proclaim "Eureka!" "I could hole up with Jessica's twin sister. We get along swell. She'd hide me. I know she would."

"Jessica's got a twin sister?"

"Yep."

"How come I never heard of her?"

"She keeps a low profile. She's a writer."

"What's she write?"

"Short stories."

"She . . . married?"

"Of course not. Who'd marry a woman built like her?"

I could name a dozen, starting with yours truly. "Let's pay her a call."

"Eddie Valiant," said Roger, "meet my beloved sister-in-law, Joellyn."

I never learn. When dealing with a Toon, always watch for the ringer. She was a dead duplex for her redheaded sister, except for one thing—she was only six and a half inches tall.

"I didn't say she was an *identical* twin," Roger whispered.

Joellyn lounged on the windowsill, oblivious to the pigeons eyeing her hungrily from outside. Her tropical-patterned halter top could moonlight as a bow tie on a Tahitian waiter. Her matching wraparound sarong possessed less substance than the chintz drapes cheap eateries hang over their windows to slow down the sun. She tied her hair back with a piece of green thread even a dandy wouldn't bother to pluck off his lapel. The tiny shoes on her tiny feet didn't have the heft to leave footprints in a bowl of mashed potatoes. "I'm pleased to make your acquaintance." Her lettering had the exact same curvaceous rise and fall as her sister's. Except her entire balloon couldn't fill the bottom of a thimble. I squinted to read it. "Everybody except Roger calls me Jo." Figures. Short woman, short name.

She extended a petite hand. It sported a Bakelite bracelet the size of a pet collar—if your pet was an inchworm. I touched her palm with the tip of my finger, carefully. Hit her with a jolt of static electricity, and she'd fricassee like a broiled sardine.

WHO P-P-P-PLUGGED ROGER RABBIT?

Roger summarized his troubles in ten or twelve thousand unchosen words. He had read her right. She consented to hide him out as long as necessary.

That settled, I made for the door.

"Wait a minute," said Roger. "You promised I could tag along, assist you with the case."

"No, I didn't."

"Yes you did. I distinctly remember. I know. I wrote it down." He flipped through his notebook. "It's in here verbatim. I'm certain of it. Give me two seconds. I'll find it."

"Whether I did, whether I didn't, it's a moot point. To stay out of trouble, you stay out of sight."

"Oh sure. I forgot." He closed his notebook. Dick Tracy still smiled on the cover. I tried my best not to do the same. "Gee, what a disappointment," said Roger.

"That's life," I proclaimed. Call me the old philosopher.

"I've got an idea," said Miss Microscopic. "Since Roger can't go with you, why don't I take his place? I am a writer, a trained observer of the human condition. I have a terrific memory for details. I'd be able to report everything that happens."

"What a swell idea," Roger proclaimed. "She'll be my eyes and ears. Take her with you. P-p-p-please."

"I'd enjoy the change," said Shorty. "I don't get out nearly as much as I should."

Small wonder when the neighborhood cat's likely to mistake you for lunch. I put the quick kibosh to this proposal. "Sorry, toots. I don't work with women." Especially ones who barely stand shoelace high to a Little League shortstop.

"I can be of help, immense help," said Little Jo in a wafting balloon with the lacy pink sweetness of cotton candy. "I can go places, see things a normal-sized person can't."

Come to think of it, she was every private eye's dream. A self-actuated burglary tool. She'd also be better than binoculars in the Peeping Tom department. And for eavesdropping, she beat a glass to the wall six ways to Sunday. I might be able to use her at that. All right. Come along.

I left with the frail riding tourist class in my breast pocket. She grabbed the edge and peeked out, making me look like I had Kilroy for a handkerchief.

When we got to the car, I transferred her into the glove compartment. "Help yourself to the bourbon," I said, "and don't touch the gun."

She refused to let go of my thumb. "I'm not riding in there." Two inches to the left and her BB-sized balloon would have taken my eye out.

"Okay. Give me a minute. I'll have the maid make up the ashtray."

Hard to tell without a jeweler's loupe, but I swear the edges of her perfect lips turned up into the faintest hint of a perfect smile. "How about if I ride up here with you?" She caught the bottom of my steering wheel, somersaulted up to the dashboard, and took a seat in the curved hollow that framed my speedometer. And did it wearing a sarong. Dorothy Lamour, eat your heart out.

What the heck. Let her stay.

I pulled out into traffic and flipped on my turn signal. The light flashing behind her sarong silhouetted her gams. I drove clear around the block, four turns worth. Even if they're only three inches long, great legs are great legs.

When bungalow apartments started renting for more than the price of a pilfered pullet, the slyest foxes bought up the henhouses they'd been raiding, evicted the chickens, and rented the refurbished coops to struggling clucks like Vivien Leigh.

I knocked on her door. The banging didn't faze my minuscule passenger. She was dead to the world, rocked to sleep by my rolling gait. For neatness' sake, I pinched off the string of Z's dangling out of my pocket.

Vivien let me in. Combining cheap decoration with acting inspiration, she'd wallpapered with Southern voice balloons. They dripped jasmine and mint in such quantities my shoes stuck to the floor.

As we drove to lunch, she slid my Luckies off the dashboard and lit two. She put one between my teeth. "I fancy you as quite the adventurer," she said.

"Old rough and tumble, that's me, although lately it's been mostly rough."

She didn't leave an inch of space on the seat between us. "I've never met a real private eye before. What exotic and dangerous cases have you worked on recently?"

"It's only exciting in the comic strips, honey. My best case wouldn't run three panels."

"My, but you're forthright."

"You want polish, date a guy with candelabras instead of brass knuckles."

I fool easy, especially concerning women, but I swear she didn't learn her laugh in acting school. "I believe I'll stick with you."

She requested a stop. She'd been invited to a formal party at Selznick's house next evening and needed a new dress. She asked me to help her pick one. "I need a gentleman's opinion."

"I'll try and find a gentleman to give you one." Me and fashion don't mix. Doris once dragged me to a clothing consultant who studied my skin color and told me I was a winter personality, harsh and colorless and cold. That meant I could wear anything I wanted. What's the big deal? I do anyway.

Warren Woodpecker, the owner of the dress shop, swished out to meet us. He wore a gold lamé vest, Kelly green frill-fronted dickey, maroon leggings, and a fuchsia beret. He had augmented his bustle with a fistful of peacock feathers and had waxed his beak with red polish. His chest and shoulder nap were fluffed out into a feather boa. I'd hate to see what other splendors hung inside the closet he came out of. "Vivien, my love, how wonderful to see you again." His balloon smelled of lemon drops.

Vivien described the look she wanted.

Warren conjured up a string of thought pictures portraying what he had in mind. An assistant snagged his balloons in a sterling-silver net and shook them onto a cutting table. Vivien separated his glad rags into two bales, the out-and-out rejects and the possibles. The rejects went into a back room to be shellacked, fitted with tabs, and sold as high-fashion clothing for the well-decorated paper doll. Vivien's chosen few were pumped full of air and given to her to try on.

"You pretty tight with Selznick, are you?" I asked her through the dressing-room door.

"Not particularly." She came out and sallied around in front of me dressed in a vagrant's outfit, by which I mean it had no visible means of support. "Mr. Selznick likes to have pretty girls at his affairs. I suspect he regards me the way he would a party decoration."

I doubted it. That was her photo, not a roll of crepe paper, Selznick tried to hide from me. "What do you know about his lieutenant, Pepper Potts?"

She returned to the dressing room. Her voice came out muffled as she slid another creation over her head. "Uncouth, belligerent, and brash. Not at all the sort I would expect to function as Mr. Selznick's right hand."

"Quote me specifics."

"He exercises his casting couch."

"Along with half the producers in Hollywood."

WHO P-P-P-PLUGGED ROGER RABBIT?

"But with Potts, it's different. He's not interested in girls like me, if you follow."

"He doesn't like his women bright, charming, witty, and beautiful?"

"He doesn't like them human. Pepper Potts goes strictly for Toons."

Little Jo crawled out of my pocket, her hands rubbing circles around her eyelids. "What are we doing here?"

Vivien appeared wearing another stunner. "I believe this is the one." She spun in circles in front of me. "What do you think?"

"Terrific."

Vivien returned to the dressing room.

Shorty belted the underside of my chin. Her sock gave me a bruise that added an hour to my five-o'clock shadow. "You've got a client fearing for his life, and you recess for a fashion show? What kind of detective are you?"

"The kind who doesn't take lip off a squirt."

"Get back on the job."

"Make me."

She slid down my tie the way a fireman descends a brass pole. She dove into my trousers.

I stood with a jerk.

Vivien came out of the dressing room holding a large dress box. "What's wrong?"

"A mild case of ants in the pants."

She handed me the box. "I hear jitterbugging's the cure. I know a terrific dance club nearby. Care to give it a go?"

Little Jo snapped the elastic on my boxers. Hard. And low. "Sorry, Viv. I just remembered a job I've got to do." I tossed her the dress box and broke the world's record for the eight-and-a-half-yard dash to the door. "I'll call you later."

"You do that," she said. She didn't give me much reason to suppose she'd answer.

Little Jo rode my shoulder like Long John Silver's pet polly. "Where to, boss?"

I stopped at a pay phone. I gave the operator Ferd's number.

"Hey, watch it," said Thumbelina. "You nearly strangled me with the cord."

A balloon came out of the mouthpiece. "Flatfoot."

"Ferd, Eddie."

His balloon dropped from pure black to a shade of gray. "I eyeballed Wrightliter's film." The weight of his words nearly crushed my cheekbone. "Shame on you, Eddie. You've been a scamp."

"If I want an editorial, I'll read the *Telltale*. Spill it to me simple. Did she sing?"

"Long, loud, and way off key."

"How bad is it?"

The mouthpiece bulged and strained. His balloon popped out the size and shape of a thundercloud. "As bad as it comes." His stormy words drifted out of the phone booth and rained down foul weather for two blocks around.

"Wrightliter stumbled across a deal between Kirk Enigman and your old friend Tom Tom LeTuit. Seems rum's the main ingredient for a new drug they're peddling. Wrightliter figured to cop an exclusive exposé. When Enigman bit the weinie, she went looking for LeTuit. He's not an easy man to find. She figured to buttonhole him at the end of a smuggling run. She greased the sedan, and he carted her along."

"What's this drug all about?"

"Wrightliter only knows one thing about it." His balloon hung in the air like the black flag flying from the mast of a plague ship. "It'll destroy the fashtumping human race."

He hung up without saying good-bye.

Billing Dingles as a cabaret equated to calling a skunk a perfume container. For seedy, the place rivaled a Burpee's display rack.

It occupied an old movie house that had finished its run playing to what movie moguls euphemistically call the adult trade. Flyers advertising the theater's final feature still inhabited the row of cracked glass poster frames out front. To save the price of new signs, the management named their establishment Dingles after that last picture show. To prove they had a modicum of taste, they whitewashed out the part about *Diddles Dubuque*. The broken-down ticket booth featured a dress dummy modeling the latest lack of fabric from Frederick's of Hollywood.

Plaster another travel sticker on the steamer trunk of a wayward civilization.

"This is no place for a lady," I told Half-pint. "Wait for me in the car."

"Not on your life. There's nothing on display in there that I don't see every day in my bathroom mirror."

"Except here it's not in miniature."

She stomped her foot hard on my shoulder pad. "That's very funny, Eddie. Ha ha ha. What do you do for an encore? Tell little moron jokes? Ridicule dwarfs? Kick a cripple? Just because I'm small doesn't mean I don't have feelings."

"All right, lay off. You want to slum, fine."

She cozied herself into the crook of my neck and anchored her arm to my collar. "Fine." She crossed her stems. I can honestly say I've never seen it done better. "To show you there's no hard feelings," she said, "the first round's on me." She flashed her China-doll smile. "Two short beers."

Dingles's barker, a slimy, bloated slug, wore a raggedy straw boater and a threadbare red-and-white-striped sport coat that came to him as a hand-me-down from a melted barber pole. He was slippery as sin. I'd bought vacuum cleaners off door-to-door sales-men not half as persuasive. He conjured up picture after perfect picture of the naughty antics awaiting us inside, basically bawdier versions of the comic-strip nonsense your neighborhood paperboy dumps on your front steps every morning for a quarter. Here it cost six bits. I negotiated half price for the snub. I paid our dues, and we went in.

The interior retained the movie's sloping floor. The incline ran straight downhill from the bar to the alleyway exit, a great conve-nience for patrons who needed a rolling start home.

The air reeked of drain-plug gin. A thick, interlocked layer of wall-to-wall peanut shells kept us from falling into the cellar.

Every watering hole attracts its own unique crowd of regulars. At Dingles, it was barflies. I counted at least one of every variety—common house, horse, shoo, May, fire, and gad. Three-, some-times four-fisted snifters, these guys, and nothing sissy. Boilermakers, straight down the thorax. Imagine the racket when these loop-de-loopers got a buzz on.

Bowl snacks consisted of gruel regurgitated by yesterday's clientele. Behind the bar, where most barkeeps hang a sap, Din-gles kept a swatter.

A self-appointed music critic had smashed a blunt instrument through the jukebox. The management had shoved the juke into a corner and replaced it with a honky-tonk piano, its bass keys worn to nubs by years of lowdown boogie.

Little Jo and I sat at a table a better saloon would burn in its fireplace. A printed notice beside a wine bottle candle holder advertised two for one on well drinks. From the taste, Dingles's well pumped mostly water.

The female crab louse waiting our table wore an apron, a pasted-on smile, and nothing else. Her pendulous, hairy antennae swung free and loose. So did her lips when I slipped her a fin and asked about the woman Baby Herman left with last night.

The waitress told me the woman came in from time to time. She was tight as a tick with the club's songstress. The *Telltale* had pegged her looks right. She was so plug ugly, the scaliest regulars wouldn't touch her with a ten-foot proboscis. The waitress didn't know her name. I tucked my card under her vestigial wing along with the promise of a double sawbuck if she'd call me the next time the woman showed up. I ordered us another round.

"What next?" asked Little Jo. She flipped idly through the pictures in the billfold I'd left on the table.

"We stick around for the floor show. Maybe the chanteuse will sing us a better song."

The crab louse returned with our drinks. "What do you know," said the waitress as she set our glasses on the table. "That's her!"

"Who?" I asked.

"The horsey-faced trixie who left with Baby Herman." She tapped a picture in my wallet.

I slipped it out of its cellophane holder and handed it to her for a closer look. "You sure?"

She pointed at her multifaceted eyes. "Honey, with these, you take in everything, whether you want to or not." She gave the picture a long, hard once-over. "That's her, no question about it." She handed the picture back. "Great job of retouching. You'd never know she was a Toon." The waitress scuttled off to the next table, where she took an order from a randy mosquito who couldn't keep his stinger off her carapace.

Little Jo indicated the snapshot clutched in my fist. "Who is that?"

"Nobody you'd know." Maybe nobody I did, either. The waitress had plunked her pincer on my photo of Heddy.

The lights dimmed for the floor show. Without introduction or fanfare, out came my second shock of the evening. The club's featured blues belter was none other than Lupe Chihuahua.

She wore sling-back pumps with high heels only a stilt walker could love, a pair of tattered elbow-length white gloves last used by a Rose Parade beauty queen to whip the horse pulling her float, an assortment of the jewelry that gave the five-and-dime its nickname, and a dark blue gown, skintight and cut low enough to lose Dingles whatever slim shot it had at a family trade.

Lupe drew a healthy round of applause, not surprising considering every patron had six arms to work with. She sat at the piano, took a few sallies up and down the keyboard, and started to sing.

I've gotten more melodious music out of a comb and tissue

paper. I took a hefty swallow of bourbon, but, short of pouring it
in my ears, there was no way for it to improve the quality of her
voice. Thank goodness she suppressed her balloons. If they'd
looked like she sounded, they would have sawed holes in the
ceiling. I hailed the waitress and took another dive into Dingles's
well.

None too soon for my tortured eardrums, Lupe finished her
set. Insects must be tuned to a different wavelength, because they
gave Lupe a hearty ovation. She acknowledged the clapping and
ducked out through a curtain in the rear.

I drained my hooch and went after her.

"What's going on?" said Little Jo, hanging on to my lapel for
dear life. "You act like you know that woman. Who is she?"

I opened the glass door you're supposed to pop only when a
fire erupts. Well, my world was blazing. "Sorry, runt. I might have
to get harsh with the thrush, and I don't want interference." Or
witnesses, either. "Call it one I owe you." I locked her inside with
Dingles's leaky hose.

Lupe's dressing room doubled as the ladies' john. I figured any
lady patronizing Dingles had run out of modesty long ago, so I
opened the door and walked in.

I found Lupe sitting at a rickety makeup table that took its
illumination from a ten-watt glowworm hung from the ceiling by
a cord looped around its middle. She had her face covered with
more cream than most hash houses serve on a piece of pecan pie.
She had swapped her gown for a green chenille bathrobe that hung
on her like seaweed on a beached dolphin.

"Wrong door, *asno*," she said. "*El potty es uno* down the hall."

"Hi, Lupe. Remember me?"

She gave me a once-over that would have done credit to the
beefcake judge at a 4-H fair. "*Madre mia*, let me give the guess.
You got an inquisitive manner about you. I know. Newspaper
reporter. Critic of music for el *Telltale*, *si*? Well *amante*, I hope you
got *muy* sharp pencil 'cause I got plenty to tell. First, I never take
voice lesson in my life."

"No kidding."

"*Es verdad!* I know. Hard to believe." She put her hands on
her ample bosom. "Especially for one with my vibrato. You want
to know, I bet, why is classy singer like me stay in dive like

WHO P-P-P-PLUGGED ROGER RABBIT?

Dingles. My *aficionados*, my fans, I am loyal to my fans. Did you not hear the buzz-buzz-buzz from the crowd? To me that mean more than a concert at Carnegie *Corredor*. As long as flyboys keep to cheer me on, I will sing out my lungs for them. Is that the, how do you say it, *punto de vista* you seeking?"

"Not quite." I leaned against the edge of the sink. "I'm Eddie Valiant. Remember me? Freddy Valiant's brother?"

From out of a ring on the wall, she took a towel that had last wiped dipsticks in a gas station and used it to scoop away her cleansing cream. "You have confused me with another, *hombre*." She peeled off a pair of eyelashes the size of small butterflies. When I took a closer look, I saw they *were* small butterflies.

I pointed to her musical instruments, looped over the coin slot on the toilet-stall door. "The old maracas tell me otherwise."

"Si, si, Eddie." She re-did her makeup for the second show, applying her foundation with a mortar and trowel. "You can no blame a *señorita* for telling lie. Singing for buggy boys is big, how do you say it, down come from what I do in Cuba. You saw me at Baba de Rum, no? I do the chickee-boom pretty good. And not to forget the movies. I was what they call a rising starlet."

"Matter of fact, I just saw one of your flicks at Grauman's. A thriller called *Shadow of Evil*."

She blew into her hand and caught her breath in her palm. It turned a gaudy shade of translucent red. She broke it in half, stuck a piece on each cheek, and smoothed the edges flat with her finger. "One of my best."

"Starred Kirk Enigman. Also featured a peg-legged Toon named Pepper Potts. Remember him?"

She squinted into her mirror, trying to bring her face, or maybe the past, into clearer focus. "*Muy gigantico*. Ugly. And mean."

"That's him."

"I don't know the peg-legged one so good. He is palling out more with Kirk."

"And they both hung around with your boyfriend LeTuit, right?"

"Tom Tom, he is very struck with the stars. When they come to Cuba, he is eager to meet them."

"He ever meet Roger Rabbit?"

"I think he do. The rabbit come to Cuba to gamble. He big American film star. Tom Tom show him the pretty good time. Tom Tom and Pete and Kirk and the rabbit, they knock around together."

"You seen Potts or Enigman lately?"

She shook her head. "We no travel in same circles any more."

"Let me bring you up to date. Early yesterday somebody turned Enigman into a slick spot on the floor of his screening room. Just before he died, he was watching a home movie of you. And LeTuit. And my brother Freddy. Remember Freddy? The sap you turned from a decent, hardworking stiff into a zombie Toon?"

She didn't flinch. "I have *nada* to do with that."

"Sure. Just like you got no idea what's in a certain little black box that half the civilized world's after."

Her composure slipped and took half her makeup with it, leaving her with a quadruple chin. She needed a backhoe and a year's supply of Kleenex to clear away the landslide. "If you know what is good for you," she said, switching to balloons so she could keep her mouth still while she repainted her face, "you will forget about Tom Tom, you will forget about *Señor* Enigman, and you will *especialamente* forget about that *caja*, that box. *Comprende?* You fool here with sinister powers you no understand."

"You mean hocus pocus dominocus? Sorry, sister, I only shiver once a year, and that came last Halloween."

"You do not want to know about this. It is too *horroroso*."

"Sweetheart, I've seen a rabbit with his clothes off. What could be worse?"

"You have no idea, Mr. Valiant. I will tell you. That box it contain only copy of formula for *Tonico de Tura*, what you would call Toon Tonic."

"People are committing murder over a cola?"

"No, no, no, fizzy cola. *Diabolico concoctione*. Dr. Jackal"—she crossed herself with her makeup brush—"he discover Toon Tonic. Tom Tom promise to bottle, sell, and split proceeds, but instead he murder Jackal to keep all for himself."

"What's this stuff do?"

"You saw. Toon Tonic what Tom Tom slip to your brother."

"That's what turned him into a zombie!"

"No. Zombie turn him into a zombie."

WHO P-P-P-PLUGGED ROGER RABBIT?

"Don't double-talk me."

"Zombie, zombie. You know." She formed a hitchhiker's fist and poured her thumb toward her throat. "The *bebida*. The bar drink. It often have that effect. Especially on *turistas*. The Toon Tonic, it work different."

"Give me a hint."

"It turn a human into a Toon."

It sounded impossible but so did the concept of Pop Tarts the first time I heard it. "This Toon Tonic. Does it wear off?"

"Nunca." Never.

"You're telling me a human who drinks this stuff is doomed to spend the rest of his life as one of you?"

"Unless he drink it again. It also turn the *vicio* into the *versio*. The Toon into the human."

I've seen men hanged, shot, poisoned, and gutted. I've seen Bela Lugosi in *Dracula* and Boris Karloff in *Frankenstein*. None of it held a candle to the horror of Toons becoming humans. "Where's your boyfriend planning to make this stuff?"

"Ex-boyfriend. We through for good."

"Ex-boyfriend then."

"Tom Tom he rent an *alamacen*, a warehouse in Toontown." She wrote down the address and handed it to me.

I grabbed her mitt and squeezed it hard. My torture technique didn't work. Her hand had the substance of foolscap. I might as well massage a wad of tissue paper. I switched persuasions, flipping out the file built into my nail clippers. In this light, she'd never know the difference between that and a shiv. I held it against her throat. "Where's my brother?"

When she shrugged, her bathrobe fell open, uncovering one of her shoulders and half her chest. She'd slipped a lot since the old days. "I no see him since Cuba. If I guess, I say he with Dr. Jackal. They swim together in ocean with the *mortos* and fish." She buffed her thumbnail on my intimidator and pushed it to one side.

She finished off her makeup with a spray coating of varnish. "You got nothing else you want to know, you ask it quick, cause my *publico* awaits."

"Who's the trixie left last night with Baby Herman? I hear you and her are bosom buddies."

Again she humped her shoulders, exposing another square

yard of sagging flesh. "I know not her name. She come to hear me often. She relish my vocal talents. She big Lupe fan of which I tell you I got *muy mucho*."

"There's a few of your admirers at my place, hanging off my flypaper. I'll drop them in an envelope and mail them over." Just as I reached for the knob, the door opened. Two ladybugs staggered in. They didn't seem surprised to find me there.

I tipped my hat, and bid one and all a good day.

WHO P-P-P-PLUGGED ROGER RABBIT?

"**Y**ou needn't have locked me away," groused Little Jo. "I wouldn't have interfered." She was back riding tourist class in my breast pocket.

"Squirt, I don't trust anybody except myself. 'Cause I'm the only Gus who's never sold me out."

"In other words, strike three on me. Besides being small and a woman, I'm also not and never will be Eddie Valiant." She smoked a dandelion fuzzy extracted from a pack that would fit in my nose with a carton to spare.

"This case wobbles in oddball directions, short stuff, Roger's only a minor part of it. There's aspects you can't comprehend." I ferried her up the stairs to my office.

"Try me," she said. She dropped her weed on the floor. I snuffed it with my toe to prevent it setting a dust kitten on fire. "I might surprise you."

I opened my door.

Clark Gable had settled into the overstuffed armchair I vacuum for loose change after every client. A trick of the trade you learn at Gumshoe U. "Where have you been?" Gable bounded to his feet. "I've been waiting for hours."

I slipped out of my suit coat and dropped it on my rack. I angled pip-squeak toward the wall. "What brings you to my side of the tracks?" I asked Gable.

"I intended to hire you to find Roger Rabbit," said Gable. Little Jo leaned out of my coat and tried to straighten my college diploma. At ten bucks a copy from Fast Frankie's Printshop, it was too crooked. She turned her attention to forming my pocket hankie into a parachute. "I'm determined to see that he pays the maximum price for killing my buddy the Babe."

"You're barking up the wrong rabbit. Roger didn't rub out Herman."

"Clark. Catch." Little Jo hit the silk.

Gable hadn't lost his Air Corps fighter pilot's reflexes. He snagged her in midair. "Jo. What are you doing here?"

"Research for a new story." She gave me a scornful glance. "Called *The Man Who Wouldn't Bend*."

"Catchy title. There a part in the movie for me?"

"The lead, if you can portray a die-hard chauvinist."

"I'll pass. It's too much of a stretch." Gable nestled her into the crook of his arm, pushing his coat sleeve to the elbow to pillow her head. He loaded the cap from his hip flask and handed it to her on a silver dollar. For a napkin, he offered his shirt cuff. While she drank, he fanned her with the end of his paisley ascot. Add a bath in goat's milk, and she'd be the Queen of Sheba.

"How do you know the rabbit's innocent?" Gable asked me. Always skeptical, movie stars. Never take your word for anything. An occupational hazard. Results from overexposure to the phrase "Trust me."

"I'm his alibi. He was with me when it happened." Except for the eight hours I racked out when he could have flown to Rio and back without me knowing. "Be realistic, Clark. Roger Rabbit's goofy as a sotted seersucker saphead, but he's no murderer."

Gable showed me an upraised chin and a perfect left profile. The bugger didn't have a bad side, at least not one visible from the exterior. "If not him, who?"

I lit a gaffer. "For starters, maybe you."

"Me?" He smacked his hand to his chest, upending Little Jo from his forearm. She clung to his leather elbow patch for dear life. "Why would I kill my best buddy?" His pearly whites sparkled with the luster of a brand-new porcelain sink.

"I got a flash for you, chump. He was beating your time with your girl."

Gable tumbled backwards into my armchair. He landed heavy, with a jingle of falling coin. Hallelujah. There's gold in them there cushions tonight. "The Babe? And Carole?" Little Jo lost her tenuous grip on his arm and tumbled into free-fall. "That's ridiculous," Gable proclaimed. Little Jo caught Gable's pants cuff with the agility of a trapeze artist, slid down his argyles to rest on the toe of his shiny cordovans. It's true what nuns say. Black patent leather does reflect up, though in Little Jo's case you'd need a microscope to see what. "The Babe wouldn't do that to me."

WHO P-P-P-PLUGGED ROGER RABBIT?

"He would, he could, and he did." I tiptoed Gable through the wilted tulips, past the huggy bear photo of Herman and Lombard hanging on Roger's wall, Lombard's love letter in Herman's baby buggy, and the picture of Lombard in Herman's trick frame.

"The insufferable jerk!" Gable said when I'd finished. He smacked his palm repeatedly against his chair. His crossed leg bobbed in tight circles. Little Jo rode his size nine like a bucking bronco. "If he wasn't dead, I'd kill him."

"Bulldog Bascomb might make the case that you already did." The high-low, high-low motion of Gable's foot turned Little Jo slightly puce. Eddie Valiant, knight in tarnished armor, to the rescue. I sucked my Lucky deep and blew a smoke ring at her. She grabbed a hold, swung inside the billowy circle, and rode the air currents up to desktop level. She dismounted with a half gainer worthy of Johnny Weissmuller. She took a seat on my ink bottle. A whiffet of smoke encircled her bright red hair like the halo on a chain puffer's dashboard Madonna. "Clark," I told him, "you're in chowder up to your eyeballs."

He dropped his head to a level that showed me the top of his scalp. "It does appear that way." The man had every hair he was born with, and half of mine, too. "Let me ask you a hypothetical question." He reached to his inside coat pocket. "Is this likely to clean my name?" He dropped a huge wad of green on my blotter. It landed beside my photo of plain Jane and her two kids. A ready-made family I bought framed in a Santa Monica hock shop. It gives clients confidence. The stable family man.

"Depends how dirty it turns out to be."

"How much Borax can I buy for that?"

I tapped his wad with my finger. It weighed the same as a small pineapple. "Enough to rinse your underwear."

"I don't wear it."

"Then for sure it's plenty." I scooted his mound of moola toward my top desk drawer.

"Don't open that," shouted Gable.

I raised an eyebrow. So did he. On him it looked better, but he is a professional. "Roger Rabbit's inside."

I inched the drawer out anyway. I never believe Wet Paint signs or Dangerous Curve warnings, either. I ought to learn. True to Gable's word, the drawer contained a compressed brick of white fur and red corduroy. Roger the Rectangular Rabbit.

Little Jo walked to the edge of my desk top and took a peek. "How did Roger get in there?" she asked me.

I snared her dime-sized balloon and flipped it at Gable. "You tell her, Clark."

He pulled out, and on, his hip flask. "As I mentioned," said Gable, "I came here to hire you to find Roger Rabbit." He wiped his mouth like an everyday working stiff, with the back of his hand. "I found him in your office when I arrived. We tussled a bit, I prevailed. I bound him with your phone cord and imprisoned him in that drawer. With the phone disabled, I had no way to call the police. I didn't want to leave the rabbit unguarded. They're slippery, these Toons. I assumed that once you returned, one of us could watch him while the other went for the law." He took another tug of liquid consolation. "If you believe he's not guilty, it appears I made a mistake. I hope the rabbit's not upset."

"Naw, rabbit's love tight, dark spaces. That's why they live in loamy burrows with nobody to talk to but earthworms." I leaned close to the drawer and spoke into what appeared to be one of the rabbit's ears. "You were supposed to stay at pip-squeak's."

A balloon leaked out of him the way residual foam escapes from a squashed beer can. "I couldn't abide twiddling my toes while you did the work. I'm a rabbit of action, Eddie. When there's a tough, nasty, dangerous job to be done, I'm the rabbit to do it. Put 'em up, gunsel. I got you covered. Bang. Bang. I nailed him, Elliot. Rat-a-tat-a-tat. Pass me more bullets, J. Edgar."

"How hard did you sock him," I asked Gable, "before you gave him the squish?"

Gable flicked his forefinger off his thumb like a kid shooting marbles. "A love tap."

"Love tap?" said Roger. "You fibbery fighting fiend. You nearly unscrewed my head."

"You're a felon, wanted by the police for murder." Gable joined me and the tadpole around the outer edge of the drawer. "What was I supposed to do?"

"For starters, *stay away from my wife*." Roger's balloon sprayed a stream of hot venom across the front of Gable's pressed linen pants.

WHO P-P-P-PLUGGED ROGER RABBIT?

Gable slammed his flask on my desk, yanked the drawer out of its slot, and upended it. Roger fell squarely to the floor. "Maybe if you weren't always off on location shooting those stupid, worthless cartoons, maybe if you spent more time at home with her, you wouldn't have to worry."

Gable was right. Toons are slippery little cusses. Roger freed himself of his bindings in seconds. "Shows how much you know about women," said Roger. "Absence makes the heart grow fonder."

Gable caressed his mouth into that sly, knowing grin that makes movie theaters keep smelling salts on hand to revive fainting women. "The version I heard has it that when the cat's away, the mouse will play."

"Oh, yeah, smarty britches?" Roger pulled himself up where his nose reached Gable's boutonniere. "For as little as you know about the fair sex, you know even less about adages. What about 'Absence reopens the springs of love'?"

"Out of sight, out of mind."

"Love does not rust," Roger said belligerently. "So there."

"Old love, cold love." Gable lit a smoke with a lighter fashioned from a gold molar yanked out of the Colossus of Rhodes.

"True love never ages," shot back Roger.

"New love drives out old."

Roger folded his arms across his chest. "Love conquers all."

"Never rely on love or the weather."

Roger assumed a soapbox posture, hand raised, finger extended even with his orange topknot. "Love blossoms at marriage."

"Marriage is the tomb of love." Never trade maxims with an actor. They eat axioms for breakfast and spit them out at the afternoon matinee.

Roger gave it one last, desperate shot. "Marry in haste, repent at leisure."

"Marry in haste"—Gable took a long, leisurely drag off his Chesterfield—"repent at Reno."

Roger swelled his head to twice normal size to prevent the escape of his spontaneous giggle. "Gigolo," he spat at Gable when he had himself back under control.

"Fool," Gable countered.

Gable walked to the window, where he finished his smoke. Roger tested the workmanship on my filing cabinet.

I helped myself to a shot from Gable's bottle, poured a thimble for the weinie and a double for Roger. I handed Gable the slim remains. "Go home," I told him. "I'll call when I turn up a lead."

He shook his head. "You take my money, you take me along with it."

"Wait a minute, Eddie," said Roger. "You can't take him. You promised you'd take me."

"Why can't he take us both?" asked Gable. "We're grown-ups. We ought to be capable of setting aside our animosities to help solve a murder."

Roger stuck out his tongue.

"See," said Gable to me. "Best of buddies, already."

"I got to make a call," I told them. "Since Clark used my cord for a hog tie, I'll use the pay box in the hall. If you two can kiss and make up by the time I get back, I'll take you both."

I left them to mend their fences while I called Ferd.

"Your time's almost up, Eddie," he warned me. "I'm not kidding. You produce one killer, signed, sealed, and delivered, or I rat you out to Bascomb."

"Sure, Ferd, I got the case under control. A few loose ends, and I hand it over. That's not why I called. I need to know about Heddy. How's she been acting lately?"

I thought his balloon took a trifle long to squeeze out of the mouthpiece, but it could have been my imagination. "Same as usual. Brassy as Barnacle Bill's buttons."

"She hasn't been doing anything . . . strange?"

"How so?"

"I don't know. Like . . . different than she normally does."

"You mean is she getting more headaches than usual? That kind of different? Or is she growing hair on her face during full moons and going out for a romp in the woods?" He laughed. I didn't.

"I'd say the latter."

"What are you insinuating, Eddie? You suggesting my wife's a freak?"

"Ferd, she's my sister."

"You intimating that my wife, your sister's a werewolf?"

WHO P-P-P-PLUGGED ROGER RABBIT?

"Worse Ferd, lots worse."

This time there was no mistaking it. His balloon took forever to swell out of the mouthpiece. "What could be worse than that?"

"I think Heddy's turned into a Toon."

He produced a ha-ha bubble the size of a dinosaur egg. "She should be so lucky."

"The waitress at Dingles identified Heddy as the Toon woman who left with Baby Herman."

His hand came through the line and grabbed me by the throat. I had to bash him with my gun butt to make him let go. "You've tried slimy tricks before, Eddie, but this wins the cake. Setting up your own sister to take the fall for your crime. I ought to noogie your fattfarking nuggets."

"Ferd, you don't believe me, go to Dingles, ask the waitress yourself. Incidentally, you'll find Lupe Chihuahua working there, too. You starting to see this tie together?"

"I'm gonna check, Eddie. Don't think I won't. You better not be foofarfing me, that's all I got to say." He slammed the phone in my ear.

I returned to my office. Unfortunately, Gable and Roger were both still alive and eager to go. I had no choice. "Let's move out."

Roger, sitting next to the small fry on the edge of my desk, hopped to his feet. So did Gable in my armchair. Only one difference. Gable keeled over and fell flat on his face. His shoelaces were tied together.

Roger spread his hands open palms up at shoulder level. He smirked.

While Gable fumbled with his laces, I pulled Roger aside. "You ever been to Cuba?" I asked him.

"Never," said Roger. "Doctor's orders. I'm deathly allergic to bananas, mangos, papayas, guavas, and sugarcane. I sneeze when I walk past fruit stands. I blush to mention what happened to me the time I danced with Carmen Miranda."

Gable offered Little Jo a ride in his trousers. She declined. Oddly, she chose my pocket over his. Imagine that.

On our way out, Gable read my door's fading inscription, EDDIE VALIANT, PRIVATE INVESTIGATIONS, INCORPORATED. "You're a publicly held corporation?" he asked.

"More or less. I'm the only stockholder. Keeps the annual

meetings short and friendly. My pencil pusher suggested it. Said it would save me money."

Gable gave me a double take. "I wouldn't have imagined excessive taxes to be a problem for you."

I got into the elevator. "Brother, sometimes you can't believe your eyes." I punched the button marked "absolute bottom."

We drove Gable's Ford. I had him pull close to the front of LeTuit's warehouse so passing cars couldn't see me break and enter.

I wedged a tire iron into the doorjamb. The lock snapped like a fresh wad of Juicy Fruit. I nudged the door. It refused to budge. I put my shoulder to it. No luck. Gable and Roger joined in. The three of us got it open wide enough for me to squeak in with my gun drawn.

I tripped over the doorstop, a hundred and eighty pounds of decomposing dead man. I rolled him over. Tom Tom LeTuit, plug ugly as ever with his flatiron snout; double row of crocodile chompers; round, open, sightless eyes sliced off the bottoms of rusted tin cans; Oop Shoop forehead; and Gravel Gertie hair. He wore white linen slacks. His rickrack-embroidered cream-colored Guabaya shirt contained an extra buttonhole just about the size of the studs in my stolen gun.

I knelt beside him and frisked him. Little Jo stuck her head out of my pocket. To her credit and my surprise, she didn't faint. The game little trouper hopped onto the body and searched those places I couldn't or wouldn't reach.

Gable and Roger inched up behind me. "Is he dead?" asked Roger.

"No, chum," said Gable. "He's sleeping with the angels."

"That's not funny," said Roger.

"Who says it's supposed to be?" said Gable. "I'm not out to draw a laugh every time I open my yap."

"And I am?" said Roger. "That's what you're implying?"

"If the shoe fits, buddy boy," said Gable.

"Hah. There you go, showing your stupidity again. I don't wear shoes." He held up his foot. As advertised, no shoes. "Anybody with half a brain can see that."

WHO P-P-P-PLUGGED ROGER RABBIT?

Little Jo crawled out of LeTuit's nether regions. She handed me her findings, an engraved invitation to David Selznick's house, the selfsame affair Vivien Leigh was dolling up for. My case was closing quicker than a Broadway play about alley cats.

LeTuit's warehouse was a dipsomaniac's daydream, stacked floor to ceiling with bottles, jugs, cases, barrels, casks, and flasks of rum. A glass-walled lab in the back boasted more copper tubing than Snuffy Smith's outdoor cocktail maker.

We tossed LeTuit's office. By mutual agreement, we divvied labor according to stature. Gable took six feet and over, Roger tackled three feet and under, Little Jo explored the mouse holes, I handled what fell in between, an ersatz leather sofa, war surplus desk, and a decrepit chair.

Roger held up a fist full of lint balls. "Are these clues?"

"To your IQ," said Gable.

We didn't find squat.

I left LeTuit where I found him. I took his party invitation and twelve bottles of his rum.

I paid my respects and three bucks to the desk clerk at Dyke's Auto Camp. He passed over the key to Cabin Six.

The room was tackier than the business side of Scotch tape. It reeked of a disinfectant that kills germs by plugging their noses. Scorch marks pocked every surface capable of supporting a cigarette butt. The twin beds swayed worse than a pair of elderly plow horses. The drinking glasses exhibited a thick, waxy buildup, a malady they caught from the linoleum floors.

Gable carried in the overnighter he kept in his trunk. I expected a Cock Robin like him to crow bloody murder once he took a gander at our hideout's rustic accommodations, but years of living on location had prepared him for Dyke's and worse. In two shakes of a lamb's tail he changed into lounging apparel, stretched out on one of the beds, and made himself comfy.

Roger, who I expected to treat the place as a joke, turned out to be the priss. Keeping his fingers clothespinned over his beezer, he pointed out the room's major shortcomings. The clothes hangers had more kinks than a Saturday night party at Fatty Arbuckle's. The dresser drawers were lined with newspapers Gutenburg printed to carpet his canary cage. Roger vowed he'd let his kidneys explode before using the bathroom. He flopped onto the unoccupied bed. The mattress sunk through the frame, sandwiching him between twin walls of plunging bedsprings. He emitted a string of tiny blue gurgles filled with despair.

Little Jo was dead to the world. Dyke's lacked a peewee-sized bed. Gable volunteered his padded Italian leather house slippers. I put one on the dresser top, laid her inside, and covered her with six plies of toilet paper.

I removed my coat and tie, opened a jug of LeTuit's rum, and splashed out a round for me and my two colleagues.

"Mud in your eye," I toasted.

"Chin chin," said Gable.

"Wrinkle my nose, cross my eyes, make my next one twice this size," said Guess Who.

I stood back and waited for Roger's explosion but none came. Seems rum affects rabbits the same way it does normal people.

I poured again. And again. And again.

My cohorts' mutual antagonism dropped away as quickly as the bottle's level.

"Bugs Bunny performs nude," said Gable with a noticeable slur. "Why do you wear pants?"

"Simple," said Roger, his lettering as fuzzy as a tippler's logic. "To hold my suspenders down." He indicated Gable's velvet smoking jacket and silk pajamas. "Who's your tailor? Dr. Denton?"

I cracked open bottle two.

"Roger, I can't figure you out," said Gable. "Sometimes you act like a mature, responsible adult, sometimes like an infant. How old are you, anyway?"

Roger tilted his head and made a whoozy, shame-shame motion with his ears. "That's one of the two questions you never ask a Toon."

"What's the other one?" asked Gable.

"What's the other one," answered Roger.

"Right. What's the other one?"

"What's the other one. That's the other one."

Gable laughed so hard he fell off the bed. Roger hopped over to give him a hand up. Gable grabbed his outstretched paw, pulled him to the floor, and tickled him senseless.

I uncorked bottle three.

As happens when you heat men with rum, they eventually stewed over women. "In the evening," said Gable to Roger as they sat side by side on the floor, their backs braced against the wall, "when you're alone with Jessica in the bedroom, what do you have that a human doesn't?"

A five-watt bulb appeared over the rabbit's head. "My own night-light!"

"Seriously," said Gable. "What's it like being married to the world's most beautiful woman?"

"It's awful." To support his sagging noggin, Roger undid his bow tie, looped it under his chin, tied the ends together, and hooked them over a nail in the wall. "I spend every waking minute worried that she'll leave me for somebody taller, handsomer, wittier, less rabbity." The nail pulled loose. Roger's head flopped sideways onto Gable's shoulder.

Gable patted the rabbit's ears. "You should have stayed single, like me," he said.

"I like being married. Marriage is wonderful," said Roger. "It's a swell institution."

"If you like living in an institution," said Gable.

Bottle four. "Let's take a poll," said Roger. He and Gable stood between the beds, bent over at the waist, breathing hard. Roger had just taught Gable the bunny hop. "What's the best present to get a woman? I vote for candy in a heart-shaped box."

"Flowers," said Gable. "Expensive, exotic hothouse varieties. Accompanied by a card dripping with mush. Women go nuts over that."

Roger and Gable turned to me. Except for the drinking part of it, I hadn't participated much in the evening's revelries. I owed them this. "Best present I ever gave a woman was a gift box of grooming aids. Pearl-white tooth drops, ear squeegee, hair trimmer with special nose attachment, mustache plucker, and a compound for removing corns. I've got the same selection myself. Had them for years. I use one or the other every day. Know what? She tossed the lot out her window and me after. Accused me of being an unromantic boob. She'd rather have yellow teeth? Corns? Or a mustache?"

"Go figure women," said Gable.

"Who can? I can't," agreed Roger.

By the end of bottle five the two were decently loaded and ready for bed. To preserve Roger's modesty, I strung a clothesline across the room and hung it with a bedspread.

Before long both of them were soundly sawing timber.

I went into the bathroom. I sobered up by splashing my face with water and my tonsils with a stiff shot of rum.

I put on my coat and tie.

Dyke's only nod to decor consisted of a carnival glass vase filled with plastic flowers. I plucked one and stuck it in my lapel. From farther than five feet away, I defied anybody to tell it from a real chrysanthemum. Glue, tape, a crayon for touch-up. It would last forever. The Garden of Eden should have had it so good.

I took Little Jo out of her leather slipper and stuck her back in my pocket. She didn't wake up.

I left my two sleeping beauties to their dreams and drove Gable's Ford to Selznick's house.

Selznick's place sat in the center of a two-acre banyan grove bounded by ten-foot privet. As I neared the front door, Selznick's night watchman, Horrible Hawk, a Hollywood legend, buzzed me by. A plug-ugly flying canker, he packed steel-tipped talons, the speed of a supercharged P-51, and a taste for criminal canapés.

Unfortunately, his radar set lacked a tube. His first night on the job, he mistook an elderly bovine for a cat burglar. He dive-bombed that old bossy smack in the middle of her nightly jump. She kicked him over the moon.

I flashed the bird LeTuit's invitation and entered Selznick's inner sanctum.

Selznick's home furnishings came secondhand from Napoleon Bonaparte's going-out-of-business sale. His matching sofas stretched the length of a prone giraffe. A senior citizen with good health and a modest standard of living could retire to Miami Beach with the gold leaf melted off one of his chairs. His Persian rugs had more knots to the inch than a string salesman's sample case. Resewn into trousers, his gray striped silk draperies would outfit Foggy Bottom. His wallpaper had more flocking than an autumn's worth of migrating geese.

A French maid with plenty of oo-la-la treated me to a glass of champagne. I spilled it into a potted plant, used my awesome powers of detection to uncover Selznick's private stock, and re-filled my tulip glass with Four Roses.

The crowd contained roughly the number of stars I spotted on my high school field trip to the Griffith Park Planetarium. The Dorsey brothers, Benny Goodman, and Harry James sat in with the band. Jimmy Cagney cut an impressive rug with Myrna Loy. When Ricardo Cortez cut in, the Yankee Doodle Dandy grabbed Helen Twelvetrees and continued his two-step without missing a beat. Dolores Del Rio sat on John Barrymore's lap. Charlie Chaplin sat on hers. Barrymore had no problem supporting the weight.

In a dark corner Zasu Pitts and Ramon Novarro created headlines for Louella Parsons. Sheldon Leonard and Edward G. Robinson cleared an end of the dining-room table for arm wrestling. Their only matchup ended in a draw.

Jessica Rabbit sat on a chaise lounge, huddled in whispered conversation with Carole Lombard. Gable would love to eavesdrop on those two comparing notes, and so would the population of every burg larger than Tiny Town. Out of respect for her lover baby's murder, Lombard wore the front of her dress at half mast.

"Where are we?" yawned Little Jo. She threw her arms up and stretched. The sheer fabric of her halter top and sarong left no doubt she packed the right parts in the right places.

"Selznick's party."

"You took me along?" She climbed onto my shoulder and planted a peck on my cheek. "How sweet. Our first date."

"Cut the sap, Lilliput. I brought you with me because you can spy into places I can't."

"Right now, I'd like to investigate the ladies' room." She asked her sister to take her. I told Jessica to keep a close watch on the squib to make sure she didn't fall in.

Aside from me, Vivien Leigh was the only nonentity present. She looked sensational in the dress I'd sort of helped her pick out. Her countryman Larry Olivier thought so, too. He had her backed against the wall, his stiff arms trapping her on either side. Not that she minded. She swizzled her drink with her finger and placed it to his lips. After he sucked her pinkie dry, he started on her ear.

Olivier, in his three-piece navy blue suit, had the look of a dandy who beams when his personal tailor runs the tape around him and remarks that his measurements haven't varied by an inch in the past twenty years. I waved to Vivien over Olivier's shoulder. She gave me the longer half of Winnie Churchill's V for Victory gesture.

Little Jo came back to me, safe and sound. She whispered in my ear. "Let's case the dance floor."

I raised an eyebrow.

"You think that's forward?"

"I think it's ridiculous."

WHO P-P-P-PLUGGED ROGER RABBIT?

"I know. You never dance with anybody but yourself because you're the only one who's never stepped on your toes."

I hate being hoisted by a woman half the size of my petard. I took her on my hand and joined the other couples. We waltzed face to cheek.

"You know everybody here?"

She scrutinized the crowd. Her balloon hit my skin with the softness of a cotton ball. "Most of them."

"Keep an eye peeled for anybody likely to be found on a wanted poster."

"In Hollywood?" Her smile widened to the size and shape of a fingernail clipping. "Accountants in this town conduct seminars on ways to avoid paying dues on the seven deadly sins."

"You ever attend one?"

"No need to. I pay as I go."

"Run up much of a bill?"

"A dollar seventy-five last time I checked. I'm a piker compared to most."

"You date much?" I asked her, mainly to fill the dead space between quarter notes.

"Not a lot. Most of the men who invite me out are movie stars. I find them generally a notch too handsome. I prefer my men with a few imperfections."

"We'd get along great. I'm loaded with them."

"How come you're not married?" she asked.

"Never found the right woman. Anybody who'll go out with me twice."

Her eyes spoke volumes, none of it printable in a family newspaper. "You have now."

Dead actors, wounded rabbits, cheating wives, missing boxes, suddenly nothing mattered except for the very light fantastic nuzzled into the tender spot under my chin.

I had myself halfway convinced a slight difference in stature didn't matter when I caught a nose full of her perfume, a fruity aroma, not oranges or apples or grapes, but rather the exotic varietals, pitangas, cherimoyas, jaboticabas, feijoas, durians, guanabanas, and sweetsops. It conjured up a vision, but not the one of passionate nights and reckless abandon promised by ads in *Vogue.* What I saw had a more heinous aroma. Little Jo smelled like the scented balloon that had tipped Delancey Duck to Jessica and Gable's romper-room antics. With a sister like this, Jessica didn't need enemies.

The music played itself out right along with my budding infatuation.

I flipped out a smoke. She lit it for me with her tiny gold Dunhill. I nearly developed a hernia sucking in her baby flame.

I spotted Pepper Potts at the buffet table.

I shrugged my shoulder, sending Shorty sledding into my breast pocket. I joined Potts at the food.

"Pepper," I said, employing the proven premise that everybody likes to hear the sound of his name. "Pepper, Pepper, Pepper." He ignored me. Maybe the heather growing out of his ears deflected sound waves. Or maybe, two million copies of *How to Win Friends and Influence People* notwithstanding, Dale Carnegie got it wrong.

Potts used Selznick's sterling silver ice pick to hack slivers off a swan sculpted out of frozen Cherry Heering. "You're treading a mighty fine line, Valiant."

"I come from a long heritage of tightrope walkers."

"Then you know how badly a fall can mess up your vitals."

He rammed the ice pick through his trousers at kneecap level. It stuck into his wooden leg. He scooped up the ice shavings, popped them into his mouth, and crunched them like candy. "I ain't seeing a whole lot of progress from you in retrieving Davey's box."

"The going's slower than expected."

He stomped his gam. The pick popped loose and somersaulted into his outstretched hand. He poked it into the swan's eye. "I ain't a patient man." He twisted the pick. The swan's head snapped at the neck. He sucked on it like a Popsicle. "Produce, and quick, or you're liable to die trying."

"That what happened to your partner in crime? You slabbed him for being a slacker?"

With uncanny accuracy, he stuck the pick through the exact same hole in his trousers. "What partner?" He slapped two slices of pumpernickel on a plate and slathered them with horseradish.

"Tom Tom LeTuit."

"Never heard of him." He layered his sandwich with jalepeño

WHO P-P-P-PLUGGED ROGER RABBIT?

peppers, hot mustard, and chili powder. He spiced it with ground pepper and a splash of Tabasco.

"LeTuit was setting up to manufacture a concoction called Toon Tonic."

He bit into his culinary creation. "News to me." An acid stream of juice squirted through the gap in his teeth. It seared a hole in the Irish linen tablecloth, the oak buffet table, the hardwood floor, the cement basement, and three quarters of the Earth.

"Funny stuff, Toon Tonic. In the wrong hands, it could make half the world furious except for the few it made rich. It turns Toons into humans."

"You casting aspersions on my pedigree again? When you gonna learn?" In a swift, efficient motion worthy of a Marseilles assassin, he yanked the ice pick out of his leg and flipped it to the floor. It imbedded between my big toes and rocked side to side like the pendulum overhanging Poe's pit. "Don't bog your brain with where I came from, how I got here, or where I'm going. You got one goal in life, and that's finding me Davey's box. Don't muff it."

Rodan shambled by and challenged Potts to an ugly contest. Potts won in a walk.

Little Jo stuck her head out of my pocket. "Is that true about Toon Tonic?"

"Every word."

"What frightening ramifications! Toon Tonic would turn civilization topsy-turvy."

"To put it mildly."

"We wouldn't know who was whom."

"Or what was where, when, or whyfore."

Her ruby-red lips puckered to the ripe fullness of a dwarf cherry tomato. "Are you making fun of me?"

"More or less."

She crossed her arms the way nannies do when chastising wayward shavers. "You're not supposed to pick on people smaller than you are."

"Who does that leave to keep *you* honest? Jiminy Cricket?" I thumbed her back into my pocket.

Selznick loomed on the party's horizon, circulating amongst the celebs. His poise, charm, and bearing, the cuts of his jib and his tuxedo, would have landed him a starring role in any of his own drawing-room comedies.

When he spied me watching him, he took abrupt leave of Constance Bennett and threaded his way toward me through the crowd. Lewis Stone extended a hand. Selznick squeezed it quickly on his way past. When he shook with me, he didn't let go. "I'm surprised to see you here, Mr. Valiant. I wasn't aware you received an invitation."

"I dug one up."

"Might I ask where?"

"A gent named Tom Tom LeTuit lent me his."

"Really." He reinforced his shake by grabbing my elbow. A few large, loutish gentlemen with bulgy armpits moved in our direction. "Might I inquire why Mr. LeTuit chose not to come himself?"

"He got another invitation. One he couldn't refuse. He's dead as the oft-mentioned doornail, murdered by person or persons unknown."

"You're not insinuating that I'm implicated in his demise?"

"Only if you're in any way, shape, or form involved with a demon brew called Toon Tonic. Seems LeTuit underwrote the mad scientist who invented it."

Selznick tilted his head slightly. His goons veered off and went back to watching the silverware. He spirited me into his den and shut the door behind us.

The walls boasted framed posters for Selznick's movies. To make room for his next film he'd have to build an addition or move to a bigger house. He braced his outstretched arms against a fake mantelpiece installed exclusively to provide display place for his six Academy Awards. A high flush crept into his face. Light beads of sweat popped out on his forehead. "I am going to confide in you, Mr. Valiant." To cool himself, he removed a slim, leather-bound volume of Shakespearean sonnets from his bookshelf and fanned the pages. When that failed to baffle his heat, he switched to the first volume of the Encyclopedia Britannica. "A deep, dark secret I have never told to another living soul." Moist half circles appeared under his arms as his Five-Day Deodorant Pads reached the weekend. "Contrary to appearances, I am not a wealthy man."

"Next you'll tell me there's no Santy Claus."

WHO P-P-P-PLUGGED ROGER RABBIT?

Selznick slipped out of his tux jacket and hung it on a mahogany valet. "I have reached the absolute end of my monetary resources. In order to finance *Gone With the Wind,* I desperately need a large influx of cash." He stared out his leaded glass window. There was nothing to see but blackness. "A sum easily raised by bottling and selling Toon Tonic."

"You don't feel a slight twinge of guilt about peddling a potion which turns Toons into humans?"

"Of course I do." He reached into his pants pocket and extracted an antacid tablet sufficient in size to throttle ulcers in a rhinoceros. He swallowed it dry. "I consider my course of action morally reprehensible." He brushed against a windup Flash Gordon rocket ship he kept on his desk. It tipped over and laid there Earthbound, whirring, spinning its wheels, and sparking green. "I take comfort in the knowledge that the money earned from this abominable enterprise will give me the financial independence to produce my films with the utmost levels of artistic integrity." Selznick's toy rocket ship toppled to the floor. Its slim chance of ever becoming airborne vanished when its wings buckled on impact.

"What's a few murders more or less and a total upheaval of society compared to a few hours of quality entertainment?" Selznick kept a dozen cigars soaking in brandy inside a large glass bell jar. I decanted three fingers of their pickling solution into a snifter and drank in their essence. "How did you get the formula?"

"I bought it from a Toon."

"Animal, vegetable, or mineral?"

"A woman, but only in the most generous application of the term. Brusque, hard-bitten, and horribly unattractive." He touched his thumbs together, raised his index fingers, and framed me in the three-sided square. "Odd. She bore a remarkable resemblance to you."

My Heddy gets around. "What's the nature of your business with LeTuit?"

"I have none. I don't know the man. I never heard his name mentioned until this evening."

"How'd he get a slot on your invitation list?"

"Perhaps Pepper invited him. Pepper has my full and complete permission to ask whomever he chooses."

"What part does Vivien Leigh play in this production?"

Selznick mopped his face with a delicate white silk hankie. It didn't have near the absorbancy. He needed a bowling towel or maybe a beach blanket. "Vivien's involvement is of no concern to the matter at hand."

"Let me judge."

"She's a promising, attractive young actress. I'm a producer. Let that suffice."

"And I thought you were different." I stepped in close to him. His cologne smelled like a tropical drink. I punched him once, a short, hard jab to the gut. First he lost his balance, then his lunch.

"Why did you hit me?" he gasped.

"Payment in kind for the telegram your messenger boy Potts delivered."

He crawled on hands and knees into his private washroom. I grabbed him by his starched wing collar, pulled him up, and sat him on the toilet. "Pepper roughed you up?"

"On your orders, according to him." I wetted a monogrammed washcloth and placed it on his forehead.

"Ridiculous. I'm a man of pacifist principles. I would never condone the use of physical violence, not for any reason."

I opened his medicine cabinet. His stock of pills would supply a small pharmacy. The ones to wake him up outnumbered sleeping potions by a considerable margin. I handed him my standard cure for his condition: three aspirin tablets and a slug of Listerine.

For myself I prescribed an unopened bottle of his best bourbon and a hasty exit.

Me and the smidge pulled into Dyke's. I found a note thumb-tacked to our cabin door. The Gold Dust Twins had moved their headquarters to a nearby all-night Laundromat.

We found Gable alone, sitting on a slatted wooden bench piled high with lady's magazines. The one he was reading featured an article about detailing a hundred and one new ways to make meat loaf. The washer next to him alternately gurgled, wheezed, and thunked. "Where have you been?" Gable asked. "We thought you'd deserted us."

The washer spun to a halt. Gable opened it and hauled out Roger, fully clothed, dizzy as a dodo and soaking wet. Gable shook him free of residual bubbles and wrung him dry.

"Thanks, Clark, old bean," said Roger in a balloon sloshed with rinse water and civility.

"My pleasure, sport," Gable answered cordially.

They stood so close you couldn't slip a cold shoulder between them. "You two have mended fences," said Little Jo.

"You betcha," Roger proclaimed. "Turns out we go together like Laurel and Hardy, Abbott and Costello, Mutt and Jeff." He scratched his pate. "Who else?"

Gable suggested, "Caesar and Mark Antony."

"I'm forum," said Roger. "They've got Gaul."

Gable nearly choked laughing. "You send me to the moon."

"Remember to remove your space helmet before you spit," quipped the rabbit.

"What a stitch." Gable slapped his knee.

"I laugh any harder, I'll bust an adenoid," I said.

Roger extracted a harmonica from his pants, crammed it lengthways into his mouth, and blew a fanfare. Soap bubbles and notes emerged in a fifty-fifty ratio. "Lady and gentlemen," he announced, "a ditty appropriate to the occasion." He pointed his pinkie at Gable. "Pick it up where we left off."

Roger pecked on the harp like a rooster eating an ear of sweet corn. Gable sang along. "Twenty-four boxes of soap on the wall, twenty-four boxes of soap, if one of those boxes should happen to fall, twenty-three boxes of soap on the wall."

Little Jo slipped back into my pocket. I wanted to join her except that would leave nobody to wear the coat.

We returned to Cabin Six. I discovered the sunshine boys had founded their mutual admiration society on the remaining schooners of rum. I cracked into Selznick's bourbon and poured around.

"Tell me what you know about Pepper Potts," I said to Gable.

"David Selznick's right-hand goon?" Gable stretched out on the bed and balanced his glass on his slab-muscled chest. "I'd hate to be on the receiving end of *his* bad intentions."

"How is Potts involved in our caper?" asked Roger. He flopped onto his bed. He tried to imitate Gable, but his glass kept skiing off his prow-shaped sternum.

"He wants the box bad."

"What makes you think that?" Roger eliminated his booze-balancing problem by draining his tumbler and storing it upside down on the end of his nose.

"He told me so."

"Oh." Roger stuffed a whole pack of Fleers into his mouth. His first bubble contained four baseball cards.

Little Jo decided to take a bath so I filled the ceramic washbasin. Gable rummaged through his Dopp kit and produced a bar of fine English soap. He shaved off a sliver with a silver pocketknife.

The Gideon Society provided a dressing screen. Little Jo stripped off between Luke and John, then she slipped into the water. I caught her reflection in the dressing table's mirror. She had the porcelain-smooth skin of a Dresden doll. She backstroked the length of the bowl. Her suntan extended without interruption from hairline to toe tips.

I poured myself a hefty dose of reality. "Potts has committed at least two murders I know of, maybe more."

"Grounds for a citizen's arrest," proclaimed Gable.

"I'd love to. Except Potts has got a certain piece of merchandise I have to relieve him of first."

"Let's storm his bulwarks and take it by force," said Roger, buoyed by the false bravado that coats the bottom of a bottle.

WHO P-P-P-PLUGGED ROGER RABBIT?

"He has it hidden. I don't know where."

Little Jo stepped out of her makeshift tub. "Ask Potts's wife." She dried herself with the end of the Good Book's satin marker. "I suspect she'd like nothing better than to do him a bad turn."

"How come?"

With a nip and tuck, Little Jo transformed one of Gable's silk socks into a dress. It looked better on her than it did on his foot. "Potts killed her, or so she asserts."

"I thought dying put the kibosh on conversation."

"The first rule of detecting, class." She combed her hair with the serrated edge of a quarter. "Never take anything for granted. Potts's wife is a Toon. She foiled his murder attempt by refusing to expire after she died."

I decided Jo, the rabbit, and I would interrogate the dead woman. I instructed Gable to find and tail Potts.

Gable and Roger floated a raft of better ideas, but my powers of persuasion and the rest of Selznick's bourbon convinced them to do it my way.

Pepper Potts's murdered wife lived in a castle which had the ersatz regality of a honeymoon hotel catering to newlyweds with more money than taste.

Naked, pudding-thighed Cupids substituted for legs on tables and chairs, for columns on archways, for spouts on fountains, and for spigots on faucets. The chandeliers contained more crystal hearts than the souvenir stand at a cardiologists' convention. Everything that wouldn't look right painted red had been anyway.

An alcove displayed a rose quartz bust depicting a stunner of a woman. Delicate ringlets of hair and a flowing wimple framed a face that could launch the Navy's next thousand ships. "Meet Pepper Potts's wife," said Little Jo. "The Queen of Hearts."

Her royal nibs in person sat on a high-backed gold throne worthy of a king's leer.

Forget what I said about her puss luring dinghies off the dock, and cancel that hoary chestnut about death being the mother of beauty, too. The Queen of Hearts suffered from a bad case of cardiac arrest. Facially, she resembled a lump of suet discarded by a butcher. If her eyeballs sunk any lower, they'd roll out through her nostrils. As for her hair, Godzilla picked less scraggly from between his teeth. Her flat, rectangular, playing card body contained more rips, tears, creases, and bends than a noisemaker laced through the spokes of a boy's bicycle. She'd shred to tatters half-way through a game of fifty-two pickup. Her patched, papery flesh looked like Hell and smelled to Heaven.

She wore an ankle-length red robe cut to fit a shape that existed only in her memory book. Red, open-toed buskins seemed an odd choice of footwear since eight of her little piggies had shriveled to sausage. A golden, heart-shaped crown sat atop the bright red turban encasing her magpie's nest coiffure. Rouged red hearts adorned her cheeks. A lipstick heart framed her mouth.

A sign on the back wall displayed the number of shopping days left until Valentine's Day.

"Identify ourself." She spoke with the wavery whine of an unbalanced power saw.

I bowed from the waist. "Eddie Valiant, Your Highness."

"Ahhhh," cooed Queenie. "Sir Valiant. A fabled handsome stranger of story and song. Pray tell us, where have we been all of our life? Have we come to court our favors? Well, we have but to say the magical word, and we win ourself an Arabian night of a thousand and one delights." She gave the regal hip a grind that powdered her seat cushion with pulverized pasteboard.

She hadn't taken a look in a mirror lately. No man in his right mind would touch her without first donning a suit of armor. "I'm not here to toot the flute, lady. I'm private heat dogging your hubba-hubba."

She poured herself a flagon of port. In her decaying condition, I wouldn't have thought she'd have the stomach for it. The mouth or throat, either. "We beg our pardon?" With nothing but empty light sockets showing, her blank stare was as blank as blank can be.

Little Jo climbed onto my shoulder and curtsied. "If you'll permit me to translate, Your Highness. Sir Valiant regrettably declines your generous offer of a royal indulgence. In actuality, the good knight is embarked on a very important crusade. To the fulfillment of that quest, he would like to query you about your husband."

Queenie sipped her libation. A wet circle grew on her robe as the liquid leeched out of her shredded border. "We would die, if we had not already, for dear Pepper Potts. How we loved us. And how did us repay we?" She opened her robe and showed me. A paring knife penetrated slightly above the spot where other women wear their boyfriends' fraternity pins. "And we escaped scot-free by calling us a cooking accident. We insisted our hand unintentionally slipped while we sliced shallots with a dip-tipped dagger."

"Your yoke mate's whiffed two since you. Deliver me the straight skinny, and I'll make him guest of honor at Sing Sing's next Friday felon fry."

Queenie raised a deteriorated eyebrow containing more empty spaces than SOS in Morse code.

"Your husband has murdered two other people," said Little Jo in the Queen's English. "Tell Sir Valiant what he wants to know, and he will guarantee that your husband is brought to justice."

Queenie fondled her orb the way Salome caressed John the Baptist before relieving him of his upper echelon. "We would truly adore witnessing brimstone and flames arising from the pantaloons of our nefarious consort." The heart around her mouth cracked in half, giving me a peek into a black hole that would make an Indian homesick for Calcutta. "Ask what we will. We will reply forsoothfully."

She handed Roger a sheaf of pink paper, a bottle of dark red ink, and a cardinal feather. "We appoint us official court posterian. Make careful note of what we utter."

"Ay, ay, Your Royalship." Roger dipped his quill.

I started with the obvious. "Why'd your helpmate whisk you?"

Little Jo lobbed my question into Queenie's court. "Sir Valiant would like to know the reason your husband murdered you."

The screech of bone on bone hackled my back as the end of Queenie's thumb rolled around her fingertips "We committed our deed most foul for lucre." A mosquito erected its derrick on her nose, sunk a shaft, but struck no juice. It departed for warmer blooded climes. "We requested funds from our royal treasury to finance a scheme to produce a magic potion. We refused us. We be old-fashioned. We subscribe not to the theorem of 'Better living through alchemy.'"

"Is alchemy spelled with one K or two?" asked the royal scribe. "And did you say 'potion' or 'lotion'?"

"When you and Potts got hoppled . . ." I asked.

"Married," said Little Jo.

". . . what flavor was he?"

"Was your husband a human or a Toon?"

Queenie arose and paced her dais. Her footsteps clanged like a Chinese gong. No wonder it's impossible to sleep in a haunted house. "We be Toon through and through." Queenie ran her hand up and down the strand of pearls encircling her neck. It produced the sound of rattling chains. Another ghostly legend debunked. " 'Twas only quite recently we began to exhibit distressing symptoms of humanity." The flickering candlelight gave her face the waviness of a badly patched two-lane blacktop. "Whence we pointed this out to us, we possessed the abject temerity to deny the obvious." Her cold, hollow words explained why people listen to ghost stories with the lights on. "Mark this well." Roger scribbled to beat the band. "We do not argue with a queen. We do not tell the royal personage what is right and what is not. We tell us!"

"You want a translation?" said Little Jo.

"Rest your tonsils. I caught the gist. Your Highness, where would your bunkie hidey-hole a rebus about yay big?" I spread my hands the length of Selznick's Colt.

"What he wants to know," said Little Jo, "is—"

"We begin to grasp the nuances of our odd bodkin speech. There be but a singular location. Whatever we possess of grave value we hide between merkin and cod."

"Do you spell that with an E or a U?"

Little Jo stuck her head halfway up my semicircular canal. "That's—"

"I know. I'm not a total ignoramus."

"Tell me, tell me," said Roger.

I pointed to his corresponding locale.

"Oh, my gawsh!" He blushed so deeply he disappeared against the crimson wallpaper.

That goes ditto for me, in spades. My case had been breaking quicker than a set of dime-store dishes, until this dead queen dumped her husband's lap in mine.

22

Against my better judgment, we stopped at Roger's place. I told him the cops would likely have it staked. He insisted. His overalls and his underwear had shrunk in the dryer and were putting a bad squeeze on his gentility. He needed looser.

Outside his front door, Roger produced a key ring rivaling the one worn by the innkeeper at the Bastille. He went around the perimeter, flipping through the unlockers, jingle-jangling louder than Kris Kringle's sleigh on Christmas Eve.

On his third revolution, I took over the search. "I'll find it. What's it look like?"

"This." He held up a single Yale connected by a long spring to the inside of his back pocket. He grinned devilishly.

A Toon woman with a heaving chest yanked open the door. "I was clear in the back of the house." The screen door's mesh turned her winded balloon to confetti. "Do me a favor, Mr. Rabbit. Hide a key under the mat like normal folks."

"It's funnier this way," Roger explained.

"Not if you travel on my aching bunions." Her breathing imitated the desperate gasps of a blocked vacuum cleaner. She stepped aside and let us in.

Whoever built this woman drew his basic inspiration from an upended cement mixer. He topped that with a honeydew melon, pounded in a carpet-tack nose, glued on a serrated bar coaster for a mouth, and made eyes out of the thin pencil lead that drew the plans. He crowned her with a thicket of hair Daniel Boone shot on a beaver hunt. She wore a shapeless black dress with starched white collar and cuffs, a frilly white maid's cap, and a matching apron. She cased her dogs in black, sensible shoes.

"Eddie, Joellyn, meet Harriet," said Roger. "My cleaning lady."

Instead of shaking hands, she dusted my shoulder, removing

the leftover husks of the popcorn Little Jo and I shared for lunch. "Use a dandruff shampoo," she advised.

"Any visitors since I've been gone?" asked Roger.

"Not if you don't count half a dozen policemen," she wheezed.

"I don't," he said.

"Not a soul." She collapsed into an easy chair, her legs spread-eagled, building strength for her return voyage.

"I brought you a present," said Roger. He folded his arms across his chest. "Presto!" He pulled an exquisite bouquet of silk flowers out of thin air.

"Oooooh," gasped Harriet. "Thank you." She clasped the flowers to her ample breast.

Harriet levered herself out of the chair. To make room in her apron pocket for Roger's flowers, she removed the object of my desires. "By the way, Mr. Rabbit, I found this in the trouser cuff of your formal overalls, the ones with the brass buttons. Looks like a prime hunk of junk to me, but I didn't want to chuck it without asking first." She handed Roger a small box made of pitted gray pot metal, its rusty hasp secured by a heart-shaped iron padlock.

Roger gave it a cursory once-over. "You're absolutely correct. A worthless piece of trash. Toss it in the garbage pail." He flipped it back to her.

Stan Musial couldn't have snagged Roger's pop-up better than I did. I shoved the box directly under the rabbit's nose. "You've never seen this before? This gray metal *box*?"

His eyeballs marched front and center for a better look. "Abso-right-o-rootie-toot-tootly. I'm like an elephant. I never forget. I don't know what this is."

"Rummage deeper in your trunk, mammoth mind."

It still took a revolution or two for his sprockets to haul in the slack. "That's Mr. Selznick's box!"

"Bingo."

"I had it all the time and didn't know it. Those overalls, the ones with the brass buttons. I wore them the day me, Baby Herman, and Kirk Enigman went to Mr. Selznick's office. The box must have accidentally fallen off his desk top and landed in my cuff. Doesn't that beat all? Thank you, Harriet, thank you, thank you, thank you." He gave his maid a juicy smooch.

WHO P-P-P-PLUGGED ROGER RABBIT?

Harriet returned to work wearing the befuddled look of a safari guide crossing the dark continent without a flashlight.

"Let's see what's in here." I set the box on the floor.

Roger pulled out his key ring. "One of these ought to work. If not, I have two hundred more in the garage."

"Spare yourself the trouble," said Little Jo. "I can reach my fingers through the lock's keyhole and work the tumblers into place. It won't take longer than half an hour."

I pulled my pistola and blasted the lock to pieces.

"Ooooh," said Roger, "Mr. Selznick's not going to like you destroying his property."

"I'll buy him a new one, engraved, for his birthday." I sprung the hasp and opened the lid. Selznick's precious box contained a single piece of plain, blank, empty, vacant, bare, unmarked, white bond paper. I studied it front and back, right side up, upside down, edge-on. I held it to the light. Nothing.

"That's what I call a secret formula," muttered Little Jo.

"May I?" asked Roger. He took the paper, contoured it into his underarm, clasped his arm against it, and rubbed the sheet vigorously in tight circles.

"Sanding your pits?" I asked him. "You need a courser grit."

He removed the paper and held it up. It now contained fifty-five lines of chemical gobbledygook. He handed it to me with a self-satisfied smirk. "It was composed with disappearing ink. Heat and friction restore the writing. I thought every detective knew that."

"Every one does now." My knowledge of chemistry stops at mixing alcohol with water. I couldn't make heads or tails of what that paper contained.

"You go to college?" I asked Little Jo.

"I've taken a few short courses at UCLA," she said without a trace of irony.

"Can you decipher this?"

She shook her head. "Sorry, I studied creative writing and fine arts. Check with me if you want to parse a sentence or make orange out of yellow and red."

"May I see it again?" asked Roger.

What the heck. The rabbit was on a roll. I handed it over.

In less time than it took him to say "Please pass me a purple-pointed pencil," Roger hauled out his Captain Midnight Decoder, spun the dial to inorganic whoozits, ran it across the formula, and read off the results. "Add two parts of ethyl methyl U-bethyl to one part of oxie moxie Biloxi, toss in a splash of chlorofloro boro-boro, and before you know it, you've got . . ." He studied the dial. "The decoder's baffled. It's only seen one concoction remotely resembling this."

"Is that one dangerous?" asked Little Jo.

"For adolescents with complexion problems. It's the formula for Coca-Cola." He gave the paper back.

There I stood, holding in my hand the most horrendous scientific discovery since the A-bomb. If I had the slightest trace of social consciousness, I'd rip it to shreds and flush it down the commode.

Instead, I tucked it into my wallet.

The doorbell chimed. It wasn't the cops. They never bother to ring. They smash in with hatchets. Even on social calls. That's why cops have no friends. Invite a badge to your Saturday night poker game, you can't win back what it costs to replace your portal. Taking no chances, I hid Roger behind the sofa before I opened the door.

I found Gable slumped against the jamb. "You lost Potts," I said.

"No, he didn't." Pepper Potts stepped out from behind a bramble bush. He held an Army-issue .45 automatic. A massive weapon. I knew big, strong galoots who needed two mitts to fire it. Potts carried it as lightly as a water pistol. His knockwurst finger barely fit through the trigger guard.

"Sorry, Eddie," said Gable. He moved his hand away from his forehead, showing me a lump the size of a darning egg. "I wasn't the detective I thought I was."

Potts motioned Gable and me inside and followed after us. The bulge in Potts's trousers told me Selznick's Colt was stowed exactly where Potts's ex indicated it would be.

Potts spotted Selznick's open box. "My, my, my, what have we here?" He picked it up. "Congratulations, Valiant. You pulled it off. To tell you the truth, I didn't give you a snowball's chance in the Sahara." He turned the box upside down and shook it. Nothing fell out. He threw the empty box at my chest. It hit with the force of a Howie Morenz slap shot. Potts leveled the gun directly between my eyes and waggled the fingers of his free hand. "Give with the formula."

I shook my head.

He shifted the gun a fraction of an inch, maybe figuring to shoot me a piece at a time beginning with my earlobe.

A tiny round gasp swam down my tympanic canal. I remembered Little Jo perched on my shoulder. Potts had pointed his big bore at her midsection.

"The bullet's twice her size, gumshoe. There won't be enough of her left over to spread on your morning muffin."

"Don't cave in, Eddie," she said gamely. "Let him shoot me."

Carefully, so Potts could monitor every move, I extracted the formula from my wallet and handed it over.

Potts tucked it into his safety-deposit box, right next to Selznick's Dragoon.

"You have what you came for," said Gable. "Now beat it."

"Don't be naive, Clark," I told him. "He's got us slated for a recital of the Hallelujah Chorus performed by the original cast."

"He's going to kill us?" asked Gable incredulously.

I nodded. Potts did, too.

Gable's knees buckled. He collapsed into a chair. When he faced death in the movies, he always knew he'd survive and win the girl in the end. He'd never been written out completely before. He didn't know how to play the role. I hoped he was a quick study. He didn't have much time to rehearse. And he only got one take.

"Say good-night, Gracie." Potts pointed the gun between my peepers and thumbed back the hammer.

"Don't despair, Eddie," proclaimed Roger Rabbit. He jumped up from his hiding place behind the sofa. "Help is on the way." Stealing a page from Mighty Mouse's manual, he sprung off a sofa cushion, sailed through the air with the greatest of ease, and landed on Potts's head. He hung on by wrapping his skinny arm around Potts's throat. He might as well have hooked a shark on a spool of sewing thread. Potts had only to wiggle his Adam's apple to free himself of the rabbit's grip.

Potts swung the .45 around and fired point-blank at Roger. It punched a hole through the crotch in his overalls. One inch higher it would have eliminated his worries about tight underwear.

Roger slid down Potts's back. He hit the floor, contracted his body into a six-inch coil, and sprung open with full force directly into Potts's nether region. His startlingly potent impact popped the formula and Selznick's .44 out of Potts's waistband.

Roger snagged them both on the fly.

Potts shot at Roger again, adding a smoking blank polka dot to Roger's bow tie.

Clutching the formula and the gun in his paws, Roger hotfooted out the front door.

Potts went after him, traveling as fast as a man can run on one leg and a mop handle.

Score one for the amateur. Time for the old pro to step in and write the finale.

I caught Potts at the door, grabbed him by the elbow, spun him around, and cocked my arm.

Potts jellied me with his gun butt.

I woke up with a tiny angel stroking my forehead. "Heaven's a lot smaller than I imagined," I said.

"Are you all right?" asked Little Jo.

I blinked, but her balloon stayed fuzzy. It wasn't my eyesight. She shook so badly everything she said came out like scribbling on the wings of a palsied moth.

I put her in my hand and stumbled to my feet. Her shivering rattled my palm worse than a fistful of Mexican jumping beans.

"What happened after I hit the floor?"

"Pepper Potts ran out chasing Roger. Clark pulled himself together and went after them both."

I stretched out on the sofa. I put her on my chest.

She walked up my necktie and stood next to my chin. "I was so scared, Eddie. Not because he was going to kill me. But because I thought I'd never see *you* again." She stood on tiptoe and kissed me on the lips.

To my surprise, I kissed her back. I went easy on the suction for fear of swallowing her whole. Ridiculous as it sounded, I seemed to have fallen head over heels for a woman who could sleep in my mitten. Go figure love.

"What do we do next?" she asked.

WHO P-P-P-PLUGGED ROGER RABBIT?

I knew what I had in mind, but I figured she meant the case. "Not much except hope Roger can stay away from Potts."

She ran her delicate hand along my cheek. "Since we're momentarily stalled, how about we break for dinner and whatever?"

Beauty, brains, and a mind reader, too. "My place or yours?"

We settled for hers, it being closer. While she changed into something more comfortable, I went for a bottle of wine. This being a special occasion, I splurged on one without a screw cap.

I stopped at a florist and bought a bouquet. Miniature roses, naturally.

When I returned, she had changed into a black satin dressing gown that clung to her the way gum sticks to a sidewalk.

She cooked a great dinner, though the portions were a little skimpier than I prefer.

I threw a platter on her turntable.

I sat on the sofa. She lounged on my shoulder. Sinatra crooned hello to young lovers. I turned my head. We took Frankie's advice and kissed in the shadows. Her perfume made me want to club a mastodon, invent fire, or scribble stick figures on a cave wall just to impress her.

I sniffed her again. "That's a different scent from the one you had on at Selznick's."

She ran the underside of her wrist beneath her nose. "No, this is my usual."

"I'm positive you wore another."

"Oh, I remember." She snuggled into my neck, pressing her contours against my racing pulse. "That was Jessica's. I borrowed a drop in the ladies' room."

"She use a common brand?"

"Hardly. It's called Jessica's One and Only. She has it specially blended by a perfumery on Rodeo Drive. Why?"

"Only curious." About why Jessica ratted herself to Delancey Duck. "I like yours better."

"I'm glad." She stuck her tongue, and other portions of her anatomy, into my mouth. I licked off her clothes. She preserved her modesty by ducking into my waistband. Things were starting to get complicated when somebody knocked on her door.

I took a deep breath, a cold shower, and went to answer.

The stranger at her door was a squat, redheaded, albino-skinned human. His ice-blue eyes would look natural floating in the Arctic Ocean. The size of his ears put Gable's to shame. His trench coat reached to his feet, which, oddly, were bare. "Hello, Eddie," he said in a mildly grating voice.

Inside my pants leg, Little Jo unhooked my elastic sock garter and rode my argyle from calf level to the floor. She crawled out from under the ribbing.

"What's going on?" she asked

"Joellyn," said the stranger, "slip some clothes on before you catch a chill."

"Friend of yours?" I asked her.

She wrapped my pants cuff around her. It went all the way with plenty to spare. Dame fashion dictated wearing cuffs wide this year, and I'm a slave to convention. "I've never seen him before in my life," she responded.

"Are we supposed to know you?" I asked him.

He flashed me a goofy gleamer. "You bet! I'll give you ten guesses."

"Grumpy, Sneezy, Heckle, Jeckle, Tom, Jerry, Dasher, Dancer."

"Here's a hint. You're not even warm. Keep trying. You've still got two guesses left."

I unfurled my gun and hoisted it up his large nose. "I give up."

"Oh, Eddie. You're such a killjoy. If that's the way you want to be, I'll come clean!" He opened his coat, exposing a pair of red corduroy overalls. "Sur-p-p-p-prize!"

I would have staggered backwards into the next county except an end table got in the way. My pants cuff snapped out, spinning Little Jo across the floor like a top. "Roger?" I asked him.

"One and the same." He pushed one leg forward, bent over double at the waist, tucked an arm into his craw, and extended the other behind him. A Toon can pull off a bow like that without looking ridiculous. Don't try it if you're human unless your first name's Basil, Errol, Cecil, or Prince. "I bought a toy chemistry set at F.A.O. Schwarz," he said. "I had a splash of rum left from the motel. I used it to concoct a batch of Toon Tonic. It's easy. Any

WHO P-P-P-PLUGGED ROGER RABBIT?

fool can do it!'' He executed a pirouette. "Great disguise, huh, Eddie?"

"What about the formula?"

He extracted the sheet of paper from his trench-coat pocket. "Safe and sound." He handed it over. "And take this icky thing, too." Holding it by the barrel, between his fingertips, he gave me Selznick's other gun.

The now human Roger studied his hands in a mirror. He stuck his twidlers into his mouth and pulled the loose flesh sideways to its natural limit. He crossed his eyes and bracked his tongue, begetting the ugliest face this side of a mud hen with mumps. The sight nearly scared him to death. "Eddie, what's wrong with me? My best funny face isn't funny anymore. It's downright doubly disgusting."

"Maybe the mirror's set to the wrong station."

He jacked up his brows to the level of a pedant's pomposity. "What a ridiculous assertion."

"It's a joke, numb knuckles."

That rocked him harder than the recoil from a misfired blunderbuss. "A joke? Honest?"

"As I live and breathe."

"You made a joke, and I didn't get it." Roger's knees collapsed. He grabbed my arm to stay erect. "Oh, no. It can't be so! Eddie, I've lost my sense of humor."

"Buck up. Maybe it's only taking a breather. Building up strength. Like hair does when you lop it. Plenty of mugs shave their scalps in summertime to thicken their thatch for fall."

"One problem. I know of cases where it never grew back." Roger umbrellaed his laced fingers over his noggin to protect himself from the pieces of his crumbling world. "What would I do if I had to spend the rest of my life hairless?"

"There are worse things than being a cue ball."

"I don't mean baldness literally." His raspy voice rose to a pitch midway between tenor and terror. "It was a metaphor. I'm talking about my sense of humor."

"There's worse than being serious, too."

"Name one."

Before I could, the doorbell interrupted me.

Gable stood on the threshold. I hardly recognized him. He'd

combed his hair by sticking it under a ceiling fan. Dark blue stubble bandannaed his jaw. His trousers and shirt harbored more rumples than stiltskin. "You're here," he said. The whiskey in his voice could keep a booze cruise afloat for a week. Where are the flash bulbers when I need them? The *Telltale* prints one snapshot of Gable in this condition, it ushers in a national fashion trend suiting yours truly to a positive tee.

"Congrats. Your detective skills are improving."

"Not really. This was my last resort." He staggered inside with the lathered, stiff-legged gait of a war horse hobbling through the curtain stanza of the Light Brigade's farewell poem. "I already tried your place, mine, Roger's, and every gin mill in between."

Roger had already killed my mood. Gable now killed my wine. He glugged it straight out of the bottle, belching when he hit bottom. "I'm sorry, Eddie," he said. "I lost Potts again. Detective work is tougher than I supposed."

Roger stood next to him, pantomiming his moves.

Gable shoved the rabbit away by levering out his elbow. "Ease off the monkey see, monkey do routine, sport. It's not funny."

"It's not funny?" Roger opened his arms to God or whomever else lived in the apartment above. "Mercy me," he wailed. "I'm not funny!"

"Who is this idiot?" asked Gable.

"Clark Gable, meet Roger Rab— Rabs. Roger Rabs. A passing acquaintance of mine."

Roger's hands formed a U and framed his face. "We've got a common vocation, Clark. I'm in the movies, too."

Gable unpacked a cigarette from a monogrammed gold case. He tapped it on his thumbnail while he contemplated the rabbit skeptically.

"Honest Injun!" Roger tallied his most recent roles on his fingers. *"A Harey Escape; Beach Blanket Bunny; Grab It, Rabbit; Somethin's Cookin'."* He stopped at four, discombobulated by his newly sprouted fifth digit.

"I saw them." Gable put match to tobacco dogface style, his palms cupping the flame to shield the glow. "I don't remember you."

"He was in the booth," I said. "He's a projectionist. Show business, get it? Rog's idea of a joke."

"Pretty lame, sport," said Gable.

"Rog isn't known for his wit."

"I am so." Roger popped to attention and saluted. "Scout's honor. I'm a fetchingly funny fellow."

"Right, Rog." I winked at Gable. "No argument. You're a barrel of monkeyshines." I nudged him toward the kitchen. "We'd drink to it if given a beer."

He shuffled away, fanning the empty air behind him to disperse the baleful black bubbles which usually shagged him whenever he grew depressed. Another plus to being human. Henceforth when he wore his heart on his sleeve, nobody expected to see a literal translation.

"Your friend needs a month in the country." Gable whirligigged his finger next to his temple.

"Cut him a yard of slack. He's a recent arrival."

"From where?"

"State of confusion."

Little Jo came out of her bedroom wearing a head scarf, sneakers, baggy slacks, and a plaid work shirt. Add smoked goggles, a welding torch, a half-inch steel plate, and she could replace Rosie the Riveter on a battlewagon assembly line. "Hi, Clark." She crawled into my lap and curled up like a bad cat or a good book. "You look like death warmed over."

"I feel even worse." He flopped onto the sofa and stretched out.

Roger returned with a Blue Label long neck in each hand, and a third balanced precariously on his forehead. He endeavored to pry them open with his nostril. Needless to say, he failed gruesomely. Same song, second and third verses, when he tried his teeth and his inner ear.

I snatched them away before he maimed himself, and popped them the normal way.

"What happened to Roger?" asked Gable. "Did he escape from Potts with the goods?"

"A clean getaway," I told him.

"At least the day hasn't been a total washout." Gable closed his eyes.

Roger leaned over the back of the sofa. "Haven't we met before?" he asked impishly.

WHO P-P-P-PLUGGED ROGER RABBIT?

"No," mumbled Gable from two inches this side of Dreamland.

"I seem to recall us rinsing our skivvies together."

Gable's eyes snapped wide. He grabbed the rabbit by the front of his trench coat. "I'll tell you once and once only, buddy boy," he growled. "I'm straight as string."

"No, silly. At the Laundromat. Across the highway from Dyke's." Roger broke into song. "Ninety-six boxes of soap on the wall, ninety-six boxes of soap, if one of those boxes should happen to fall, ninety-five boxes of soap on the wall."

Gable gave the rabbit a closer look. "Roger?"

Roger flashed Gable a peek at his overalls and toasted him with a swallow of suds. "Hare's looking at you, Clark."

Gable pinched the rabbit's cheek. "Astounding." He tugged Roger's crop of red hair. "I've never seen a better makeup job. I'd swear you were human."

Roger flashed him the thumbs-up sign, proof positive of human genus. "You'd be right."

"What . . . How . . ." An actor lost for words. Mark the date. It'll never happen again,

"Roger glugged a potion called Toon Tonic," I explained. "It changes them into us. Also works the other way, for any fool eager to make the trip."

I explained how Pepper Potts, Kirk Enigman, Tom Tom LeTuit, and probably Roger's unscrupulous cousin Dodger had been partners in a scheme to manufacture and sell Toon Tonic. Potts won sole control of the business by ash-canning his three associates. "Potts is one dangerous snake. He'll stop at nothing to get what he wants."

"Whew," said Little Jo.

"Double whew," said Gable.

"That goes triple for me," said Roger. "Whew, whew, and whew again."

"Where is the formula now?" asked Gable.

"Tucked away." In my coat pocket alongside Selznick's Dragoon. I tried and rejected Potts's hiding place. Safe as a bank vault, great for the silhouette, but murder on the inner seam.

"My compliments, Eddie," said Gable. "You appear to have solved the case."

If you didn't count a few minor, unanswered questions. Like who muffed Baby Herman? Did Jessica really dish her own dirt to the *Toontown Telltale,* and if so, why? What happened to my brother Freddy? How does Heddy fit into this mess? And my two biggies. What's the secret of life? And, Does the light go off when you shut the icebox door?

Morning kicked a hole in the window and lobbed in a shaft of daylight. "Time for me to hit the road. I have to see a dog about a bigger dog."

"I'm coming with you," said Roger.

"Pass," said Gable. "I'm going home. I've decided I'm functionally ill suited to this line of work."

"I'll stay here, Eddie," said Little Jo. She bussed me on the earlobe. "And keep your home fires burning."

Outside Little Jo's building Roger, Gable, and I encountered a beat cop, a brick-solid, red-faced shillelagh of a man twirling a four-pound billy club the way a kid elevators a yo-yo. "You three," he barked the instant he spotted us. "Hold it right there."

He slid his billy into its sheath. His steel-cleated boots sparked on the concrete sidewalk as he walked in our direction. His gun hand rested on the mahogany butt of a long-barreled Police Special.

A half dozen ribbons for bravery underscored a name tag identifying him as Officer Meany. I hoped Roger decided to go along quietly. This wasn't a fight any man smaller than a steam shovel was likely to win.

"You who I think you are?" asked Officer Meany.

Roger hung his head and prudently extended his hands for the cuffs. "One and the same, Officer."

"Not you, nitwit. Him." He pointed at Gable. "Aren't you Clark Gable?"

Gable flashed his pearly whites. "Guilty as charged, Officer."

"My wife drags me to every one of your pictures." Officer Meany hauled out his ticket book and handed it to the star. "How's about signing an autograph to her?"

"My pleasure," said Gable. "What's her name?"

"Timothy." The cop flushed when he said it. "And don't write nothing gushy. She's a hard-nosed, two-fisted, can-do kind of broad."

"Right." Gable inscribed his name and added a small self-caricature.

"What about me?" Roger asked the cop.

"What about you?" Officer Meany tucked his ticket book into his large rear pocket.

"Don't you want my autograph?"

"Not particularly."

"But I'm— Ooooof!"

I elbowed him hard in the cowcatcher. It slowed his chugging but didn't knock him off the track.

"I'm Roger Rabbit!" He did a slipshod buck-and-wing.

The cop gave him a long, slow once-over. "And I'm Fearless Fosdick."

"Hi, Fearless." Roger pumped the cop's hand. "P-p-p-p-pleased to make your acquaintance. Jumpin' jiminy. Your jaw's rounder than I recall. You're taller, heavier, fairer, lighter haired, and younger, too. Have you been sick?"

"I'll be dipped." The cop reached under his hard brim and scratched his scalp. "That's the best take on Roger Rabbit I ever heard. How long you been working on that?"

"All my life."

"Keep it up, fellah." Officer Meany strolled away. "You nearly got it perfect."

We dropped Gable at home.

Roger and I went to my place to select the former rabbit a less conspicuous wardrobe.

He browsed my closet and emerged decked out in a suit I'd worn once, a conservatively cut, dark blue, double-breasted banker's special I bought for Heddy's wedding. Heddy steered me towards it. She wanted me to fit in with Ferd's family. Fat chance. I would have blended better wearing Dad's old clown outfit. I was the only one in attendance whose carnation didn't squirt water.

I plucked that selfsame withered flower out of Roger's button-hole and tucked it into my wallet.

When we left, Roger lugged along the leather briefcase I keep to disguise myself as a nine-to-fiver. "For carrying briefs," he told me when I asked him why. He opened it and showed me. He'd filled it with my underwear. Another axiom validated. You can take the man out of the rabbit, but not the rabbit out of the man.

We drove to Malibu Beach.

I walked to the water alone.

I bought Selznick's second Dragoon a one-way, first-class accommodation on board the biggest rock I could lift and throw.

The Mug Shot saloon offers no atmosphere, no food, no live entertainment, no dance floor, no Happy Hour, no mixed drinks, no draft beer, and no clean glasses. What keeps it in business? It's a hop, skip, and a coffee break away from the Toontown Police Station.

Even this early in the morning, the place was filled to standing room. Assuming the typical ratio, I figured two out of three for cops, though I recognized only one.

I made introductions. "Ferd Flatfoot, Roger Rabs."

Roger propped his foot on the bar's dented, tarnished brass rail and extended his hand. "Eddie tells me you're a minion of the law. Here's a riddle you might find amusing. What are old pennies made of?"

Ferd turned his back on the rabbit and signaled the barkeep. "Dirty copper!"

I'd guessed wrong when I estimated two thirds of the patrons enforced the law. A quick show of hands, those reaching for guns to blast Roger to kingdom come, indicated nearer ninety-five percent.

"What a rib tickler," said Roger. His proffered shake hung empty. Rather than waste a reach, he scooped his mitt full of peanuts and tossed them toward his mouth. He scored a perfect zero. The goobers ricocheted off his nose, his chin, and every piece of face in between. Undaunted by failure, he grabbed for more.

Ferd slid the bowl down the unvarnished, splintery pine bar. "I can't shuffle that fumpadumping woman from pillar to post much longer, Eddie. She's screaming bloody murder. Sooner or later, Bascomb's gonna hear her. Then my fat hits my friggetytooting fan."

A group of long-term residents cancelled their lease on a booth, and we moved in.

"You got 'til the end of my shift tonight. After that, all Hell and Louise Wrightliter both break loose."

Our plain-featured, stoop-shouldered, mussy-haired, flat-footed waitress worked as hard as Tillie the Toiler. You have to in a bar serving liquor to cops. We ordered two slugs apiece to spare Tillie a second trip.

"I need another extension."

"No dice, Eddie. You've collected what you're owed. Read my balloon." It displayed a parcel of words the Brits never envisioned when they invented English.

"You're forgetting about Heddy."

"Who's Heddy, Eddie?" asked Roger. "Your steady?"

"I thought we agreed," said Ferd. "You bring her into it, you sink in a wink."

"You whiff in a jif. Spin it in a minute. Sour in an hour. Crash in a flash. You're lice in a trice."

I smacked Roger hard in the ribs. "Hush."

"In a rush!"

I gave him a dime and a shove toward the jukebox.

I motioned Ferd closer. I didn't want my sorry story noised around a crowd with a sworn duty to eradicate crime. "Heddy's in bonafide Dutch involving a dastardly brew called Toon Tonic. It changes humans into Toons and vice versa. I know for certain Freddy swigged a dose. I got reason to believe Heddy did the same. To snare the formula, and the big money that comes with it, she bagged and dusted Baby Herman."

Ferd's response ascended out of him slowly, like once-burned bread rising from a twice-shy toaster. "Peeeeeeeeeee-you. I ain't biting, Eddie. Not again. That's the biggest fooping fairy tale I heard since Cinderella."

"I admit I'm lacking proof. But the facts line up like a row of dominoes with Heddy the first to topple. I want to keep her clean, but that's gonna be easier said than done. She's messed in a big, ugly way."

Roger and my ten-cent piece returned together. "What kind

of establishment stocks twenty-five different versions of the Marine Corps Hymn?" He slid into the booth.

"Heddy never leaves home." Ferd tossed back his first and second shooters and mine for good measure. Tillie would earn her tips today. "The woman cooks, cleans, tends to the kids. When's she have time for mischief?"

"Lois Lane thought the same about Clark Kent."

Ferd's cogitations resembled a basic arithmetic primer. No matter how he rearranged the numbers, two plus two kept adding up to four. "I'll stall Bascomb," said Ferd, "provided you reciprocate."

"How so?"

He pulled out a Wanted poster advertising Roger Rabbit's particulars. "Turn in the rabbit. For as much as Bulldog wants you, he wants Roger Rabbit more."

"Let me make sure I understand you right. If I hand the bunny to Bascomb, I save my beloved sister and get myself off the hook in one fell swoop?" I looked at Roger. "What do you think, *compadre*? Would you snap at a deal like that?"

Roger clutched his shot glass so hard I feared for exploding shards. "I'd have to give the matter a great deal of thought. Speculate, cogitate, meditate, ruminate, contemplate. Weigh the respective pros, the disrespective cons, the whys, the wherefores . . ."

"I'd do it in a whisker." I addressed Ferd. "You want Roger Rabbit, he's yours." I slid out of the booth. "As soon as I find the slippery cuspidor." I grabbed Roger by the arm and hustled him out.

Roger slouched in the front seat twiddling the car radio. He bypassed the chuckleheads—Baby Snooks, Groucho Marx, Lum and Abner, The Great Gildersleeve—in favor of hillbilly music about busted wranglers, jilted lovers, out-of-gas truck drivers, and similar washouts knotted together by a common thread of off-key misery.

"Relax, bunkie. I won't roll you out of the frying pan to save my own bacon."

"I know, Eddie. You're my friend, my chum, my pal, my crony, my sidekick." Roger hung the upper half of his body out of the moving car and pressed his face against the window of the bus chugging along parallel to us in the next lane. The strap hanger on the receiving end of Roger's attention responded by smacking the glass with a rolled-up newspaper. Roger hauled himself back inside. "See there? That's my problem."

"You're a world-renowned movie star, but everybody takes you for an ordinary Joe?"

"Merciful Mergatroyd, no! That's not it. Next to rhubarb, humble's my favorite pie. I can live with obscurity." We stopped at an intersection. He made a face at a kid entering the crosswalk. The kid started to bawl. The kid's mother shook her fist at us. "I've lost the ability to make people laugh."

I punched the accelerator and sped away before the angry mother took down our license number. "You're fighting a losing battle, *amigo.* Humans regard buffoonery as a social disease. If it shows up in your blood, you're not funny. You're sick."

The Oriental ruddy who functioned as Delancey Duck's butler *cum* bodyguard was big as the pressed sumo entrées you wrestle with during the main event in a Chinese restaurant. Except when you melted down this quacker, you wouldn't wind up with much fat on your skillet. He was as solid as the cement goose anchoring a middle-class front lawn.

He admitted us into a living room containing enough potted foliage to reforest the Bikini Islands. I unhinged the machete in my Swiss Army knife and hacked through to the backyard.

I found the duck in his pool. It wasn't as big as Gable's, but then neither was the Indian Ocean.

Delancey floated on a plastic inflatable created in the likeness of Esther Williams. When he saw me and Roger, he slid off her stomach and paddled towards us. I'd rank his swimming ability at the underside of a stone.

He waddled out of the water and onto the Mexican tiled apron. He wrapped himself in a Turkish towel the thickness of lawn sod.

"You need help with your backstroke," I said.

Ever see a duck sheepish? "I'm ashamed to admit," he said, "I can barely tread water."

"I thought it came natural."

"To Donald and Daffy perhaps. Not to me." Delancey slipped into a formfitting bathrobe that doubled as the cover for his outdoor gas grill. He stuck his tootsies into boat shoes that could flagship a flotilla. "Introduce me to your companion."

"Delancey Duck, Roger Rabs."

They shook.

"Ah-ah-ah-ah-chooooo!" said Roger. "Ah-ah-ah-ah-chooooo! Excuse me. I seem to be catching cold."

"Perhaps you're allergic to Toons," suggested Delancey. "The *Telltale* recently chronicled a score of humans suffering from the malady. Have you ever sneezed in the presence of a Toon before?"

"Always," said Roger. "Whenever I sneeze there's a Toon in the room."

"Mystery solved," said Delancey. "Stay away from Toons." Delancey offered us breakfast. Bowls of seed corn. Packed with the six essential vitamins and minerals required for strong webs and shiny feathers. I didn't need either. On the other hand, what was Kellogg's Corn Flakes but this once removed? I dug in.

"I'm pleased you stopped by, Mr. Valiant." Delancey's morning exercises entailed filling his cereal bowl with seconds. "My ace reporter has disappeared. I wondered if you might know her whereabouts."

"If you're referring to the lovely Miss Wrightliter, we might be talking turkey, Duck."

"Ah-ah-ah-ah-chooooo!" Roger resorted to a Toon's standard cure for the sneezies. He submerged his head in the pool.

"An extreme remedy for a human to undertake," marveled Delancey.

"When in Toontown . . ."

Delancey poured a brace of eye-openers. He kept the bigger glass. I didn't argue. He had more eye to open. "What's become of my Louise?"

I gave it to him straight, hard, fast, and bitter. Rum running, Wrightliter's arrest, Toon Tonic, Freddy, Enigman's murder, Le-Tuit's murder, Dodger's murder, Herman's murder, Potts, Selznick, the whole ugly shebang except for Jessica and Gable, Roger's disguise, and Heddy.

He crossed his spindly legs and oscillated his foot, provoking a breeze that rustled my tie. "Can you prove any of this?"

"Not so's you'd notice."

"What, then, do you expect me to do with the information?"

"Print it anyway." I noticed Roger had stopped bubbling. I grabbed him by the belt, hauled him out of the water, and laid him faceup. His skin had a bluish cast, and his breath wheezed out in fits and starts. At least he wasn't sneezing. I slapped his eyes open and bequeathed him what remained of my drink.

"You can't be serious, Mr. Valiant." Delancey patted his long expanse of bill dry with his linen napkin. By the time he went up the left side, across the front, and down the right, I was ready for lunch. "You actually want me to run an unverified story implicating several of Hollywood's most powerful men in a quadruple murder? You're asking me to bring a rainstorm down on my head."

"I heard that was lovely weather for ducks."

Roger and Delancey both got a cackle out of that, or rather the buck got a yuck and the duck got a cluck. Me, I wished the ASPCA had a branch to protect us from them.

"I'll consider it." Delancey leaned over in his chair and brought his head to mine, giving me the sensation of putting on an Indian headdress backwards. "I find you extremely interesting, Mr. Valiant. We must meet socially some time."

"You bet. How about Christmas? I always have a duck for dinner."

"I'll come hungry," he said with a smile.

"You'll leave stuffed."

Judging from the moon-sized craters of dirt, a neighborhood mongrel had paid a visit to Heddy's front lawn. If a fraction of his buried bones took root, Heddy would raise sufficient beef to throw her own stampede.

"Hi-de-ho-ho-ho. Twice in one week," she said in answer to my knock. "You must be miles up the proverbial creek."

"Without the mythical paddle."

She swung the door open wide. "Come in and tell Sis all about it." If your nighttime reveries involve grocery store delivery vans, Heddy stepped out of your dream. She'd fabricated her housedress from a hundred-pound flour sack. She wore a duplicate of the red head scarf that adorned Aunt Jemima. Her white cotton apron came to her for ten cents and the box top from a package of Betty Crocker cake mix. "You're just in time for mid-morning tea." She'd invited my two oldest and dearest friends, Jack Daniels and Jim Beam.

"Let's go for a walk, instead."

"I'd love to, Eddie." My three nephews galloped through the room in a two-against-one game of cowboys and Indians. To improve his odds, Cochise had pried the rubber suction cups off his

WHO P-P-P-PLUGGED ROGER RABBIT?

arrows. He let fly a badly aimed darter that penetrated six inches into the ceiling. "I can't leave the boys alone."

"Meet my buddy Roger Rabs." I pushed Roger front and center. "He'll baby-sit the little darlings."

"I don't know. Does he have experience?"

"Four years of combat infantry."

The boys ran through in the other direction. The game had switched to aerial dogfight. The Lafayette Escadrille chased the Red Baron with a whirling electric fan.

"He's hired," said Heddy.

She corralled her sprouts. "Boys, this is your new baby-sitter, Roger. You behave for him, or it's off to the science lab with the lot of you."

We left the three-member Sioux Nation attempting to scalp General George Armstrong Custer with the Red Baron's propeller.

Heddy set our pace, a quickstep at mazurka tempo. Since we weren't hurrying to reach anyplace, I assumed she was anxious to leave where she'd been.

Once we lost sight of her house, she slowed to waltz speed, laced her arm through mine, and patted my wrist. "Tell me what's wrong, big brother."

"I brought you a present." I went into my wallet and sprung my dried carnation. "It's from your wedding."

"I'm touched." She pressed it to her breast, right over the red Pillsbury trademark. "Thoughtfulness is so unlike you. Why the sudden attack of solicitude?"

I heaved a rock at a rectilinear Toon Crossing sign. I missed by a mile. The sign showed its contempt for my pitching by crossing its O's and sticking out its double S. "I've got to ask you a few questions, Heddy. I don't want to, but it's required."

"You think I won't answer unless you're extra specially nice to me?" She removed her scarf and wrapped the carnation inside for safekeeping. "Hi-de-ho-ho-ho." She tucked the flower into her apron pocket.

"No, I think you'll tell me the truth. I'm afraid of what might happen between us when I hear what you're likely to say."

"In that case, fire away. I can't wait to hear my answers myself."

We sidestepped a Toon beer wagon whoozy from sampling its own wares. "How are you and Ferd doing in the financial department?"

"First cousins to a baker. We have all the dough we knead."

"I'm dead serious, Heddy."

She opened her tattered straw handbag, held it upside down, and shook it. A used Kleenex fell out. "My husband earns one third less than a human doing the same job. At best, we scrape by."

Clarence Centipede, a Toon of my passing acquaintance, undulated down the opposite sidewalk. To avoid him, I skidded down an embankment into a dry creek. He's a one-man receiving line. Say hello and spend the rest of the day shaking hands.

Heddy kicked off her shoes and joined me. She shut her eyes and wiggled her toes. "Isn't this pleasant?" she said. "Shut your eyes. You can almost feel the cool, clear water that ran through here in prehistoric times."

Mine caressed the rusty edges of a skeleton left over from the days when Model A's roamed the Earth. "Heddy, I know about you and Baby Herman."

She picked up a discarded coffeepot, sniffed the inside, turned the pot over, and checked the bottom for holes. "From what I read in the *Tattletale,* he's danced the baby buggy boogie with every woman in town." She threw the pot on the bank. "My bad luck. I was out shopping the day he worked his way through our neighborhood. I found his 'Sorry I missed you' note in the mail slot." She took a practice swing with a broken baseball bat. "I don't have the slightest idea what you're talking about."

"I know you hustled Baby Herman in a bar. I know you kidnapped him. What's worse, I know you've been moonlighting as a Toon."

"Hi-de-ho-ho-ho. Pull my other leg, Eddie. It plays Jingle Bells."

"Deny it until you're green in the gills, Sis. I know what I know."

"Which isn't much." She slipped on her shoes, retrieved her coffeepot, and ran towards home. I galloped after her.

A Toon and a human ambled toward us. The Toon was a big mouse, five seven, a hundred thirty pounds, Ping-Pong paddle ears, and furry face. He had "Mick" stitched on the bill of his cap. The human matched him at five seven, a bit lighter at a hundred twenty, with an equally furry face. His hat called him Steve. Both wore yellow orthopedic shoes. Heddy approached them head down like a cannonball converging with a bull's-eye. They parted to let her through.

I caught up to her, grabbed her from the rear, and spun her around. "Sis, I'm on your side. When the tango hits the fandango, I'll dance to whatever music you play. But you've got to level with me now."

"I'll level with you, Eddie. You bet. I'll level with you good." She poked my chest with her pot handle. "You're my favorite brother. I love you come rain or shine, Hell or high water, better or worse. But I'm starting to think Ferd might be right when he says you're a few spots short of a Dalmatian."

"You telling me you're not a Toon?"

"That's the looniest statement I've ever heard you utter. Even if such a thing was possible, why would I do it? Hi-de-ho-ho-ho. Why would *anybody* in their right mind want to be a Toon?"

My question exactly.

Roger stared morosely out the car window.

"Don't blame yourself, Rog. Boys will be boys. At least you smothered the fire shy of permanent damage."

He uncorked his baby-sitting wages and took a healthy slug. "I'm not disturbed by a few childish pranks. My abject melancholy stems from deeper causes. After spending an afternoon with those three delightful tots, I realize what's missing in my life." He cradled the bottle in his arms and crooned it a lullaby. "I want to be a daddy."

Did Jessica have a surprise for him! "How does the ball and chain feel about that?"

"I don't know. We haven't discussed it. I suspect she won't be terribly enthusiastic. Jessica's currently slated for a number of prominent starring roles. A pregnancy anytime in the near future would seriously stall her career. A woman of Jessica's stature can't risk sags, professional or physical."

I never drink and drive. I pulled over to the curb and idled before starting work on tomorrow morning's hangover. "It's time you and the mate talked it over."

Roger took his bottle back. "You are absolutely correct." His glugs produced no reflexive cartwheels, skyrocketing, cranial steaming, or bouncing off the walls. Liquor now affected him the subtler, human way, luring him into voluntary harm. "Let's visit Jessica, and I'll do it right now."

"Not so fast, bub." I eased into traffic. "Don't forget. You're still a wanted rabbit. You've got to stay in hiding. Plan your family after we clear your name."

"It's not the matter of children. There's another reason." He plucked a length of thread from a fray on the seat between us. "I'm handsome, wouldn't you say?"

"If you stretch the imagination." From here to Cleveland.

"Jessica won't recognize me in a week of Wednesdays, a month of Sundays, a year of Mondays, a decade of day after Thursdays." He wound the thread around his fingertip so tightly it cut off circulation. "I want to give her a tumble and see if she tumbles back."

I broke my own ground rule and had a toot on the move. If I stopped for nerve tonic every time Roger dropped a bombshell, I'd roll the road forever. "If Jessica fails your test, there's no makeup exam. School's out forever."

"I'm fully prepared to accept the consequences of my actions. Eddie, once and for all, I have to know the truth."

L.A. architects practice visual onomatopoeia, designing buildings to resemble the products sold inside. Angelenos dine in hot dogs, cheese burritos, and giant milk shakes. We push paperwork in Brillo pads, RCA radios, and flatirons. We dance to, and in, a huge drum called Jungle Rhythms.

"Tarzan sent us," I told the gorilla behind the cymbalic door.

"He should have sent you someplace else." The gorilla curled his upper lip over his nose. "Your kind's unwelcome here." He banged the door.

"What does he mean?" asked Roger. "I've been here countless times."

"You were of a different persuasion."

Roger flicked his eyelids, like a switch-hitter clearing his vision after being bopped by a beanball. "Let me make certain I understand how this works." He tick-tocked his index finger between us. "I can't go in your establishments when I'm me. I can't go in my establishments when I'm you."

"That's the gist of it. Next time I stop by the Auto Club, I'll pick up a guidebook so you can keep track of where you can enter when."

"I already have one, Eddie. It's called the Golden Rule."

I knocked on the door again. In exchange for a few bananas, which he stuffed in his mouth for safekeeping, Cheeta let us in despite our heritage.

The gorilla was right. We didn't belong. I counted on two hands the patrons who walked on two legs. As we made our way to the watering hole, rhinos, lions, hyenas, leopards, and wildebeests made me feel like the first clay pigeon of spring.

While the resident taxidermist worked up an estimate for skinning us out and nailing us to a wall, the elephant bartender squirted me a healthy snootful of gin. It reeked of peanuts, but I kept it anyway. Better that than gamble on what might dribble out of his only other spigot.

The self-drumming conga, snare, bongo, bass, timpani, kettle, tymbal, and naker orchestra launched into a ditty short on melody, long on beat. A herd of beasts charged the dance floor and launched into a cheek-to-cheek four-step laden with plenty of tusk-tusk.

Jungle Rhythms poured short on whiskey, long on atmosphere. The juiceware started life in the upper branches of a coconut tree. The grass tablecloths made the room look like an assembly of kneeling hula dancers. I angled my thatched palm chair toward the entrance. Roger sat facing a wall mural called "The Mutiny on Noah's Ark." "I am positively outraged by the bestial way these Toons glare at us," he said. "Why did we have to meet Jessica here?"

"No particular reason." Except Jessica specified it. She said she felt like dancing. In a recent MGM musical, I watched her perform a solo tap-stepping routine that Gene Kelly couldn't have duplicated wearing steel-soled shoes on a soapy floor. Maybe she intended to hoof it without a companion tonight. Maybe I'd change my name to Yul, and ascend to the throne of Siam.

Jessica entered wearing sufficient diamonds to etch her name on a five-foot-eight, hundred-and-twenty-five-pound hourglass. Her slinky green dress fit her closer than the tanning butter I slathered her with on the beach. It had lust written all over it, literally, in sequins. She peeled down one of her long green gloves the way a sea serpent sheds its skin before hopping into an oyster's bed.

I waved to attract her attention, standing so she'd see me over the heap of animals falling on top of one another for a glimpse of her.

Gorgeous women turn heads. Jessica spun them in circles until they snapped off. Swiveling her way across the club she left behind more loose noggins than the French Revolution.

"Good evening, Mr. Valiant," she said in a balloon smooth as a satin pillow. "I've been hoping you'd call." I held her chair. In the process of plunking her posterior on the palmetto she rubbed me with more body parts than other women own. "I've been in great need of male companionship lately." Her balloon wrapped its dangling stalk around my middle and refused to let go.

A snake waiter slithered to our table. "The ussssssssual?" he hissed.

Jessica nodded. "Plus a late supper. You know what I like." She toted her vitals inside the front of her dress. She reached down and pulled one out, a slender ruby-red cigarette. She inserted it between her lips, making that straight, hard cylinder the envy of every male in the joint.

Roger materialized a wooden match. He ignited it with his thumbnail and extended it to his wife. "You come here often?" His hand trembled like a wedding night virgin.

"Only for evening rendezvous with handsome strangers." She steadied Roger's shaking member while she sucked in his heat.

"Lets me out," I said.

"But not your attractive friend." Jessica pursed her Cupid's bow lips and blew on Roger's torch. "Introduce us, Mr. Valiant."

"Jessica Rabbit, Roger Rabs."

The snake crawled up with a plate of chocolate-covered cherries balanced on his head.

WHO P-P-P-PLUGGED ROGER RABBIT?

"Mr. Rabs," said Jessica. She mounted his hand and pumped it. "I'm pleased to meet you."

Roger bowed, a maneuver ill advised while sitting down. "I'm equally delighted, Miss Rabbit."

She stroked his gash, the one he acquired when he smacked his forehead on the table. "*Mrs.* Rabbit." She exposed her naked truth. "I'm a married woman.

Roger's throat throbbed. Judging from the largeness of his bulge, becoming human hadn't diminished the size of his larynx a whit. "What a shame."

Jessica laid her essentials out on the table for all to see. "Only on occasions when I meet an attractive man."

The snake returned balancing a bucket of champagne on ice. He was flanked by two armed guards. He gave me the bill before the bottle. I don't know if Jessica came easy, for sure she didn't come cheap. I authorized Mr. Wiggler to pull her popper.

Roger reached under the table, tore off a piece of grass, and used it to wipe his brow. "Does your veiled intimation of unhappiness at being a married woman mean you would venture on a date with me?" He indicted himself with his sweaty clump of grass.

Jessica ran her hand along his sodden stalk and relieved it of seed. "I love men with big vocabularies."

Roger went limp. "How about . . . *your husband?*" he ejaculated.

She leaned forward, giving Roger a close-up view of her round and firm tête-à-têtes. "What he doesn't know . . ." She climaxed with "won't hurt him."

Roger toppled over backwards onto the dance floor. A foot farther left, and he'd have been rumbaed over by a rhino. He stood up and faced his missus. "I beg to differ." A single impotent teardrop dribbled from his eye. "It would hurt him immeasurably." He turned and ran out the door.

"An odd man, your friend." Jessica filled my coconut with bubbly.

"He's adjusting to a difficult change."

"Change of the proper nature can be quite pleasurable if inserted directly into the animus." In terms of fizz, her balloon outspumed the fluid in my nutshell.

"I wouldn't know, toots. I flunked the four main ologies: psych, bi, phisi, and the."

Her wavy hair fell across one half of her face, turning her eye into a peep show. "That lets out conversation." She tongued a bit of spume off her quivering upper lip. "We'll have to find another means of stimulation."

"How about a parlor game, twenty questions. I'll start. Why did you tip the *Telltale* to you and Gable?"

She fumbled into her bosom for another cigarette, exposing a part of herself that few rarely see, her reddening fluster.

"Who fathered the Tiny Toon you're incubating? How's a pregnancy going to affect your chances to play Scarlet O'Hara? What were you and Carole Lombard huddling about at Selznick's place? Oh, yeah. Lest I forget. Does the light go out when you shut your icebox door?"

She French-kissed her cigarette. "We'll have to play a less taxing game, Mr. Valiant. I find this one far too difficult to follow." She invited me to light her fire.

A tough choice. Stay and swill expensive champagne with the world's most beautiful woman, or chase after a dumb bunny who had just learned what puts the "mort" in "mortal."

Call me concerned, call me caring, call me stupid. To settle the bill, I spiked half the contents of my wallet onto the waiter's fang. He flicked his tongue for more. By the time I finished, the evening cost me every cent in my pocket, and I didn't even pop my own cork.

As I left, Jessica put her hand, the one that should have been wearing a plain gold wedding band but wasn't, on my forearm. "What about my husband, Mr. Valiant? That's the reason I came. You said on the phone you had news of him."

"Indeed I do." I shook her loose. "The news is that he's too darn good for you, lady."

I tracked Roger to the Crying Towel, a cut-rate gin joint catering to weeping Willies.

The Yellow Pages includes a separate listing for places like this—dark, dank, dives where men drown their troubles with women. They're found under the heading of "Grief Relief" and run on for more pages than I ever cared to count. I've patronized plenty, in the company of others inflicted and on occasions when I've caught the malady myself. I've yet to set foot in one that wasn't jammed, winter or summer, day or night. Sob sisters say a good man is hard to find in this town. Bull. There's an overabundance if they know where to look.

Roger sat alone at a back booth drinking out of a snifter so large chipmunks could use it to bob for olives. "I'm surprised to see you here," he said. He hoisted his empty at the waitress. As if he needed a refill. He already had more sheets in the wind than a three-masted schooner. "I assumed you would stay with Jessica." The waitress dragged over a garden hose and topped him off with the house specialty, a Southern Suffering Sympathy, a potent mixture of embalming fluid and essence of Everglades. He tossed it back like swamp water over the dam. "I thought you two would be drinking and dancing the night away."

"Why waste time with her when I can hang out in a swell place like this with my best buddy?"

Roger signaled the waitress again. "That's most likely an unmitigated lie, but I appreciate the sentiment." The waitress poured him another hit. Roger had turned into such a steady customer, she left the hose with instructions to yank it when he wanted her to turn the spigot. Roger held his glass to the light. A baby alligator paddled around inside. "Eddie, I think we ought to swear off."

"Booze?"

He swallowed his medicine, reptile and all. "Women."

"I second that motion. All in favor, bottoms up." I ordered the Crying Towel's unique bottomless bottle of bourbon.

Roger scooted his empty glass aside and stuck the tarnished brass nozzle directly in his mouth. He yanked the hose, but the waitress refused to play. He stuck the nozzle into his glass and yanked again. This time it worked as advertised. "Did Jessica talk about me after I left?"

"You mean you the way you are now, or you the way you were before?"

"Either one."

"Nope."

"Oh." He uncased his harmonica and climbed onto the table. That spelled trouble. Unlucky-in-lovers came here to cry in their beer, not laugh up their sleeves. They weren't going to take kindly to a guy blowing comedy harp.

I needn't have worried. Roger wailed it straight, soulful, lowdown, and mean. When he finished his lick, the only rummies who weren't in tears were the ones in comas.

"I didn't know you played that well," I told him when he came down off the Formica.

"I never could before tonight." Roger signaled the waitress to resume his flow of rotgut.

"What made the difference?"

"A substantial infusion of cyaneous, cerulean, amethystine, and Prussian."

"I don't follow."

"Those, Eddie, if you'll pardon the pun, are the major blues."

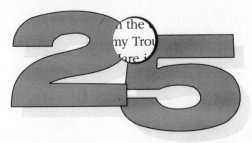

I rousted Roger off my couch. "Rise and shine, tiger."

He rose fine, but his shine fell a pallid pale short of luster. "I feel p-p-p-positively p-p-p-putrid." He had opted for my typical bedtime attire, whatever I happened to be wearing when I passed out. "My head's exploding." He yanked his earlobes. "Oooooh, that only makes it worse."

"Naturally, rum dum. What did you expect?"

He gave his danglers another tug with equally painful results. "Pulling my ears normally activates a factory steam whistle that releases the pressure caused by overimbibing."

"You're in a different union, chum." I handed him an ice bag. "Here's how humans signal a hangover that it's quitting time."

He squished the bag and heard water sloshing inside. He unscrewed the metal cap and tilted the bag to his mouth.

I felt like a foster father to a man from Mars. I relieved him of the bag, resealed it, and laid it across his cheekbones. "Leave it there until the pain goes away or your brain freezes solid, which- ever comes first." Since the bag covered his eyes, I guide-dogged him to my kitchen table. "Sit down. I cooked us breakfast."

Roger peeked out from under the red rubber cooler and stared at the T-bone I forked unto his plate. He crinkled his nose. "I can't eat that!"

"Try it first. I might not be a gourmet chef, but I know how to fry a steak."

He scooted the plate away with his fingertip. "I'm a strict vegetarian."

"No stomach for meat?"

"No teeth."

With my untucked shirttail, I polished the shiny bottom of a steel pot, and held it to his face. "Check what's protruding from your gums, horse. Courtesy of Toon Tonic you now come equipped with a full set of Grade-A choppers. Put them to the use for which they were intended."

Roger ran his tongue across his newly sprouted incisors. "I don't know."

I sliced a tiny hunk of well done, stuck it on a fork, and airplaned it toward his mouth.

"One bite," I said.

He opened wide.

We climbed the stairs to my office.

"Mere words cannot describe the experience." That didn't stop Roger from trying. "Savory, delicious, scrumptious, tasty, mouth-watering." He rubbed his hands together like Ebenezer Scrooge gleefully contemplating a visit to the vault. "I can't wait to try pork chops, quail, rump roast, beef brisket, pheasant, ham hocks, pickled pigs feet, venison, partridge, mutton, Spam, SOS."

I opened my office door.

"Hi yah, Valiant," growled Pepper Potts. "How are the old bells clanging?" Curlicued wood chips sprinkled the floor around his chair. My best piece of furniture, a polished oak desk lamp, rested on his lap. He'd removed the shade, the bulb, and the metal fittings, but not the cord. He had whittled the lamp into a new leg.

He was dressed for the links in a five-button tweed jacket, knickers, and snow-white golfing cap. The six iron he pointed at my stomach came endorsed by two scratch shooters named Smith and Wesson.

Roger grabbed me around the middle. He shook more than a chorus line of Saint Vitus's dancers. "Oh my gosh, Eddie. It's Bepper Botts." At least the cottontail was smart enough to realize that a stutter here pickled him in a peck of problems.

"I'll pass up the blindfold but not the cigarette," I told Potts. I extracted a Lucky.

"Pshaw, Eddie." Potts sighted his gun at me and pulled the trigger. A flame sprouted from the ejection chamber. I leaned forward and let him light my smoke. "You didn't think I was serious about snuffing you out? The joke's on you. I was merely spoofing."

WHO P-P-P-PLUGGED ROGER RABBIT?

"You got quite the bizarre sense of humor, Pottsie. Remind me to avoid you like poison ivy on April Fool's Day. I might die laughing."

"You're a hot ticket, Valiant. Be careful you don't burn out early." Potts waved his flaming lighter across the arm of my easy chair. My nostrils filled with the noxious odor of scorched nylon frisé.

"My interior decorator's going to be miffed with you, Pepper. She spent months searching for a chair with the proper degree of tawdry elegance, and you ruin it."

"Let's cut the crape." Potts flicked my desk lamp's light bulb at my head. It zipped past with velocity sufficient to draw applause from a V-2 rocket and popped against the wall. "Where's the rabbit?"

I moved to Potts's right, hoping to split his attention by putting me on one side of him, Roger on the other. The rabbit missed my message. He stuck to me like graft to a politician. "I haven't seen Roger since he disappeared into the sunset with you hot on his trail."

Potts tied his new hardwood leg in place by knotting the electrical cord around his stump. "When the rabbit turns up, give him a message for me." He stood, shifting his entire weight to his dowel. A floor-shaking test hop won him a loud Gypsy curse from the fortune-teller renting the office below. "Tell Roger I want to work out a trade for the formula."

Roger stuck his head over my shoulder. "You don't possess a single article Roger Rabbit could possibly want."

Potts surplused his old pivot into my wastebasket. The cup end, shaped like a giant golf tee, protruded eight inches over the trash can's lip. "Who's your loudmouthed friend, shamus?"

"My apprentice. I'm teaching him the business."

"Giving him the business more likely." Potts reached behind the easy chair. "I got plenty the rabbit wants. An item he'd die for. An item that might wind up dying for him if he don't play my game." He produced a plain brown paper grocery bag. "Here's my trade bait, Valiant." He reached into the bag. "Pass it along to the rabbit when you run into him." He tossed me the dress Jessica wore last night.

Roger nipped it out of my hands. "You've kidnapped Jessica!" He buried his face in the bodice. "You vile, heartless, degenerate, debased, ignoble, depraved fiend!"

"We've met before." Potts lifted Jessica's hem with the blade of his whittling knife. "Nothing more fun than peeling a tomato except maybe slicing one for salad."

Roger removed his puss from the fabric. Jessica's sequins had left their imprint, lust in reverse, on his forehead. "You would actually murder her?"

"What murder? Nobody said nothing about murder. I'm talking about making a vegetable salad, period. What you read into it's your problem." He stuck his mitt back into the bag. "I figured the rabbit's one and only might get lonely, so I snatched a chatterbox to keep her company." He showed me Little Jo's work shirt. Every button had been ripped off. The garment barely covered his palm. "Regular dolls, those sisters. Trouble with dolls is they break easy. Their arms crack. Their legs twist off. A risky life being a doll, especially one with an uncooperative owner." He arranged Little Jo's sleeves so they folded corpse style across the breast.

Roger grabbed for him, his arms extending outward on either side of my body.

Potts drew another gun. "Relax, friend. This one sparks more than flint." He edged around us. "The dames are safe and sound. They'll stay that way if the rabbit hands over the formula. Otherwise . . . well, I'm a volatile person." He smacked his gun against my bogus diploma. The glass shattered. "When I don't get what I want, I can't be held responsible for my own actions."

"You hurt either one of them," shouted Roger, "and I'll hurt you a hundred times worse."

"I'm quaking in my boot." Potts backed out and slammed the door behind him. The frosted panel shattered. Between that, the light bulb, and the picture frame, I'd never again be able to skip through my office barefoot.

Roger grabbed my lapels. "Give him what he wants, Eddie. I'll expire from grief if anything happens to my darling, beloved, sweet patootie."

I poured us a pair of bracers. "We talking about the woman you swore off once and forever last night?"

He bumped back his nip and splashed himself another.

"Eddie, she's my wife. When we married, I took a vow to love, honor, and obey. Through thick and thin, better and worse, rich and poor, sickness and health, tall and short, fatness and lean. I can't renounce my word over a minor peccadillo."

Myself, I'd consider Gable's cake in Jessica's oven to be the frosting on a recipe for divorce, but I wasn't the one cooking up the half-baked notions of what constituted marital fidelity.

Officer Bunk Thunker stuck his broad-beam shoulders through my shattered office door. "You want to improve your ventilation Valiant, try a fan. It's a lot less messy." Thunker came in, purposely choosing a path that let him crunch maximum glass into my parquet.

For a plainclothes cop, Thunker was far from plainly clothed. He wore a garish, Hawaiian print, short-sleeved sport shirt pulled out over baggy plaid pants. His tie was wide enough to use for a tablecloth if you didn't mind eating off a hand-painted water spaniel.

What I took for a black fedora turned out to be a thundercloud. "Bulldog wants you." He squeezed his fist, causing the dragon tattooed on his forearm to roll over and play dead.

Nobody ever won an argument with Thunker. I wasn't about to buck the odds. I told Roger to hold down my fort.

Thunker shoved me unceremoniously into Bascomb's office.

Rows of thumbtacked red streamers hung down the wall. They were blood lines, what Toons leave behind when they leak. Each came from a public enemy Bascomb had plugged on the run.

"Here, Valiant," said Bascomb. "Don't say I never gave you nothing." He split his mid-morning snack, a prune Danish, down the center and scooted half across his desk.

I bit into it. Stale as the joke about firemen wearing red suspenders. "You buy this last year and let it age? That's for wine, not crullers."

"You got complaints, take them up with the donut shop. You ought to know first that Big Mo, the pug who owns it, moonlights twisting arms for Lone Loan Shark." A morsel of prune fell onto Bascomb's desk. He licked it off without bending over. The darting motion cracked his tongue like a bullwhip.

"So much for friendly chitchat, Sarge. Let's pound brass tacks. To what do I owe the displeasure of my visit?"

Bascomb employed a miniature guillotine to lop the chaff off a rolled bundle of stinkweed pretending to be a cigar. "I'm hearing scuttlebutt, Valiant. In these selfsame hallowed halls." His lighter produced sufficient heat to fry an innocent man. "Rumors are circulating that there's pictures of Kirk Enigman's parting words." He rested his stogie in an ashtray formed from the hammered end of a spent howitzer shell. "You know what I'm thinking I'll see when I finally corral that film and give it a view?" He pointed a claw at the precise spot where my breath was caught in my chest. "I'll see a balloon implicating your rabbit pal."

I exhaled a quantity of air equal to the cubic volume of the Hindenburg. "What makes you sure?"

"Previous history." Bascomb unzipped a scarred leather vanity case and extracted a steel fingernail file. "As I recollect, Roger's the rabbit who was chief suspect in the murder of that studio exec a while back." He stuck his file into his mouth and whipsawed it back and forth across the sides of his teeth.

"I cleared him of that. You can't hold it against him."

"Oh, but I can, and I do. I'm the law in Toontown, Valiant. I'm not constrained by the normal legal niceties." He tested the sharpness of his snappers by biting into a tablet of lined paper. He left a double semicircle of holes the size of carpet tacks. "In my book, a rabbit's guilty until proven innocent."

"That the official police motto these days? I always thought it was 'We're here to serve you.' Or do I have you cops confused with the busboys' union again?"

"Clever banter don't become you, Valiant." He picked a piece of gristle out of his mouth. I'm assuming it came from a butcher shop and not his upper jaw. "If you're hiding the rabbit, you're an accessory to murder." Bascomb blew a smoke ring in the shape of a noose. It settled around my shoulders. "That's the way the D.A. will lay it out. And you know what a terror he can be."

Indeed I did. In his office, the D.A. kept a box containing the skeletons in my family closet. He had enough bones in it to build his own dinosaur, and would the instant a cage opened up at the zoo.

"If I was you, Valiant, I'd stop off at Schwab's and buy a tube

WHO P-P-P-PLUGGED ROGER RABBIT?

of Chapstick. After I find the rabbit, you'll need it to keep your lips from cracking when you kiss your sweet license good-bye."

"You're barking down the wrong warren, Bascomb. The rabbit's pure as snow."

"Toss me one other name had a reason to bump Enigman and Herman, both."

I did more than that. I tossed him the morning edition of the *Toontown Telltale*.

"You win, Pottsie," I told him over the phone. "The rabbit capitulates. The formula swapped even Steven for the women."

His voice dripped with smugness. "That's real smart of him. You instruct the rabbit to bring the goods to the end of Lonesome Canyon Road in an hour. If the formula checks out, I'll contact him tomorrow and tell him where to find the broads."

I clanged the mouthpiece on the edge of the phone booth.

"Hey! You want to give me an earache?"

"I'm only making sure I've got your undivided attention. Listen close, Pottsie. I'm rewriting your scenario. Here's how it plays out. I make the delivery, not the rabbit. It happens in a public place. When you get the formula, I get the girls. On the spot, immediately, no waiting. Those are my terms, and they're not negotiable. You want the formula, or not?"

He wanted it, and bad.

The Museum of Visible Locution was a tiddlywink of a building, as flat and white as the art it displayed.

The museum's gift shop prominently featured *The Word on Words,* Ring Wordhollow's latest scholarly tome cogitating on the semantic and aesthetic aspects of Toon balloons. The shop also peddled actual-sized reproductions of utterances from the museum collection, though I can't imagine why anybody would pay for a balloon jigsawn out of painted plywood when you could strangle the real McCoy out of a Toon for free.

The main exhibition hall boasted a major extravaganza, a hanging of Toon balloons from what the museum catalog grandly titled "The Neo-Comical Era." It proved my own personal rule of thumb—beware the pretensions of any art form with more than three syllables in its description. The turning lane of this cultural crossroads consisted of *duh*, *grunt*, *ugh*, *booga booga*, and that giant linguistic leap forward *kowabunga*.

The sparse batch of culture vultures viewing the exhibit included a fidgety and bored grade-school class on a field trip and a half dozen bereted and bespectacled art students copying the balloons line for line, syllable for syllable, onto large sketch pads.

I entered a small auxiliary salon housing turn-of-the-century Western word work, *yippies*, *giddyups*, *woopie ti yi yos*, and their ilk. These priceless creations were being watched over by a guard with more years on him than most of the museum's antiquities. Judging from his buzz-saw snoring, he had mastered the same, and only, skill I had learned in high school, the ability to sleep with his eyes open.

I perused the artistic creations. To my surprise, I saw several I'd nail up in my apartment. They were exactly the right size to cover the cracks in my plaster.

The dull clatter of hardwood limping across the museum's polished marble floor cut short my excursion into cultural appreciation. I braced for trouble on the oaken hoof. "Swell place you picked for a meet, Valiant." Pepper Potts showed me his ticket stub. "I had to fork over a buck to get in."

"That why I don't see the ladies? You couldn't afford the entry fee?"

He swung his yard-long arm in a motion that took in here, there, and everywhere. "They're close by. Within screaming distance, if you follow my drift." He held his meat hooks with their palms up, one higher than the other. "You give me the formula . . ." He dropped his high hand and raised his low. "I produce the dames. You don't . . ." He squeezed his mitt into a fist.

"That wasn't the deal."

"I'm cutting a new deal. You turn over the goods right here, right now, or the doxies expire." He extended a pincer and wiggled his nippers.

I dipped into my pocket, extracted the formula, and passed it over.

Potts gave it a browse and grinned wolfishly. "Thanks, Valiant." He tucked it into his underwear. "Wish I could say it's been a pleasure knowing you." He emerged from his shorts fondling a gun. "Nothing personal, but I can't let you live."

"That go for the women, too?"

"Naturally. What kind of dunce you take me for? With the stuff they know, they could put me away until the cows troop home." To preserve the hushed sanctity of the locale, Potts screwed a silencer to the business end of his rod. He pointed the final result at my head with a nod to one of the Western graphics. It read "Adios, amigo."

I jerked my thumb at another one reading "Whoaaaa." "Since this is my final chapter, at least let me close the book knowing I figured out the story."

"Make it the *Reader's Digest* version," said Potts. "You ain't got many pages left until your ending."

I ripped a triptych, "Yip yip yip," off the wall. I bent its three tails under to form a stool. I sat on my creation directly beneath the No Smoking sign and lit a gasper. I dropped the flaming match on the floor. The dozing guard didn't move. "You were in the screening room with me and Enigman."

Potts's chin stubble scraped his rayon foulard.

"You shot him with my Dragoon."

He nodded again. "I was never much for sharing, especially where money's concerned."

The guard uncorked a snuffle capable of waking the dead, though he himself slept through it. "You went in and out of Selznick's office every day. Why didn't you steal the formula away from him? You could have done it easy."

"We mere mortals ain't as quick on the uptake as you, Valiant. By the time I figured out it was Selznick who had the merchandise, somebody else had beat me to it. But I got it now." He gave it a tender pat. "Proving all's well that ends well." He thumbed back his hammer. "Which brings us to the conclusion of our fable."

"Not quite. There's another question nagging my fanny. Why'd you cancel Tom Tom LeTuit's ticket? And why did you blast Dodger Rabbit?" I flipped away my burning butt. It landed red hot in the guard's lap, burned through the loose fabric of his uniform pants and fell to the floor. He didn't stir.

"I didn't thump LeTuit. I needed him. He was in charge of procuring my raw materials. I didn't ventilate the rabbit, either. Though I got to admit I considered it more than once. That rabbit was so squirrely."

A tour group cut through the salon on the way to someplace better. Potts ripped a balloon off the wall and draped it over his gun. He removed it after the parade finished. He didn't want anything, even a sixteenth inch of cowboy babble slowing his bullet.

I jangled my coin, tapped my cleats on the marble floor, and coughed. The guard didn't budge. "Why'd you kill Baby Herman?"

"You want to live by grasping at straws, go to work in a soda fountain. I ain't guilty of that, either, and you've asked your last question." He sighted down his barrel. "Good-bye, sucker."

"Belt him hard and put him under," I said, glancing past Potts to the doorway in back of him. "Don't count on a second chance."

"No dice," said Potts. "You ain't fooling me with that old gag."

"Your mistake, p-p-p-peckerwood!" Roger Rabbit coldcocked Potts from behind with the cry of "Hi yo, Silver." The blow rocked Potts hard. He crashed into the wall, dislodging a blistered assortment of cowboy curses and the first chorus of "I'm Ridin' Old Paint." He dropped his peashooter.

"He's all yours, Eddie," proclaimed Roger gleefully. "Take him in and book him."

"My pleasure." I unholstered my .38.

Potts yanked down a round, fragrant prairie flatulence the size of a bean plate. He threw it at me. It hit my hand. My gun went flying.

"Smart mug like you ought to learn not to count his chickens." Potts picked up his gat and stood. "Let's roll this scene back to where I was so crudely interrupted." He brought the gun into firing position.

I rushed Potts, kicking the guard's chair out from under him on my way past. The guard hit the floor with a thump.

I smacked into Potts's midsection, toppling him over. I hung on to him for dear life.

The guard rolled to the baseboard, curled up into a ball, and kept sawing wood.

Potts whipped his gun hand around, trying for a clear shot at me. I didn't have the muscle power to stop him for long. "Run for help," I yelled to the rabbit.

"What for?" said Roger. "Two big, strong men like us can handle him fine." To prove it, Roger grabbed Potts's weapon. Potts lashed him across the face with the barrel. The rabbit went sprawling.

We wrestled across the floor, trundling straight over the snoozing guard. He didn't notice.

I held on to Potts's gun with one hand. With the other I pawed at the electrical cord connecting him to his phony shank. I loosened the end, but he had it knotted too tightly for me to pry his leg off.

Roger crawled toward us on hands and knees. Dark red blood gushed from the slash Potts had laid across his forehead. "Hang on, Eddie. I'm coming."

"Leave the heroics to Audie Murphy. Call the cops!"

"No, Eddie. There comes a time when a rabbit's got to do what a rabbit's got to do. I'll defuse this situation personally." He grabbed Potts's foot.

Potts kicked backwards. He caught Roger flush in the face with his heel. Roger crumpled into a bloody heap.

Potts shuffled his pins under him and stood, dragging me along for the ride. I clung to his gun with both hands, but Potts had the strength of Samson before his crew cut. He twisted his pistol around and wormed it between our bodies. I felt a hard, cold circle of destruction press into my stomach.

Potts yanked the trigger. His gun snicked, the way they do when they're wearing a muzzler over their snood.

Searing pain ripped through my gut.

I collapsed like a ripped rag doll.

I clutched my midsection. Warm, sticky blood ran out between my fingers.

Potts stood over me, straddling my chest. "Like I said, Valiant, all's well that ends well." He pointed his gun at my forehead. "So long, dick." He thumbed back his hammer.

"Geronimooooooooow!" His legs pumping full steam ahead, Roger charged Potts and tackled him around the knees. The momentum of the attack knocked Potts forward. His shot flew wild, smashing into the floor half an inch from the guard's ear. Right. The guard didn't notice.

Roger hung tough, but Potts proved too strong for him. Potts shook his leg like a dog fertilizing a hydrant. Roger sailed into the wall.

Roger carried the end of Potts's electrical cord with him. Gamely, he tried to fell Potts by yanking his wire, but Roger had taken too much abuse. He didn't have the oomph.

Potts swung his leg once quickly, forward and back, lashing the cord and smacking Roger against the hard marble floor. Roger remained there, stretched out, defenseless, a thoroughly broken rabbit. "Say your prayers," Potts growled to him, " 'cause you're a dead man." He returned his attention to me. "As soon as I polish Valiant."

Potts pointed his gun directly into my mouth. I stared straight down the long, hard, black barrel. From my perspective, it looked like the end of a road to me. "As I keep telling you, shamus," Potts snarled, "all's well that ends well."

"To paraphrase your notion slightly," said Roger, "all's well that ends in the wall." He plugged Potts's leg into a socket.

Potts lit up like a Christmas tree. A brilliant corona enveloped his entire body. His hair stood on end and sparked. His eyes bugged. His arms and legs stiffened at angles that formed him into a giant X. His skeleton glowed so brightly, I could see it through his skin.

Potts collapsed over onto me. His plug yanked out of the socket an instant before he hit, sparing me his fate.

He pressed his face into mine. "We'll finish this later," he gasped. His last words came out in a balloon. Either high voltage or death had turned him back into a Toon.

His dead weight pressed into me, squeezing out what little breath I had left. I lost my last ounce of strength and all my self-respect reaching into his skivvies to retrieve the formula.

Odd, your thoughts when you're dying. I wondered if I would spend eternity wearing what I had on when I arrived at the pearly gates. If so, I should have taken Mother's advice and put on clean underwear this morning.

My eyes closed. The last sound I heard in life was the guard snoring.

The hereafter came highly overrated. From what I heard in Sunday school, I expected trumpet symphonies, choirs of boy sopranos, angels dancing on the heads of pins, and murals on the order of the Sistine Chapel. I got public address pagings, clattering gurneys, and neutral beige walls. My celestial-issue robe exposed my backside. The only angel in the vicinity didn't dance on a pin, she jabbed me with it. My halo had the shape of a bedpan. My white cloud lumped on the edges and sagged in the middle. Saint Peter's breath reeked of Alpo.

"Welcome back to the land of the living," he said. His balloon wrapped around the high-wattage stainless steel overhead light fixture and melted into a circle of white icicles.

"Bulldog?"

"Unless you know another sucker willing to hang around City General for an hour while sawbones dig six ounces of lead out of your worthless carcass." He opened his get-well present, a two-pound box of kibble. He removed a hidden fifth of gin. "You're a lucky pug. Your redheaded buddy kept you pumping with mouth-to-mouth until the ambulance arrived."

A classic case of good news, bad news. I'm alive, but filled to the gills with bunny breath. "You find the women?"

"Just where you suspected." He slipped my glucose bottle out of its wire holder and replaced it with his smuggled crock of liquified juniper berries. "Roped to a railroad track."

"Old habits die hard."

"So, almost, did the women. We got their ropes off less than thirty seconds before the four-oh-five freight whistled through." He plugged my IV tube into the hooch, instantly correcting my blood-to-alcohol imbalance.

"They all right?"

"Tired, scared, cold. A quack here at the hospital's checking them for permanent damage. I doubt he'll find any." Bascomb sat on a slat wooden chair. He leaned back, balancing on the chair's two hind legs, with his hindquarters stretched out on the end of my bed.

I pulled the hose off my needle, leaked gin into a specimen bottle, and handed it to him.

"I'm on duty." He took it anyway and tossed it back. He yanked out the squared-off corner of my bed sheet and used it to wipe his mouth. "I had a long, intensive heart-to-heart this afternoon with your brother-in-law, Ferd Flatfoot."

"Good thing I'm in a hospital." I reconnected myself to my liquid nourishment. "I got a hunch you're about to give me a pain."

"Flatfoot's a tough little monkey, no pun intended. I had to pull rank *and* my brass knuckles to persuade him to hand this over." Bascomb held up a clear cellophane evidence envelope containing a circular spool wound with a thin strip of film. "Photographed in total darkness by one Louise Wrightliter, but surprisingly illuminating, nevertheless. I gave it a gander while you were in surgery."

"I bet you loved what you saw."

"Positive music to my eyes." He bounced the film in his paw. "I been waiting my whole career to nail you on a rap of this magnitude."

I held out my wrists a shackle's length apart. One already sported a hospital bracelet inscribed with my name, age, height, weight, blood type, and the fact that I carried no medical insurance. "What are you waiting for?"

Bascomb stuck a pencil through the spool's center hole. He yanked the film. It rolled off the reel and piled up in a tangled heap on the floor. "Unfortunately for me, your buddy supported your story. He swore he heard Potts confess to committing a quadruple dip: Enigman, LeTuit, Dodger Rabbit, and Baby Herman."

"You believe him? A friend of mine? Will wonders never cease?"

"Can any notions you might be harboring that I'm turning soft, Valiant." The last of the film hit the linoleum. Bascomb pinched the empty spool to a stop. He gathered up the snarled film and dropped it into the sink. "For two cents, I'd charge your sidekick with perjury and toss him in the cell next to yours. Lucky for you both, the museum guard corroborates. He heard Potts's confession, too."

"We talking about the same gent? Ancient sucker? Deaf, dumb, and blind? Suffers from chronic narcolepsy?"

"That's where he fooled you, Valiant. That old bucket's sharp as a tack. Doesn't miss a trick." Hard to tell exactly, since Bascomb never opens his eyes more than a slit, but I swear he winked. "Based on the overwhelming weight of accumulated evidence, I'm satisfied that Potts murdered the four stiffs in question. Hence, I'm declaring this case closed. Which means you're off the hook, Valiant. And your rabbit friend, too. Good thing, since I really get a tickle out of that chowderhead. Besides, it would have kicked the slats out from under the value of his autograph if I had to execute him for murder." Bascomb ignited a match. He threw it on top of the film. The damning evidence went up in flames, burning hot and bright.

Bascomb bit the end off a cheap cigar. He leaned in close to the conflagration and sucked his stogie to life.

The nurse, my needle-jabbing angel in white, entered my room on the run. "No smoking allowed in here, Officer," she said. "How do you expect this man to get well?"

"I got a sneaky suspicion he's feeling better already." Bascomb turned on the water and washed my problems down the drain.

My bed quaked. I opened my eyes to find Bunk Thunker kicking the leg. "Visiting hours are over," I told him.

"Don't flatter yourself, Valiant. If I had my way, they'd quarantine this room 'til doomsday and you along with it." He searched his pockets by patting them hard. "I brought somebody who wants to see you. Though I can't imagine why."

Little Jo emerged from behind his cigarette pack just ahead of a hard smack. She wore a dress cut out of sterile gauze and belted with a Band-Aid. She'd tucked her hair into a skullcap made from the amputated thumb of a rubber surgical glove. Dabbings of Mercurochrome called attention to the facial abrasions around her mouth and cheeks. Except for those, and the string burns on her wrists and ankles, she appeared none the worse for wear.

WHO P-P-P-PLUGGED ROGER RABBIT?

"Hiyah, Toots," I said. "Good to see you. You okay? Doc give you a clean bill of health?"

"Oh, Eddie, I'm fine." A tear the size of a mustard seed rolled off her eyelash. "But just look at *you*. You poor wounded dear. How heroic of you. Risking your life to help a friend." She slid down the center gully of my mattress, crawled up to my head, kneeled on my pillow, and smooched me on the cheek. "I was worried beyond belief when Sergeant Bascomb told me you'd been shot. I was afraid I'd never see you again." Her words came out in the fine, delicate line used by Victorian ladies to pen love letters.

"Aw," gagged Thunker, jamming a wooden tongue depressor down his throat, "ain't that sweet." He placed his hand over his heart but only to pull out his shirt pocket. "Come on, Tootsie. Hop back in. I ain't got time or the stomach for any more kootchie coo."

She combed her fingers through my eyebrows. "If it's all the same to you, Officer, I'll stay here with Eddie."

Thunker shrugged. "No accounting for taste." He left us to our own devices.

Little Jo graced my mouth with a passionate smacker. The astringent taste of her antiseptic tingled my lips. "I'm sorry, Eddie. I should have asked you first." She crawled under my blanket. "Do you care if I stay and nurse you back to health?"

With the type of first aid she administered, I didn't mind one bit.

My doctor prescribed an absolute minimum three weeks of hospital bed rest. I cut him short by twenty days. I'd rather bleed to death on the street than he bled to death by the room rate.

I rummaged through the paper bag containing my personal effects. I hauled out a cigarette and the formula for Toon Tonic. I used the same match to torch both.

I stopped at a phone booth and checked my answering service. Skipper read me my lone message, from publicity agent and flicker flack Large Mouth Bassinger. Large Mouth's client roster boasted many of Hollywood's most notable stars. His well-deserved reputation as the slickest fish in the pond derived from his oft-proven ability to turn horse manure into the Lippizaner stallions.

He wanted to see me pronto.

Large Mouth's secretary, a trim young perch with undulating fins and a pouty smile, sat behind her desk scissoring her boss's utterances to eight and a half by eleven and embossing them with his letterhead. An efficient way to handle correspondence. Saves a bundle on White Out. Not to mention the hours normally wasted practicing "The quick brown fox jumped over the lazy dogs."

She migrated me into Large Mouth's office. All it needed to become a fish tank was caulk, a hundred gallons of water, and a giant cat staring in through the floor-to-ceiling windows. The gritty layer of sand carpeting the floor nurtured large clumps of snaky, pastel-colored ferns. A copper-helmeted diver's suit stood in a corner. Slightly below the cornice, a plaster fisherman sat on the end of a mock dock. He was reeling in a scuba diver.

Large Mouth's desk replicated a sunken ship. Telephone and

intercom resided on the bridge. Work in progress occupied the poop deck.

Large Mouth shook my hand with the vigor of a thirsty man priming a pump. "I'm pleased to make your acquaintance, Eddie."

"It's mutual, Mr. Bassinger."

"L.M., please. All my intimate, close, sincere, good friends call me L.M." His gills labored to suck in air, shrouding his lippy face. Large Mouth's glassy peepers bulged outward with the curve of cat's-eye marbles. His dorsal fin undulated as daintily as a Japanese fan. A liberal coating of fish oil gave his scales the shimmer of interlocked rainbows. He stood on his tail, flattening the ends to solidify his base of operations. "Simply because we've only just met doesn't preclude you from joining the immense, worldwide fraternity comprised of my oldest and dearest acquaintances."

"Fine by me, old buddy, old pal. What's on your mind?"

He opened a gold-foil-lined tin box of expensive English blends, the brand advertised as decorator items in better fashion magazines. He slid one out and inserted it into an ivory holder the size of an elephant's toothache. He flipped open his lighter and removed an eel. The eel grabbed a deep breath, flicked its flinty tongue across its ratchety incisors, and belched an impressive electrical arc which Large Mouth used to light his smoke. He extinguished the eel by dipping it headfirst into a bowl of lemon-scented water with a gardenia floating on top. Nero burned Rome with less showmanship. "I invited you here to hire you on behalf of a client of mine, Baby Herman."

"He's got no friends? His publicity agent has to pay six men to carry him to the grave?"

Large Mouth dipped a manicured flippertip into a pink shell filled with sea salt. He sniffed the crystalline residue up one of his double-barrelled, sixteen-gauge nostrils. "Suppose I were to assure you, Mr. Valiant, quite confidentially, that the rumors of Baby Herman's demise have been greatly exaggerated."

I grabbed a smoke of my own, a garden-variety Lucky right from the pack, and lit it with a plain wooden match. "I'll believe that when I hear it straight from the horse's toothless, pacifier-sucking mouth."

"Unfortunately, that won't be possible. Baby is in strict seclusion, under a doctor's care. Recuperating from an extremely frightening experience." His words emerged as a string of bubbles the size of seed pearls. They barely made it into my field of vision before popping to smithereens. "Baby was kidnapped. Threatened with death. He escaped from captivity only hours ago. Baby has been quite traumatized by the whole, horrible ordeal."

"How does that involve me?"

"Baby requires your aid in the resolution of a rather delicate personal matter, totally unrelated to his recent tribulation." His balloons orbited his head like tiny moons, slowing slightly as they passed his eyes so he could have the pleasure of watching himself talk. "Baby committed a minor peccadillo, a slight malfeasance, a bit of an indiscretion."

"Skip the disclaimers. Open the floodgates and spill the swill."

With a clanking of heavy chains, the drawbridge descended from the ersatz castle that functioned as Large Mouth's private toilet. "Jeez, L.M., throw a squirt of Lysol in there. The whole place reeks of silt." Baby Herman toddled out.

"Baby, I don't believe it's advisable for you to make an appearance quite yet," counseled Large Mouth. "Wait until I've had an adequate opportunity to outline your situation and justify your position."

"Route it out your snout. I'm not hiding in a fish crapper while you bleach my dirty diapers." Herman ripped the cellophane off a cigar. Large Mouth hastened to offer him the eel. Herman kept it, dropping it into his nappie. "Here's my problem, Valiant. I need muscle. To protect me from one of my soon-to-be-former buddies."

"What's the beef?"

Herman waded across the sandy floor. "Do something about your carpeting, L.M. It makes me feel like the fritter in a cat box." He halted at a leather sofa sewn to the shape of a snail. "Seems I started this quaint little rumor concerning a friend of mine."

"Let me guess. Clark Gable."

Large stooped over and let Herman use his spine as a stair step onto the sofa. "You heard it?" Herman waddled to the sofa's apex.

"Of course he heard it," stated Large Mouth. He brushed the sandy outlines of baby feet off his sofa's buttery leather. "The entire Hollywood community heard it. That rumor couldn't have spread faster if I'd planted it myself."

"Why'd you slice that particular hunk of phony baloney?" I asked.

"My way of discrediting the competition." Herman spit on his balloon, slipped it under his bumpus, and rode it down the sofa's spiral curved spine. "Wheeeeeeeee." He hit the floor and skidded on his ample rump, cutting parallel ruts in the sand. He stood and pulled his chappie away from his legs to drain out the grit. "Five foot two, eyes of blue, anything I want she'll do."

"Carole Lombard."

"The man wins twenty-four silver dollars." Herman opened a pirate's treasure chest containing a fully stocked bar. "I don't know where you got your scoop about me and Carole, but every word was true. I went for Carole"—Herman ground his pudgy pelvis—"as bad as she went for me."

"You're a lucky stiff."

"You got that right." He flicked his solid-gold diaper pin. "Women go ga ga over my goo goo." Herman poured two fingers of rye into a baby bottle.

"I'll issue a press release at once," Large Mouth enthused. "Herman and Lombard hear wedding bells."

"Save your balloons," said Herman. "I dumped her. Love 'em and leave 'em, that's my motto. I sent her packing back to Gable."

I saw his problem. "Now you're afraid of what Gable will do when he finds out his best so-called buddy vamped his best so-called girl."

"He'll turn me over his knee and spank me black and blue. Or worse." Difficult to tell which Herman enjoyed more, the taste of the liquor or the act of sucking it through the nipple. "Unless I find a bigger bullyboy willing and able to paddle him first. How's about it, Valiant? Are you my man?"

"Probably. First, answer me a question. Where you been the last few days?"

He cocked his head. His blue-ribboned topknot flopped sideways like a reaped shock of wheat. "What's that got to do with me and Gable?"

"Maybe nothing, maybe everything. Give me the gories, and let me decide."

He hauled himself onto a knotty-pine chair carved in the shape of a mermaid. "I was crawling saloons night before last, hunting for company of the female persuasion." He stowed his bottle in the cleft formed by the mermaid's wooden brassiere. "This Toon doxie ambled up and gave me a how-do-you-do. I asked her the sixty-four-dollar question, and she won my jackpot. We were no sooner out the swinging door than she bopped me with her purse. Knocked me silly. Next thing I know, I'm tied up and blindfolded. Which I normally enjoy, except here the only action I got was this bimbo grilling me as to the whereabouts of Dave Selznick's box."

"You knew the box she was talking about?"

"Sure." His wiggly pink fingers explored one of the mermaid's knotholes. "I dropped it into Roger Rabbit's pants cuff the day me and him and Kirk Enigman met in Selznick's office."

"Why'd you do that?"

He chinned himself on the mermaid's bosom. "The three of us were up for the same role. I figured if Selznick thought Roger was light-fingered, it would cut the competition."

Large Mouth's secretary fishtailed into the office bearing a stack of unsigned balloons.

Herman winked at her lewdly. "I could get hooked on you in a big way, butterfish." He jostled his diaper. "Want to feel my eel?" Sparks came out.

"I'd swim up *her* stream," he said to me after she'd gone.

"Did you tell your kidnapper that Roger Rabbit had Selznick's box?"

"You kidding? I'll give a dame half the night but never the time of day." His diaper ballooned out, lifting his rear end with it. "I told her to soak her head in a bucket of Dip."

"How did you escape?"

"I didn't. That's L.M.'s concoction." He tugged out his waistband, releasing a string of bright green bubbles. His posterior sunk to its normal level. "The ditz let me go. Dumped me in a ravine across town. I figured I'd better check with L.M. before I squealed to the cops. See how to get maximum mileage out of my plight." He touched the glowing tip of his cigar to one of the floating bubbles. It burst into flames, leaving behind an airborne smudge of green soot and the smell of Limburger cheese. "Maybe parlay it into a sympathy bump or two."

"Describe your kidnapper."

Herman rolled his baby-browns. "Supremely ugly sucker. The kind I'd la-de-la only if she wore a bag over her head, and another over that in case the first one broke." He tilted his head and gave me a once-over lightly. "She kind of resembled you. Oh, yeah. One other thing. Every third sentence she repeated the same stupid phrase. Over, and over, and over. Hi-de-ho-ho-ho. If she said it once, she said it a jillion times."

Herman motioned to Large Mouth. The fish obligingly lifted the Baby so he could throw a fat, dimpled arm around my shoulder. "How's about it, Valiant? You want to guard the body that's going to win the Academy Award playing Rhett Butler in *Gone With the Wind*?"

"I'd be foolish to refuse."

On my way out, I handed Large Mouth the photo and bio of Charlie's niece. "L.M., do an old, dear, sweet, longtime friend a favor. See what you can arrange for this young lovely."

Large Mouth took a gander. His jaw dropped open. "What a face! I can make this woman a star! She has that . . . that . . . raw animal quality."

To put it mildly.

29

The story, under Louise Wrightliter's byline, made page-one headlines in the *Toontown Telltale.*

BABY HERMAN ALIVE AND WELL.

Herman had been kidnapped, so the story went, by a stunningly beautiful and exceedingly amorous female fan. "She forced me to perform unspeakable acts," said Herman, who went on to speak about them in graphic detail. A satyr in season would have been hard-pressed to match his alleged performance level. Wishful thinking? Or good advertising? The police department's composite sketch of his kidnapper bore a distinct resemblance to Marlene Dietrich.

A paragraph on an inner page caught my eye. Seems a red-headed, stuttering albino in a trench coat pasted acerbic film critic Nono Nuttingood in the kisser with a custard cream pie.

"I realized I'd never again have such a splendid opportunity. So I took it," said Roger. "Nuttingood never utters a kind word about anything or anybody. I detest the man. He's ruined countless careers. It gave me immense satisfaction to strike a blow on behalf of the entire acting fraternity. Best of all, there's no way for him to retaliate. I invented the perfect crime. I'm no longer who I was when I did it."

His balloon extended the full width of my office like a banner welcoming a traveler home. "Thank goodness Toon Tonic works both ways. Being a human was the worst experience of my life. I don't know how you tolerate an existence so mundane and boring."

"I take it one day at a time and manage to struggle through."

"The world isn't ready for Toon Tonic, Eddie." Roger handed me the small flask containing the remnants of the batch he'd mixed up. "If I were you, I'd destroy this immediately, or at least squirrel it away until humans and Toons can accept its consequences."

"You realize Toon Tonic could make us both rich beyond our wildest dreams."

"What dreams? I wouldn't be able to sleep nights knowing the horror I'd inflicted on civilization. Smash, bash, trash, mash, lash, hash, gash, and dash Toon Tonic, Eddie, and then do it again for good measure."

"I've got one final use for it, then it's gone." I shoved the flask into my top desk drawer, removing my office bottle to make room. I poured myself a nip. "Here's to another case wrapped up in ribbons."

"Not quite." Roger plopped his head on my desk top. His features flattened out and lost their definition, like a wax doll face gone spongy in the sun. "I still have to confront Jessica."

"Yeah." I cleared everything breakable off the walls and poured him a nip, too. "I suppose you do."

"I want you there with me." He spun his glass between his paws, creating a whirlpool that sucked in his words and swallowed them whole. "To keep me from falling apart at the seams."

"If you want to be propped up, buy a two-by-four and hire a carpenter."

"Eddie, I saved your life!"

"That was your choice, not mine."

"P-p-p-please, Eddie. Do this for me, and I'll never, ever, in my whole life ask you for anything again. I p-p-p-promise. Scout's honor, cross my heart, and hope to die."

"Put it in writing, and we've got a deal."

I hit Gable hard—with a handful of rice.

Lombard giggled. Then she excused herself and went to powder her nose. She was a vision in white, from her platinum hair to her low-cut ivory dress, to the bouquet of colorless roses she clutched to her milky chest.

"Thanks, old sport, for coming down on such short notice," said Gable. He brushed my rice off the shoulders of his simple, expensive, double-breasted, dark blue suit. He lit a smoke. The flame sparkled off the plain gold band he wore on his third finger, left hand. "You made a superlative best man." He slipped me a century note. I swapped it to the Justice of the Peace for Gable and Lombard's marriage license, signed, sealed, and delivered. The JP threw in free a souvenir copy of their marriage vows printed on imitation parchment.

I gave the two pieces of paper to Gable along with my best wishes. "Since I won't be seeing you for a while, I'll use this auspicious occasion to deliver my final report."

He folded the license and the vows lengthwise, being careful not to crease any of the important words, like "love," "honor," and "obey." He tucked both into his jacket pocket, where nothing in the world could touch them. "Save your breath. I got what I wanted. I married the woman I love. What she did prior to today, before she said the words 'I do,' well, it doesn't matter anymore."

"I suspect it will."

A thumbnail of ash fell off his ciggie and hit his shoe, marring a perfect shine. "You're going to tell me even though I don't want to hear it."

I nodded.

He bopped one of the chapel's large, silver, cardboard bells. Instead of pealing, it split up the middle. "Speak your piece and be done with it."

I borrowed his smoke and lit one of my own off the end. "There was nothing going on between your new missus and Baby Herman. She only pretended to be cuckoo about him to get you to pop the question. I think you ought to know that, because it's not often a guy finds a woman who adores him that much."

Gable stared at me a minute, then grabbed me by the ears and kissed me flush on the forehead. "Thanks Eddie." He stuffed my breast pocket with a fistful of crisp, new one-hundred-dollar bills. "For a job well done."

"All in a day's work." The first lesson you learn when driving in my neighborhood is how to toot your own horn.

Lombard came back from the hooter. The three of us walked out onto the JP's front porch.

A hundred reporters milled around on the front lawn.

Large Mouth Bassinger stepped forward and inserted himself

WHO P-P-P-PLUGGED ROGER RABBIT?

between Gable and Lombard, two of his most prominent clients. He hooked his fins through their elbows.

"You promised. No press," carped Gable to the fish.

"I did, I know, and I kept that promise. I have no idea how word of your nuptials leaked out." The glare of flashbulbs gave a preview of what it would be like to stand on this porch a billion years from now on the day the sun exploded. "As long as they're here," said Large Mouth, "you might as well give them an interview."

The reporters formed a tight circle around the newlyweds.

Gable mouthed the words "Eddie, the car."

I headed toward it, shouldering a path through the minions of the fifth estate. Gable and Lombard followed me.

Large Mouth, abandoned to his own devices, composed a half page of razzmatazz set in newsprint, justified on either end, ready to be pasted into the afternoon edition. The news hawks pushed forward the long-handled butterfly nets they use to scoop quotes. The few extraneous comments they left behind wouldn't make up a three-line filler.

I shoved Gable and Lombard into their car. "Happy honeymoon."

I leaned inside and whispered to Gable. "A word of advice. Man to man. Shave the caterpillar. Women hate smooching a gent with a furry lip." He promised to think it over.

Her eyes glued to mine, Lombard extended her slim, shapely, nyloned leg and propped it on the dashboard. She reached beneath her skintight, calf-length white skirt.

As their car pulled away, Lombard leaned out the window, winked, and threw me her black-lace garter.

It was my day for glamour girls.

Jessica Rabbit opened her front door wearing a glimmer of perspiration and a thin cotton red-and-white-checked sundress. She carried a tall, chilly glass of iced tea to ward off the oppressive midday heat. "Hunny bunny," she sighed when she spied Roger on her threshold, "you're back!" She picked up her spouse and hugged him to her chest.

I took her tea. The outline of her hand remained on the glass. The frost had turned to steam beneath her fingers. I helped myself to a swig. She drank a gunpowder blend but it was the peppermint taste of her lipstick on the straw that fired my cannon.

She let her husband go. She had clung to him so tightly his head displayed her bosom in full relief, hatcheted outward from forehead to chin, dished on either cheek.

She planted me with a smacker so scorchy it singed my socks. One more, and my shorts would come crashing down in flames. "Thank you, Mr. Valiant, for bringing my punkin puss home to me safe and sound." She indicated the open door. "I hate to appear rude, but I would like to be alone with my sweetums. We have a bit of catching up to do."

I gave her gunpowder brew a touch more bang by adding half an ounce of the liquid explosive I tote in my arsenal. "Roger needs to ask you a few questions. He wants me to stick around awhile to check his punctuation, grammar, and spelling."

"Of course," said Jessica. "Whatever my lord and rabbit desires." She lead us onto the veranda. We took seats around a glass table containing an ice bucket, a large pitcher of her tea, a stack of fashion magazines, and the screenplay for *Gone With the Wind*. "Ask away, darling. As you are wont to say, I'm all ears."

Roger moved his mouth silently, like a ventriloquist's dummy trying out a solo act.

His better half glanced at me and raised an eyebrow. I shrugged. "Go ahead, Roger." I gaffed him in the side. "Shoot."

The rabbit shut his eyes and scrunched his face. His head swelled to the size of a watermelon, but not a word came out.

"What's wrong with you?" I asked him.

He opened his mouth and showed me his tongue tied into knots.

His wife leaned in close to me so the fall of her flaming red hair blocked her words from her husband's sight. "What's causing my snookie ookums such grave consternation?"

I boiled it to the essence. "You and Clark Gable."

She straightened her head and aimed her word-filled bubbles directly at her husband. "Clark Gable and I are extremely good friends. We've known each other for years, ever since we were both struggling to break into the movies, long before you and I ever met. Ours is a strictly platonic relationship. We have never had the slightest romantic involvement." She pointed her left index finger at Roger and rubbed it with her right. "Shame, shame, silly, silly rabbit, if you suspect otherwise."

Roger pantomimed his response. I quit playing after guessing that the correct answer contained thirty-seven words, first word sounds like "herbaceous." "You can't blame Roger for jumping to the obvious conclusion. You and Gable have been spotted together a lot lately, in most of the wrong places."

"Of course we have. It's the essence of our plan." She fished an ice cube out of the pitcher and rubbed it across her breastbone. The melting water soaked through the front of her dress and plastered it to her skin, revealing plenty of hidden assets, but you had to look quick. Her body heat dried the fabric almost instantly. "When Carole Lombard, the love of Clark's life, left him for another man, Clark and I concocted a phony romance to make Carole jealous."

Do tell. The flip side of the fib I gave Gable.

Jessica drummed her fingertips on the arm of her chair, daring one or the other of us to contradict her.

Roger stuck two fingers in his mouth and whistled to signal another session of Pantomime Party. I declined to play, choosing to press ahead on my own. "You personally leaked the story of your big romance to the *Toontown Telltale.*"

"Naturally." A fly landed on her bare ankle. She ended his brief moment of bliss with a quick swat of the latest *Harper's Bazaar.* Noisier than a spider's web, but every bit as deadly. "For our charade to succeed, Carole had to hear about it."

"Why not let your husband in on the gag?"

She stroked Roger's knee. His whistling sunk lower and fizzled out. "I didn't tell you, sweetie pie, because you know you can't keep a secret. You would have blabbed every detail of our ploy to the first ten people you met."

She leaned back in her chair and crossed her legs, exposing a generous expanse of thigh. Roger gave one last whistle, of the wolf variety. Jessica rewarded him with a wink and a purse of her lips. "I never imagined you would suspect there was anything actually going on between Clark and me. Not the Roger I married. He doesn't have a jealous bone in his body. Our relationship has always been built on mutual trust."

Roger's tongue unraveled. "What about night before last at Jungle Rhythms?" He jumped out of his chair, put his fists on his hips, and spread his legs wide.

Jessica's green eyes narrowed and the slightest trace of a line appeared on her brow. "What about it?"

Roger thumped a yellow thumb on his scrawny chest. "You agreed to go out with me!"

"What are you talking about?"

"That was yours truly there with Eddie. Me, myself, and I." He folded his arms and tapped his foot. "What do you say to that?"

She glanced back and forth between us. "I consented to date my own husband." She reached forward and caressed Roger's cheek with the back of her hand. "Hardly a federal offense."

"But I was a *human*!" He ripped the word out of his balloon and stretched it out beneath his chin. "You didn't recognize me."

"Of course I did." She took him gently by the paw, relieved him of his "human" label, sat him down, and plunked herself on his lap. She wound him around her little finger, starting with his ear. "What kind of wifey poo would I be not to recognize my own precious hubbie wubbie in whatever form I happen to find him?" She kissed him full on the mouth with such force she sucked his nose into his head.

"Makes p-p-p-perfectly good sense to me," said Roger nasally when she let him up for air. He smacked himself on the back of the noggin. His beak popped back into place. "How about you, Eddie?"

"If you're happy, I'm happy."

"Oh boy, am I happy," sighed Roger, leaning forward for another lip lock.

Jessica left his pucker dangling. She jumped up. "Stay right here. I have a present for you."

She disappeared into the house, returning with a large picture draped in red velvet. "For you, honey bumpkins." She pulled the velvet away to reveal her portrait, the one we saw hanging over Gable's mantle. "It's your birthday present. Clark's been storing it for me. But I can't wait. I want you to have it now."

WHO P-P-P-PLUGGED ROGER RABBIT?

Roger couldn't decide whether to hug the painting or the model. He made the right choice in my book. "Oh, Eddie, isn't she wonderful?"

"A regular peach."

"I've got another, even bigger surprise for you." Jessica's eyes flicked for the briefest instant from his to mine. "I'm expecting a baby."

Roger's orbs irised to the size of the winning ticket in the Irish sweepstakes. "You mean I'm . . . I'm . . . going to be a p-p-p-poppa! A p-p-p-pater! A p-p-p-parent!"

"Yes, Roger, you're the father of my child." She hung her head and clasped her hands girlishly behind her back. "I've known for almost a month. I put off telling you because I feared you might be upset. We've never talked about a family. I have no idea how you feel about children."

"Are you kidding? This is the happiest moment of my life!"

Mine, too. According to the notarized promise in my pocket, I was now officially through with Roger Rabbit forever.

Gable and Lombard. Roger and Jessica. All those lovebirds billing and cooing only made my next task that much harder.

Little Jo sat cross-legged on the white linen tablecloth of our restaurant table. She kicked away the gold-rimmed plate bearing the meal I ordered special for her, shoestring potatoes, baby Brussels sprouts, petite filet. "What do you mean, you're breaking it off?" Her words sloshed around on a jigger of tears. The hovering headwaiter snagged her tiny balloon with a pair of sterling silver ice tongs and handed it to a busboy for disposal. He didn't want it floating away, snagging on a salad fork, breaking open, and irrigating one of the other patrons. The mark of a fancy place. Nothing but the best when I give a dame the air. "I repeat what I've been saying ever since we met, Eddie. Size doesn't matter to people who truly love one another."

"We're not only two different sizes. We're two different worlds."

"And never the twain shall meet." She rejected my handkerchief—it was the size of her bedspread and smelled of laundry starch—for one of her own, a swatch of lace as delicate as a leprechaun's antimacassar. She dabbed it under her eyes. "I won't buy that, Eddie. It's too trite."

"I'm sorry, pidge. I don't know how to do this gracefully. I haven't much practice at it. I'm usually on the receiving end."

"Here's a suggestion. Come straight out with it. Try, 'So long, Shorty. It was fun while it lasted.' "

I took her advice. It only made matters worse.

Junior Selznick sat hunkered over Abe Lincoln's desk. He was playing with a flea circus.

"Your juggler's passable, but your clowns stink, and I've seen squirrels perform better high-wire acts on a telephone line."

"I have no desire to replace Barnum and Bailey." With the tip of a pencil, he edged a few of the tiny critters around into different positions. "I use insects to block out my big crowd scenes. Here, for instance, they're set up for Scarlet's visit to the railroad yard, where she hunts for Dr. Mead to deliver Melanie's baby."

"Imagine that. I've seen thousands of those little tykers cavorting on the backs of junkyard dogs, and never once recognized the dramatic possibilities."

"Paint on the brush of a master becomes the Mona Lisa. Applied by a journeyman, it merely covers the side of a barn." Selznick put a miniature megaphone to his mouth. "Take five," he announced. The flea playing Scarlet crawled into a matchbox with a gold star pasted on the sandpaper striker. Even in flea circles, rank has its privileges.

"How are you managing without Potts?"

"Not well." Selznick emptied his overheaped ashtray into his wastebasket to make room for the butt in his hand. He had started smoking again. Pressure will do that. I took the one he offered me. "Pepper was a man uniquely suited to expediting film projects."

"He was a crude, oafish, unprincipled, murdering lout."

"I won't deny he had his faults." A moving van screeched to a halt outside. Selznick watched morosely through his window as a sweaty team of knuckleheads loaded the truck with period furniture. He winced when a muscleman banged a highboy into a commode. "My creditors have called in my notes. I'm being forced to sell off my props to meet my payroll." He closed his blinds so he wouldn't have to watch any more of his castle crumble to dust. "I need my box, Mr. Valiant." Selznick laced his hands together. His fingers were long and artistic, the kind that connect tuxedos to keyboards.

"No movie's worth the consequences of unleashing Toon Tonic on an unsuspecting world. That's why I heaved it into my neighborhood smelter."

"You *what*?"

"I melted your box to slag."

He slammed his hand on his desk, severely rattling his cast of thousands. "You've done the public a great disservice. The money I derived from selling Toon Tonic would have financed one of the greatest moving pictures of all time." He uncapped a pill bottle, shook out a rainbow assortment, and popped them dry.

"You could always make the flick on the cheap." I pointed to the fleas. "Shoot it with these peewees and a telephoto lens."

"You're displaying your ignorance, Mr. Valiant." He mobilized his circus and sent it back to work. The ones playing the dead and wounded had it easy compared to poor six-legged Scarlet. She scampered frantically across the desk top, searching, searching, searching. "If I wanted to scale back the budget, I'd simply substitute humans for Toons."

"How would that save moola?"

Selznick punched a string of calculations into a huge adding machine. He pulled the handle and handed me the strip of paper that popped out. It displayed an awfully large number. "For starters, that's the amount I'd save by staging the battle scenes with blank ammunition instead of whipped-cream pies. But it's an academic question. Audiences would never accept it."

"Don't be too sure. I'm no movie critic, but I know what I like, and I'm tired of seeing every topic played for a laugh."

He cupped his chin and stroked it. "Hmmm. Take a serious approach to *Gone With the Wind*. Is that what you're saying?"

"It might play in Peoria."

He rearranged his miniature performers into a tableau depicting the burning of Atlanta. "It would be a gamble." An ember from the end of his smoke landed on the corner of his blotter, adding an unplanned touch of realism to his miniature scene.

"I hear risk's never bothered you before."

He reached into his desk drawer and removed a file. Vivien Leigh's. "You were curious concerning my interest in young Vivien. It's strictly professional. She's a woman of remarkable acting ability. I don't want word of her talent leaking out to other producers. I've been seasoning her with bit parts before launching her as a full-blown star. Perhaps the time has come. What do you think? Vivien Leigh as Scarlet O'Hara." He studied Vivien's glossy. "She's no Jessica Rabbit."

"Who is?"

He pointed at a flea piloting a Tootsietoy carriage across the smoldering desk. "And for Rhett Butler, I'd cast Ronald Colman. Or better yet, Errol Flynn."

I suggested Gable. My way of saying thanks for the C-notes. Selznick didn't see it. He considered Gable nothing but a pretty face. I told Selznick to picture Gable without the fuzzy lip.

I stuffed in a quarter, but the Automat refused to fork over my breakfast. I banged the glass window with the flat of my hand. The door stayed closed.

"You need another dime. Chocolate cake went up last week to thirty-five." Louise Wrightliter stood behind me. She dropped two nickels into my slot. The cubbyhole popped open. I carried my cake, her cornflakes, and a brace of coffees to a table near the wall.

"Sorry I had to have you locked away," I said. "You happened to be in the wrong place at the wrong time."

"Don't apologize." She laced our javas with half an ounce of brandy from her filigreed flask. "I appreciate a man of action. And I'm none the worse for my stay in the pokey." True. No jailhouse pallor, no knife scars, no self-inflicted tattoos, at least none visible. "I'm very impressed with your style, Eddie. It's not every day I meet a man as lacking in principles as I am."

"Let's form a club."

"I have a better idea." She scooped a bit of my cake onto her finger and licked it off with her tongue. "I'd like to become your Boswell. I want to write a book about you, about your cases. Eddie Valiant, private eye to the stars. I'm positive it will make a mint. Imagine the publicity. It would supercharge your career."

WHO P-P-P-PLUGGED ROGER RABBIT?

"The duck'll squawk up a storm if he finds out you're writing my life story on company time."

"That shan't be a problem. You say yes, and I'll take a sabbatical from the *Telltale.* I'll work on you exclusively. Think about it, Eddie." She put her hand on top of mine, halting the progress I was making shoveling frosting into my mouth. "We'll be together side by side, day and night. Naturally, I'll reward you handsomely for your cooperation. In any form of currency you desire."

I demurred. It was a generous offer, but I didn't need any more notoriety. I'd gotten enough in the past few days to last me a lifetime.

I finally received the message I'd been waiting for. It came in the form of a balloon mailed to my office. It told me to be at Ten Pin Lane's bar that evening at eight.

The lettering style duplicated that left behind by the mug who sapped me, and shot Roger during his session with Ed Murrow.

There wasn't much difference in shape between Ten Pin Lane and the long-necked beer bottle he delivered to my table. Ten Pin had been one of the greats on the pro bowling circuit. He and the other nine members of his team, the Splinters, worked the far end of the alley, dodging the likes of Cannonball Spin and his Rolling Rockets. Ten Pin wore the old uniform, a bright red neck stripe. I tried engaging him in conversation, but found him too wooden for words. He fell twice on his way back to the bar, once taking a table of four out with him.

At the stroke of eight, the pinsetter door lifted open, and my brother Freddy more or less walked in.

I stress "more or less" because he didn't exactly walk. He couldn't. His body had shrunk to a height of eighteen inches, but his feet remained size ten. He reminded me of a clown balloon stuck through footprint-shaped cardboard, and he traveled the same way. Hop, boing, hop, boing. He reached the bar in six arcs. He needed three launches to order a short beer.

He bounced to my table. Embracing him was like hugging Froggy the Gremlin. When I squeezed, his tongue poked out, his feet expanded, and his belly button made rude noises. "You've changed, Freddy," was the best I could manage.

"I'm a Toon now, Eddie, in case you hadn't noticed." His balloon paraded proudly across the space between us, without the slightest trace of shame. "I can be whatever shape and size I want. Small, tall, anything at all." To prove it, he metamorphosed into

WHO P-P-P-PLUGGED ROGER RABBIT?

the Freddy I knew from the old days except this version came in a single plane, no deeper than a sheet of glass, and totally transparent.

We drank in silence. Neither of us wanted to start this conversation because we both knew how it would finish. Finally, I took the leap. "As soon as I spread out the whole puzzle, I knew the missing piece was you."

Freddy mock-punched my jaw. His hand felt as icy cold as a dead man's. "I knew you would, Eddie. You always were the brainy one." His lettering left no doubt. Freddy was the mug who rapped me, and the shooter who plugged Roger Rabbit. "Me, Teddy, at best we tagged along on your coattails. Neither of us could hold a candle to you when it came to solving crime." He glugged a swallow of lager. The foamy liquid gurgled through his visible esophagus.

"Stop it. You're making me sick. It's worse than watching you chew with your mouth open."

"You always offended too easy, Eddie. I only ate that way to get your goat." He opaqued out his innards anyhow. "What next? You arrest me? Toss me in the hoosegow? Put me on trial?" He stretched his neck to the length of a hoe handle. "Swing me from the highest tree? Hi-de-ho-ho-ho."

"I'll decide that after a few questions."

"Why bother asking?" He expanded, quadrant by quadrant, like a rubber doll filling with air. He ended up thinner than I .remembered him. "You generally have all the answers."

"I always like to confirm what I already know."

"Same as ever. You, death, and taxes never change." He flashed me a perfect smile. At least in his new, Nutty Putty existence, he'd had the good sense to straighten his teeth. "Fire away."

"What's it mean, Freddy? 'Box, and you could get hurt'?"

"Hi-de-ho-ho-ho." He pushed his balloon out slowly, proofing it letter by letter, word by word, to make sure he got it exactly right. "It should have said 'Suppress the contents of the box, and you could get hurt.' I left off the first part. Chalk it up to inexperience speaking visually." With the backside of his hand he batted his round, white, grammatically perfect balloon across the table like a Ping-Pong ball.

"Why'd you want to shoo me off?"

"I know how you feel about Toons." His expression of distaste was almost human. "I knew you'd try and queer any plan to peddle Toon Tonic."

"Are you kidding? Selznick, Potts, Enigman, LeTuit, they intended to sell that stuff to anybody with the cash to pay for it. Men, women, old people, kids on the street."

"So what?"

"Freddy, look at yourself. We're talking about a brew that turns a human into a Toon!"

His balloon came out with its edges softened to the point of blurriness, like the billowy clouds that Peter Pan rides around on in Never-Never Land. "Eddie, this will be hard for you to believe, harder still to accept, but my life began the day I became a Toon. Every day's a barrel of sunshine. I don't age. I have no cares, no worries. I have nothing but fun. It's the perfect life. Being a human was never this good. Hi-de-ho-ho-ho. I want every person in the whole world to experience the rapture of Toonhood."

"How do you jibe your newfound, jovial, elevated nature with the fact you murdered Tom Tom LeTuit?"

He scratched his nose, rubbing too hard, pushing it an inch off center. "He had it coming."

"Nobody deserves to die."

"LeTuit turned me into a zombie!" Freddy tried to float a balloon picturing what it was like, but the form wouldn't come. He'd suppressed the memory of it. "Hi-de-ho-ho-ho. Thank goodness Lupe weaned me off those infernal cocktails before they did permanent harm."

"We've both got a lot to thank her for. It was Lupe who tipped me to Toon Tonic."

"She thought you'd back off if she made the situation sound deadly."

"She was wrong. How'd you come by the formula?"

"Lupe heisted it from LeTuit." Freddy finished his glass of suds. He left the foam that circled his lips, like he did in the old days when he drank a root beer. He'd tell me he'd been bitten by a mad dog and had gone stark raving crazy. It never frightened me then. It scared the daylights out of me now. "Me and her hopped a tramp freighter from Havana to Miami, and hitchhiked from there to L.A."

WHO P-P-P-PLUGGED ROGER RABBIT?

"Where you figured to raise cash by ransoming the formula back to LeTuit's partners, Pepper Potts and Kirk Enigman."

"I don't know what you need me for, Eddie." He scaled a balloon to the bar. Ten Pin loaded a beer on it and scaled it back. "Hi-de-ho-ho-ho. You're chalking up a perfect score. One hundred percent accurate."

"There are a few questions left that might lower my curve. What happened when you contacted Potts?"

"He put me off." Freddy laid his balloon on the table and smacked it with his hand, shattering it to pieces. "Potts told me he needed to think it over. I suspect he wanted to devise a way to cut me permanently out of the picture so he could grab the formula free."

"How'd you hook up with Selznick?"

"Lupe's idea. She read a story in *Variety* about Selznick needing to raise big money." Freddy salted a piece of his broken balloon and popped it into his mouth. "Potts's office and Selznick's sit side by side. Hi-de-ho-ho-ho. I slipped out of one and into the other. I pitched Selznick my terms. He met my purchase price on the spot, and even tossed in a percentage of net."

"You made the deal disguised as a woman."

"To protect my true identity." He handed me a piece of his balloon. I took a bite. It had the crunch and taste of fried pork rind. "All of us superheroes travel incognito. Hi-de-ho-ho-ho."

"Selznick contacted you later. Told you the formula had been stolen."

"Yeah." He picked my hat off the table. He exhaled a brown balloon and folded it over my fedora. When he peeled it off, it formed a perfect duplicate of my headgear. Freddy always envied my Stetson. "Selznick asked if I had a copy. I told him no. I suggested he hire you to find out which one of his three suspects robbed him blind. After I thought it over, and factored in your attitude toward Toons, I regretted giving him your name. Hi-de-ho-ho-ho. The only way I could think of to get you off the case was to spook you off."

"As usual, your timing stinks. You tried to scare me off before I was on. Why'd you take a potshot at Roger Rabbit and kidnap Baby Herman?"

"I wanted to frighten one or the other into returning the

goods to Selznick." He tore off a hunk of his foamy white balloon and formed it into a phony beard complete with ear hooks. He put it on and studied his reflection in the waxed tabletop. He liked what he saw well enough to shape four more pieces into a wig, mustache, and bogus eyebrows.

"You broke into Baby Herman's place and searched it for the goods."

"Yup, sonny." His lettering was cracked and broken to match his wizened visage.

"Why'd you shoot Dodger Rabbit?"

"Brotherly concern." A rapid shake of his head dissolved his ersatz gray beard and the wisdom that went with it. "I saw him trail you into the graveyard. He was packing a gun. I figured he was planning to blast you."

"He wasn't toting so much as a peashooter when he died."

"Okay." Freddy stroked his naked chin. "Suppose I shot him for sport, for the fun of it." He flashed the devilish grin seen on young scamps who amuse themselves by overturning outhouses. "What's the crime in that? Hunting rabbits out of season? It made a major star out of Elmer Fudd." He toyed with his words, with his clothes, with his hands, with everything in reach. "I take it you found the formula."

I nodded.

"Hi-de-ho-ho-ho. When does Selznick start to manufacture?"

"Never. I destroyed it. It's gone for good."

"I should have known big brother would come through." He ate another handful of salted words. "As usual. Hi-de-ho-ho-ho."

I pulled out a flask and handed it to him. "Drink this, Freddy."

He gave the bottle a shake and examined the contents through the glass sides. "It's Toon Tonic!"

"Right. The world's sole remaining dose. It'll turn you back into a human. You do that, and I'll forget everything you've done."

"Sorry, Eddie, but I can't oblige." He gave me back my container. "I've got a better idea. You drink it. Turn Toon and experience the bliss I'm talking about. Hi-de-ho-ho-ho."

"Nothing doing. I was born human, and it's human I'll remain."

He settled into his seat. He put his hands behind his head and crossed his legs in front of him, as relaxed as if we were discussing nothing more important than the relative merits of loafers over lace-ups. "I guess you're faced with a major dilemma. You going to collar your own baby brother for murdering a sadistic bum and a no good Toon rabbit?"

I waffled. Yes, no, yes, no. In the end, I let him bounce away laughing into the night. I had no choice. He's my little brother! Besides, the way I saw it, spending the rest of his life as a Toon was punishment aplenty.

I returned Ferd's car. I thanked him and meant it. I told him he wasn't such a bad farfafoofaloofing guy, once you got to know him. Not that I planned to.

Heddy walked me to the garage, where I retrieved my heap.

She stood beside it, with her foot propped on the running board, while I warmed the engine. I scrutinized her through the open side window.

"Why you staring at me?" she asked. She wiggled her fingers. I reached under the seat and handed her my traveling companion. She uncorked it and took a swig.

"I never realized how much you resemble Freddy. Stick him in a dress, and I couldn't tell the two of you apart."

"Hi-de-ho-ho-ho." She swallowed one for the road, gave me the flagon, and I did the same. "Fine detective you are. People have been commenting on that ever since me and Freddy were kids. Most people take us for twins. Hi-de-ho-ho-ho. We even talk alike."

"So I notice." I stepped out of the idling car, took her in my arms, and hugged her close.

She pushed me away, flustered. "What was that for? You're not going mushy on me, are you?"

"Heddy, you're the only family I've got left."

She staggered backwards, colliding hard with Ferd's tool bench. His set of left-handed wrenches fell to the concrete floor. A quarter-inch hex head skinned her ankle. She didn't flinch. "Freddy?"

"Forget him, Sis. Put him out of your mind. I'm sorry, but he's never coming back."

Tears welled up in her eyes. She wiped them away with a page she ripped off Ferd's wall-hung girlie calendar. "Was it quick, Eddie. Did he suffer?" She uncrumpled her makeshift hankie and realized she had been wiping her misery on a baboon's backside.

"Not a bit. He went fast and painless. Take comfort in knowing he's gone to a better place where the living is easy."

With tears streaming down her cheeks, she tore Ferd's calendar off its nail and ripped it into tiny pieces. She left them heaped on the bench top, weighted by one of her husband's hardened blue profanities.

I climbed back into my car. Heddy reached through the window and ran her fingertips gently over the stitches lacing my head together. "Take care of yourself, Eddie."

"Don't worry about me, Toots. I plan to die an old man in bed."

She walked along beside the car as I backed down the driveway. "Eddie, there's something else we've got to clear away. This foolish notion of yours that I'm a Toon."

I pointed to my banged-up noggin. "I've been imagining all sorts of goofy stuff the past couple of days. Chalk it up to delusions."

"I told you so."

"I know. I should have listened."

WHO P-P-P-PLUGGED ROGER RABBIT?

Apartments in this town come with a special closet for storing broken dreams. The residue from this case filled mine to overflowing. One more busted fantasy, and I'd have to pop extra for a storage locker.

I emptied a bottle of Smith Brothers Cough Syrup and refilled it with my dose of Toon Tonic. I tucked it into my medicine cabinet behind my razor blades and corn plasters. Horrible though Toon Tonic might be, I wanted to keep it handy on the off chance Freddy one day came to his senses and realized his terrible error.

I went into the kitchen to build myself a sandwich.

A single large cupcake sat in the middle of my Formica table.

It hadn't been there when I left.

A booby trap? I debated dunking it in water, but the smell of fresh vanilla dulled my judgment. If I had to go, what better way than in a blast of flour, butter, milk, sugar, and eggs.

I reached for the confection.

The top sprung off.

Little Jo uncurled herself from inside. "Hi, Eddie." She was in hair by Veronica Lake, jewelry by Mrs. Rockefeller, makeup by Max Factor, evening gown, what there was of it, by sister Jessica. "Sorry for the cheap trick, but I wanted to make certain I had your undivided attention."

"You succeeded." I lifted her out of her pastry.

She kneeled on my palm and placed her delicate hand on my inner wrist. Her fingers caressed my artery. The tingle plucked my heartstring. "I couldn't let you go without a fight, Eddie. I love you, and I believe you love me. Let's at least give our romance an opportunity to blossom. We're not as incompatible as you think. Not if you put your imagination to work."

I did. And guess what? It worked fine.

AFTERWORD

I escorted Joellyn to the party Roger and Jessica threw to introduce their offspring to the world.

Jessica greeted us at the door. The men of our proud nation would be happy to know Jessica got her figure back in no time flat, if "flat" is a term you can use in the same breath with "Jessica Rabbit."

Roger stood proudly beside the bassinet holding his triplets. Joellyn and I took a peek. The girl was the spitting image of Jessica, the bunny a spitting image of Roger. Then there was the baby boy. He was spitting, period.

"He looks just like Baby Herman," I whispered to Joellyn.

"All babies look alike," said Jessica over my shoulder.

"Not under the sheets, they don't," smirked Baby Herman, sticking his head beneath Jessica's skirt.

"Aw, Baby," said Roger. "You're sooooo funny."

For the first time in his furry life, Roger Rabbit didn't get the joke.

THE AFTERNOON AFTER THE AFTERWORD

My office door banged open. Roger Rabbit stood on my threshold. "Eddie, I'm in terrible, terrible trouble. Nono Nuttingood was murdered last night. The police are turning the town upside down looking for the redheaded fellow who pasted him with a pie. They think he, I mean I, I mean me, I mean myself, came back later and killed he, him, whomever. Oh, Eddie. I don't know what to do, done, ditty. I is positively un*grammatical*! You have to help me Eddie, p-p-p-please, p-p-p-pretty, p-p-p-pretty p-p-p-please."

I reached into my desk, pulled out his sworn promise to leave me alone, and waved it under his fuzzy pink nose.

He rolled his eyes and unrolled a wad of money, no bill smaller than a Cleveland.

How could I resist?

"And one other thing, Eddie," he said after he had me, and his note, in his pocket. "About Jessica. I think she's dating Cary Grant."

ABOUT THE AUTHOR

GARY K. WOLF'S short stories have appeared in *Orbit, Fantasy and Science Fiction,* and *Worlds of Tomorrow.* His science-fiction novels include *Killerbowl, A Generation Removed,* and *The Resurrectionist.* His novel *Who Censored Roger Rabbit?* became the basis for the Academy Award–winning movie *Who Framed Roger Rabbit,* produced by Steven Spielberg for Walt Disney Studios. His screenplays include *The Flying Tigerfish* and *Typhoon Lagoon* for Walt Disney Studios, and *The Curse of Cali Caliph* and *Genie Man* for Talking Rings Entertainment. Moreover, he and his wife, Bonnie, have written a number of screenplays together, including *Attitudes* and *Worlds Apart.*

Mr. Wolf grew up in Earlville, Illinois. He now lives in Boston. He is currently at work on the third Roger Rabbit novel.